PRECIOUS THINGS

A MOTHER'S EMPTY ARMS
A DAUGHTER'S EMPTY HEART

ANDREA BOESHAAR

BARBOUR
PUBLISHING

PRECIOUS THINGS

For more information about Andrea Boeshaar, please access the author's Web site at the following Internet address: www.andreaboeshaar.com

Published by Barbour Publishing, Inc., P.O. Box 719, Uhrichsville, OH 44683, www.barbourbooks.com

Our mission is to publish and distribute inspirational products offering exceptional value and biblical encouragement to the masses.

 Member of the
Evangelical Christian
Publishers Association

Printed in the United States of America
5 4 3 2 1

DEDICATION

To my husband, Daniel, and my mother, Janice Kuhn. . .
two people who know precious things when they see them!

I shall surround myself with precious things,
To keep my sorrow at bay.
Books and letters and photographs,
Pieces of heart, broken along the way.
A cradle, pink blanket, a lock of her hair,
A watch, record album, the shirt he used to wear,
These precious things will do me no harm—

If I could only forget who they are from.

AKB

It's amazing what people throw away. My husband, Daniel, once watched in disbelief as the city workers tossed a Victorian chest of drawers into the back of the garbage truck. It had been discarded as worthless trash. The owners didn't realize what they had—but all too soon the antique dresser was gone. Destroyed.

On the flip side, it's remarkable what people hang onto. My husband's grandfather was a collector and, consequently, the woods surrounding his house were cluttered and littered with all sorts of. . .dare I say "junk"? From rusty metal bed-springs to cracked porcelain toilets, to cars and automobile parts to even the kitchen sink, Grandpa had some plan and story behind everything he acquired. Of course, not all of it was junk, either.

But how true it is that one man's trash is another's treasure. Sometimes trash can be renovated into treasures, given time and a new coat of varnish or paint. Other times treasures just need to be rescued from the rubbish.

I rather think God sees us as the latter. Diamonds in the rough. Lost sinners in need of salvation. It was sin, mine and yours, that sent Jesus Christ to the cross. He died so that we might have eternal life. He saw a glimmer in humanity's garbage pit and gave His life to make us free.

So if you're reading this, feeling bogged in life's miry mess of woe, please know that there is hope—because there is Jesus Christ.

PROLOGUE

MARCH 2000

A week's worth of mail covered the top of Blythe Severson's one-hundred-year-old rolltop desk. As she sorted through the bills, magazines, and flyers, she wondered where the past seven days had gone. She'd allowed herself two "junk hunts," as she fondly termed her excursions. They took her in and around Chicago and sometimes even into neighboring states. During these little trips, she accumulated miscellaneous items for her antique store, Precious Things, and with the exception of this past week's junk hunts, she hadn't been far away from her shop's back office. Where had all this mail come from?

A white frilly envelope caught her eye, and Blythe reached for it, noting the return address. It belonged to a friend of hers. That is, Allie Drake—now Allie Littenberg—*used* to be a high-school friend. But they had lost touch some thirty years ago.

Then, last fall, Allie phoned out of the blue. She was in Chicago. She wanted to have lunch. Get together. Talk about old times. Allie even stopped by the shop one afternoon and handed Blythe a copy of a faded photograph. Allie had gone so far as to frame the silly thing. It had been taken in March of 1969, at the end of an antiwar demonstration in front of Oakland Park's City Hall. In addition to Blythe and Allie, Jack Callahan and Wendy Chadwyk were pictured. Wendy held a picket sign and Jack was clad in his policeman blues. What an odd foursome they were: three anti-Vietnam War hippie chicks and one law-abiding, law-enforcing, Christian cop!

Unable to contain her curiosity, Blythe tore into the envelope. While she felt glad that Jack and Allie had renewed the romance they'd begun decades ago, Blythe wasn't interested in exhuming the past. Those were painful days for her—so painful Blythe had experienced an emotional breakdown. In fact, just a glimpse of that old photo caused her heart to crimp in misery. And if Allie ever found Wendy. . .

Shaking off her sudden angst, Blythe removed a lovely wedding announcement from its matching envelope. She told herself she shouldn't feel surprised. Of course, Jack and Allie would marry. Jack hadn't ever stopped loving Allie. Blythe sensed it from the little bit of contact she'd had with him over the years. Out of their group of four, only she and Jack had remained in the Chicago area. Allie had moved to California and Wendy to—

The chime above the shop's front door signaled an entering patron. Setting aside the announcement, Blythe left her cluttered office and stepped into her shop. In contrast, it was neat, organized, and decorated with all the trinkets and treasures she'd collected.

"Can I help you?"

The dark-haired woman wearing a teal suede coat glanced her way and Blythe recognized her at once. Kylie Rollins.

Blythe stopped in mid-stride and cold dread poured over her being. What was she doing here? Then Kylie stepped forward, and Blythe thought she looked different somehow. Her usually blissful countenance appeared troubled and sad.

What happened? What's wrong?

The younger woman quickly scanned the shop, devoid of other customers. "You know who I am, don't you?"

Blythe tried to speak but couldn't force out a single syllable.

"Your name is Blythe, isn't it?"

Where's your mother? Wendy. . .Wendy, how could you let her come here without telling me first?

"I apologize for putting you on the spot like this," Kylie said, inching towards her, "but my mother recently died, and—"

"She died?" Blythe staggered at the news and set her hand on a nearby display table. If she didn't hang onto something, she was certain her knees would give way from the weight of the shock.

Wendy was dead. Her friend. Dead!

For a moment, the room seemed to spin. "I—I didn't know. . ."

"It was very sudden," Kylie eked out, obviously distraught herself. "Mom fell and hit her head."

"Oh, I'm so sorry." Blythe ached for Kylie—for the both of them. She took several steps forward then stopped. As much as she longed to comfort this young woman, she couldn't. She'd given up that right almost thirty-one years ago.

Kylie reached into her purse and extracted an oversized brown envelope. "Last week, I got this in the mail." She held it out.

Blythe hesitated before accepting it. Examining the front of the envelope, she saw Allie's return address. Taking a quick peek inside, she winced, seeing that cursed, faded photograph. Had just thinking about it minutes ago somehow conjured up this nightmare?

Bringing her gaze back to Kylie's lovely face, she said nothing. *Does she know?*

"When I saw the photograph," Kylie began, "I thought you looked familiar, and then I remembered seeing you here at this store. My mother took me here every year—ever since I was a little girl."

Blythe didn't reply. She couldn't. There were no words to describe how she felt.

Clearing her throat, the young woman continued, "But what I can't figure out is. . .if you and my mom were once friends, how come she didn't say so? Why didn't she introduce us?"

Oh, Kylie, why are you asking me something I can't answer? Lowering her gaze, Blythe stared at the brown envelope in her hands. *Oh, God, how could You take Wendy home and leave me to deal with this all by myself? You know I'm not strong enough. . . .*

"I, um, didn't come here to upset you," Kylie said. "I just wanted to ask a few questions. You see, I've been talking to Allie Littenberg, and—"

"Oh, that Allie!" Anger welled up in Blythe, threatening her austere composure. "What did she tell you?"

"Well. . ." Kylie hesitated, as if she were suddenly unsure of herself. But a heartbeat later, she managed to forge on with her reply. "Allie said that the three of you were friends and that you. . .um. . .dated my mom's brother. I wondered if you could tell me where he's buried."

"Oh, dear Lord. . ."

Blythe closed her eyes. *Rob. She's asking me about Rob. I loved him so much. . .Kylie's living proof of that!*

Feeling a hand touch her shoulder, Blythe looked up to find her daughter standing just inches away—so close.

"I'm sorry. I didn't mean to cause you any pain by bringing up the past," Kylie said. "I'm just confused. I didn't even know my mom had a brother."

Blythe hoarded her silence, yet allowed her gaze to wander over Kylie's features. She'd memorized every one of them. Her round face, so much like Rob's, her flawless, ivory complexion and coal black eyes and hair, like Blythe's own. And those pink rosebud lips—lips Blythe had kissed good-bye. . .

Kylie's dark gaze suddenly widened and her jaw dropped with realization. Blythe knew at once that she'd guessed the truth. How could she not? It was staring back at her!

Oh, no, Lord, I'm not ready. I'll never be ready.

Kylie took the envelope from Blythe and pulled out the photograph. "You–you're pregnant in this picture, aren't you?"

She knows.

"You need to leave." Blythe felt her lower lip quiver. "My store closes at noon and I've got an appointment in an hour. I don't have time for this conversation."

"Could I come back tomorrow or Monday? I need to talk to you."

Blythe didn't answer, but gathering her wits, she placed a firm grip on Kylie's elbow and propelled her toward the door.

"Please," Kylie begged, "please talk to me. I'm confused. I need answers."

"I c–can't."

Tears gathered and Blythe noticed her sorrow mirrored in Kylie's eyes.

"Please?"

"You don't understand," Blythe told her. "I made a vow."

"To whom?"

Again, Blythe didn't reply. It seemed impossible to articulate the consequences that would befall her if the truth came out.

With a hand on Kylie's upper back, she guided her toward the exit. Once the younger woman stepped outside, Blythe closed the door and locked the deadbolt. However, she wasn't fool enough to think mere metal and wood were going to stand in the way of Kylie's determination. Hadn't Wendy told her more than a few stories that illustrated Kylie's stubborn streak?

Pivoting and placing her back against the door, Blythe put her face in her hands and sobbed.

CHAPTER ONE

B lythe, I'm worried about you."

From where she sat in the creaking, cherry-wood rocker, she glanced up at her friend, Wendy Chadwyk, and managed a smile. In truth, Blythe felt a little worried about herself. At nine months pregnant, her baby due in a matter of days, Blythe felt exhausted and emotionally spent. She hadn't recovered from Rob's death and still had nightmares of his beating on the streets of Chicago during the Democratic National Convention last August. It shouldn't have happened, but the unspeakable horror occurred right before Blythe's eyes, and now the memory of it haunted her night after night.

"You don't have to come today." Wendy flipped several strands of her long, chestnut-brown hair over her shoulder.

13

"Jack said he'll arrest us if we demonstrate in front of City Hall and, who knows, he might actually do it this time."

"No way." A rare chuckle escaped Blythe, but the thought of Jack Callahan arresting his friends was mind-blowing. Overall, she didn't trust *pigs*, not after what they did to Rob. But Jack was different. He'd won Blythe's confidence, even though Rob never liked him. However, since that terrible night seven months ago, Jack had been a great source of encouragement to Blythe. "Jack's hip—for a cop."

"For sure."

Blythe stood and smoothed her red, blue, and green printed smock over her protruding midsection. Since the moment she learned she was expecting a baby, she loved this child. This little he or she was all Blythe had left of Rob. Glancing around her bedroom, which she'd decorated with knickknacks and furniture she'd picked up from the curb, Blythe's gaze stopped when it came to the psychedelic drawings Rob had created on two of the four walls. The sight of his artistry caused her heart to twist, and she wished once more that she could somehow turn back the hands of time and take back that hot August night downtown.

"Josh said he'll be there today."

Blythe pivoted and looked back at Wendy. "What?"

"Josh. He'll be at the demonstration."

"Oh. Right."

"I don't want to push you, Blythe, but you're going to have to decide soon whether you're going to let Josh and me adopt the baby. I mean, it could be born any time. If I'm going to be a mother, I need infant paraphernalia like a crib, diapers, bottles. . .a place to live, as in moving to northern Wisconsin and into the house Josh bought up there."

"It's a heavy decision." Blythe paused, considering her friend. She knew that her unborn child was all Wendy had left of Rob, too. "Do you really think you'll dig living up there in the north woods, away from everything and everybody? I'd go crazy. I'm a city chick."

"I'll be happy."

"And you'll really marry Josh?" Blythe had a hard time envisioning Wendy making such a commitment. But since Rob's death, she'd changed a lot. Even so, Blythe had to be sure. She wanted her child brought up in a stable environment, unlike her own growing up years. Blythe had never been able to trust her parents, who acted like kids themselves. "I can be a single mother, too, you know."

"Sure, you could. But is that what you really want?"

Very slowly, Blythe shook her head.

A satisfied expression settled on Wendy's face. "Josh and I will get married. I promise. Josh is cool, even if he does have *establishment* ideas. But, like you once said, he's crazy about me." Wendy paused and took a deep breath. "I just pray we won't turn into my parents."

A bittersweet plume rose up in Blythe. She knew how much Wendy loathed her parents and blamed them for Rob's death. Wendy believed that if they had understood and supported his beliefs, he wouldn't have been in Chicago last August 28. Instead, he would have been well on his way to Canada, dodging the draft. Blythe, on the other hand, wasn't so sure. Rob had been a free spirit. Who knows where he would have been seven months ago. All Blythe knew is she had wanted to be with him. She would have followed him to the ends of the earth.

"I still think you should let your folks know about Rob."

"What for? They don't care about Rob or me." Wendy's naturally husky voice sounded calm despite the emotion behind it. "I'll never speak to them again. My decision is final."

Blythe tried to cover her wince. If Wendy made up her mind, it was usually set for good.

"And now *you* have a 'final decision' of your own to make."

"I know, Wendy. I know. . ."

Blythe was all too aware of the choices she faced. Unfortunately, since Rob's death, all she'd been able to do was cry.

Wendy stepped forward and placed her hands on Blythe's rounded belly. She grinned. "Is he kicking?"

"No. 'Junior' usually moves around while I'm trying to sleep at night." Blythe mustered a grin.

Wendy's smile grew. "I hope it's a boy."

"I just hope this kid is healthy." Tipping her head, Blythe narrowed her regard and studied Wendy's features. She looked a lot like Rob, who'd had the same hair color, round face, delicately sculptured cheekbones, and full lips. Wendy also had a stocky build like Rob, but on a feminine scale. Hanging out with Wendy was a constant reminder of the man Blythe loved and lost. The similarities brought her both pain and comfort.

This baby will be a constant reminder of him, too.

The deepest part of Blythe wanted to hang onto everything associated with Rob, everything he touched, his clothes, his poetry, his drawings. . .his child. But could she manage it. . .alone?

As if reading her thoughts, Wendy chimed in. "Blythe, you and my brother were beautiful together." She continued to run her hands over the swell of Blythe's midsection as if somehow the caress reached the infant inside. "This is a real person in here. I never valued an unborn life 'til now."

Blythe saw tears gathering in her friend's eyes. Wendy had told her about the abortions she'd had during her wild days in high school.

"I love this baby."

"I know, Wendy." Blythe touched her friend's shoulder.

"I would be the best mother on the face of this earth, not like mine. . .not like yours. And you could have a place in this child's life if you wanted one, Blythe."

She sucked in her lower lip, working it between her teeth.

"But just think of all the responsibility taking care of a kid involves."

Blythe needed no reminder of the enormity of the task. Fear and uncertainty had haunted her for months.

"Now think about your parents tossing you out of their house. You don't have a job and even if you did, who's going to watch 'Junior' while you're at work?" Shaking her head, Wendy stepped back. "Man, your folks are one bad trip these days. I thought they were hip, but they're, like, acting their age."

Another piece of Blythe's heart crumbled at the mention of her parents. Pete and Lydia had been anything but supportive during Blythe's pregnancy. They acted as if they were in denial that she was even expecting a baby.

"Remember, I was there when they said they didn't want a kid around in a house that was open to everybody—except their grandchild. No room for a baby here, which means you, Blythe, would have to find another pad if you keep this child."

Wendy took her hand. "Now, look, you could easily find a place to crash. But what kind of life will you be offering this little one? Don't you want to give 'Junior' here," she said, patting Blythe's belly, "a better world than you had growing up?"

"Yes. . ."

"Well, then—" Wendy's eyes darkened with earnest. "Let Josh and me raise this baby."

Blythe knew Wendy had a point. At least with Josh and Wendy as parents, living up north in a small town, this kid would have a fighting chance at a good life, away from the noise, pollution, and riots of Chicago. Moreover, Wendy was a strong person, so much stronger than Blythe. She was smart and sensitive—in essence, Wendy Chadwyk was everything Blythe wanted to be but wasn't. If Wendy married Joshua Rollins, a guy graduating from med school in two months, they'd make the perfect adoptive couple. Josh had been good for Wendy these past few months. She'd grown up a lot. Then, again, senseless tragedies, such as Rob's death, forced reality on their victims and robbed them of their inner peace. But because of it, Wendy had a vested interest in this child too. She had idolized her older brother. This baby would be in the capable hands of a woman who would love him or her nearly as much as Blythe did.

But could she really give away her child? Rob's child?

"Listen, we'll rap more about this later. I've gotta split," Wendy said, glancing at the rustic pendulum clock that hung on the far corner of Blythe's cluttered room. "The demonstration starts in an hour and I still have picket signs to paint. Are you coming or not?"

"I'm coming." Blythe squared her slender shoulders. She felt she owed it to Kyle, her older brother. He'd been killed in Nam less than two years ago. Moreover, she owed it to Rob. He had been against the violence overseas and he'd refused to fight, even after he got drafted—

How ironic that he died in a street battle here in Chicago.

The jangle of the telephone jarred Blythe from her reminiscing. Her frayed nerves served as a reminder of how much she needed this vacation and time away from her shop.

Now if only she could escape her memories.

"Hey, phone call for you."

Standing, Blythe turned in time to see her friend, Twila Babcock, stepping out onto the deck through two wide, glass patio doors. A heavyset woman in her fifties, Twila always looked fashionable. Like today. Clad in a flattering, black, one-piece swimsuit, both she and Blythe were enjoying this first day in April, sitting near Twila's heated backyard pool and relaxing in colorful plastic lawn chairs.

Twila handed Blythe the portable phone. "It's your mom."

"Oh?" Puzzled, Blythe put the receiver to her ear. Her mother wouldn't call unless the matter was urgent. "Lydia, what's up?" She and her mother had been on a first-name basis since Blythe was in junior high.

"Hi, hon. How's the weather in Houston today?"

"Gorgeous."

"Lucky you."

Blythe grinned. "What can I do for you?"

"Well, I just had to call you." Lydia Severson sounded a bit winded from years of cigarette smoking. "You'll never believe who just left the shop."

"Who?"

"A couple from—are you ready for this?—from South Carolina."

Tingles of apprehension climbed Blythe's spine. Rob's parents were from South Carolina. "Did you get their names?"

19

"No. I never got the chance. Sorry."

"Don't worry about it. You're doing a great job minding the shop in my absence."

"Well, thanks. I've had a lot of practice over the years."

In spite of her sudden trepidation, Blythe smiled and reclaimed her seat on the deck.

"You know, these people said they might stop back. You don't suppose that Kylie somehow tracked down the Chadwyks, do you? This couple was about the right age and—"

"Lydia, please, stop it. Your paranoia is beginning to make me feel crazy."

"I'm not paranoid. I'm practical—and you need to do something about Kylie before she ruins our lives."

"What do you want me to do?" At the mention of ruined lives, Blythe felt sick. Her stomach knotted, tears welled in her eyes, and her throat constricted. She'd never been a strong person, and she'd always despised that weakness in herself. "Wendy's dead," she forced herself to continue. "Josh has been dead for years. Kylie has no one left." Blythe paused to swallow a lump of sorrow. "No one but us."

"No, not 'us.' You chose adoption. You're not responsible for Kylie's well-being. Good grief, she's thirty years old!"

Blythe watched with a weary spirit as Twila took a seat in the adjacent lawn chair. A curious expression lit her friend's amber eyes and caused her brows to furrow with a hint of concern.

"Need I remind you that your Christian uncle will have apoplexy if he learns about your so-called 'love child'? If that happens, you can kiss your shop good-bye, Blythe."

She winced, hating the gauche way in which Lydia described the situation. And yet it was true. Despite his faith,

Uncle Garth was not a man of deep sensibilities. "I need to tell him. I should have told him years ago."

"Don't be ridiculous. Garth will never listen. All he knows is you signed that contract." Her mother expelled an audible sigh. "I wish you would have asked me to read it over first. You were in no emotional condition to sign anything back then."

Blythe clenched her jaw, hating the rehash of her past, particularly this aspect of it.

"Well, just remember, you made me a promise. I don't need to tell you that we could lose our home!"

You don't need to tell me, but you will anyway. Blythe sighed. "Look, Lydia, we'll have to continue this discussion when I get home, all right?"

"Of course." Her mother's voice lost its edge. "I'm planning to pick you up at O'Hare tomorrow evening."

"Thanks."

"Hope you've had a nice vacation."

"I have."

"See you soon."

"Yep. Bye."

Pressing the END button, Blythe set the portable phone on the plastic side table and glanced at Twila.

"Everything okay?"

"Not really." Blythe sat back in the chair and raised her face to the heavens. "It seems my past has come back to haunt me."

"Yeah, pasts have a way of doing that. Just ask any politician."

Blythe laughed, grateful for Twila's ability to find something amusing in every situation. They'd met at an auction gallery in Chicago seventeen years ago where they coveted the same side table with its inlaid satinwood top. They'd bid against each other, but neither won the prize. Two days later, Twila visited Precious Things, and she and Blythe discovered they had more in common than a love for antiques. Both were committed Christians who described themselves as "terminally single" women. Not much had changed in almost two decades.

"Are you having family troubles or business woes?" Lifting her can of diet cola, Twila took a long sip.

"A bit of each."

"Bummer. Is that why you're so stressed and needed to come visit me? You never did get specific, not that you're obligated." Twila laughed. "I'm just nosy."

Blythe didn't know where to begin. "It's a long story, but I appreciate you letting me escape to your house for a couple of weeks."

Twila stood. "Let's go for a swim. If you feel like talking, we can discuss whatever's bothering you in the pool. I'm all ears." She grinned and smacked the sides of her ample but tanned thighs. "Well, maybe I'm more hips than ears, but I'm a good listener."

Smiling, Blythe stood and followed her friend across the deck and into the oblong, heated swimming pool.

❦

"Your birthday is five days away. We'd better start making plans for your party."

A dish towel in her hand, Kylie Rollins turned from the sink and faced her grandmother, Kathryn Chadwyk, who appeared quite comfortable where she sat at the white-painted kitchen table. Brownish red hair gracefully framed the older woman's age-lined face, but her hazel eyes sparked with enthusiasm. It was still difficult for Kylie to believe she'd only met her grandparents a little over two weeks ago. She felt like she'd known them forever, particularly Grandma Kate.

"Do you want a large or small gathering?"

"Small, I guess. Thirty-one isn't a benchmark age. Besides, Mom threw me a huge bash last year."

Kylie lowered her gaze and fidgeted with the towel. Mentioning her mother, who had died this past January, brought on that familiar wave of anguish. Kylie had been through so much this year—her mother's death, a broken engagement, a shattered friendship, discovering she was adopted—and it was only April! However, through it all, she'd become a Christian, and God, in all His goodness, had given her back what she'd lost. Kylie now had grandparents whom she'd never even known existed up until a month ago, and she'd made new friends while journeying from her small rural town of Basil Creek, Wisconsin, to Chicago and then Sabal Beach, South Carolina.

Nevertheless, the losses in her life still caused Kylie's heart to ache.

"Shall we just have cake and punch or would you like to serve dinner?"

"Cake and punch would be simpler." Kylie turned, and from her vantage point in the kitchen, she could see past the dining room and through the windows where a sturdy FOR SALE sign stood on the front lawn. "And, who knows, we might have prospective buyers walking through the house."

"We can schedule any walk-throughs accordingly. But, you know, Kylie, we could have your party somewhere else. A restaurant of your choosing, perhaps."

Kylie shook her head. "Then everyone has to drive a long ways. Basil Creek only has the Captain's Café on the edge of town or the hamburger joint attached to the new gas station, and I refuse to have my birthday party at a gas station. The Red Rocket Lounge is a bar in town, but I vowed never to step foot in there again." She grimaced. Nothing good ever happened in that place.

"I completely understand. I wouldn't want my birthday party in a gas station or a barroom either."

Kylie looked up and grinned. "Thanks, but Captain's Café isn't much better. We'll have to go to La Crosse for a *real* restaurant, and no one wants to do that on a Monday night."

"Hmm. . .well, we could have your party on Sunday afternoon."

Kylie thought it over and realized what she really wanted to do was escape Basil Creek and the wounds she'd suffered these past months and move to Sabal Beach where she'd live happily ever after with her grandparents. That was the plan, although it would take time before Kylie could be ready to leave. In addition to selling the Cape Cod-style home she'd inherited, she had to sort through thirty years of memories. Thankfully, she had her grandparents here to help her.

"Kylie?"

She blinked. "Sorry, Grandma. I started thinking about everything I have to get done in the next few months."

"Don't look at the whole picture, dear. It's too over-whelming. We'll take it one day at a time." Grandma Kate cleared her throat. "Now, about your birthday party. . ."

Kylie laughed. "All right. Let's make it Sunday afternoon."

With an agreeable nod, Kathryn lifted a pencil from the kitchen table and began to jot down specifics. "Sunday afternoon it is."

Allie stood in the well-lit parking lot trying to tamp her impatience. Several feet away, the three Callahan men—Jack, Steve, his brother, and Logan, Jack's son—were huddled beneath the open hood of a Mercury Sable. The vehicle hadn't been running properly for the past few days and now, after church, it wouldn't start. Allie wondered why they didn't just call a tow truck and be done with it.

"If and when the guys ever get Logan's car started, do you want to go out for a bite to eat?"

Glancing to her left, Allie saw Nora Callahan, Steve's wife, had come to stand beside her. She wore a tan trench coat that was belted at the waist, and as the cold April wind whipped around them, strands of Nora's chin-length, sandy-brown hair blew onto her cheek. Pushing them aside, Nora added, "I'm starved. I didn't eat supper tonight. I was so busy getting the kids ready for church. Wednesdays are always so hectic."

"I'm sure they are." Allie gave Nora a sympathetic grin. She'd raised her son, Nicholas, but she still knew the meaning of "hectic."

"So what do you think about going out to eat?"

"Sorry to disappoint you, Nora, but I think I'll have to pass. I need to get Patrice home. She has to get up early tomorrow morning and she hasn't been feeling well."

"Nothing serious, I hope."

"No. I think it's just the usual morning sickness. I keep telling Patrice that once she's into her second trimester, she'll feel better. But I don't think she believes me."

"Where is she now?"

"She's with Marilee. They went to find Patrice a soft drink."

"Hmm." Nora seemed momentarily pensive. "Is the living situation going all right?"

Under the bright glow of the tall halogen lights, Allie could see her friend's blue-green eyes narrowed in concern.

"Not to worry. Things are fine. For the last week and a half Patrice has behaved herself. I'm praying her good behavior will continue."

"You're a regular Mother Teresa in my eyes, Allie."

"Hardly." She laughed. The truth was, Allie loved people. So when Logan's younger half-sister, Patrice Rodriguez, showed up here at Parkway Community Church, homeless, unwed, and three-and-a-half months pregnant, Allie didn't think twice about offering her a place to stay. Since then, Logan had found Patrice a job in the church office. Being the youth pastor, he had a bit of clout. Nevertheless, Patrice seemed determined to show up every day and work hard. It was obvious that the younger woman had a high regard for her half-brother and didn't want to disappoint him.

"Any more talk about Logan and Marilee adopting Patrice's child?"

"Not that I've heard," Allie replied. "Although, Patrice refers to the child she's carrying as Logan and Marilee's baby."

"Oh, my! I hope she doesn't call it 'Logan's baby.' A rumor like that could damage his ministry."

Allie smiled. She understood the concern. Nora had

practically raised Logan and there were times, like now, when the mother in her surfaced.

"Relax, Nora. I've discussed this very subject with Patrice and she understands. What's more, I think she makes it known she's Logan's sister. She's also very open about Logan and Marilee—both—adopting the baby."

"But Logan hasn't agreed to it, has he?"

"Not officially, but I can't imagine he'd refuse."

"Yeah, I s'pose you're right."

Allie didn't reply, but she *knew* she was right. It wasn't any secret that Logan's fiancée, Marilee Domotor, couldn't bear children as a result of a car accident she'd been involved in last fall. Marilee wanted the child, if Patrice decided for certain to go the adoption route. Since Logan and Patrice shared the same mother, Patrice and her baby were Logan's blood relatives.

Nora expelled a weary-sounding sigh. "I hope it's not trouble that I see brewing on the horizon."

"Me too." Allie sobered, sensing how very disappointed Marilee would be if Patrice decided to keep her child. "But first things first. Right now I'm going to try and convince three macho guys to call a tow truck so I don't have to stand here and freeze anymore."

Nora laughed. "Good luck."

CHAPTER TWO

B lythe cradled her newborn daughter as the two of them reclined in the hospital bed. Only four days old, and already Blythe could tell her child possessed a strong will and healthy set of lungs. Due to the nature of the delivery, Blythe had been advised to stay a full week—and her baby was allowed to stay with her. One week. That's all the time she'd have with her precious daughter. She'd already signed the legal documents.

Blythe held Kylie closer.

Her friends Josh and Wendy Rollins, who also were her baby's adoptive parents, had graciously allowed Blythe to choose a name. At first, she'd pondered Roberta or Robyn. However, the pain felt so intense that she could barely form the syllables on her tongue, let alone say the names aloud.

Blythe was still devastated by Rob's death. So she decided, instead, on a variation of her brother Kyle's name. Kylie.

Kylie Dawn. Her middle name was indicative of her arrival as the first pinks in the dark eastern sky had just appeared on the horizon as Josh and Wendy rushed Blythe to the hospital.

Kylie Dawn. Blythe decided the name was cute. Hip. Like the name of the most popular girl in school. And that's what Blythe wished for her daughter. Everything good and wonderful. But most of all, she wished her child happiness.

Baby Kylie smacked her lips and then turned her head into Blythe's arm. She sure was a snuggler. Loved to be held. Of course that's all Blythe had done since Kylie's birth, and Wendy accused her of hopelessly spoiling the infant.

Well, so be it. The time would soon come when Blythe's arms would be forever empty.

The future loomed before her like a boundless black hole. After Wendy and Josh took Kylie home, Blythe planned to return to Chicago. Go back to school. Get a job. Pete and Lydia said she could live with them; however, Blythe felt as though she'd surpassed her parents' forever-young and irresponsible attitudes. Rob's death and Kylie's birth and imminent adoption had shaken Blythe into reality. She knew now that life consisted of more than dreams, debates, and political protests. Life was filled with heartache and painful decisions. The fight had gone out of her, replaced by an inexplicable void, and yet something deep and fathomless beckoned her. But it all seemed so complex, and Blythe felt too exhausted to try to make sense of such ambiguity.

She returned her attention to Kylie and stroked her daughter's inky black hair with the side of her left forefinger.

Kylie had inherited Blythe's coloring: dark hair and lashes and skin so creamy white it resembled bone china. But Blythe could see Rob in their child too.

Blythe bent her head and placed a soft kiss on Kylie's rosebud lips. The baby scrunched her tiny face as if to say, "How dare you disturb me while I'm sleeping."

My little princess. Tears gathered in Blythe's eyes, distorting her vision. "I hope you'll always know in your heart that I love you, Kylie. I'll always love you. . . ."

" 'Scuse me, ma'am."

Blythe snapped from her daydream and moved aside to allow a man and two children to pass by her in the greeting card aisle. She swatted an errant tear and wondered why she was standing here staring blindly at an array of birthday wishes. Having been gone the past two weeks, she had a hill of paperwork and messages to catch up on at Precious Things. Additionally, she'd never before sent a birthday card to Kylie, even though she thought of her every April 10. But this year was different. Wendy wasn't there and Blythe had been fretting that Kylie would spend her special day alone.

She's got a fiancé, Blythe reminded herself. Wendy had e-mailed her at the end of December to say Kylie was engaged to a nice young man named Matt Alexander. A dairy farmer. Responsible. Very much in love with Kylie.

Blythe couldn't have asked for more for her daughter. She was thankful that, throughout the years, Wendy secretly kept her informed and, once a year, the day after Thanksgiving, she would bring Kylie into Precious Things. Wendy started the tradition when Kylie began first grade. Perhaps it courted disaster year after year, but Blythe always looked forward to getting a glimpse of the child to whom she'd given life. She carefully kept her distance; she'd made a vow, after all, and Wendy promised to help keep it.

Of course, Kylie had been clueless that the shop's owner was actually her biological mother—clueless until recently, that is. Blythe felt certain Kylie knew the truth now, or at least she knew the biggest part of it, thanks to Allie and that awful faded photograph.

Bringing herself back to the matter at hand, Blythe began an internal debate. *Do I buy Kylie a birthday card or not? Will it encourage her in an impossible way or will it show Kylie how sorry I am that Wendy's gone and sorry that I so rudely shooed her out of my shop a month ago?*

Blythe lifted another birthday card and read its message. No. It wouldn't work. Replacing the greeting in the rack, she took a step backward and turned down the aisle. She wasn't a strong person, not since Rob's death. Part of her had died with him, and the emotional breakdown Blythe suffered shortly after giving Kylie up for adoption had stolen much of her zest for life, her spirit. Had she not gleaned just enough strength from the Lord to go on living day to day, she'd hate to think of where she might be right now.

I turned fifty last August. When will I start living again?

She made an abrupt halt at the end of the aisle. The question startled her into seeing her life in the light of reality. Perhaps now was the time that she'd been living for all these years.

Kylie might need her.

Blythe glanced over her shoulder at the colorful cards,

then walked toward them and plucked another from the rack. It was pink and sparkly, and after reading its inscribed birthday wishes, Blythe smiled. She suddenly knew that this was the card to send Kylie along with a special memento.

Kylie might need me. . . .

Blythe knew if that were the case, she could never deny her daughter any request. *Lord God, You'll have to help me bear the consequences.* She drew in a deep breath, but her resolve didn't waver.

Squaring her shoulders, she strolled to the checkout.

───────

The "small" gathering on Sunday afternoon turned into a packed house party. Word about Kylie's birthday party spread around town faster than a juicy tidbit of gossip.

Finding a rare moment alone, Kylie cornered her grandmother in the dining room. "We don't have enough cake."

"Don't worry, dear, I sent Lee to the store for more of. . . *everything.*" She glanced around the dining room table at the rapidly diminishing bowls of snack foods.

Kylie took a step closer to Grandma Kate. "Where did all these people come from? We only addressed seven invitations."

"It's my fault. I handed one to your coworker at the library and offhandedly told her to tell anyone we might have missed."

"Oh. Big mistake in a small town."

"Yes, I see." Kathryn's cheeks pinked with embarrassment. "Sabal Beach is such a touristy community that we don't have such problems."

Kylie had to laugh—that is, until she saw Matt walk in through the back door. Dena Hubbard, Kylie's former best friend, trailed in behind him.

"They came together? To *my* birthday party? Of all the nerve!"

Kathryn followed Kylie's line of vision then turned back around. She enfolded Kylie's hands in her own. "Be polite. You don't want to make a scene."

Pulling her gaze away from her uninvited guests, Kylie peered into her grandmother's face. "I am not in the habit of making a scene. My mother taught me better than that. Besides, it'd make the front page of our local newspaper."

Kathryn chuckled. "I'm afraid you're right."

Matt reached them first. "Happy birthday, Ky, although I know it's not really 'til tomorrow."

"Thanks."

She forced herself to smile at the man she'd intended to marry up until a few weeks ago. After discovering that he and Dena had closed the Red Rocket Lounge together one night last January and spent the rest of it making out like a couple of shameful teenagers in Matt's pickup truck, Kylie decided she didn't trust him anymore and broke their engagement.

Nevertheless, it still hurt to see him, and Kylie realized that love didn't disappear just because a decision had been made.

Matt's blue-eyed stare captured her gaze. The last time they spoke to each other was exactly a week ago. Kylie told him she was selling the house and moving to South Carolina with her grandparents. Matt hadn't taken the news well.

"I bought you something," he said, extracting a long, narrow box from the side pocket of his red-plaid flannel jacket. "I planned to give it to you tomorrow, but seeing as your party is today. . ."

"You didn't have to get me anything."

"I know, but I wanted to. Besides, I ordered it over a month ago, when. . .well, you know." He shrugged.

"When you two were engaged," Dena finished for him.

"Right." Kylie was surprised at how much those words hurt. But the gift wouldn't change anything. Nevertheless, she held her tongue and only hesitated a moment before accepting the blue and gold box. "Thanks."

She noted the shiny gold ribbon that had been meticulously tied around the box, and Kylie guessed Matt's mother, Lynellen, had wrapped it for him.

Then, before she knew it was coming, Matt pulled her into his arms for a quick hug. In the process, Kylie's nose was pressed into the shoulder of his jacket, and the familiar scent of fresh air, hard work, and dairy cows enveloped her. She squeezed her eyes closed to stave off the threat of tears. Part of her wanted to cling to Matt, while another part wanted never to see him again.

She stiffened and he released her.

"Thanks," she muttered once more. Kylie glanced at Dena in time to see the smirk on her face. Then, turning her gaze to Kylie, she smiled.

"May I take your coat, Matthew?" Grandma Kate asked with a polite grin.

"Um. . .I don't know if I'm staying."

Was that a question? If so, Kylie didn't know how to reply. She studied the box in her hand.

"Well, of course, you're staying. Lee will be back any minute and he's going to need a bit of help. Would you mind carrying in the groceries?"

"I don't mind, but it's up to Kylie."

She glanced from her grandmother to Matt and back to

Grandma Kate again. The words *don't make a scene* echoed through her mind, and she knew now was not the time for an honest answer.

"You're welcome to stay if you'd like." Adding a perfunctory smile, Kylie figured she'd done her duty.

"Let me hang up your coat, Matthew," Kathryn said.

He still appeared unsure but shrugged out of his jacket and handed it to Kathryn. Next, he combed strong fingers through his thick, straw-colored hair.

Dena stepped around him. Petite and blonde, with expressive hazel eyes, she'd been Kylie's best friend since kindergarten. "I brought you a present, too, but I can't stay. The kids are at Todd's folks," she said, referring to her ex-husband. "I have to pick them up at four-thirty." She glanced at Matt, then back at Kylie. "My timing is really bad. . .as usual."

So they didn't come together after all.

Unfortunately, the admission only solidified Kylie's desire to leave Basil Creek forever. Dena's "bad timing" would always stand in the way of Kylie's happiness with Matt. Dena had confessed to wanting him. Well, now she could have him.

Except the very idea filled Kylie with misery.

Dena handed her a large, colorfully wrapped rectangular box, then whirled around and left the dining room.

Kylie watched her ex-best friend's retreating form, aware that Matt had remained at her side. She looked over at him in time to see him pop a handful of peanuts into his mouth.

"Mom says hi. She couldn't come today because she twisted her ankle in the barn and it hurts her to walk on it."

"Sorry to hear that." She'd always been fond of Lynellen, who, in fact, had been Kylie's mother's best friend. "Tell her hi from me."

"Will do."

Kylie crossed the room and set the two gifts on the oak buffet beside several others.

Within moments, more people had entered the dining room, and separate conversations ensued. Kylie was only too glad that her guests provided her with the perfect excuse to avoid Matt. She strolled into the living room and began chatting with Pastor John Hanson and his wife, Sarah.

All seemed well until a short while later when Grandma Kate called Kylie into the dining room to cut the birthday cake. Everyone sang "Happy Birthday," then Kylie managed to blow out all thirty-one candles with a single breath.

As she sliced the vanilla-frosted, three-layer cake, guests took their portions and headed into the living room and den. When the dining room emptied, Matt came up behind Kylie.

"Hey, Ky, you really think you'll be happy living on the beach in South Carolina?"

His warm breath tickled the back of her neck, but she dared not turn around. She didn't trust herself or her emotions.

"You with your milky white complexion," Matt continued. "Somehow I just can't picture you as a beach bum. I mean, I don't ever remember seeing you in a pair of shorts, let alone a bikini."

"And you never will, either." Because of her fair skin, Kylie stayed out of the sun. But that's not exactly what she meant. Their engagement was over. Finished.

Irritation overruled any love-sweetened sentiments she harbored for Matt, and she whirled around to face him. In reply, he took a step closer, all but pinning her between the dining room table and the side of his left hip. Kylie realized her mistake in reacting to his teasing, but she wasn't about to back down now.

"Did it ever occur to you, Matt, that 'beach bum' isn't the only occupation on the island of Sabal Beach? And even if there were, Charleston is only minutes away. I could get a job anywhere."

A tiny grin curled the corners of his mouth. "Good cake. Here, try some."

The fork came at her so fast, Kylie opened her mouth in fear that if she didn't, the bite of cake would end up in her nose.

"You two look so romantic," Lauren Kendricks declared, entering the dining room with an empty paper plate in her hand. The bubbly brunette worked with Kylie at Basil Creek's new library—or at least she had until Kylie quit last Monday. "I see you've patched things up. I'm so glad. You two are such a cute couple."

"Thanks," Matt said with a wide grin.

"Lauren, there's been a misunderstanding. Matt and I—"

Before she could finish her explanation, he leaned over and kissed her. Kylie pushed him away, so breathless with anger that she wanted to sock him.

"Oh, listen, you don't have to give me any details," Lauren said, slicing herself a second helping of cake. "Every couple goes through their difficult times. I know Ed and I did, and look how happy we are."

She smiled, licked the frosting off her forefinger, and left the room.

Kylie gave Matt a shove. "Get away from me."

"Oh, now, Ky. That was funny. Laugh."

She folded her arms, not the least bit amused.

"You've got frosting on your cheek."

Matt attempted to remove it, but Kylie slapped his hand away.

"You just don't get it, do you?" she said with a clenched jaw. "We're not engaged anymore, so don't act like we are. Don't tease me. Don't kiss me." Tears gathered in her eyes and she looked away, hoping Matt didn't see.

"Kylie, I love you," he whispered.

Those words were the last thing she wanted to hear.

Exasperated and still deeply hurt by his betrayal with Dena, she fled from the dining room. She rushed past her grandmother, ignoring the look of surprise on the older woman's face. Running up the stairs, Kylie reached her bedroom and locked the door. She stayed there, alone with her sorrow, for the rest of the afternoon.

Dark, ominous clouds swirled in the distance, and a flash of lightning zigzagged across the balmy Sunday evening sky. An angry rumble of thunder followed, and TJ McGwyer grinned. Positioned on the gravel shoulder of a lonesome highway, he lifted his camera and snapped several shots. By the looks of it, this storm was ripe for spawning funnel clouds, and should that actually occur, TJ didn't want to miss the action. Twisters weren't exactly a typical event around the Charleston, South Carolina, area. In fact, in this part of the country, they were history-makers.

"Hey, I've decided storm-chasing isn't my kind of fun."

Holding his camera in place, TJ glanced at his long-time buddy, Seth Brigham. He chuckled at the younger man's worried expression. "Kinda late to decide that now."

"Yeah, well. . ." Seth returned his brown-eyed gaze to the brewing storm. "Shouldn't we be running for cover?"

TJ laughed again. He'd been chasing storms all across the United States for the past five years and this was about as exciting as it got. He wasn't about to hide and miss all the fun. "We're not in any danger."

"Yet."

A smirk tugged at one corner of TJ's mouth. "Time to test your faith."

"Or tempt God."

Still looking concerned, Seth smoothed back his straight, mahogany-colored hair that, in the last year, he'd taken to wearing in a short ponytail. TJ detested the style—thought it made guys look too feminine. On the other hand, TJ had gone to the opposite extreme and shaved his head completely bald. His hair had been falling out anyway, so TJ had decided to speed along the natural process. He had to admit that it sure felt more comfortable in the summer months.

"Isn't that one of the ten commandments? 'Thou shalt not tempt the Lord your God.' "

"No, it isn't, and the way I see it, we're admiring one of God's most awesome creations." TJ laughed. "Now quit being such a wise-guy and start filming the storm. Maybe one of the local TV stations will buy some footage. It's happened before."

Sporting an amused expression, Seth retrieved the video camera from TJ's Silverado and began recording the squall. Moments later, the temperature fell and the wind picked up. The long grass in the nearby field bowed in respect.

"Um. . .should we run for cover now? It's pretty windy."

"Naw. Keep filming."

"Wind has always given me the frights."

TJ chuckled. "Stop being such a sissy."

Seth shot him a look of mock exasperation and TJ laughed again. They'd been friends for a good part of ten years—long enough to razz each other. At the time of their meeting, Seth was in college, and every Saturday night he'd volunteer at a storefront church in downtown Charleston. TJ had just hired on with the Chadwyks at their bed-and-breakfast, and at the older couple's suggestion, he gave the church a try. Seth had immediately befriended him and, even though TJ was more than twenty years his senior, the two had bonded and remained comrades over the years.

And TJ owed him his life. Had it not been for Seth Brigham and the Chadwyks, TJ figured he'd be dead—or worse.

"Whoa, look at that!"

TJ snapped from his reverie in time to see a twister begin to form. If it touched down it'd likely be a mile wide—might be categorized as a "wedge" tornado. TJ had heard this variety of funnel described as "boiling balls of black fog." But fortunately for all in its path, the funnel cloud stayed near the heavens. Then all too quickly, it dissipated.

TJ felt mildly disappointed.

"That was amazing! I've never seen anything like it!"

TJ grinned at the enthusiasm in Seth's voice but kept photographing the storm as it moved off to their right.

Minutes later, the clouds burst opened and rain poured down. The men hastened into TJ's Silverado.

"That was awesome!" Seth grabbed his sweatshirt from out of the backseat and wiped his face.

TJ grinned. He had a feeling his friend might have just gotten bit by the storm-chasing bug.

Chapter Three

The tears wouldn't abate. Sitting at the wooden table in her parents' orange, yellow, and white kitchen, Blythe knew she'd made a terrible mistake.

"I want my baby back."

"You made your decision. You can't go back on it."

Through bleary eyes, Blythe stared at her mother. Petite with midnight black hair that hung to her tiny waist, Lydia Severson was oftentimes mistaken for Blythe's older sister. "But I changed my mind. I want my baby. . . ."

"Blythe, get your head together," her father, Peter Severson, said. His tone wasn't harsh, just insistent.

As she rested her sad eyes on her dad, she thought he appeared every bit the hip college professor in his blue jeans and tweed jacket. He knew Joshua Rollins and liked him.

41

He'd brought Josh home on several occasions, and that's how Wendy met him.

"But—"

"No 'buts.'" Peter folded his six-foot-four-inch frame into an orange vinyl upholstered chair. He was fair-skinned and wore his riotous, curly tangerine-colored hair to his shoulders. His beard, a shade of reddish brown, covered the lower half of his face. "Babe, it's over." He reached across the table and set his hand on top of Blythe's. "The legal documents have been signed. It's over. But look on the bright side. You're no longer saddled with an infant. You've got your life back, your whole future to consider. So what are you going to do with the rest of your life?"

Blythe couldn't think past the misery in her heart long enough to even ponder the question.

"I think you need to go back to school," Lydia said.

"I'm all for that," Peter concurred.

At that instant, a skinny young man in tattered jeans and a wrinkled camouflage T-shirt stepped into the room. He had a head full of bushy blond hair. "Hey, like, what time are you dishing up the grub?"

"In a few minutes, Beaner." Lydia turned to the stove and stirred the vegetable soup simmering in the stainless steel kettle. Homemade rolls baked in the oven.

"I'm feeling like a refugee in a Third World country," the young man drawled on a facetious note. "I haven't eaten, like, all day and these far-out smells are driving me wild."

Peter smiled and turned to the latest hippie taking refuge in the Severson household. While the neighbors complained about the "weirdos," Pete and Lydia—and Blythe, too—believed in extending kindness to strangers and reveled in meeting new people. Pete and Lydia called the experience "mind expanding."

"Dinner will be worth the wait. I promise," Pete told Beaner with a smile. "My better half's a great cook."

"My nose agrees with you, man."

Lydia turned to her husband. "Beaner is from Oklahoma. He's attending the university but was forced to leave the dormitory."

"Yeah, they, like, caught me with a nickel," he said, referring to the amount of marijuana found in his possession.

"So he needed a place to crash for a while," Lydia continued, "and he heard about us."

"Welcome." Pete stood, grinned, and extended his right hand. "Nice to meet you, Beaner."

While introductions got underway, Blythe stood and slipped out of the kitchen unnoticed. Grabbing her raincoat, she left the house, feeling as though no one in the world cared how wretched she felt.

Outside, the sky was gray and it had rained most of the day. The weather was a true reflection of Blythe's present state of mind. Her life had no purpose. Too bad she hadn't died with Rob on the streets of Chicago.

Heading east through Oakland Park's business district, she thought about taking her own life. The idea of drowning herself in Lake Michigan gained momentum with her every stride. With her thoughts tangled and skewed, she heedlessly stepped into the bustling traffic on Central Avenue. Several cars screeched to a halt with horns blaring. Blythe wished they had hit her. Reaching the other side of the street, she kept walking, wondering where the tallest peak overlooking the lake was located.

Then someone caught her upper arm and spun her around.

"Blythe! What in the world are you doing? You almost got yourself run over back there!"

She tried to focus on the face of the man standing before her but realized she couldn't make out his features through the thick veil of her tears. However, she did notice his dark blue uniform.

"Jack?"

"Yeah." He leaned closer to her. "You're crying. What's wrong?"

Blythe covered her face with her hands and sobbed. How could she describe the utter hopelessness and despair that filled her being?

Jack set a brotherly arm around her shoulders. "Hey, c'mon, things can't be that bad."

"Things are worse than 'that bad,'" she choked in reply.

He gave her a little hug. "Let's go have a cup of coffee. I can take a few minutes' break."

Blythe shook her head. "No. I—I have. . .plans."

"What kind of plans?"

Blythe shrugged out from under his arm. "None of your business. Just because you're a cop doesn't mean you have the right to interfere in people's lives."

She turned to walk away, but he caught her arm again.

"Hey, Blythe, I've got two eyes. I can see you're upset, and as a *friend*, not a cop, I'm concerned about you."

"Leave me alone." She twisted out of his hold and continued on her way. When she'd gone a block, she looked over her shoulder. Jack was watching her with that piercing brown-eyed gaze of his, but he made no attempt to follow.

No wonder Allie fell in love with him. What girl wouldn't succumb to Jack Callahan's charm and good looks, not to mention the fact that he was just an all-around nice guy?

Blythe slowed her pace and Jack's words replayed in her mind. . .*as a friend, not a cop, I'm concerned about you.*

She felt bad for lashing out at him. He had tried to be a friend. She was simply incapable of opening her wounded heart and allowing anyone else in.

But her pain and misery would end soon.

She pressed on, making her way along Central Avenue. The rain pelted her face, but Blythe didn't care. She'd be a whole lot wetter when she drowned herself.

Turning left, she decided on a shortcut through Central Park to the lake. She strolled along the quiet, tree-lined street adjacent to the park where the lawns were wide and well groomed. Likewise, the homes stood tall and proud.

Suddenly, Blythe spotted a heap of trash on the curb just ahead. It seemed so out of place in this upscale neighborhood. Reaching the debris, she saw the battered, white wooden crib, and stopped.

Why would someone throw away a child's crib?

A quick inspection of the bed told her it had seen better days. The wooden legs on both headboard and footboard were split; obviously, they could no longer sustain the weight of the metal mattress springs. The crib appeared unsafe and beyond repair.

But then something else caught her eye. It was the sweet face of a teddy bear. Sticking her hand into the rubble, she pulled it out and realized the painted wooden figure was part of a bookend. Was there another?

Blythe rummaged through the junk and found the match.

She turned the pair in her hands. They appeared unscathed. A closer inspection revealed that each bookend was shaped like a storybook on which the teddy bears sat. One bear wore spectacles and the other a red beret. Both held books in their paws and were posed as if reading. Instinctively, Blythe held them closer, shielding the wooden creatures from the rain.

Then, all at once, she knew she couldn't end her life. Kylie might need her someday.

A vehicle pulled up alongside the curb, startling Blythe. At second glance, she realized it was a police car. None other than Jack Callahan, one of Oakland Park's finest, was seated behind the wheel.

He rolled down the window. "Can I give you a lift home?"

Very slowly, she nodded.

Standing behind the counter in Precious Things, Blythe thought of the teddy bear bookend once more. Today was April 10. Kylie's birthday. Would the card and gift Blythe sent arrive in time?

For the last three decades, Blythe had kept the bookend bear with the spectacles—the same one she'd mailed off to Kylie last week. But, thirty years ago, she'd sent its twin to Wendy, who promised to place the gift in Kylie's room on the shelf. It would hold her storybooks in place.

Does Kylie still have it or had she discarded it along with all her other childhood toys and books?

Deciding it didn't matter, Blythe sprayed the counter with foaming cleaner. Kylie would soon be married. Perhaps she'd use that bookend in her own child's bedroom someday.

How ironic, Blythe thought, wiping the glass with a piece of paper towel, that tonight was her scheduled evening to work at the crisis pregnancy center.

Kylie traipsed through the kitchen where her grandparents, Lee and Kathryn Chadwyk, stood at the long counter, preparing lunch. Both greeted her with a smile and she returned the gesture, even though awkwardness filled the airspace between them. Kylie sensed her grandparents were disappointed with her for stomping off from her birthday party like a spoiled child. But if they only knew how Matt had trifled with her feelings yesterday and how hurt she still felt from his cheating on her with Dena, maybe they'd understand.

Unfortunately, Kylie couldn't get herself to explain. If she started talking about it, she'd dissolve into tears. As it was, she'd cried herself to sleep last night. And all this in spite of the fact she'd made the decision to forgive both Matt and Dena.

But Kylie was in the throes of learning that forgiveness didn't make the hurt disappear. Her heart had been severely wounded and, like a skier who'd broken his leg in a fall, these things took time to heal. Why could no one understand?

And Matt. . .he'd won her grandparents over. Kylie still couldn't figure out how that happened. Nonetheless, they all seemed to expect her to snap out of her funk and miraculously return to the person she'd been a month ago, before she received the faded photograph Allie sent.

Unfortunately, that person didn't exist anymore.

"I'm going out to get the mail," Kylie muttered, reaching

the small back hall just off the kitchen. Dressed in faded blue jeans and a hunter green pullover sweater, she slipped her feet into a pair of winter boots.

"You still have presents to open from your party."

"I know, Grandma. I'll open them later. . .and don't worry. I plan to write everyone a thank-you note."

"I'm not worried."

Kylie caught the note of amusement in her grandmother's tone and grinned as she walked out the back door. Despite thirty-plus years of estrangement, her mother and Grandma Kate were remarkably alike. Sometimes when Kathryn Chadwyk spoke, it was like hearing her beloved mother's voice again. Kylie missed her.

Except the mother who raised her was her biological aunt—not her biological mother. Kylie wrestled with that truth upon learning it, and she'd since concluded that Wendy Rollins was "Mom" and always would be—especially since her natural mother didn't want anything to do with her.

Trudging down the soggy gravel driveway, Kylie avoided the potholes that were filled with rainwater after this morning's April shower. As she reached the mailbox on the side of the road, she heard a vehicle approaching. Looking up, she recognized Matt's pickup and clenched her jaw.

Please don't let him stop here. I don't want to talk to him.

To her dismay, Matt turned his truck into the driveway and sped uphill.

Great. Just great.

Kylie glanced down the highway, suppressing the urge to run. But where would she go? Her nearest neighbor lived half a mile away. Even if she did flee, it'd only be temporary. She'd have to come home sometime, and she'd have to face Matt.

Lord, this is harder than I ever imagined. Help me handle this situation with dignity. I blew it yesterday, but I want to manage things better today.

Pulling out the wad of mail that had been banded together, Kylie tucked it under one arm and shut the postal box's lid. Then she made her way up toward the house.

Matt met her halfway. "Happy birthday."

"Thanks." She halted, sensing he had more to say.

"I, um, well. . .I came over to tell you I'm sorry about yesterday. I shouldn't have teased you."

Kylie swallowed a retort and managed to produce a charitable reply. "Apology accepted."

He took a few steps forward and in spite of herself, Kylie noticed how attractive he was with his tousled blond hair and sparkling blue eyes. He wore the same red plaid jacket he had on yesterday, and the color enhanced his wind-reddened cheeks.

"All things considered, I haven't been very sensitive, I guess."

Kylie arched a brow.

"Mom pointed out that you've been through a series of traumatic events. I understand that, but. . .well. . ." Matt shrugged. "I guess I've selfishly wanted you to be the Kylie I know and love, the one who's always been there for *me*. I mean, you listened to me go on and on for hours about Rochelle and Jason," he said, referring to the wife and son he tragically lost in a car accident years ago.

And that was another sore spot between them. Matt was forever bringing up Rochelle and Jason, and Kylie didn't think she could live with those ghosts.

Matt took another step toward her. "You've always been

so strong, Ky. Strong and independent. It never seemed like you needed anyone or anything. But, see, all this time, I *needed* you and now that the table's been turned, I really don't know what to do."

It was on the tip of Kylie's tongue to remind Matt that no tables were turned when he parked his truck last January and pulled Dena into his arms. Every time she imagined the scenario, her stomach pitched.

"Matt, look, it's like I told you last week. I need time—time away. All I want to do is sell this house and get out of Basil Creek. Maybe after I'm away for a while—"

"Why? Why do you need to move away? Why can't you sell the house and stay here—with me?"

He was pushing her emotional buttons, but Kylie willed herself not to react.

"Kylie, I made a mistake. I was drunk." She could tell Matt did his best to conceal his exasperation, but Kylie heard strains of it in his tone. "I'm in counseling and I've recommitted my life to Christ. God's forgiven me—why can't you?"

"Because forgiveness has nothing to do with it. I forgive you."

"Then what is the problem?"

The lid suddenly blew off Kylie's boiling emotions. "The problem is, every time I see you, Matt, I feel like slapping your face."

There. She said it.

"Well, slap me, then. Get it out of your system."

His offer was so tempting, Kylie's palm itched. However, she had never struck another human being in all her life, and she wasn't about to start now.

She moved to walk around him, but Matt sidestepped into her path.

"Matt, please. . ." Kylie squeezed her eyes shut. "I'm hurt. I'm angry. And I don't like the feel of either emotion. They're foreign to me." She opened her eyes and stared at him, praying he'd go away. "Let me be. I'll work things through, but on my timetable—not yours or anyone else's."

"All right." Matt raised his hands in surrender. "You win. I'll leave you alone. I won't call or come over here anymore if that's what you want. But let me get one thing straight because I do need to get on with my life. We're not engaged anymore, right? You broke our engagement, so everything's off. No wedding come September. Is that correct?"

Her eyes welled up with such remorse that another piece of her heart chipped off. She wondered if she'd have anything left.

Letting the mail fall to the ground, she covered her face with her hands, wondering how, after last night, any tears remained.

"Is that a yes or a no?"

Kylie lowered her arms and glared at Matt through bleary eyes. How could he behave like such a brute? Hadn't she just admitted how hurt and angry she felt? How could he stand there and demand answers?

Matt shifted his stance. "A simple answer, Kylie, that's all I want. Because, see, if you're really calling things off between us, I'm going to need to heal too. I love you—more than I've ever loved anyone. Yeah, I was stupid a few months ago and made the biggest mistake of my life, but I already promised to spend the rest of my born days making it up to you. What else can I say?"

"Say it won't happen again. Ever." Kylie ran her fingers across her moistened cheeks.

Matt seized her gaze, and the light of sincerity in his eyes was unmistakable. "I swear it'll never happen again."

Still, Kylie didn't feel convinced. "How do you know?"

Matt blinked. "Because I just gave you my word."

"But you gave me your word before. I mean, we were promised to each other and you broke that promise."

Matt's cobalt eyes darkened, and he pointed a long calloused finger at her. "Kylie, you're holding that one incident against me, which means you haven't forgiven me at all. And that's not my problem. That's *your* problem."

All hope sunk and discouragement filled her being as she stooped to gather the mail she'd dropped.

And that's when she spotted it. The package with the shiny gold return address label. The way it had been banded between the magazines, catalogues, and bills, Kylie never guessed a small parcel was in the mix.

"Kylie, you know, I think I can take blatant rejection over a cold shoulder any day. Will you just say. . .*something?*"

She glanced up at Matt and held out the package. "It's from my biological mother in Chicago."

He held her stare and his stony façade seemed to crumble before Kylie's eyes. Hunkering beside her, he gave the parcel a quick inspection.

"What do you think it could be?"

"Don't know." Matt grinned. "Only one way to find out."

Standing, he took Kylie's hand and led her the rest of the way up the driveway and into the house.

CHAPTER FOUR

APRIL 1969

Blythe sipped her hot coffee and felt some of the chill leave her bones. She hadn't realized how cold she'd become out in the rain. When Jack pulled up in his squad car, Blythe decided to accept his proffered ride, and he made mention of her shivering in the passenger seat. Then he insisted on stopping for coffee.

"Won't Allie be jealous that we're sitting in this place together?" Blythe teased.

"Nah, she knows it's all in a day's work for me."

Blythe arched a brow. "Well, all right, *Superman.*"

Jack smirked at the retort before picking up the small bookend bears that she'd set on the table. He turned them in his hands. "What are these supposed to be?"

"I found them in that heap of trash on the curb."

"I figured that much out. . .but what are they?"

"Bookends."

Jack inspected each one. "What are you going to do with them?"

"I don't know." Blythe gazed into her *café au lait*. "I know they might seem useless, but they saved my life tonight."

"What?"

Blythe looked across the table at Jack and decided to confess. "I had every intention of drowning myself. That's where I was headed when you first stopped me on Central Avenue."

Leaning forward, he set the bookends down and placed his arms on the table. A deep frown furrowed his dark brows. "Why would you want to drown yourself?"

Tears gathered in Blythe's eyes. "Because I concluded life isn't worth living anymore. Not since Rob died. Not since I gave. . .gave my baby away. But when I found these bookend bears, I realized I couldn't end my life. Kylie might need me someday."

"You regret it? The adoption?"

Blythe managed a weak nod.

"Call Wendy and tell her you changed your mind."

"And then what? Lydia and Pete said they don't want a bawling baby in the house. I have no bread. No job." Blythe shook her head. "Kylie is better off with Josh and Wendy. I really believe that, even though it hurts so bad."

Jack shook his head in disbelief. "Your parents seem so. . . *accepting*. They take in every freak that shows up on their doorstep. Why wouldn't they allow you to keep your baby and stay with them?"

"Because, for one thing, they've despised their parental

roles since I was twelve or thirteen years old. So grandparent-hood is one unfathomable state of being for them. Pete and Lydia refuse to go there. To make matters worse, they never liked Rob. He wasn't intellectual enough for them. He was a dreamer. An artist. He wanted to change the world through nonviolence and beauty, and I know he could have done it, given the right opportunities."

"Well, I hate to tell you this, but I didn't appreciate Rob's, um, *talents* much either."

"No newsflash there, Jack."

"I know." He grinned and lifted his cup, and Blythe thought Jack's deep brown eyes and hair were the same color as his creamless coffee.

Her thoughts went round and round, from Jack to Rob and Rob to Kylie.

"I think I made the right decision about adoption. You should have seen how happy Wendy and Josh looked. They seemed like a real family." Blythe paused and relived those last moments when she'd placed her daughter in Wendy's arms. Then she blinked, realizing more tears were on the way. Quickly, she wiped them off her cheeks with shaky fingers. "Josh is crazy in love with Wendy. He just graduated from med school—"

"Blythe. . ." Jack reached across the table and grasped her hand. "I think you need some professional help."

She pulled away, feeling insulted—even threatened. "Like a shrink? Is that what you mean?"

"Maybe. You've been through a lot, emotionally and physically. But the Person you really need is Jesus Christ."

"Right. You've told me that before."

Blythe turned her head and gazed out the window. All

she saw was rain and gloom. It felt like the whole world was a lonely, desolate place.

Maybe she should have drowned herself after all.

"Blythe, will you let me tell you one more time about Jesus? He's the One who'll give you hope to face the rest of your life without Rob and your baby."

Blythe put her head in her hands. "I don't have the strength to face the rest of my life without Rob and Kylie."

"No. . .no, you don't. Not on your own. But Jesus Christ will lend you His strength—and He's Almighty God."

Blythe let her arms fall to the table. She gazed at Jack through misty eyes. She felt desperate and he seemed so confident about the answer to her troubles. "All right, Jack. Tell me again about Jesus. I'll listen this time."

"Let not your heart be troubled: you believe in God, believe also in Me. . . . Peace I leave with you. My peace I give to you. . . . Let not your heart be troubled, neither let it be afraid."

The Savior's words, as recorded in the fourteenth chapter of Saint John's Gospel, soothed Blythe's anxious soul. She reverently closed her Bible. Indeed, the peace that Jesus Christ offered filled her heart. Then again, Blythe knew God's Word rang true. The Lord hadn't let her down yet.

Sitting in her office in the back of Precious Things, she glanced at the old wooden kitchen clock, ticking off the minutes. She wondered if Kylie's mail had arrived yet. Had Kylie received the gift? What would she think of it? Would she be insulted that it wasn't something more valuable? Maybe she would see the teddy bear bookend for what it really was. . .an old piece of trash.

Feeling another wave of unease crash down around her, Blythe reopened her Bible to the book of John and read over those soothing words in chapter 14 once more. . . .

With her grandparents and Matt seated at the kitchen table watching her, Kylie peeled off the brown paper, revealing a small, four-inch-square box. Next, she opened its white cardboard lid and dug through the tissue paper before extracting a—

Kylie felt her brows pull together as she examined the bear. Small, but weighty, the wooden creature was seated on a pile of books. It looked familiar. Did she have one of these already?

"What is it?" Matt asked.

"It's a. . .a bookend."

"Just one?" Grandma Kate's expression matched the confusion Kylie felt. "Usually bookends come in a pair."

"Yes, that is rather odd to give only one as a gift."

Kylie glanced at her grandfather, Lee Chadwyk. His snowy white hair framed a face that disguised his age. No one would guess he was pushing eighty.

Then, suddenly, realization hit Kylie. She did have one like this. Just one. . .and this bookend was its match.

"Oh, my. . ." Her limbs felt weak as several implications whirred in her mind.

Matt stood. "Ky, are you okay? You look a little pale."

"I know where the other one is."

She headed to the stairs. Pure adrenaline allowed her to

take them two at a time. Kylie reached her bedroom and walked to the far wall where, years and years ago, her father had erected four long shelves. There, holding up her childhood favorites, sat an identical bear on a stack of wooden books, only he wore a red cap. The one in her hand sported reading glasses that slid halfway down his adorable little nose.

Inching the classic fiction works forward, Kylie placed the other bookend on the shelf. She imagined satisfied sighs emanating from both little fellows, now that they'd been reunited.

But what did it mean? Did Blythe have a change of heart?

Kylie stood there, staring at the bear bookends and pondering the idea for an immeasurable amount of time. Then two strong hands on her shoulders startled her out of her musings. Turning slowly, she looked up into Matt's face and saw his worried expression.

"Matt, I've had this one bookend forever." She took it off the shelf to show him, wondering if he'd understand. Up until now, he'd been impatient and seemingly uncaring of her journey to uncover the truth about the past. "Blythe sent its match. See?" She removed the other little bear, and *Cinderella, The Three Musketeers, The Nutcracker,* among others—including her *Anne of Green Gables* collection—toppled like dominoes. "What does it mean?"

Matt took the colorfully painted objects, scrutinizing them in his calloused palms.

"Blythe had to have sent this other bookend to me on purpose. What is she trying to say besides she remembered my birthday?"

"I don't know."

Matt handed back the bookends. After straightening the hardbound stories, Kylie set the bears in their rightful places.

"Ky, why don't you give the woman a call and start off by thanking her for the gift? See what she says."

"Yeah, maybe I will."

Spinning on her heel, Kylie faced Matt once more.

"I can't even imagine what you must be feeling right now." His voice was so soft that Kylie had to strain to hear him. "I just know that I want to help you through this trial. Will you let me?"

What could she say? Love and anger, mingled with a profound sense of loss and betrayal, all warred within the depths of her being. There were no words to describe how she felt.

Matt gathered her into his arms, and this time Kylie didn't push him away. With her hands on his waist, she felt the thickness of his leather belt beneath the flannel shirt he wore hanging over his blue jeans. Resting her cheek against his shoulder, she felt the softness of his blue and green plaid shirt and inhaled the woodsy, outdoor smell she'd come to associate with Matt.

"I love you, Ky." He spoke the words into her hair. They soothed her like a caress.

His hold on her tightened, and Kylie slipped her arms around his trim midsection. It seemed the most natural response in the world, and despite her roiling emotions, she suddenly felt like that little bear bookend, reunited with its created equal.

———— ❦ ————

"Allie, you're making me nervous."

"Not to worry." She grinned before placing a cup of steaming coffee in front of Jack. Then she joined him at the kitchen table of the home they'd purchased not too long ago. While he still kept the condo he owned and shared with his son, Logan, Allie lived here by herself—or she had until Patrice moved in with her. But all that would change in less than two weeks, after she and Jack married. She wouldn't live alone anymore and Patrice would have to leave.

"Not to worry? We're getting married in ten days, Patrice still doesn't have another place to go, and you're telling me *not to worry?*"

"Honey, relax." Allie placed her hand on Jack's forearm. "Logan, Marilee, and I. . .we're trying to find other living arrangements for Patrice. What's making it difficult is that no one seems inclined to want to house her indefinitely, or at least until her baby is born."

"I figured as much."

"A few weeks while we're gone won't be a problem, though."

Jack shook his head. His dark hair was peppered with gray. "Allie, we can't start off our marriage living with a crisis like Patrice."

"I think we could. She's been on her best behavior. She hasn't done drugs or alcohol—"

"That you know of," Jack cut in.

"She hasn't." Allie wasn't that naïve. She could tell. "And Patrice has been going to work every day. Logan picks her up and drops her off. She's always ready on time."

"For a week." Jack sipped his coffee. "It's only been a week. Anyone can behave for seven days."

Allie's patience wore thin under Jack's negativity.

"Look," he said, sitting back in his chair and regarding her with intense brown eyes, "its fine for the two of you—you're both women. But if Patrice continues to live here after you and I are married, I won't feel comfortable in my own home. I mean. . ." He shrugged. "What if I want to watch TV in my boxers?"

Allie smirked but decided against making a smart remark. And she had to admit Jack had a point, although she wished he could think outside of his own desires. After all, Patrice's stay would be only temporary.

"What, no reply? I expected better from you, Allie."

"I'm exercising self-control."

"Ah. . ." Jack chuckled and took a gulp of coffee.

"But since I don't know how long I'll last, don't goad me."

He gave her an amused look but said nothing.

"Besides, we have a lot to accomplish in just a few hours."

Jack glanced at his wristwatch. "What's on the agenda?"

Pushing back her chair, Allie stood and fetched her "to-do" list off the kitchen counter. She rattled off the first five tasks and Jack groaned.

"And if you don't complain, I'll buy you dinner at a restaurant of your choice."

Jack's deadpan expression said he wasn't impressed by her ultimatum.

"Come on now. Don't play hard-to-get."

"Allie, I hate shopping. An afternoon driving from store to store is as bad as going to the dentist. The mall is *worse* than the dentist."

She folded her arms. "If we work together, we can make it a fast trip. Tell you what. If we get done in time, I'll cook for you tonight."

Heaving an exasperated sigh, Jack stood to his feet. "Okay. But once we're married, I'm not going shopping anymore."

"Fine. Just give me your credit cards and the checkbook and I'll go all by myself."

Jack narrowed his dark gaze. "Kind of a frightening thought—you and my money on a shopping trip."

Allie gave him a tight smile then made her way into the foyer where she pulled her spring jacket from the front closet. She didn't want to hurt Jack's feelings, nor did she want to start an argument, but Allie had her own money. She didn't need Jack's. And if she wanted to go shopping, she would!

Jack had followed her through the house and now stood behind her, politely assisting her into the black, short-waist coat.

"Allie, I was being facetious back there in the kitchen. Something tells me you didn't appreciate my humor."

"No, I guess I didn't. But I've got a lot on my mind right now."

She turned and faced the man she'd marry at the end of this month. She loved him so much—ever since she was seventeen. They'd both made grave mistakes in their lives, but by God's mercy and grace, they were now free to spend the rest of their lives together as husband and wife.

"I apologize for offending you."

"All's forgiven."

Meeting her gaze, he stroked her right check with the backs of his knuckles, and Allie was once again reminded of the many errors she'd made in the past.

Like marrying Erich. She would forever bear the consequences of that disaster in the form of the scar on her cheek—the very one Jack now caressed.

Yet in spite of his tenderness, a wave of uncertainty washed over her being. Where had it come from? Allie thought she'd gotten past all her doubts and insecurities. She'd prayed about marrying Jack. She sensed her heavenly Father's approval. Perhaps their mixed views on Patrice, money, and shopping had caused her to feel suddenly unsure about her future with Jack. Even so, she'd known all along that they weren't going to agree on everything in life.

"Allie, what's wrong?" Jack frowned. "You look troubled."

"I think I'm having an anxiety attack," she admitted.

"The idea of shopping will do that to a person." Jack grinned.

"Oh, you!"

Allie smiled and playfully slapped his hand away. The stress that had settled around her like an invisible fog dissipated. She hoped and prayed it would vanish forever.

Inhaling a deep breath, Allie felt her pragmatic side emerge. She strode toward the front door and beckoned Jack to follow. "Come on. We'll compromise. You can wait in the car and I'll shop."

"Such a deal," he groused.

Allie just laughed.

CHAPTER FIVE

"Blythe, why were you in that squad car? You blew my mind. I thought the neighbors called the cops again. Are you in trouble?"

Entering the living room, Blythe watched as her mother let the drapery panel fall back over the window. "Lydia, everything's cool. That was Jack Callahan. He gave me a lift home."

"What's that you're carrying?" Pete asked before drawing deeply on the pipe he held in his hand.

Blythe glanced at her father, who sat in a rust-colored wing-backed chair in the far corner of the living room. From the sweet smell filling the air and seeing how her father held his breath before expelling a cloud of bluish smoke, she knew it wasn't tobacco in the pipe. He'd probably bought dope from Beaner.

She looked down at the items in her hand before replying to her dad's question. "I found some cute bookends in the garbage and then Jack lent me his Bible. He's a born-again Christian and he wants me to read the book of John. Really heavy stuff. Jesus is, like, the Savior of mankind and it's all documented in four different Gospels."

"I've read the Bible cover-to-cover," Pete said. "You're right. It's heavy." He handed the pipe to Lydia, who took a hit. "I've concluded God is whoever you want Him to be. That's the beauty of being free."

"Not according to Jack. There's only one way to God and that's through His Son, Jesus Christ." Blythe raised the Bible to emphasize her point. "That's why I want to read about it for myself."

Pete nodded his approval, and Blythe knew he was all for people searching out what they believed.

"Blythe, um. . .your dad and I have been rapping about what to do with you. . .you know, since you're so bummed out. We think it might be a physical thing. Postpartum depression. Very common after having a baby."

Tingles of foreboding worked their way up Blythe's spine as she stepped farther into the room. "What to do with me? What do you mean?"

"Babe, we think you need a change of scenery, like *bad.*" Pete reclaimed the pipe. "Garth called tonight and when I told him how down you've been on life, he said you could visit him."

"Garth? Uncle Garth?" A vision of a blond giant with keen blue eyes flashed across her mind. "But doesn't he live on the other side of the world or something?"

"Singapore. Yep, that's him," Pete replied.

Blythe's heart squeezed in disbelief. "You're kicking me out and banishing me to a Third World country?"

Pete chuckled at her sarcasm. "No, we're not kicking and banishing here. Relax. You're way too uptight. As for Third World living, that doesn't describe my younger brother's existence. He's made a fortune and owns a sprawling estate."

"With servants," Lydia added with a sneer. "Garth claims he pays them, but it sounds like those people are no more than slaves."

Pete pursed his lips in thought, and his forehead crinkled. He appeared every bit the philosophical professor. "We're all slaves if you think about it. Slaves to our own minds." He took a hit off the pipe.

"Oh, that's heavy, Pete."

Blythe glanced upward. Her parents were stoned. Little wonder they'd freaked out when Jack dropped her off minutes ago.

Ignoring them *and* their crazy idea about visiting Uncle Garth, Blythe tucked Jack's Bible under her arm. She made her way upstairs and into her bedroom. There, she shelved the bookend bears before undressing and climbing into bed. She turned the delicate pages of the Bible to the place Jack had marked with a paper napkin. The Book of John. Then she began to read about Jesus and how He had come not to condemn the world, but that the world through Him might be saved. . . .

⊶⊷

The ringing of the telephone brought Blythe's thoughts back to the present. She made her way across the shop to where the phone sat on the counter near the cash register.

"Thank you for calling Precious Things. This is Blythe speaking."

"Blythe?"

"Yes. Speaking." She paused, wondering if the female voice at the other end sounded familiar.

"This is Kylie. Kylie Rollins."

Pushing a smile to her lips, Blythe ignored the hammering of her heart. She'd hoped Kylie would call. "Well, hello, and happy birthday."

"Thanks. I got the present you sent in today's mail."

"Glad to hear it. I had hoped it would reach you by your birthday."

"I must confess that I was sort of puzzled when I opened the box and found only one bookend. Usually they come in a pair."

Blythe held her breath.

"But then I remembered that I already have the other one. I've had it forever. Did you know that?"

"Yes." Blythe inhaled a steadying breath. "I sent one bookend shortly after you were born. There's a story behind those little bears, you see, and at the time I couldn't get myself to relinquish the second one."

"Um. . .well, I'm sorry, but I don't get it. You gave me up easily enough. Why would you hang onto a bookend?"

Blythe felt as though she'd just been delivered a mighty blow. Her arm went across her abdomen as she fought for the air to return to her lungs. Is that really what Kylie thought? That adoption had been a flip decision? Blythe had cried a river of tears after giving up her daughter to Josh and Wendy.

But how would Kylie know?

At the other end of the phone line, the younger woman expelled an audible sigh. "I'm sorry, Blythe. That was a thoughtless remark and totally unfair of me. I know nothing about you. I shouldn't have passed judgment. It's just that I'm dealing with so much right now. You have no idea. In addition to missing my mom who, as I told you, died in January, my fiancé cheated on me with my best friend, and then I come to find out I'm adopted and you're my birth mother." She paused. "You *are* my biological mother, aren't you?"

"Yes."

"Thought so."

A weighty pause.

"Well, in addition to that discovery, I also found out that I have grandparents who live in South Carolina. I went to visit them. They're wonderful people. But my mom lied to me my whole life! She said her parents were dead and that she was an only child. Mom said she was from around here, but the truth is, she'd grown up out East."

By now, Blythe had seated herself in a cane-back chair. It was either sit down or fall over from shock. Words escaped her. She'd always thought Wendy should have been truthful with Kylie regarding Rob and her parents. But telling part of the truth would have led to all of it, and then everything Blythe had worked so hard to achieve would have been jeopardized. Wendy had felt she stood to lose just as much.

And, in Blythe's case, that still could happen; however, Blythe couldn't turn her back on Kylie now, especially when her daughter was facing such great emotional hardships. The death of her mother, a broken engagement, discovering she'd been adopted—any one of those would have pushed Blythe over the edge of sanity, let alone all three combined. And then to learn she had living grandparents. . .

Oh, Lord, how do I encourage Kylie?

"Blythe, are you still there?"

"Yes."

"Good. I was afraid you'd hung up on me. I guess I would have deserved it."

"No. . .I didn't hang up."

"I hope you don't have customers in your shop; I should have asked if this is a good time to talk. I usually try to be polite and conscientious."

Blythe smiled. "I know. Josh and Wendy did a fine job bringing you up."

"I loved them very much."

"I know."

Kylie sighed audibly. "When I was in your store several weeks ago, you didn't want to talk to me. You said you made a vow. But, seeing as you sent me a birthday present, I'm thinking you changed your mind."

"Yes, I changed my mind. I started thinking that. . .well, if you needed me, I wanted to be there for you."

"Thanks, Blythe, that's very kind of you."

"It's the least I can do."

"I have so many questions. . . ."

"I'll try to answer as many as I can."

Another pause.

"Did you and my mom keep in touch over the years?"

"Yes." Blythe pulled a tissue from the Kleenex box on the counter and dabbed the tears that had suddenly filled her eyes.

"And my mom's brother, Rob Chadwyk, is actually my biological father?"

"Yes." It amazed Blythe that she still felt the pangs of a

thirty-two-year-old heartache.

"Did you ever meet my grandparents?"

"No."

"They're really terrific. They're here in Wisconsin with me now. I'm selling the house and moving to Sabal Beach with them."

Blythe's jaw dropped as she tried to grasp the meaning. "You? You're moving. . .in with your grandparents? Wendy's folks?"

"Yep. We get along great and I want out of Basil Creek in the worst way."

"Wendy must be turning in her grave."

Momentary silence.

"My mom couldn't ever forgive her parents, could she? My grandmother told me all about their falling-out."

"Well, there's more to it. Wendy blamed them for Rob's death. She always thought that if they would have supported him, given him money, helped him get to Canada and avoid the draft, then Rob wouldn't have died."

"Do you believe that?"

"No. In fact, I don't think I ever really did."

"Well, my grandparents were devastated to find out their children are dead. All this time, they thought Rob and my mom were alive and well and living. . .*somewhere.*"

Blythe's heart went out to the older couple.

"They'd like to speak with you. They stopped by your shop one Saturday, but you were on vacation."

Blythe closed her eyes in anguish. So Lydia's hunch had been correct after all.

"My grandparents are nice people, Blythe. They're like me, looking for answers so they can bury the past and move on."

"What about your fiancé?"

"I broke our engagement about a month ago. He wants to get back together and. . .maybe I do too. I don't know. I'm confused. Matt hasn't been very understanding, but I think he's trying." Kylie blew out a breath of exasperation. "I'm not sure. Anything's possible at this point."

Yes, she sounded confused.

"So, can they talk to you?"

"Who?"

"My grandparents."

"Oh, um. . ." Blythe took a moment to consider the request. "Kylie, I. . .well, see. . ." She swallowed and began again. "Look, I don't think I'm up for getting grilled by your grandparents. I've been an emotional mess ever since that Saturday you entered my shop."

"Could my grandmother e-mail you? Maybe that way you wouldn't feel pressured."

Blythe mulled it over. "Okay, we can try E-mail."

"Great. And what about me?"

"You can e-mail me too."

"Just e-mail?"

"Um. . ."

"I guess what I want to know, Blythe, is do you want a relationship with me?"

She almost laughed. Her daughter sounded so much like Rob and Wendy. Those two had been get-to-the-point people. They spoke their minds and possessed wills of steel.

"I'd like for us to. . .to get to know each other. I'd like to be your. . .well, your friend, Kylie."

"I'd like that too."

There was a smile in the young woman's voice, one that

caused Blythe to relax. Until now, she hadn't realized the tension building around her shoulder blades.

The door suddenly opened and the tiny bell above it signaled the entrance of her uncle. It was his daily practice. He liked to check on his "investment."

"I need to hang up," Blythe said in a hushed tone.

"Sure. Just tell me your E-mail address first."

"Blythe at Precious Things dot com."

"Got it. Thanks. And thanks for the birthday present."

"You're welcome. Talk to you later." Blythe placed the receiver in its white plastic cradle then turned to the tall man leaning on his shiny wooden cane. "Hi, Garth." She pushed out a smile. "You're just in time. I was about to brew some coffee."

───◦◦◦───

Kylie pressed the OFF button on her portable phone, feeling a measure of satisfaction intermingled with relief. Blythe wanted to know her better. She wanted to be Kylie's friend.

Lord, that's more than I had hoped for. Thank You!

Seated on the edge of her bed, Kylie fell backwards into the fluffy down comforter and gazed at the white ceiling. Maybe things in her life were improving. She'd begun to feel depressed since returning from her mini-getaway in South Carolina. Then, again, April in Basil Creek could do that to a person.

An unfamiliar presence around her left wrist caused Kylie to remember the gift Matt had given her. She never did get around to opening it at her party yesterday evening, but after their embrace hours ago, he'd insisted she unwrap his present.

Lifting her hand, Kylie inspected the lovely gold and silver watch. Engraved on the backside of its gold-trimmed face were the words *Matt & Kylie forever*. When Matt clasped the watch on her wrist, he'd whispered that their love would last 'til the end of time. Kylie wanted so badly to believe him.

The phone rang and Kylie lifted the handset to view the Caller ID. She grinned when she saw the call originated from South Carolina. Pushing the TALK button, she put the phone to her ear.

"Hello, Rollinses. . ."

"Kylie?"

"Yep."

"Hi, it's Seth."

She smiled. "I thought it might be you."

"It's me, all right."

Her smile broadened, hearing Seth Brigham's baritone voice with its perpetual note of amusement. Kylie had been introduced to Seth during her stay in Sabal Beach. He was a friend of TJ McGwyer, the guy who managed her grandparents' bed-and-breakfast.

"Happy birthday. Hope you're having a good one."

"You sound like a greeting card."

"Thanks. I've been practicing all afternoon."

Chuckling, Kylie rolled onto her stomach and bent her legs, crossing them at her ankles.

"So, what's new?" Seth asked.

"A lot of things. Matt and Dena showed up at my party yesterday. Both brought gifts."

"Peace offerings?"

"I don't know. . .maybe." Kylie glanced at the watch.

She'd poured her heart out to Seth one Sunday afternoon, so he knew the situation. "Matt obviously put some thought into the present he bought me since he had it engraved. And Dena purchased the most gorgeous lilac-colored sweater I've ever seen. It's a perfect fit. She knows me that well."

"Well, now I feel bad that I didn't get you anything."

"I'll cut you some slack this year."

"This *year?* Are you implying that the two of us have a future?"

Kylie laughed, unsure of how to reply. When she thought of her future, she could only imagine sharing it with Matt. And, although she enjoyed the easy banter with Seth, she knew it wasn't right to lead him on.

After learning of her broken engagement, Seth had asked her out and, needing a diversion, she'd accepted the offer. They dated a couple of times, and then Seth requested that she pray about a romantic relationship between the two of them. Kylie promised she would, and it was obvious that Seth, a successful computer programmer in his early thirties, wanted to settle down with a wife and raise a family. While Kylie desired the same thing, it was painfully evident that she still loved Matt.

Oh, God, what do I do?

Her heart ached for Matt, but common sense leaned toward developing this friendship with Seth.

"Hey, let me tell you about my afternoon yesterday."

Kylie forced herself to pay attention. "Sure. Let's hear it."

"TJ talked me into chasing a storm with him, and it was awesome."

Kylie imagined Seth's toffee-colored eyes growing large with enthusiasm.

"A huge, black funnel cloud dropped out of the sky, but it didn't touch down. No damage done, other than it snapped off a few tree limbs. For the most part, the twister just sort of blew over and disappeared. But TJ took pictures of it and I filmed it. Today we learned a national weather station wants to buy our footage for a documentary."

"Congratulations." Kylie smiled, feeling proud of her friend's endeavor, and if nothing else, Seth was her friend.

"I've got to admit, I was scared silly at first," he told her. "TJ called me a sissy."

She bit the inside of her cheek to keep from laughing.

"So I got to thinking about it—the 'sissy' thing, that is—and I decided to get my hair cut. Happened this afternoon. Walked into one of those chop shops and got it all cut off."

"All of it?"

"Well, no. That is, I don't resemble TJ or anything."

"Oh. . ." Kylie couldn't hide her disappointment. "I rather liked that avant-garde style on you, Seth."

"Not to worry. You can still run your fingers through my hair. I'm not bald like TJ."

Kylie cast a glance upward and grinned. "I said *avant-garde style* and nothing about running my fingers through your hair."

"Well, that's okay. You still have my permission—as long as I can return the gesture."

Laughing, Kylie barely made out the words, "You are such a nut." But moments later, she heard tires crunching the gravel on the driveway outside her bedroom window. She knew Matt and Lynellen had arrived for dinner. Grandma Kate had extended the invitation while Kylie opened birthday presents this afternoon, and Matt accepted, much to

Kylie's both pleasure and dismay. She wished she could figure out exactly how she felt about Matt. The confusion was wearing her out.

"Seth, I have to hang up. Company just arrived. I'll e-mail you later."

"Sounds good. Take care."

"You too."

Kylie disconnected the call then pushed herself off her bed. She straightened her shirt, then walked to her dresser and inspected herself in the mirror. Deciding she looked presentable, she headed downstairs to greet her guests.

CHAPTER SIX

APRIL 1969

Blythe's gaze wandered around the magnificent ivory-colored foyer of her uncle's enormous home. Even with her limited knowledge of artistic design, she could appreciate the intricately carved arches over four separate entryways, which led into other parts of the house. Glancing at her feet, she marveled at the polished stone flooring on which she stood.

"I think you'll be comfortable here, Blythe."

She regarded her aunt Sabina. The woman bordered on pleasingly plump, and her disposition was all sunshine and smiles. "I'm sure I'll be fine. Thanks for inviting me."

"Of course. Garth and I are glad you took us up on our offer."

Blythe pushed out a polite grin. Truth be told, she hadn't

been given much of a choice. Pete and Lydia determined that Blythe's blues were generating bad karma in the house, so they gave her an ultimatum. She could check herself into a sanitarium, one they'd heard about in the Upper Peninsula, or she could spend the summer at Uncle Garth and Aunt Sabina's mansion in Singapore. Or she could move out altogether. Since the latter would take more money and energy than Blythe possessed, she nixed that idea. The sanitarium option conjured up images out of Ken Kesey's novel, *One Flew Over the Cuckoo's Nest*, so Blythe chose Uncle Garth's place.

Besides, after one phone call, she'd learned her aunt and uncle were born-again Christians like Jack, Allie, Wendy, and Josh. For that reason, Blythe felt safe with her relatives, even in a foreign country that was in the same hemisphere as Vietnam.

What would Rob say if he knew. . . ?

"Let me show you to your room where you can take a rest before dinner," Sabina said. "I'm sure you're exhausted. The flight from the States seems endless, doesn't it?"

Blythe nodded.

"I'll have one of our hired men bring up your suitcases." Sabina escorted Blythe through the foyer and up a grand staircase that rivaled something from *Gone with the Wind.* "God has really blessed us. Shortly after Garth and I arrived in Singapore, we met a man named Thurman Wallace. He was an entrepreneur who had the wisdom to see how manufacturing companies would benefit by bringing their business to this country. Thurm helped revolutionize Singapore and he made millions. Garth began working for him and was soon running the company. Now Garth owns it." Reaching the top of the steps, Sabina turned and beamed over her husband's success. "We feel God blessed us, so we try to share our wealth and help others."

"Very generous of you." Blythe stood in awe as she took in her opulent surroundings. "This place is outta sight."

"What?" Sabina pulled up her dusty-blond eyebrows in a frown.

"Oh, that means I like it. I'm impressed."

"Ah. . .well, pardon me for being so far removed from the U.S.A.'s popular culture."

"Hey, it's cool." Blythe smiled.

Sabina smiled right back. "Come along now, dear, let's get you settled. . . ."

———— ∞ ————

The vehicle behind her honked and Blythe realized the stoplight had changed to green. She stepped on the accelerator and continued up Michigan Avenue, heading toward the Lincoln Park area and the home she shared with her mother. Years ago, Lydia had sold the house in Oakland Park shortly after Pete's death, and then she and Blythe pooled their funds and purchased a duplex, or "two-flat," in the upscale neighborhood of Lincoln Park. Lydia lived downstairs and Blythe right above her. With Lydia's health somewhat of a concern, Blythe wanted to be close by; however, both women wanted—and needed—their own "space" too.

Pulling alongside the curb, Blythe parked, climbed out of her minivan, and then made her way to the house. The rain had stopped and the sky was clear. The April air smelled fresh and felt cool against her face as she lifted her mail from out of the metal postal box beside the front door. Letting herself into the house, she walked up the steps to her apartment. She noticed the days were growing longer now; the living room wasn't quite as dark as usual. Nevertheless, Blythe closed the vertical blinds that hung over her front windows, coveting the privacy they provided.

Ambling through the living room, she entered the dining room and paused beside the mission-oak table where she set down her purse, tote bag, and the small stack of bills and catalogs. With her arms free of their burdens, Blythe headed for the kitchen, and thoughts of Aunt Sabina and Uncle Garth filled her mind again.

Blythe had remained in Singapore for three years before coming home. Since they'd never had children of their own, Sabina and Garth fondly referred to Blythe as the daughter they never had. Blythe was, in fact, their "daughter in the faith," as it'd been Sabina who explained God's simple plan of salvation in a way she clearly understood and accepted. Moreover, without Uncle Garth's generosity, Blythe wouldn't have been able to start up her business, Precious Things. Back then, banks wouldn't give her the time of day, much less a loan. But in allowing her uncle to finance her endeavor, she'd signed a contract with an ambiguous moral turpitude clause. If violated, according to the agreement, Garth gained control of Precious Things, and his investment had to be paid back in full, plus interest—and that amount of money was no small change.

Garth bought the building in which Precious Things was located, and Blythe all but gutted the place. She had the ancient rubber tiles removed and the wooden floor repaired, sanded, stained, and varnished. She installed new light fixtures and built an office in the back of the shop along with a bathroom and kitchenette. The space above the shop was turned into a workshop and storage area. Her uncle paid for everything.

Next, Blythe purchased her inventory even though about a third of the items in her store at the time were *precious things* she had collected over the years. Throughout the process, she consulted her uncle, the silent partner, and he encouraged her each step of the way. Hundreds of thousands of dollars later, her shop announced its grand opening. But, like many small business owners, Blythe experienced lean times and, as a result, she incurred some debt. Garth, of course, helped her out financially, but he insisted she do her part—and she did, by second mortgaging the house she owned with her mother. Lydia had conceded to the second house note on the condition that Blythe never violated her contract with Garth.

Oh, God, when I signed that contract I wasn't thinking about the past, just the future. Will Uncle Garth understand that—that my relationship with Rob and Kylie's birth both occurred before my salvation?

Blythe extracted a frozen entrée from her freezer, peeled away the package, and stuck the dinner in the microwave to cook. Those three years in Singapore had done wonders for her psyche, although the pain of losing Rob and Kylie never ceased. So Blythe created a minuscule compartment in her heart and stuffed those memories inside, sealing them off forever, lest they ever wound her again. Later, when Wendy began bringing Kylie into Precious Things, those memories fought for release, but Blythe never allowed it. Instead, she rejoiced year after year as Kylie grew into a lovely, intelligent, and very capable young woman.

Now Wendy's dead and Kylie might need me. . .but what do I do about Uncle Garth? And what about Lydia? The two of us could end up homeless.

She thought of her uncle, who had moved back to the States. Sabina had passed away almost two years ago, so Garth decided he needed to be with his "family," a unit that consisted of only Blythe and her mother. He resided in a nearby senior citizen complex, and for all his wealth, he lived a no-frills existence. He gave money to charities and funded after-school programs. He set up scholarships at Christian colleges and donated his time at the local Christian radio station—a pastime he enjoyed enormously.

But while Lydia thought him a religious fool who lived like a pauper, Blythe respected the man. For the three years she lived in Singapore, Garth had been more of a father figure to her than Pete had been during all her growing-up years. But as her uncle aged, he became rigid in his beliefs and more controlling of his funds. A donation had many strings attached to it. Blythe knew that much to be true.

That's why she dared not tell him about Kylie. Thirty-one years ago, Garth might have understood. If not him, then Sabina. Oh, how she wished she had confided in her caring, loving aunt!

Except, she thought they had known.

For years, Blythe had assumed Garth and Sabina were aware of her situation. Simply, she thought Pete and Lydia had told them. As for herself, Blythe hadn't been emotionally able to talk about losing Rob or to discuss Kylie's adoption. She had wanted to heal and move on with her life. She viewed her uncle's financial offer as a godsend. So, upon learning of the contract, Blythe signed it. However, years later, when

Lydia heard of their agreement, she had a fit. She saw the vow, the pact, as an infringement on Blythe's freedom. It came out then that Garth and Sabina were never told about Kylie. All they knew was that Blythe's "boyfriend" had been killed in a riot and that Blythe had a "breakdown."

Lydia swore her to secrecy. Because of that moral turpitude clause, they stood to lose everything—their home and Precious Things—so Blythe vowed to keep quiet. It had been easy to do while Garth resided in Singapore; there seemed to be little chance of him ever finding out about Kylie. But now that he was back in the States, living close by, there was more of a chance that he'd discover the truth. Therefore, he had to be told. . . .

Or did he?

Blythe mulled over her options. Would it be unethical if she didn't tell him? After all, falling in love with Rob and giving birth to Kylie happened prior to her conversion to Christianity. Was she, therefore, obligated to inform her generous but somewhat judgmental uncle of every past transgression simply because he happened to be the financial backer of her shop?

The microwave beeped and Blythe pulled out her dinner. Still feeling troubled, she ambled into the living room and turned on the evening news. Maybe after viewing the world's upheaval, she might actually start believing her problems weren't that bad after all.

—⦿—

"This lasagna is the best I've tasted." Kylie smiled at her grandmother, who was seated at one end of the dining room table. As always, she looked classy in her beige pants and brown and cream sweater.

"I'm glad you're enjoying it, dear."

"Everyone makes lasagna differently, don't they?" Lynellen Alexander remarked. She sat across from Kylie and beside Matt. "Mine has more of a casserole appearance to it. Then, again, Italian cuisine isn't my specialty, but my Norwegian meatballs will knock your socks off."

Chuckles flitted around the table and even Kylie laughed. She loved Lynellen. Redheaded and spunky, Lynellen Alexander appeared at least ten years younger than her actual age of sixty-three.

"You'll have to come to my place for dinner next time."

"We'd enjoy that," Grandpa Lee said from where he sat at the other end of the table. The hue of his bushy white hair seemed subdued beneath the dim candlelight. "Wouldn't we, Kathryn?"

"Absolutely, although, Lynellen, you were gracious enough to invite us to lunch last Sunday."

Lynellen waved her hand in the air, trivializing the matter.

"In any case, we accept," said Grandma Kate. "What do you say, Kylie?"

"Sure. Lynellen's meatballs are a favorite of mine."

Kylie made a point not to peer across the table and look at Matt, although she had to admit to feeling impressed by his behavior tonight. He hadn't nudged her once under the table if she said something that wasn't to his liking. Nor had he cleared his throat to make her look his way so he could send her back a meaningful glance. While that aspect of their relationship, the one in which Matt made her feel like a child, had always annoyed Kylie in the past, she never said anything. She had wanted to marry Matt and just figured it was part of his personality and something she'd have to learn to live with. Besides, she'd decided his overall benevolence made up for it. But now, she reminded herself, she didn't have to live with him. . .or his paternal, and slightly chauvinistic, ways.

I should be happy we're not engaged anymore. So then, why do I feel so depressed?

Dinner ended and Grandpa Lee fetched a deck of cards and began shuffling them. "Game of bridge, anyone?"

Kathryn and Lynellen stopped clearing dishes long enough to nod.

"Great." Grandpa Lee's gaze moved to Kylie. "You and Matt are welcome to join us."

Kylie glanced at Matt before pushing her chair back and standing. "Thanks, Grandpa, but I don't know how to play bridge."

"Me neither. Let's go out for a while, Ky."

"Sure, you two go and have fun," Lee said.

"Leave us old folks to our card game," Kathryn added, re-entering the dining room and settling back into her chair.

Kylie regarded her grandparents and Lynellen then looked over at Matt. Everyone in the room wanted to see her and Matt reunite. But what did she want?

He nodded toward the living room and Kylie followed him there.

"Tom's having some people over to watch the basketball game. Wanna go?"

Having little to no respect left for Matt's drinking buddy, Kylie shook her head. "Tom's house is the last place I want to go. No, make that the Red Rocket Lounge is the last place I want to go. In fact, I'll never set foot in there again."

Matt raised his hands, palm sides out. "Okay, okay. . ."

"But you're welcome to go if you want to."

"Ky, I want to spend time with you."

She laughed and its bitter ring echoed in her ears. "You want to spend time with *me* at Tom's place, watching basketball and drinking beer? Right. I really believe you."

"I wasn't planning to drink." Matt's voice was but a whisper.

"You know what? I don't care." Kylie folded her arms, trying to keep her temper in check.

"Want to go for a drive?"

"Nope." She narrowed her gaze, remembering how he'd parked with Dena that wintry night last January. "I'll never set a foot in your lousy pickup truck again either."

"Why? What did my truck do?"

"Nothing. It's what happened inside the truck that makes me sick."

Matt expelled an exasperated breath. "Give me a break, Kylie. Can't we just put that incident behind us. . .forever?"

"No, because it'll never be 'behind us.' Tom will always be inviting you to his house for sports and beer, the Red Rocket Lounge will be—"

"All right. Forget I asked!"

Matt slid his hands into the front pockets of his blue jeans. Anger reddened his complexion, all the way to his hairline. He shot a look into the dining room before his gaze returned to Kylie, and she figured he was about to tell her off and leave.

Good. She just wished he'd be quick about it.

Matt lowered his gaze and studied the floorboards. But

then he looked up at Kylie again and she could see sincerity in his eyes.

"Could I stay here with you? Could we talk? I mean, I'd like to hear about your trip to South Carolina—and about your biological mother. You haven't told me much. Just bits and pieces that I managed to put together along with everything your grandmother has told my mom."

His request put a chink in Kylie's defenses. But swallowing down the lump of pride was another matter.

"Two Sundays ago, your grandparents told me you became a Christian." Matt shook his head. "I thought you already were a Christian, and last week I realized that your accusations were right. I don't know you as well as I should. But I want to change that."

"Won't happen over a basketball game," Kylie muttered, leaning against the wooden doorframe that led into a narrow hallway.

"Forget the game. I was using that as an icebreaker. I thought you might feel more comfortable with me if other people were around." He shrugged. "It was just a suggestion."

Pulling his hands from his pockets, Matt reached out and entwined his fingers through hers. "Let's talk, Ky, okay? Let's talk about you. I want to know how you became a Christian. I'll tell you how and when it happened for me." He grinned, albeit ruefully. "Our faith should have been one of the first things we ever discussed—and it's my fault it wasn't."

He was saying everything Kylie wanted to hear, and Matt wasn't one to play games. Ironically, she knew him very well.

"What do you say?"

Kylie glanced at their clasped hands then stared up into Matt's face. He was trying to repair things between them.

She could see it in his Norwegian-German baby blues. As much as she once loved him—or maybe she still loved him like she always had—in any case, she felt obligated to give him another chance.

A tentative smile curved her lips. "Do you want to talk in the living room or the den?"

A look of gladness mingled with relief wafted across his features. "In the den."

Kylie led the way and, once inside the room, she dropped into the forest green swivel rocker, tucking one leg beneath her. Matt lowered himself onto the sofa across from her.

"You know, Ky, all this time I assumed you were a Christian."

"I thought I was," she confessed, "but the new friends I made in Chicago, Allie and Marilee, helped me see that I was trusting something other than Jesus Christ for salvation. I was trusting. . .me. I always tried to be a 'good girl' and do things right. In essence, I was trying to earn God's grace."

Matt winced and stared at his hands resting on his knees. "I just wish I had been more focused on spiritual matters. Maybe I could have helped you. But until recently, I haven't been close to Christ. If I'm not close to Him, I don't have the strength to act like a Christian. That's what Christian counseling has helped me see. Learning God's Word will keep me on the straight and narrow."

Kylie mulled it over and Jack Callahan came to mind. He had come back to Christ after thirty years of feeling like the things he'd done were unforgivable. If Jack could turn his life around, why couldn't Matt? It seemed to Kylie that God was all about second chances.

"I'm making a concerted effort to read some Scripture every day."

Kylie sent him a smile. "Both Marilee and my grand-mother have told me the importance of reading God's Word and praying every day—in other words, staying close to Christ. Grandma Kate has her devotions first thing in the morning with her coffee or a cup of tea."

"I like to have mine after the milking is done and once I've eaten breakfast. Sometimes it doesn't work out, though, and I have to put off my Bible reading. But then I try to get it in later. And I've been praying all the time, in the barn, on the tractor. For the first time in years, I really do feel close to God."

Kylie glanced at the seam of her slacks, contemplating Matt's remarks. She'd never heard him talk like this, and she couldn't deny feeling pleased if not downright encouraged. She had envied Marilee for having a fiancé who was such a devoted Christian. And one of the things that had attracted Kylie to Seth was his faith.

"Hey, Ky?"

She brought her gaze up and looked at Matt.

"Why don't you come over here and sit next to me?" He patted the seat beside him.

Hopefulness shone in his eyes, and it, along with his soft-spoken request, crushed any remnant of her resolve to end their relationship. In that very moment, she realized she truly did love Matt.

Standing, she crossed the room. Matt pulled her in beside him, one arm around her shoulders, the other across her midriff.

"I love you so much," he whispered.

His lips touched her ear, sending delightful shivers down her neck.

He pulled her closer still. "Look at me."

She did. His face was just inches from hers, his expression somber.

"I love you, Ky. I think about you day and night. Tell me you love me, too, because I don't think I'll be able to stand it if you don't."

"I love you, Matt. I love you!" The words erupted from the depth of her being. "The truth is—I never stopped. I tried to because I felt so angry. But it didn't work."

"Thank God!" Matt suddenly looked misty-eyed himself.

Then he kissed her and, like a miracle from above, Kylie's broken heart began to heal.

CHAPTER SEVEN

B lythe, we need to discuss your future."

"Why?" She stood at the window, watching the rain pour down, but then whirled around to face her uncle.

"You've been here for three years now, and—"

"You're sending me back to the States?" Suddenly she felt unwanted, first by her parents and now her uncle. "What did I do wrong?"

Garth chuckled and lowered his lumberjack-like body into a gold-upholstered armchair. "Blythe, my dear, you may stay here forever if you like. I'm not sending you any-where. But Sabina and I are concerned about you. You seem so. . .down."

Blythe nodded. "I think April will always be a difficult month for me." *It was three years ago that I gave away my baby*. She choked on the thought before it ever became spoken words.

"Hmm, I see, well. . .Sabina and I think you need a purpose in your life. It's not enough that you do a little bookkeeping for me. You need your own reason for being."

Collecting her wits, she looked at her uncle askance. "Such as?"

Garth steepled his fingers. "You tell me."

Blythe was speechless.

"If you could do anything in the world, and make a living at it, what would it be?"

"Pete would say I should finish college."

"Bully for Pete. I want to know what *you* want."

A slow grin pulled at her mouth. "That's easy. I'd have perpetual rummage sales."

"Really?" Garth's steely-blue gaze alighted with curiosity. "What would you do when your, um, *rummage* was gone?"

"I'd find more."

"Find?" Garth blinked.

Laughing, Blythe sat on the gold and brown sofa and detailed her talent of finding treasures among junk piles.

"Fascinating. And what sort of 'treasures' have you procured?"

Blythe shrugged as she recollected. "I've found everything from jewelry, clocks, and crystal vases to desks and dressers and lamps—and sweet little bookend bears that saved my life."

"Saved your life? How so?"

"I think I told you about how depressed I was before I came here. I contemplated suicide."

Garth dismissed the subject with a wave of his hand.

"We're not going backward, Blythe. We're discussing your future now."

"Right." She forced off any remaining emotion she felt. Garth was not overtly sentimental, although he did enjoy helping others. But once a need surfaced, he acted, and he preferred to be spared all the heart-wrenching details.

"Perpetual rummage sales, huh?" Garth mulled over the idea. "What about an antique shop?"

"Antiques are cool, but my finds are more along the lines of—of precious things. They're unique and sometimes valuable, but they aren't always old."

"Precious things. . .hmm. . ."

Blythe grinned as her uncle processed information like a human CPU, those monstrosities he was so taken with of late. Computers, Garth claimed, would someday be as much a household item as vacuum cleaners. Blythe and Sabina, of course, couldn't foresee that ever occurring. Why, people would need to build an extra room onto their homes just to store the things!

"Blythe," he began at last, sitting forward in his chair, "let's open a shop and sell 'precious things.' If we do it right, we could make quite a nice profit."

"Are you serious?"

He nodded his blond head. "I am."

A brand new hope bubbled up inside her. She hadn't felt so enthusiastic about anything since she became a Christian two-and-a-half years ago. "Uncle Garth, do you really mean it? Open a shop? Where will it be located? How will we begin?"

He laughed and stood, then stretched his arms over his head. "Let me get Sabina and the three of us will discuss this matter over dinner."

Blythe snapped from her musings when she heard the tiny bell above the front door of her shop jingle, signaling the entrance of a customer. Rising from her chair in the back office of Precious Things, she hurried into the shop only to see her uncle enter through the front door.

She smiled. "You're early."

"It's our monthly fund-raising day at the radio station." Closing the door, he stepped forward and unbuttoned his spring jacket. "I said I'd man the phones and record donations."

Blythe shook her head. "Uncle Garth, you could buy that radio station."

"Perhaps." A sheepish grin curved his thin lips. "But I wouldn't have nearly as much fun."

They shared a laugh as the telephone began to ring. Blythe moved to the checkout counter and reached for it.

"Thank you for calling Precious Things. This is Blythe."

"Hi, Blythe. It's Kylie. Got a minute?"

"Um. . ." She flicked her gaze in Garth's direction. "Not really."

"Okay, I'll let you go. But first let me just quickly tell you that my thirty-first birthday marked a turning point in my life. On that day I established a relationship with you, my natural mother, and I also decided to give Matt a second chance. We're engaged again."

"That's wonderful. I'm happy for you."

"I'm happy, too. For the past couple of days, Matt and I have done a lot of talking. I think we've worked through most of our issues."

"Super. I want to hear all about it. But let me call you back, all right?"

"Sure. I'll be here. I'm packing stuff up. Sorry to babble when you're busy. Want my phone number?"

"It's on my Caller ID. Talk to you later." Blythe disconnected the call before returning her attention to her uncle.

"You didn't need to end your conversation on my account," he said. "Was that Twila?"

"No, just another—friend." Blythe headed toward the kitchen area. "Cup of tea, Uncle Garth?"

"Not today. I want to hear about your friend on the phone."

Blythe halted her steps and tried to keep her stomach from forming a nervous knot. Slowly, she turned back around.

"Is it a gentleman friend? You look. . .chagrined." Garth took a seat in the ladder-back side chair that Blythe had found scuffed and battered at the side of the road. A bit of sanding, stain, varnish, a new seat cover, and it appeared brand new.

But regarding her uncle and his request, Blythe wished her emotions weren't so obviously written across her features. "It's a young lady, Uncle Garth." Oh, how to explain? "Um, well, she and I just met. We're just beginning a friendship—"

"Ah." A knowing look entered his rheumy eyes. "Someone from the crisis pregnancy center. Say no more." He crossed his leg. "Now, tell me, how's business?"

<hr />

It was some time later when Blythe found a few minutes to return Kylie's phone call. "I'm glad to hear you and Matt are back together. Wendy was so excited after you got engaged last year. She felt certain Matt was the one for you."

Silence.

"Blythe, why did my mom lie to me my whole life?"

Sitting at her desk in the back room, Blythe began to fidget with a paper clip. "Why did she lie regarding your grandparents? I can't answer that. But regarding me and Rob and your adoption. . .well, Wendy lied about it because I asked her to."

Another pause.

"I guess that makes me feel a little better. Lying to protect someone else is almost honorable in sort of a weird way."

"Oh, Kylie, at first I wanted you to know the truth about me as soon as you were old enough to understand. But then, after I returned from Singapore—"

Blythe halted her explanation, realizing she was getting into some heavy subject matters, ones that couldn't be dealt with in an afternoon's phone conversation.

"Kylie, I suppose we should get together and talk face-to-face."

"Great. Why don't you come up here and visit? I'll introduce you to my grandparents and Matt."

"I'd like to meet Matt, but—"

"Listen, my grandparents are as nervous about meeting you as you are about meeting them. The hilarious thing is you'll probably all end up being the best of friends."

"Kylie, I don't know. . . ."

Blythe pondered the idea of making the Chadwyks' acquaintance. What, exactly, had Rob said about his folks? After all these years, she couldn't remember.

"Would you come as a special favor to me, Blythe? I promise to play mediator, but I really doubt that'll be necessary."

Blythe wrestled with a reply.

"What are you doing this weekend? Can you hop in your car and drive up here? I'll give you directions." Kylie's laughter rang through the wire. "I sound like my impetuous friend Seth."

"Kylie, today is Friday," Blythe replied on a note of incredulousness. "You can't possibly mean this weekend, as in *tomorrow*."

"Well, yeah, that's what I meant. But you've probably got plans, huh?"

Blythe didn't have a single one, other than do laundry, dust, and vacuum her apartment. Those things could wait. . . but, she'd have to see if her mother would mind the store during the day tomorrow.

I can't believe I'm actually considering this!

"Are you still there, Blythe?"

"Yes."

"You're so quiet."

"Kylie, please, let me think a moment," she said on a little laugh. "My brain doesn't run as fast as yours does."

"My apologies. I drank too much coffee this afternoon."

Blythe heard another chuckle waft through the miles of phone lines.

"Rob was like that without caffeine," Blythe muttered. "He was a real take-charge sort of guy. Wendy had that ability too, but not quite as much."

"I know. . . . I mean, people always said I was like my mom."

Blythe sifted the idea of traveling to Wisconsin through her mental sieve, then took a deep, steadying breath and sent up a prayer for wisdom. "I know this will sound very selfish of me, considering everything you're going through, but I don't want to get hurt again. Losing Rob was a nightmare. Kylie, he died in my arms. Can you even imagine that?"

Blythe fought back the sudden rush of emotion. "Giving you up for adoption wasn't easy, either. I regretted my decision as soon as I got home from the hospital. But there was no turning back. Those were extremely painful years in my life."

Now it was Kylie's turn at momentary silence.

"I promise you won't get hurt again," Kylie finally said, and Blythe could hear the strains of earnestness in her voice. "We won't badger you or pelt you with questions. We'll just. . .get acquainted. You can tell us as much as you want to. If you choose to say nothing, that's fine too. At least lines of communication will have been drawn and that's a start."

"Yes, it's a start," Blythe agreed. What's more, she believed Kylie's every word. "Okay, you're on. But I'm an early riser, so have breakfast ready. No, wait. I'm guessing it's a five-hour drive. . . ."

"Six, actually."

"Hmm. . .better make it brunch."

"You got it. I'm famous for making an awesome egg dish with bacon, potatoes, onions, mushrooms, and green peppers. You mix it all together, turn it over into a glass pan, and then bake it for an hour."

"Sounds incredible. My mouth is watering already."

"Regular or decaf?"

"Regular. In fact, I wouldn't mind if you threw in an extra scoop."

Kylie laughed. "You and I are going to get along great."

———⦵———

TJ descended the stairs, having just carried up a basket full of clean linens, and now Lissa Elliot, a part-time employee at The Light House, would make beds and straighten up rooms in preparation for the weekend's guests. Walking through the spacious foyer, TJ rounded the corner and entered the living room. He halted when he saw Seth sitting on the floral-upholstered sofa and wearing a gloomy expression. He must have come in when TJ was upstairs, and he hadn't yet changed out of the suit and tie he wore to work.

"What's the matter with you? You look like you just lost your best friend."

"Close." Scooting forward, Seth shut down his notebook computer where it sat on the coffee table. "Just checked my E-mail and read one from Kylie. She's back together with her cheating boyfriend."

"Mmm. . ." TJ thought it over and then shrugged. "Guess I called that one, eh?"

"This is no time to gloat."

Pursing his lips, TJ tried to stifle a grin. "Listen, Kylie was up front with you from the start. She said she still loved that dude. . .what's his name?"

"Matt."

"Oh, right."

"Yeah, I know what she said." Seth leaned back into the couch cushions. "But I was hoping Kylie would stay mad at him long enough to see what a great guy I am."

TJ laughed and collapsed into a nearby armchair. "She knows what a great guy you are. She just loves. . .Matt."

"She's making a big mistake." His expression set in all seriousness, Seth stretched his arm out along the back of the sofa. "I e-mailed her back and told her so. Once a cheater always a cheater. That guy can't be trusted."

TJ didn't really believe that, but he refrained from voicing his opinion. He sensed his friend was hurting right now.

"Hey, weren't we supposed to rent a moving truck and drive to Wisconsin and bring Kylie back here?"

TJ nodded. "That was the plan. But I imagine it's changed now."

"We don't know that for a fact. I say we make the trip this weekend."

TJ chuckled out of sheer incredulousness. "Listen, buddy, it's time to throw in the towel. You lost this round."

Seth didn't reply, but the stony look in his brown eyes spoke volumes.

TJ decided to change the subject. "Any other interesting news?"

"What?" Seth snapped from his musings. "Oh. . .yeah, Kylie said her biological mother planned to visit this weekend."

"No kidding?" TJ let out a long, slow whistle. He recalled seeing the dark-haired woman in the same faded photograph that pictured Wendy Chadwyk. Kylie had it with her when she came to The Light House. Kylie also said when she made the initial contact, her natural mother wanted nothing to do with her. "Man, that just goes to show you how fast things in life can change."

"Yeah, whatever." Seth stood. "Look, I'm not much company right now. I think I'll change and go work out at the gym for a while."

"Sure."

Seth left the room, and a swell of empathy lodged in TJ's chest. Getting dumped by a woman never felt good—no matter how gently the lady tried to choose her words. Knowing Kylie, she let Seth down easy. But it still hurt. Poor Seth was smitten the first day he met her.

Then, as TJ's thoughts moved from Seth and Kylie to her birth mom and this weekend's impending visit, a rush of protectiveness filled his being. TJ couldn't stand the thought of Lee and Kathryn getting hurt. One broken heart around here was all he could stand.

He blew out a breath, thinking that menacing clouds were surely gathering to the north. Except this storm TJ had no intentions of chasing.

CHAPTER EIGHT

B lythe awoke before dawn and tossed aside the colorful
hand-sewn quilt covering on top of her bed. She showered and dressed, realizing that, for the first time in many
weeks, her grievous memories weren't haunting her. Perhaps
it was because she felt more nervous than melancholy this
morning as she rushed around her apartment, readying herself for the trip to Wisconsin. Lydia said she'd tend to the
shop, although she didn't like the fact that Blythe refused
to tell her any details about her "appointment." However,
Blythe was rapidly concluding the truth is what would set
her free. Secrets would keep her bound in the past, and she
didn't want to live the remainder of her life there.

Would Lydia and Garth understand that?

Lord, You're going to have to carry me through all this. . . .

Blythe left her upper apartment and walked to her red and
white Pontiac Montana. The sun hadn't yet appeared on the

eastern horizon, and the predawn air felt cool and clammy against her skin. In darkness, she drove downtown to her shop, parked in front, and put on her flashers. Then, letting herself inside, Blythe hurried upstairs to her workshop/warehouse. Turning on the overhead light, a bare bulb that dangled from an unfinished ceiling, she made her way through the collection of "junk," as Lydia dubbed it. A scuffed chest of drawers, a Pembroke table with a broken leg, a Chippendale chair in need of a new slipcover, a Queen Anne loveseat with upholstery tattered and torn—one had to look beyond its ugly shade of green paint to see the beauty beneath. Blythe planned to restore it and fix up her other curbside acquisitions too. Then they'd be placed in her shop.

Nearing the dusty back area of her workspace, Blythe opened another door to a small crawlspace. She pulled out several boxes, opening each until she found what she sought. Rob's things.

Blythe's heart felt as though it plummeted into her midsection. *Rob's things.* What precious keepsakes they were, but it had been almost a chore to hang on to them. Twice in the past three decades, Lydia had stumbled across the brown cardboard box containing Rob's belongings and had thrown it away. Both times, Blythe had managed to rescue it before the city's garbage crews arrived.

But now, Blythe sensed God telling her it was time to let go of Rob's things. So she would, albeit reluctantly. She could still hear Kylie's voice stating how "devastated" her grandparents felt, learning their children were dead. If that were the case, then this box would go to them. The Chadwyks might want remembrances of their son.

Carrying the weighty parcel through her storeroom and

workroom, Blythe shut off the light and descended the creaky steps. She traipsed across the polished wooden floor of her quiet shop and let herself out. After locking up, she used the button on her keychain to pop open the back of the Montana. Dropping the box inside, she pushed the door closed, climbed into the minivan, and headed for the interstate.

⥊⥊⥊

Allie awoke feeling worried and anxious for the third morning in a row. She didn't know how to express what brewed inside of her other than it felt. . .troubling. Was its cause her impending marriage to Jack Callahan?

Lord, I've prayed about this. I've sensed Your approval of this marriage. So what's wrong with me?

Slipping from beneath the bedcovers, which included a fluffy blue and white floral down comforter, electric blanket, and coordinating top sheet, Allie scooted out of bed and pulled on her fuzzy bathrobe. It seemed she was always freezing, but the first time Jack caught a glimpse of the layers of bedding she slept beneath, he told her she'd piled too many covers on the bed for his liking.

There are so many things about Jack and me that are different, Lord, and I've been on my own for a long time now. . . .

Tying her bathrobe at the waist, Allie padded into the hallway, stepping softly so as not to disturb her houseguest. She entered the kitchen and flipped on the overhead light. Lifting the teakettle off the white stove, she filled it with water and then replaced it on the burner and set it to boiling. She glanced around the kitchen feeling a measure of satisfaction as her gaze lingered on the new, polished oak cupboards. Since she and Jack had purchased this house together, they had invested in various updates like the recently installed linoleum floor with its various shades of green, gray, and white and the marble countertops. They'd also recarpeted the house, and Jack had installed a lovely new vanity in the bathroom. With only a week before the wedding, it was ludicrous for Allie to have second thoughts now.

As her gaze wandered around the room, Allie spotted the white portable phone. The desire to call Jack, express her concerns, and hear his strong voice was almost irrefutable. However, one glance at the round-faced kitchen clock above the sink reminded her of the time.

You can't call him now, you ninny. He'll ring your neck!

But then she wondered what he really would do if she called him at six o'clock in the morning and said she needed to talk to him. . .now. Would he get mad?

Allie figured Jack would be at least irritated with her for waking him up. But suddenly she wanted to test the waters and see how deep they ran. Leaning over the counter, she plucked the cordless phone from its base. She pressed out Jack's number and it began to ring.

He's going to kill me, she thought on a facetious note.

"Callahan." His voice was raspy with sleep, but he'd picked up in only three rings—even though he sounded like he expected the precinct to be calling.

"Good morning, honey. It's Allie."

He sniffed and sort of moaned. "Good morning yourself." Then the sound of a wide yawn reached her ears. "What are you doing up so early on a Saturday? It's not even light outside yet. . .is it?"

"It's getting there and. . .I couldn't sleep." She paused, ordering her thoughts.

"You've seemed a little preoccupied lately. Everything okay?"

"No. . ."

"What's wrong?"

"It's so absurd that I'm ashamed to tell you, and yet. . .oh, I don't know."

"Just spit it out, Allie."

She nearly grinned. Jack was a man who preferred the direct approach any day to niceties and skirting issues.

"Okay, Jack, here it is. There are six days until our wedding, and I'm. . .well, I'm getting cold feet."

Her confession was met by a wall of silence. And why not? She'd done something similar to him thirty years ago. She'd broken his heart. Hers too.

Allie shook off the past, reminding herself that thirty years was a lifetime ago and things were different now. Still, marriage was a commitment, and to Allie it meant "Till death do us part." Forever was a long time to endure anything less than marital bliss. One lousy marriage was enough for Allie. She didn't want to make the same mistake twice.

Nevertheless, she loved Jack. He loved her. In her heart of hearts, she believed this was their chance at happiness. So, why did she suddenly feel so unsure?

"I'm sorry. I don't mean to upset you. I love you, Jack. You know that. I'm just. . .struggling. But I can't figure out why."

"Allie, if it's any consolation, the Lord already warned me that this was going to happen. I mean, I didn't realize it at the time, but now I do—now that I know what's eating you."

"The Lord forewarned you?"

"Sure did."

Allie felt the burden ease up off her shoulders. Then the teakettle whistled. Removing it from the stove, she opened the cupboard and pulled out a ceramic mug along with a box of green tea.

"Hang on a sec. Let me go find my notebook."

Allie heard Jack set the phone down while her confidence began to grow. He wasn't anything like her first husband. How foolish she'd been even to entertain that notion. Jack was a Christian man who communed with the Lord on a regular basis—now that he'd reestablished a personal relationship with Christ. Jack even kept a log of the special things God showed him.

"Okay, Allie. . .you still there?"

"I'm here."

"I wrote this down Thursday. I won't read it verbatim because I'm no William Shakespeare. But I noticed that something was bugging you and I was worried because you seemed so. . .*tormented*. I guess that's the word I'd use. So I jotted down my thoughts, and sometime later the Lord gave me this verse out of the book of James: 'For he who doubts is like a wave of the sea driven and tossed by the wind.' "

Allie knew the verse well, and a wave driven and tossed by the wind certainly was "tormented." What's more, "driven" and "tossed" accurately described her insides this past week.

Had she been suffering the consequences of doubting God and His Word?

Oh, Lord, I'm sorry!

"Maybe I'm not making any sense here."

"You're making perfect sense, Jack, and you shared exactly what I needed to hear."

"We prayed about getting married. I'm at peace with it, Allie. God showed each of us from His Word that He would honor our union."

"I know. . ."

Contrition, like the warmth from the hot tea she sipped, spread throughout her body.

"So are your feet getting a little warmer now?"

"Yes, as a matter of fact, they are." She smiled, feeling juvenile on one hand, but on the other, she reveled in the fact that she could turn to Jack with her doubts, fears, and insecurities. "I love you."

"I love you too. But. . .um. . .for waking me up there is a price to pay."

All at once, Allie felt daring. "Name it."

"Breakfast. At Jerry's Deli over on Deerfield Road. Meet me there in half an hour."

"Half an hour? I can't be ready to go out in public in a mere thirty minutes. I'm not one of the guys, you know!"

"Yeah, I know. *Boy,* do I know!"

"I hope you mean that in a complimentary way, Jack, and you aren't referring to the times you've had to wait for me to get ready."

"Sweetheart, you're worth the wait."

"Mm-hmm, that's what I thought you meant."

Smiling, Allie shook her head. Poor Jack. For the past three decades, he'd lived in primarily a man's world as a police officer and single dad, raising his only son. The latter, of course, waned, as Logan became a man. But then Jack worked longer hours and picked up extra shifts. There were no women in his life to pander to, no female sensibilities to deal with, not to mention shoes, clothes, cosmetics, and other frills.

Jack's in for a real shock when he moves in with me. I've already taken up most of the bedroom closet and occupy all but one drawer beneath the bathroom vanity.

"Now about the breakfast that *you're buying,* how 'bout I pick you up in an hour?"

"That's a little better." Then she couldn't help teasing him. "I'll have coffee ready for you while you wait."

He feigned an exasperated sigh, she laughed, and suddenly everything in her world seemed right again.

Kylie hung up the phone located on the wall in the hallway and returned to the kitchen. Decorated in country blues and whites, it had a homey feel to it—or at least Kylie thought it had until her mother died several months ago. Now this house and everything in it brought Kylie little comfort.

Well, maybe with the exception of the little bear bookends. Each time she glimpsed them on the shelf in her bedroom, Kylie was reminded that there was hope in all of life's perilous situations.

"Was that Blythe who just called?"

Kylie gave her grandmother a nod. "She's about an hour away."

"I have to hand it to Miss Severson," Grandpa Lee said, sipping his morning coffee. "I didn't think she'd show."

"Why not?" Kylie pulled out a white Windsor chair and joined her grandparents at the kitchen table.

"Rob was notorious for making promises and then breaking them. I imagine Miss Severson is just like him. That old cliché about 'birds of a feather' is on my mind."

"Let's pray that isn't the case." Grandma Kate shook her reddish-brown head in dismay.

"Whoa! The 'birds of a feather' thing was a lifetime ago, guys." Kylie looked from one grandparent to the other. "I'm sure Blythe's changed in thirty-one years." Kylie reached across the table and placed her palm on top of her grandfather's hand. "She seems like a nice person, and she strikes me as being extremely sensitive. I promised she wouldn't be hurt by coming here. You both agreed to cooperate. Remember?"

A rueful smile pulled at the corners of her grandfather's mouth. "You needn't remind me, young lady."

"I do hope to learn where Rob is buried," Grandma Kate said, looking somewhat sad herself. "But you have my word, dearheart. I won't judge her or pelt her with questions."

"Good."

"Nor will I," Grandpa Lee promised.

"Thanks. Both of you." Kylie retracted her hand and lowered her gaze, studying the woven placemat in front of her. "I have a lot of questions, too, and it won't be easy for me to hold them back. But I'm going to try. Blythe admitted to being 'an emotional mess' since the day I entered her shop exactly four weeks ago today." Kylie shook her head. "Hard to believe it's only been four weeks."

"Yes, it is." Kathryn gave Kylie's arm an affectionate pat.

"In time, I think Blythe will share information with us. We just have to be patient." Kylie sighed, hoping the curiosity burning in her heart wouldn't make her a hypocrite this weekend.

CHAPTER NINE

Blythe admired the scenery as she continued her drive into northwest Wisconsin. Rolling hills sloped downward into fertile farm fields, and as she maneuvered her van around a curve, she passed a rustic old red barn. To her left, she spotted cattle on a hillside, and miles later, she saw several horses grazing in a pasture that was flanked by a white rail fence. Remnants of winter in the form of occasional patches of snow could still be seen, and the treetops were barren for the most part. It appeared that spring hadn't yet made it this far north.

Blythe smiled, recalling the adjustment Wendy had been forced to make decades ago. She and Rob had grown up in Maine but spent the latter part of their teenage years in South Carolina. Wendy had forgotten how long and snowy the winters could be, especially in this part of the United States. Blythe recalled one of Wendy's letters in which she'd stated that she now knew the meaning of "cabin fever." Nevertheless, Wendy never regretted adopting Kylie, even though Blythe rued the day she let her baby go. But she knew it had been for the best.

And it had.

Hadn't it?

Blythe shook herself. It was far too late in life for second guesses. Of course she'd done the right thing. Kylie was intelligent and. . .strong, like Rob and Wendy. She was a well-adjusted young woman, and Blythe had been correct to stay out of the way and let the Rollinses become a real family. Blythe was just grateful that, over the years, Wendy saw fit to send her cards and letters containing precious photos of Kylie as she grew and blossomed. Those happy reminders always put her mind at ease.

Yes, she'd done the right thing.

But what about the Chadwyks? To be honest, Blythe hadn't given the older couple much thought over the years. Would they condemn her for not informing them of Rob's death and Kylie's birth?

Lord, that was Wendy's obligation and right, not mine. Oh, God, I'm so afraid—afraid the Chadwyks' questions will set me back emotionally. I'm frightened of this path I've chosen to take. I could lose my shop, my home. . .everything! And yet I believe You're leading me onward because You know I want so badly to be part of Kylie's life.

A Scripture passage flitted through Blythe's mind and served as a divine reminder to her prayer.

"For God hath not given us a spirit of fear, but of power and of love and of a sound mind."

How well she knew that verse from the Second Book of

Timothy. She'd hung onto that portion of God's Word, knowing the promise to be true. No, she wasn't a strong person, but God was all-powerful and His Holy Spirit resided within her. She took a deep breath and willed herself to relax. She'd be all right.

Entering Basil Creek, Blythe followed Kylie's directions through town and found the highway that led to the Rollinses' home. More countryside met her as she exited town. Five miles later, she turned into the gravel road that took her up to the house.

"Kylie, I think Blythe just arrived."

Hearing her grandmother's call, she rose from the sofa in the living room where she'd been keeping company with her grandfather, Matt, and Lynellen. Taking a deep breath, Kylie did a quick mental check and found everything in order. Burning logs glowed from the cozy fireplace, the egg dish cooked in the oven, and the freshly baked cinnamon loaf had been extracted from the breadmaker and now cooled on a wire rack on the kitchen counter.

Matt stood and took her hand. "Everything's going to be fine, Ky."

Leaning toward her, he kissed her cheek and she returned a smile. "I feel kind of nervous." She glanced at Grandpa Lee. He sent her a nod of encouragement.

"You're going to be just fine," Lynellen said.

Matt gave Kylie's hand a gentle squeeze, and as she walked through the house, she sent up a quick prayer. Another one. *Oh, please, Lord, let this go well. . . .*

With a grin for her grandmother, Kylie exited the back door and met Blythe on the narrow walkway that led to and from the house.

"Hi! I'm glad to see you made it here safely."

"Not a single problem."

In two quick up-and-down glances, Kylie noted Blythe's willowy figure over which she wore a thick lavender sweater that came to her knees. Funky-patterned black, blue, and lilac knit pants covered the rest of her slim legs.

Kylie decided to break the ice with a bit of humor. "So why couldn't I have inherited *your* body shape, huh?"

Blythe smiled and a blush rose up her face and colored her cheeks pink. "You're beautiful just the way God made you."

So much for being funny. The reply caused a lump of unshed emotion to form in her throat.

Blythe looked misty too.

Kylie stepped forward and pulled her biological mother into an embrace. The woman felt so slight and fragile, unlike Kylie, who was a woman physically able to assist Matt with some of his toughest chores.

Blythe sniffed and Kylie pulled back in time to see a tear slide down her cheek. Reaching up, she brushed it off Blythe's face. Then, staring into ebony eyes like her own, Kylie smiled.

"No more crying, okay? Not for either one of us. We're going to have fun this weekend, beginning with the brunch I made."

"Sounds good." Blythe appeared to collect her wits. "I'm starving."

"Yeah, and I almost believe that." Kylie laughed as Blythe gave her a look of mock annoyance. Then, putting an arm around her shoulders, Kylie led her to the house.

"It feels so weird to be here. At Wendy's place. . ."

"You share my grandparents' sentiments exactly, only they're still struggling with Mom's rejection. All this time they'd been hoping my mom and Rob would have contacted them. My grandfather hired detectives to find them, but it cost a lot of money and turned up nothing."

Blythe came to an abrupt halt, causing Kylie to do the same.

"I'm a little nervous."

"Don't be." Kylie whirled around so that her back was to the door. She didn't want her grandmother to overhear their conversation. She lowered her voice to a whisper. "Everything will work out. I think you'll like my grandparents. Besides, I promised you wouldn't get hurt, remember?"

"Yes, but some things are out of your control, Kylie."

Hearing her name brought to mind a subject that came up not too long ago. Kylie folded her arms, feeling suddenly too curious to hold back. "How'd I get my name? Is it a contraction of my grandparents' first names? Kathryn and Lee? If it is, then my mother couldn't have really *hated* her parents, right?"

Confusion followed by uncertainty crossed Blythe's delicate features.

"Please. Tell me."

"I named you." Sorrow laced her soft voice. "Josh and Wendy granted me that privilege, and your namesake is my brother Kyle, who was killed in the Vietnam War."

"Killed? How tragic." Kylie spoke the words on an exhaled breath while more questions filled her head. But seeing Blythe glance toward her van then back at her, she wondered if her birth mother was thinking of making a run for it. If that were so, Kylie couldn't let it happen.

"Okay, interrogation's over." She smiled, praying she could put Blythe at ease. Opening the door, she propelled Blythe into the back hall. "You'll like my grandparents. They're nice people."

"We certainly are," Grandma Kate said with a soft chuckle. Then she smiled at Blythe and extended her right hand. "I'm Kathryn Chadwyk."

"Blythe Severson."

The two women clasped hands.

"Please come in. Kylie's going to serve us brunch in a few minutes."

"I made a fresh pot of *strong* coffee too."

Blythe replied with a tremulous little smile.

Matt, Lynellen, and Grandpa Lee entered the kitchen and Kylie made the introductions. She saw by Matt's expression that he noticed the resemblance between herself and Blythe. Same dark hair, black eyes, and bone china complexion.

"Why don't we all sit in the living room and get acquainted," Grandma Kate suggested. She appeared every bit the professional hostess, but, of course, that didn't surprise Kylie. Grandma Kate was in the habit of making guests feel at home since she and Grandpa Lee ran an ocean-side bed-and-breakfast.

The men ambled out of the room, but seeing Blythe's tentative expression, Kylie decided to ask her to stay.

"Blythe, would you mind giving me a hand?"

"Oh. . .not at all. I'd love to help you."

Kylie turned and gave her grandmother a wink, lest she earn herself a reprimand for putting a guest to work.

Grandma Kate took the hint and followed Lynellen, Matt, and Grandpa Lee into the living room.

"Would you mind slicing the cinnamon bread?"

"I wouldn't mind a bit."

Kylie opened a drawer and pulled out a serrated knife and handed it to Blythe.

"Your fiancé is a very handsome young man."

"Yeah, he is." Kylie pulled on a pair of oven mitts. She recalled telling Blythe how he'd cheated on her with Dena. "He's got a good heart and I can't imagine my future without him. I love him. But I warned him that if he's ever unfaithful again, he'll be dead and I'll be in jail." Kylie sighed. "I was being facetious but, to my shame, I think he believed me." Opening the oven door, she shot a speculative glance at Blythe. "I don't sound like much of a Christian, do I?"

"You sound human."

Kylie thought it over as she pulled out the egg casserole. "This thing with Matt caused me to see that I have a horrible temper. Who did I inherit that from? I don't ever recall my mom flying off the handle. I mean, she occasionally got angry, but it wasn't to the same degree that I lost my temper with Matt. It sort of scared me."

"Given the circumstances, anyone is capable of anything. That's why it's so important for Christians to walk closely with God."

"If I'm being too personal let me know, but. . .are you a Christian?"

Blythe nodded.

Placing the rectangular Pyrex pan on the stovetop, Kylie removed the mitts. "Jack Callahan said he was the one who talked to my mom about Jesus Christ and salvation."

Blythe stopped slicing the bread. Her expression was one of surprise. "How do you know Jack?"

"I met him when I was in Chicago. I stayed with Allie, and she and Jack are engaged."

"Yes, I know they're engaged, but—" Blythe turned to face her. "How did you become acquainted with Allie?"

"She's the one who sent my mother that faded photograph of the four of you along with a wedding announcement. I called Allie to tell her about Mom's death, but the picture sparked off a ton of questions, and—"

"And Allie told you everything." Blythe's tone had an accusatory ring to it.

"No, she didn't. I figured it out. I thought you looked familiar when I saw that old photo, but it wasn't until a week or so later that I recalled seeing you in your shop. I asked Allie about it and she confirmed my suspicions, but that's only after I begged her for the truth. It was my idea to visit Precious Things and ask you about Rob Chadwyk, and it was my idea to drive to Sabal Beach in order to discover if I really had grandparents living there. I found them on the Internet."

Blythe's slender shoulders seemed to sag in defeat.

"A lot of women give up their children for adoption," Kylie said in a whisper-soft voice, "and for many different reasons. I don't fault you for yours. I really don't, although I'm still confused about a great many things. But I can't complain. I had an idyllic childhood." She grinned. "That's not to say I didn't get my share of spankings when I deserved them."

Blythe smiled and returned to the task of bread slicing.

"My mom and I were good friends. I loved her." Kylie swallowed hard. "And I miss her so much."

"I know you do. I'm so sorry for your loss, Kylie."

Blythe was beside her in a flash, and this time it was she who initiated the embrace. But Kylie felt foolish for attempting to cry on Blythe's shoulders. They weren't made to carry such a burden. She was, however, grateful for the hug all the same.

"Ladies, can we be of any help?"

Kylie turned to find her grandmother and Lynellen standing in the doorway that led into the dining room.

"We'd love your help." Kylie wiped away her tears. "Blythe and I got sort of sidetracked."

"So we see." Grandma Kate smiled and Kylie noted the pools of empathy in her hazel eyes.

Kylie stood back as Lynellen strode to the cupboard and pulled down a stack of plates. She glanced at her grandmother, then at Blythe, hoping and praying that her newfound family would find a place of permanence in her life.

CHAPTER TEN

B lythe felt grateful for inane topics that dominated the table conversation. The dreary spring weather. The upcoming Easter holiday and what that meant for business at The Light House, a bed-and-breakfast owned and operated by the Chadwyks. It sounded like a hectic time, and Kathryn seemed concerned that their manager, a man named TJ, wouldn't be able to handle the volume of guests without more help.

"He's gone solo before," Lee said.

"I guess that's true enough." Kathryn put on a smile; however, she still had a light of concern in her hazel eyes.

Meanwhile, Matt leaned over and whispered something to Kylie. It appeared unrelated to the present topic. She grinned and nodded in reply.

Watching the couple interact, Blythe hid her amusement. They were cute together. But sitting across from her daughter,

Blythe felt as though she might as well be sitting across from Wendy. Kylie had inherited many of the Chadwyk traits. Like that smirky smile.

"Well, Miss Severson, did you have a nice vacation?"

"Excuse me?" Confused and thrown somewhat off guard, she glanced at Lee Chadwyk, who sat at the end of the table.

"Kathryn and I stopped by your store a few weeks ago," he explained. "Your mother said you were taking a 'much-needed' vacation."

Suddenly it clicked. "Yes, I did. I went to see a friend in Houston. Had a very nice time. Thanks." After picking at her eggs, she looked back at Lee. "But how did you know Lydia was my mother?"

"She told us. She said her daughter owned the shop, yada, yada, yada. . ." He grinned.

"You never told me that, Grandpa! All you said was that Blythe wasn't there." Kylie sent the older man an exasperated look.

"I'm sorry, darling. I assumed your grandmother told you."

"And I thought you told her, Lee." Kathryn smiled. "So, sorry, Kylie."

"That's okay." She glanced across the table at Blythe. "Then, I have another grandmother, huh?"

Blythe felt her insides begin to twist. Lydia? A grandmother? Not a chance! Lydia had never been the maternal sort.

"My mother is still living," Blythe stated carefully.

"Does she know about me?"

"Yes, but I don't want you to get your hopes up, Kylie. It's doubtful that Lydia will ever be any sort of grandmother to you, and a friendship seems equally as unlikely."

"Can I ask why?"

"Yes, but. . ." She glanced around the table, detesting the awkward silence. "Let's talk later, okay?"

"Of course." Kylie looked immediately chagrined. "I didn't mean to put you on the spot."

Blythe sent her an affectionate wink. "No harm done."

"Do you have other children, Blythe?"

She looked at Lee. "No, I don't, Mr. Chadwyk. I never married."

Redheaded Lynellen Alexander piped in. "Matt's my youngest. I had five children and they're spread all over the country, but we manage to get together at least once a year, don't we, Matt?"

He nodded.

"Five children?" Blythe smiled, feeling amazed. "I would have never guessed that, Lynellen. You don't look much older than me."

"Well, thank you." Lynellen peered at Kylie. "I like this woman."

Kylie beamed. "I said you would."

Blythe felt herself relax and enjoy the easy banter. She still couldn't quite believe the fact she was actually sitting in Wendy's house across the table from Kylie. The glimpses of her daughter over the years, coupled with the letters and E-mails from Wendy, had given Blythe a fair understanding of Kylie's personality. However, nothing compared to real life, up close and personal.

She's darling, Blythe decided, watching Kylie laugh at something Lee Chadwyk just said. Smart, confident, and so full of life—she'd inherited those qualities from her father.

"Miss Severson?"

Blythe startled when someone touched her forearm.

Glancing to her left, she realized Kathryn Chadwyk was waiting for a response.

"You caught me daydreaming. I apologize." Blythe pushed out an embarrassed little grin.

"Oh, I'm so glad I'm not the only one who does that." Kathryn chuckled and Lynellen joined her. "I was asking about your shop, Miss Severson. How do you acquire your inventory?"

"First of all, please call me Blythe." She sent a meaningful glance around the table before her gaze returned to Kathryn.

The older woman nodded.

"As for the items in my store, I find them at rummage and estate sales, antique shows, or in heaps along the curb. It's amazing what people throw away."

"You know, I believe your mother told us the exact same thing," Lee said from where he sat at the other end of the table. "About it being amazing what folks toss out."

"Oh, it's incredible, all right." Blythe loved to discuss her *precious things*. They were the center of her world, after all. "In my storage area right now there sits a gorgeous love seat that I found in the garbage. Well, correction, it's not 'gorgeous' yet. But it will be once I remove all the green paint and stain and varnish it. After that's done, Lydia will reupholster it for me and then it'll be for sale in my shop."

"Lydia?" Kathryn's brows drew together. "Your mother?"

"Yes." Blythe suddenly felt the need to explain. "I've called my parents by their first names since I was about twelve or thirteen. Back then, they were forty-plus-year-old hippies, trying to prove to us kids that you *could* trust someone over thirty."

Lynellen laughed. "Oh, my! I'd forgotten that adage."

Blythe grinned before continuing. "Dad was a professor and"—she looked at Kylie—"he was the one who introduced Josh and Wendy. Josh had been one of his students. Odd thing was, Josh was a pretty straight guy. He didn't fit the usual typecast of people milling in and out of our home."

"I've been wondering how my mom and dad *really* met!"

"Well, now you know."

"Gracious me, but it just wasn't like Wendy to lie," Lynellen remarked. "I was one of her best friends. You'd think she would have at least confided in me."

"Please don't feel betrayed in any way," Blythe said. "Much of the reason for the half-truths and, perhaps, outright lies was because Wendy wanted to protect my identity."

"You told me you made a vow. . . ?"

Blythe looked over at Kylie. "Yes, but let's not go there."

"All right." Once more, her daughter appeared embarrassed. "I'm sorry I keep pumping you for information. It's just that I'm so curious about everything. A whole new world opened up to me and now that the shock has worn off, I want to know *everything*."

Blythe laughed. "Well, let's begin with Josh and Wendy and how they met. I like to tell that story." She set her coffee cup down and lifted her fork. "Pete brought him home one evening, and he was introduced to the dozen or so kids staying in our house. But when he met Wendy, I think it was love at first sight for Josh."

"They were very happy."

"I know they were." Blythe took a small bite of egg casserole, savoring the flavor of spicy sausage, onions, and green peppers. After she chewed and swallowed, she added, "Kylie, you're a very good cook."

"Thanks," she replied, appearing pleased by the comment.

"Blythe, is your father still living?" Lee wanted to know.

She shook her head. "Just Lydia."

"What are your holidays like?" Kathryn asked, then quickly amended, "I don't mean to pry. I guess I still have Easter on my mind."

"No problem." Blythe thought it over. "I guess my holidays are always different. Lydia has her own set of friends and I have mine. But occasionally she and I will travel together, and now my uncle Garth has been added to the picture. He's eighty, a widower, and I make it a point to be sure he doesn't spend a holiday alone." Blythe recalled how disappointed Garth sounded on the phone when she told him she wouldn't be at church tomorrow and cancelled their lunch date.

"You and Lydia will have to visit us at The Light House," Kathryn invited. "Bring your uncle too."

Blythe felt herself pale at the very thought. Uncle Garth with Kylie and the Chadwyks? It'd never happen.

"Does he golf?" Lee asked.

"Who?" Blythe shook herself.

Lee chuckled. "Your uncle. Does he play golf?"

"Um, yes, as a matter of fact, he does."

"Excellent! Now I just have to get Matt on the golf course."

"I'm pretty rusty, Lee," the younger man admitted.

"Well, you can't be as rotten a player as TJ. He has double-digit handicap every time we play."

Matt laughed. "No, I'm not that bad."

Kathryn leaned toward Blythe and explained. "TJ can fix just about anything. Right, Lee?"

"You betcha, and that makes up for his lousy golf game."

Kylie smiled at the quip while Matt chuckled.

After an amused glance in her husband's direction, Kathryn turned back to Blythe. "TJ's been with us for over a decade. He's more than an employee. He's like a son to us."

"Indeed," Lee chimed in.

Blythe replied to each of the Chadwyks with a polite smile, but she couldn't help wondering if the remark meant Rob had been replaced.

<hr />

Early afternoon, Allie arrived home to find Logan's car and Marilee's SUV both parked in the driveway. She immediately concluded Patrice had summoned them. But why?

She gathered her purse and Jack assisted her down from his black Ford Explorer. Together they walked to the house.

"Wonder what's up."

"I can't imagine." Allie only hoped it wasn't anything serious.

Jack unlocked the side door with his key and allowed Allie to enter first. They were met at the kitchen entrance by a very worried-looking Logan.

"Um. . .the ambulance is on its way."

Allie's heart did a swan dive. "Patrice lost her baby." It was more a guess than a query.

"I think that's what happened. Marilee's in the bathroom with her. I'm just trying to stay out of the way."

"Oh, Lord. . ." Allie put her fingertips against her lips

and reminded herself that God was in control.

Jack didn't utter a word but took her purse and helped her off with her coat. She felt like a piece of driftwood for all the aid she was administering.

Logan rubbed his shadowed jaw. He looked just as helpless.

"Maybe I should go see if there's something I can do. . . ."

Collecting her wits, Allie took purposeful strides toward the half bath off the kitchen. At that moment, Marilee exited the powder room and met Allie in the hallway.

"What can I do to help?"

"Nothing at this point. But. . .um, we owe you a new set of towels."

Allie waved a hand in the air, dismissing the remark.

"Is the ambulance here yet?"

"Right now, Mar," Logan called from the kitchen.

"Oh, good." A look of relief washed over Marilee's face.

"Did Patrice lose her baby?" Allie whispered.

Marilee nodded, and strands of her chestnut-colored hair escaped from the clip in the back of her head. "I saw the fetus—no bigger than the palm of my hand."

Allie winced. "Are you okay?"

"I'm fine, now that the paramedics are here."

No sooner had those words tumbled from Marilee's lips than two men wearing white shirts and navy blue pants rounded the corner of the kitchen, each holding onto one end of a yellow metal gurney. The second medic also carried something that resembled a toolbox, and Allie surmised it contained medical supplies. She pointed out the way to the bathroom then retreated into the kitchen so she wouldn't hinder progress.

She glanced at Jack, then Logan. "Marilee's holding up just great. I'm proud of her. For an elementary schoolteacher, it appears she's done a fine job nursing Patrice."

"She's been a pillar of strength since she got here." Logan raked his fingers through his dark hair. "I arrived first, since I'm closer," he said, stating the obvious. "But I didn't have a clue what do to, mostly because I wasn't sure of what the problem was. Patrice was doubled over and crying, and you know how she reverts to Spanish when she's upset." Logan shook his head. "I kept telling her, 'English! English!'"

"Oy," Jack said, sounding as though he were from Manhattan instead of the Chicago area. "I can just imagine the scene."

His cynicism made Allie smile. Most times, she found that part of his personality charming, if not thoroughly amusing. But after thirty years on the police force, there wasn't a lot that fazed Jack.

"Honey," she said, deciding this was no time for jokes, "think sensitivity right now, okay?"

Her remark was met by a stony expression that kept her grinning.

"Anyway," Logan continued, paying them no attention, "my instinct was to immediately call for an ambulance, but then I decided to wait for Marilee in case Patrice had just come down with a case of the flu. But guess what the first three words out of Marilee's mouth were?"

"I love you?"

"Jack!" Allie socked him in the arm for being such a wise guy. "Stop it!"

"All right. I apologize. But this is how I handle stress, and I'll have you know that my smart-aleck comments saved me and my partners from numerous nervous breakdowns over the years."

"You sure about that, Dad?"

Allie closed her eyes. She'd never win. "Logan, you are a chip off the old block."

"Yeah, I've heard that before." He and Jack exchanged amused glances.

Activity at the end of the hallway put a sudden cap on the humor. Seconds later, Patrice was wheeled out of the bathroom, looking pale and weeping.

Allie rushed to her side, but Logan beat her there. The paramedics stopped long enough for Logan to kiss his half-sister's forehead and promise her he'd pray.

"I'm going to ride in the ambulance with her," Marilee announced. "We're headed to Mercy."

"Good. That's not far from here." Allie glanced at Patrice. "We'll see you at the hospital, okay?"

"Okay." Patrice's brown eyes were filled with such anguish that Allie wanted to cry right along with her.

Stepping back, she allowed the medics enough room to maneuver the gurney outside to the ambulance. Then she spun on her heel, intending to make plans for a trip to the hospital with Jack and Logan, but seeing their stricken expressions caused her breath to catch in her throat. At the same time, it was reassuring to know how very sensitive the Callahan men really were, all wisecracks aside. In fact, Jack's tender heart was one of the things she loved most about him.

"C'mon, fellas," she said, slipping her hands around each man's elbow and guiding them into the living room. "Why don't you two make yourselves comfortable while I clean up the powder room? Afterwards, we'll head over to Mercy Medical Center together. What do you say?" She looked up at Jack.

He smiled into her eyes. "Sounds like a plan."

CHAPTER ELEVEN

APRIL 1969

Dear Blythe,

Josh and I and baby Kylie just moved into our new home. The place belonged to Josh's grandmother so he bought it for practically nothing, but it sure does need a lot of work. I don't know what to tackle first. Maybe the master bedroom. Right now, the house only has two bedrooms, but Josh says in a few years we can build on another one and add a den downstairs in the process. He's full of dreams, my Josh, and I'm beginning to dream right along with him.

Don't worry about Kylie. She's doing fine. But I think she knows I'm not you. She looks at me kind of weird when I'm holding her. Josh said I'm imagining things. He said a three-week-old baby couldn't distinguish between

131

her mom and her aunt. Josh says infants this age operate on the survival instinct. But I'm not sure I agree with him. I swear Kylie knows I'm not you.

As for me, I'm doing my best to adjust to country living. You wouldn't believe the squares in this small town. Staunch Norwegians, every one of them. The old women are barely civil to me, but Josh told me not to worry. It was at least ten years before his dad was accepted into the fold.

The talk making its way around Basil Creek is that Kylie is the result of an unfortunate "indiscretion" on Josh's part, but because he's such an upstanding person, he married me. I was about to set his mother and sister straight a couple of days ago, but he shushed me. Josh thinks we should just let everybody believe the gossip so we don't have to do much explaining. I suppose he's right. . . .

———— ✑ ————

"I'm back, bearing hot chocolate."

Blythe jumped when Kylie entered the room.

"Sorry, I didn't mean to sneak up on you."

"Quite all right. I was just preoccupied." She replaced the decades-old letter she'd been reading then turned from where she'd been standing in front of her suitcase. Blythe smiled at her daughter, who'd changed for bed already. Wearing a cream and navy floral nightshirt that came to the middle of her shins, Kylie appeared relaxed as she set the wooden tray on top of the colorful bedspread.

"Do you think you'll be comfortable enough in here?" she asked, handing a mug of cocoa to Blythe.

She accepted the steaming beverage. "I'll be fine. Thank you." She glanced around the spacious bedroom, noting the shiny light blue walls. A floral border had been secured at the ceiling line, and it matched the bedspread and draperies. Wendy had done a commendable job of decorating this place. Every room had a cozy country feel to it.

"If Mom were still alive, we'd probably give you my room and I'd sleep in here with her." Kylie sipped her chocolaty drink. "So if you feel strange at all about sleeping in my mom's bed, I can switch with you."

"Kylie, I'm perfectly comfortable. No bad vibes in here. Honest."

She grinned. "Well, I get 'sad vibes' in here. That's why I offered you this room instead of mine."

Blythe replied with a smile and lowered herself onto the edge of the bed.

"After you agreed to visit, I forced myself to come in here, clean up, and change the sheets. Before last week, I hadn't been in this room since Mom died. In fact," she added on a mournful note, "all my mom's stuff is still in her bathroom." She nodded to the full bath off the master bedroom.

Blythe reached for Kylie's hand and gave it a gentle squeeze. "I feel privileged to stay in this room. I loved Wendy."

Kylie smiled, appearing pleased by the remark.

Releasing her hand, Blythe's gaze wandered the room again. . .and then she saw it. On the bureau.

"What is it?" Kylie twisted around, following Blythe's line of vision.

"Is that what I think it is?" Blythe stood and walked over to the oak-finished dresser. Lifting the tarnished silver frame with its sculpted border, she peered at the poem inside.

I shall surround myself with precious things,
To keep my sorrow at bay.
Books and letters and photographs,
Pieces of heart, broken along the way.
A cradle, pink blanket, a lock of her hair,
A watch, record album, the shirt he used to wear,
These precious things will do me no harm—

If I could only forget who they are from.

"Mom took a calligraphy class years ago and that poem was one of her projects. She liked the way it turned out, so she made it into a keepsake."

Silver frame in hand, Blythe turned back around and watched Kylie take a sip of her cocoa.

"Personally, I always thought it was a dumb poem. The meter is off or something," Kylie confessed.

Blythe arched a brow. "Excuse me? I'll have you know I wrote this 'dumb poem'—and the meter is *supposed* to be off." She laughed at Kylie's wide-eyed surprise.

"Oops. Well, you know what they say. Poetry is like any other literary form—make that art in general—it's very subjective."

"You're quite the diplomat."

Kylie grinned. "So what's the story behind that poem?"

Blythe glanced at the black loopy letters on the sheet of parchment. "I wrote this while I was in Singapore trying to get my head together and figuring out what to do with the rest of my life. When my uncle asked what I was good at, what 'gift' had God given me, I told him I had a knack for finding precious things in garbage piles. Uncle Garth saw that as a viable way to earn a living and suggested I open a store and surround myself with *precious things*. I mulled it over, started thinking about some of the objects I owned, the ones that I held near and dear to my heart, and this poem came to me—along with a name for my shop."

Kylie held out her hand. "Let me see the poem again!"

Blythe set the framed verse in Kylie's palm and she read it aloud. When finished, she glanced back at Blythe. "The cradle and pink blanket and lock of hair. . .that's me, isn't it?"

Blythe nodded.

"The other stuff. . .that's Rob."

Again, Blythe replied with a slight bob of her head.

Kylie heaved a weighted sigh as she handed back the picture frame. "You know how many times I've read that poem? The truth was staring back at me but I didn't recognize it. I never even asked my mom where she got that piece of poetry or why she liked it enough to frame it. I figured it just had to do with her success in calligraphy."

"You never had a reason to ask." Blythe set the silver frame back on the chest of drawers. "Now, I want to show you something. Another *precious thing*." Crossing the room, she pulled the pink and white fabric-covered scrapbook from her suitcase. "Here," she said, handing it to Kylie.

"What is it?"

"You'll see."

Kylie took care in opening the book with its lacy edging. "This is all about me!"

"That's right." Blythe sat down on the side of the bed once more. "There are letters from Wendy tucked into pockets on the backs of various pages. The first letter dates back to when you were three weeks old. It was written right after she and Josh moved into this house."

The way Kylie's dark brows drew together spoke of her amazement.

"You can keep the scrapbook for a while and read through Wendy's letters. It might answer some questions you have. But I would like the keepsake album back when you're finished. It's very precious to me."

"Of course. And I promise to take good care of it."

Blythe smiled.

"So, how did you meet Rob? Will you tell me, or do I have to wait and read it for myself in this scrapbook?"

Holding her warm mug of hot cocoa between her hands, Blythe pondered the questions. "I'll tell you. Then perhaps as you page through the scrapbook, other things will make more sense."

"Thanks."

Blythe took a sip of warm chocolate before beginning. "As you may have guessed, my parents were unconventional, to say the least. They welcomed anyone needing a place to stay. When Rob and Wendy arrived in Chicago, someone told them about my folks and they showed up on the doorstep one day."

"What was he like?"

"Oh. . ." Blythe felt her heart constrict in the way it always did when she reminisced. But just this once she wanted to be strong enough to tell the truth because she believed Kylie deserved to know about her biological father. "Rob had charisma. He also had big ideas. He was an impulsive dreamer and a hopeless romantic, but that was part of what made him so charming. He abhorred any kind of violence, so when he got drafted, he chose not to fight. His plan was to seek political asylum in Canada, but first he wanted to hitchhike across America and participate in antiwar demonstrations in each state he passed through." Blythe stared into the depths of her creamy cocoa. "He made it as far as Chicago."

"Allie said Jack didn't like him."

"That's true and the feeling was mutual, I'm afraid." The thought of young Jack Callahan caused Blythe to grin. "Jack was a rookie cop who played by the book—well, except when it concerned Allie, Wendy, and me. He went easy on us. Really easy." Blythe's smile grew. "But Rob had a minor drug habit—he wasn't a junkie. But smoking pot and tripping on LSD were illegal practices, so Jack saw Rob as a guy who thumbed his nose at the law. Rob was also a draft-dodger, and that irritated Jack, who would have fought for his country in a heartbeat, but the army wouldn't take him because of some minor medical condition. Rob didn't have a job, so that made him a deadbeat in Jack's opinion. He believed if a man didn't work, he didn't eat. Period."

"Don't hate me, but I agree with Jack."

Blythe laughed. "I could never hate you, and I agree with Jack too. That is, now I do. But when I was nineteen and looking at the world through rose-colored glasses, I didn't see the moral irresponsibility in my generation's behavior. I saw freedom and originality. I heard intellectual ideology that contradicted biblical principles, and I thought it was okay to believe differently. But God is not mocked. In professing ourselves wise, we became fools. So many of us in that era wanted to make the world a better place, but instead we opened the door to decadence."

A solemn shadow crossed Kylie's features. "How did Rob die?"

The memory of that night burned like a fire in Blythe's chest. However, she pressed on. "We were demonstrating outside the building where the Democratic National Convention was being held. It was supposed to be a peaceful antiwar protest, but with the massive crowd of people who showed up, many of them drunk or high on drugs, riots broke out all over the city. The night was hot with not even a breeze off the lake. I remember seeing just about everyone with a cold can of beer in hand. The later the night got, the hotter the tempers became, and suddenly cars were overturned and set on fire. Rocks were hurled through glass windows." Blythe shook her head at the scene playing before her mind's eye. "As you can imagine, things got out of control very quickly. The police were outnumbered so they started using their nightsticks. Hitting people, cracking them over the head. People were walking the streets with blood trickling down the sides of their faces. It was ghastly.

"Then something happened farther ahead of where Rob and I stood. I'll never know what incited the cops, but minutes later, chaos broke out all around us. Men were yelling, women screaming. Police were coming toward us and I remember seeing nightsticks going up and down. Rob was in front of me, and I yanked on the back of his T-shirt, trying to get out of the way. But he was attempting to help the guy in front of him." Blythe paused to calm her pounding heart. "The next thing I knew, Rob disappeared. He got sucked into the pandemonium. Minutes later, when the crowd inched its way down the street, I found Rob lying face down on the pavement. I ran to him and pulled him into my lap, thinking that maybe if I wiped the blood off his face he'd be okay. His features were unrecognizable and his head. . ." With one hand, Blythe wiped the sudden dampness off her cheeks. "It was like the worst horror movie I ever saw, and I must have sort of gone into shock, because I've never been able to recall more than bits and pieces of the rest of the night."

Blythe set her mug on the tray. "I remember an ambulance arriving. I remember someone talking to me in what had to have been the hospital's waiting room. I think they were telling me Rob was dead, but I knew that already." Blythe hung her head back and gazed at the smooth, white surface of the ceiling. "Somehow I made it back home, and I remember Pete and Lydia freaking out. I recall being hysterical and someone's arm went around me. Wendy finally came home and managed to calm me down." Blythe shook her head as she recounted the incident. "Wendy was such a strong person emotionally. She acted more like my mother that night than Lydia. Of course, Wendy was devastated to learn Rob had been killed. We held each other and sobbed. But she cleaned me up, made me take a shower, and tucked me into bed, instructing me to get some sleep. I never saw her fall apart. *Ever.*"

Kylie nodded, wiping tears from her own eyes. "That was my mom." She stared at Blythe askance while a worry line creased her forehead. "Did you ever file charges against the cops who beat Rob?"

Blythe shook her head and blinked back a new onset of emotion. "Wendy didn't want to pursue anything because that would have meant she'd have to turn herself over to authorities. You see, she was under age and she wasn't about to trust any of the 'establishment,' like cops and lawyers. Besides, she was flat broke. Lawsuits cost money. And even if Wendy had found somebody to represent her for free and that attorney won the case, nothing would bring Rob back." Blythe raised her shoulders in a helpless shrug. "So justice was never served."

Kylie seemed pensive as she set her now empty mug back onto the tray. "I'm so sorry you had to live through all that. I can't imagine how traumatic that must have been for you."

"It was a nightmare."

Kylie set aside the scrapbook and put her arms around Blythe. A daughter comforting the mother she never knew. It was all Blythe could do to hold back her tears.

"Jack told me that sometimes God has to break us before He can use us," she said, and Blythe had to smile. Kylie was every bit as motherly as Wendy was. "Just like a wild horse has to be broken before someone can ride him, God has to break our wills so we conform to His."

Blythe thought it over. "Yes, I suppose Jack's right. God used Rob's death to help me see my desperate need for Him."

"Then the tragedy wasn't for nothing."

"Perhaps that's one way of looking at it."

"Maybe that was God's way of breaking you."

"Maybe. But I think God's heart broke the night Rob died, too. He loved Rob and, from what I know, Rob wasn't a believer. But it is true that the Lord can take even the worst of tragedies and use it for redemptive purposes."

Movement at the doorway suddenly caught Blythe's attention, and she glanced over in time to see Kathryn Chadwyk swipe tears from her eyes. She sat up straight and saw that Lee stood beside her. His face looked blotchy, his eyes red.

"Please forgive us for eavesdropping," Kathryn murmured in a shaky voice. "We didn't mean to, but we heard Rob's name several times and became curious."

"That's quite all right." Blythe stood and walked toward the older couple. She wasn't the least bit offended. In fact, she realized the Chadwyks had done her a favor. "Now I don't have to recount that awful story again."

Kathryn began to weep. She sagged against Lee and he pulled her into his arms. Guilt and sorrow filled Blythe's heart. She wished she had been able to persuade Wendy to tell her folks about Rob.

As if divining her thoughts, Lee asked, "Why weren't we notified? You'd think the authorities would have contacted us. You'd think the detectives I hired over the years would have at least been able to discover our son was dead!"

"Well, for one thing, Rob didn't have ID on him that night. I had his wallet in my purse. He told me to hang onto it because he was afraid of getting pickpocketed. I was wearing my purse across my chest and had it under my T-shirt." Blythe sniffed, realizing her emotions were getting the best of her again. "Secondly, Wendy was a minor, and she was scared she'd get busted if she went to the authorities and claimed Rob's body. I wanted to claim it and give Rob a decent burial, but my parents wouldn't hear of it. They said if I stepped forward, I would have to pay for all the funeral expenses, and I didn't have any money at the time. My parents didn't care for Rob, so they refused to lend me the cash."

"So what are you telling us, Blythe?" Lee's voice cracked with misery.

"Cook County buried Rob in a paupers' cemetery, located in Homewood, Illinois."

"No service?" Kathryn looked aghast.

"Oh, there was a service, but it was held for the multitude

of indigent and/or unclaimed buried that same day. Rob was one of many."

Kathryn paled. "In a mass grave?"

Blythe shook her head. "A mass service. Rob has his own grave."

"What name is on his headstone?" The older woman's hazel eyes pleaded for information of her son, and Blythe couldn't find it in her heart to deny the unspoken request.

"No headstone. His grave is marked with a plain white cross. I know the location and plot number. I can give it to you."

Kathryn turned to her husband. "Rob is a. . .a *number*."

"We'll fix that." Lee pulled his wife closer.

Feeling wretched, like she didn't do right by the man she loved so deeply, Blythe glanced at Kylie, then back at the Chadwyks. "I apologize that things weren't handled better. We were kids, frightened and ignorant. But I, um, have Rob's belongings in my van. Perhaps in some small way they'll help right all the wrongs. If you'll wait here, I'll get them."

Without pausing for an answer, Blythe ran downstairs and out to her Montana. When she returned, she set the cardboard box on the bed and opened it, revealing a light blue plastic bag inside. She tore it and pulled out several record albums. The Doors. Steppenwolf. Jimi Hendrix. Jefferson Airplane.

"These were Rob's favorites, but I'm afraid I didn't share his taste in music. I was more Tommy James and the Shondells, and the Mamas and the Papas."

Kylie looked over the recordings then waved her hand at her grandparents. "You don't want to know."

"I trust you, my dear," Lee said, his gaze on the next items Blythe extracted from the box.

Blythe held a black lacquer box. "I don't know where Rob got this, but. . ." She lifted the lid. The sight wasn't as painful as she thought. "I put his watch and wallet in here." She handed the box and items to Lee.

Next, she pulled out sketchbooks. "These are Rob's drawings. Don't ask me to look at them, because I'll sob the rest of the night." She gave the artwork to Kathryn, who held them close to her heart.

Then came Rob's knapsack. It contained articles of clothing. "There's not much here. Rob traveled light. He planned to hitchhike across the country, so if it didn't fit in his backpack, he didn't want it." Blythe glanced at Kylie. "I had made up my mind to go with him. I was ready to leave whenever Rob gave the word."

"Life threw you a curve, didn't it?" Kylie said.

"Yes, it did."

Kathryn said nothing but stared at the sketchbook in her arms. More tears filled her eyes. "Having Rob's belongings would have brought me some comfort decades ago. All this time. . ." The older woman shook her head. "All this time Rob's been dead."

Blythe felt awful.

Meanwhile, Lee was carefully inspecting Rob's wallet. When the room's hush reached his ears, he brought his chin up and scanned the onlookers, stopping on Blythe. "There are twenty-three dollars in his wallet. How on earth did Rob think he'd get anywhere on twenty-three bucks?"

"Oh, you'd be surprised," Blythe replied. "He sold his drawings on the street, and people like my parents were very willing to let a hippie 'crash' at their 'pad.' "

"How utterly irresponsible but oh, so typical of your generation."

Blythe folded her arms, feeling somewhat defensive. Didn't these people realize that she was trying to do them a favor?

"Maybe we should call it a night," Kylie suggested, obviously sensing the tension.

The Chadwyks agreed and, wordlessly, they gathered their son's things and left the bedroom.

Looking at Kylie, Blythe wondered if she'd made a mistake by coming here.

"You look worried."

At Blythe's shrug, Kylie crawled off the bed and crossed the room. She enfolded Blythe in an embrace, one meant to assure her. "Don't mind my grandparents. They've carried around a lot of sorrow for a very long time."

They're not the only ones. Blythe's heart seemed to break all over again. *They're not the only ones!*

CHAPTER TWELVE

Kylie felt like she could run a mile. Lying on her back, staring at the moonlit ceiling, she thought about everything Blythe had told her. Her natural mother had certainly come through some harrowing experiences. But maybe now that the truth had been exposed she would finally find happiness. Kylie closed her eyes and asked God to help Blythe with whatever vow she'd made—and had broken.

Time ticked on. Kylie tossed and turned. She couldn't sleep. Her thoughts came around to Matt. When should she tell him about her idea? She'd come up with it on Friday, and the more she thought it over the more she wanted to implement the notion. An Easter weekend wedding. How cool would that be? And moving up their wedding date would solve her grandparents' problems of coverage over a busy weekend. Moreover, marrying Matt sooner rather than later would give Kylie's healing heart the boost it seemed to yearn for.

Maybe she'd tell Matt about it today after church. No, she'd want to spend some more time with Blythe. Then when? It would have to be soon. Easter Sunday was one week away.

The digital alarm clock on her bedside table now read 4:30. *Maybe now's the perfect time.*

Kylie threw off her bed covers and decided to drive over to the Alexanders' farm. Matt rose at this hour each morning, and he was usually in the barn no more than half an hour later. Kylie hoped that if she helped him with his chores, she'd find a chance to tell him about her Sabal Beach idea. She had considered every angle. It could work.

Dressing in the dark, Kylie pulled on her blue jeans and an old sweatshirt. She tiptoed downstairs to the first floor where she found her old sneakers and slipped them on. Then she quietly left the house. Five minutes later, she pulled into Matt's driveway. After parking her Outback, she climbed out of the car. The predawn temperatures had to be near freezing, and the cold air sent a chill through Kylie. Rubbing her arms, she traipsed across the yard to the barn, glad to see the light on.

"Matt?" She stepped into the lofty wooden structure, and the familiar sweet, dank smell of straw, hay, and Holstein cows tickled her nostrils. She stepped in farther and called his name again.

No answer.

She kept walking, following the sounds of static and country music coming from a portable radio.

Then suddenly he rounded the corner of the milk room and they nearly collided. He jumped when he saw Kylie and his blue eyes widened. "You scared me half to death! What are you doing here?"

"I couldn't sleep." Her gaze roved over him, from his

Milwaukee Brewers baseball cap, thick navy blue sweatshirt with its tear in the right shoulder, faded blue jeans, frayed at the knees, to his worn, brown leather work boots.

Matt chuckled. "You'll probably sleep when Pastor Hanson starts preaching in a few hours."

Kylie laughed. "Oh, cut it out."

Stepping forward, he pressed a kiss on her lips. "I'm glad you came over."

"I thought I'd help you with your chores."

"Great. I'm just getting started."

"But, um, just so you know, I do have an ulterior motive."

Matt folded his arms and grinned. "Yeah? Let's hear it."

"I'm hoping that if I help you we'll have time to talk before breakfast."

"Sure. What about?"

Kylie grinned. "Our wedding."

He looked confused. "Can't it wait until this afternoon? Why now?"

"You'll understand after I tell you."

His wary expression made her laugh. But she refused to say another word about it until the chores were done.

Finally, two and a half hours later, they strode hand in hand to the house.

"Looks like it's going to be a nice day."

Kylie glanced upward and took note of the bright sky. "I hope so. I'm tired of rain."

"April showers bring May flowers."

She rolled her eyes at the cliché.

"Well, hey, at least it didn't snow."

"True."

They entered the house through the back door and almost

at once, the rich aroma of freshly brewed coffee filled Kylie's senses.

She kicked off her soiled canvas shoes and headed into the kitchen. "Coffee smells good."

"Want some?"

"Yeah."

Matt pulled two mugs out of the cupboard. "So what's this all-important issue about our wedding that kept you awake all night?"

"Well, actually, that's not what kept me up. Blythe ended up telling my grandparents and me about my biological father's death." Kylie shook her head as Matt poured her a cup of coffee. "Really tragic. I started thinking about everything and couldn't seem to shut off my mind."

"I've had those nights." He handed her the steaming mug.

"And then I started thinking about us and our wedding. . . and my idea."

"Uh-oh." Grinning, Matt took a sip of his coffee and then nodded toward the kitchen table.

Kylie followed his lead and pulled out a brown and tan vinyl chair. Once seated, she set her coffee on the veneer table. Matt sat to her left.

"I decided I don't want to wait until September to get married."

"Fine with me. As you recall, September wasn't my idea."

"I know." Kylie peered into her coffee. "It was Mom's."

Matt covered her hand with his, then gave her fingers a gentle squeeze. "So when do you want to get married?"

Kylie met his curious stare with one of intent. "This coming Saturday—in Sabal Beach."

Matt removed his hand, lifting it up palm-side out as if

to forestall the inevitable.

But Kylie wasn't about to be hushed. "I have it all figured out. I made some phone calls on Friday."

"Ky—"

"No, please, hear me out."

Matt complied, although the entire time Kylie listed specifics, his expression remained skeptical at best.

"I just want to do something daring and different."

"Why?" He tore off his hat and flung it over the counter toward the back hall. Then he rubbed his disheveled hair and leaned forward, giving her an expectant look.

"Because it'll be fun and we'll remember it the rest of our lives."

"We won't remember a traditional wedding?" Matt shook his head. "Look, Ky, if you don't have a formal ceremony, I think you'll be disappointed later."

"No, I won't." Kylie scooted to the edge of her chair. "Please, Matt, let's elope—well, it's not eloping in the true sense of the word. My grandparents, your mom, and, hopefully, Blythe will be there." She took his hand and held it between both of hers. "I love you. I can't imagine my life without you—even more so now, after all we've been through. I feel closer to you than ever before."

"Ditto." He leaned forward and placed a kiss on her cheek. "But I still don't understand the rush."

"I want to be your wife *now*. I don't want to be alone anymore."

"Honey, you're not alone. Your grandparents are staying with you, you've got Mom and me, and best of all, you've got God."

"I know. . . ." Kylie glanced down at their clasped hands,

wondering how she could explain herself. "My wanting to get married now rather than a month from now or even in September goes beyond just doing something daring."

"I figured."

She looked up at him, searching his face from his blue eyes to his stubbly chin. "Matt, I need you to be my husband. . .*now*. I don't know how to explain it, but I'm sure it has a lot to do with everything I'm going through. There's a part of me that was so full and happy, but it got depleted when my mom died and then. . ." Kylie took care in choosing her next words, remembering that she and Matt had agreed never to bring up the incident with Dena again. "And then everything else, like finding out I was adopted and discovering my mom lied to me."

Matt squeezed her hand. "Your world sure got rocked off its axis, didn't it?"

She nodded, feeling like she might cry, and he pulled her onto his lap. In the past, Kylie despised it when Matt treated her like a child, but at the moment, it was rather comforting to feel small and vulnerable with his strong and protective arms around her. She leaned the side of her head against his forehead.

"My second and third reasons for wanting to elope are my grandparents. They feel the need to be at their bed-and-breakfast next weekend to help with the guests. Our getting married in Sabal Beach will enable them to return to The Light House without feeling guilty about leaving me." She tightened her hold around Matt's neck. "Incidentally, guests are gone by eleven o'clock. Grandma Kate said a two o'clock wedding would work perfectly."

"What?" Matt pulled back. "You talked to your grand-mother about this before me?"

"Well, I had to be sure the idea was even feasible."

As he digested her reply, Matt's features relaxed. "Okay, that's the second. What's your third reason?"

"It's not half as good as the first and second." Kylie chuckled at Matt's deadpan expression. "Okay, here it is. I'm hoping that if I get you to Sabal Beach, you'll fall in love with the place as much as I did, and maybe you'll think about moving there."

"Ah," he said, a knowing sparkle in his blue eyes. "Now this is all starting to make sense. It's a sales job!"

"No, it isn't." Kylie laughed. "I've told you before that I want to be close to my grandparents now that we've found each other."

"Yeah, I know, but. . ." Matt turned somber. "What happens if I hate Sabal Beach?"

"You won't. But if you do, you won't hate Charleston."

"Suppose I do. Suppose I don't want to leave Wisconsin, except for an occasional vacation. What if I want to live the rest of my life here on this farm?"

"Do you?"

He paused, regarding her with an earnest stare. "I don't know."

Kylie snuggled against him again. "Can't we just take things one step at a time? I've learned these past few months that life is so uncertain. But at least our love for each other isn't. I've learned that, too, and it's sealed in my heart forever. I love you."

"I love you, too." Matt drew in a deep breath and then let it out with an audible rush of air. "This Saturday in Sabal Beach, huh?"

Kylie nodded.

"I suppose I can ask Nicky Potter if he'll come over before and after school and milk for me. He'd probably come all weekend, too."

"That would work. You hired Nicky last summer to help you, so he knows his way around and what to do."

Matt was momentarily pensive. "And you won't be disappointed that you didn't get a real wedding?"

"It'll be a real wedding. I'm not talking courthouse, and I've had my dress for months already." Kylie straightened. "We can have the ceremony at my grandparents' bed-and-breakfast. The place is like a modern-day castle. Did I tell you about the honeymoon suite? Marilee and I toured it. Totally romantic with a Jacuzzi on the deck overlooking the Atlantic Ocean."

"Hmm. . ." Nothing short of mischief entered Matt's eyes.

Kylie grinned, anticipating a wisecrack.

"A few days holed up with you in a honeymoon suite on the Atlantic? I guess that's an offer I can't refuse."

Kylie raised her arms in victory. "Whoo-hoo!"

"She wants to do. . .*what?*"

"Oh, TJ, I know it sounds spur-of-the-moment."

"Kathryn, it's Monday morning and you're talking about a wedding on Saturday!"

"Yes, I know, but Kylie has everything figured out right down to obtaining the marriage license. She discovered there's only a twenty-four-hour waiting period in South Carolina, and it doesn't matter that she and Matt aren't residents."

"Guess that's good to know," he stated facetiously—as if he'd ever have use for a marriage license.

Sitting in the enclosed sunporch, TJ leaned back in the brightly upholstered wicker chair and grimaced when he heard the thing creak beneath his weight. It was his favorite seat in the house, but TJ figured one of these days he was going to end up on the tiled floor if he wasn't careful.

"The plan is that we'll all fly in on Wednesday," Kathryn continued. "Matt and Kylie will apply for their license on Thursday, they'll pick it up on Friday morning—"

"That's Good Friday."

"Kylie was told the office is open until noon."

"Listen, Kathryn, I think this is a bad idea."

"Why?"

"Well, because. . ." TJ scratched his jaw. "All right, I'll give it to you straight. It's Seth. When Kylie e-mailed him and said she'd gotten back together with her fiancé, Seth took the news really hard. He moped around here all weekend."

"Oh, dear. . ."

"On the bright side, Seth has plans to fly to Indiana over Easter and visit his folks. I think he said he leaves Friday afternoon."

"Well, then, I think Seth, Matt, and Kylie can be civil to each other for a few days, don't you?"

"Hope so."

"Of course they can." Kathryn sounded a bit distracted, and TJ didn't think she fully understood how awkward the situation was going to be. "Now, the way we've planned it, the wedding will be held on Saturday at two. I've already talked to Sam. He said he'll be able to perform the ceremony."

"Is Pastor marrying them at church?"

"No. At The Light House. Kylie requested it and neither Lee nor I have the heart to deny that girl a single thing."

"Don't I know it!"

"Oh, now," Kathryn drawled. "Everything will work out fine. Guests have to be out by eleven o'clock, so that'll give us plenty of time to get ready for the wedding."

"If you say so." TJ, on the other hand, had his doubts. "How many people are coming?"

"Under a dozen, I imagine."

"Whew! That's a relief. I was afraid you'd say a hundred."

"No. Besides us and the bride and groom, there'll be Matt's mother, Lynellen Alexander, and a few of our closest friends, and Blythe. That's it."

"Blythe? Who's Blythe?"

"Kylie's biological mother."

"Oh, right." TJ recalled hearing the name now. "How did your visit with her go this weekend?"

"She's a sparrow of a woman, small and quiet. She's rather nondescript in my opinion."

"Is that good or bad?"

"Neither, I guess."

TJ sensed Kathryn didn't like her. "Were you able to have any sort of meaningful conversation?"

"Well, yes, and to her credit, Blythe was very honest with us about everything. She told us how Rob was killed and why she chose to let Wendy adopt Kylie. All very understandable, I suppose. But why she didn't think to notify us really troubles Lee and me. It would have been as simple as searching the Internet by using our last name."

"So, why didn't she? Did you ask her that?"

"No. The opportunity never presented itself. But it's a point of contention that neither Lee nor I know how to overcome. For thirty years, we agonized over the whereabouts of our children. Blythe had the answers all along and kept them to herself."

TJ wanted to remind Kathryn that her own daughter could have told them about Rob's death—and done it anonymously too. But he kept quiet. He could tell Kathryn was upset.

"And now Blythe's coming to Sabal Beach for Kylie's wedding? Is that wise?"

"Kylie wants her to come. As for Blythe, she'd like to attend, but she has to work out several particulars. Maybe it'll happen that she won't be able to make the trip. But enough of this doom and gloom. Let's discuss Kylie's big day."

"Sure." TJ stood and strode into the foyer, pausing at the desk where he found paper and a pen. "What do you want done first?"

Kathryn rattled off the tasks and TJ wrote each one down. At long last, they said their good-byes. TJ disconnected and set down the portable phone. He stared at his "to-do" list and couldn't shake off the unease he felt over this coming weekend. Seeing Kylie again was going to affect Seth, and if Blythe showed up, the Chadwyks wouldn't enjoy their granddaughter's wedding day.

Pocketing his list, he sauntered off in the direction of the kitchen. Was he the only one who saw danger signs flashing in the distance?

CHAPTER THIRTEEN

Blythe lay in bed in her darkened room, listening to the wind off Lake Michigan rattle her windowpanes. She thought about the strange dream she'd just had and tried to recall it, but couldn't. All she remembered was that Allie was in it. What was she doing? Directing traffic or some such ridiculous thing? And she was eighteen years old again!

Blythe smiled. Dreams could be so strange at times. Uncle Garth once said he thought dreams were the result of one's subconscious mind purging itself. Maybe he was right. It certainly fit in her situation. For the past month, Blythe's subconscious mind had been working overtime, recalling the past that she had tried to bury and forget.

Before her alarm even sounded, Blythe tossed off her covers, climbed out of bed, and began preparing herself for the day. She started a pot of coffee, then rode her stationary bike for a half hour while watching the early news. After that, she showered. But as she dressed, Blythe's thoughts came back around to Allie.

Allie Drake. Her mother had died when she was a senior in high school, and Allie had filled the void in her heart with rebellion. She fit right in with Blythe and Wendy. They hung out together, and Allie actually ran away from home and moved in—until one day the neighbors complained about the loud music blaring from the Seversons' house. That brought the Oakland Park police to the door, specifically one young cop named Jack Callahan. He knew Allie's stepfather was looking for her, so he took her into custody.

Blythe grinned at the memory of that first meeting, and then her thoughts hopped to Jack. He'd suffered his own set of trials. He didn't marry Allie, as he planned, but another woman Blythe never knew about or met. They had a son together, Logan, and then she took off with some other guy. Jack covered his hurt over losing first Allie and then his wife with an intense bitterness that changed him into an almost cruel man—one Blythe didn't recognize at times. They kept in touch, even dated, although nothing serious ever resulted. Blythe sensed she wasn't the woman he needed. She didn't have the wherewithal to pull Jack from the depths of his self-despair. Recognizing this, she began to pray he wouldn't call her for a date again—and, suddenly, he didn't. Nevertheless, she and Jack remained good acquaintances. But when Blythe bumped into him a couple of months ago, he seemed like a new man, as if the old Jack Callahan she used to know thirty years ago had returned. He even *smiled*. Then he gave Blythe a hug. Right there at the Walgreen's checkout counter.

And that's when she learned that he and Allie were back together. Blythe was happy for them—truly happy—although she'd purposely dodged Allie's phone calls and invitations to lunch. She hadn't wanted Allie to open those old wounds from a generation ago. But, without intending to, Allie managed to expose the truth in spite of Blythe's elusiveness. Now, however, after spending the last two days with Kylie, Blythe knew she had to get in touch with Allie and, if nothing else, thank her. Yes, these last several weeks had been difficult, and this past weekend had been uncomfortable with the Chadwyks. But what mattered most was that Blythe and Kylie were well on their way to becoming good friends. Blythe had fantasized about getting to know her daughter for thirty-one years. Now it seemed God had granted her a dream come true, and He had used Allie.

However, before Blythe could know complete happiness, she'd have to tell Garth about Kylie, about her past. Wouldn't she? But what if she held her silence? Did Garth really need to find out?

Through showering and dressing, Blythe pondered her options. Was keeping silent the same as lying? She knew Lydia would tell her it wasn't.

With her thoughts still weighing heavily on her mind, Blythe left her upper apartment at seven-thirty. When she arrived at Precious Things, she parked in the lot behind the building and entered by way of the back door. While her shop didn't open until nine, Blythe liked to have a bit of quiet time in her office, a practice she'd begun when Pete was still alive and she lived at home in Oakland Park. After returning from Singapore, Blythe never felt comfortable in that house again, so she took to reading her Bible and praying here at Precious Things before the store opened.

Sitting down at her desk, she reached for God's Word,

when the phone rang. Blythe ignored it. She didn't take calls until nine. The answering machine picked up: "Thank you for calling Precious Things. The store is closed at this time. Please call back between the hours of nine a.m. and six p.m. or leave a message. . . . *Beep.*

Blythe opened her Bible, intending to continue her reading in a portion of the Old Testament and a portion of the New Testament.

"Hi, Blythe, it's Allie. I'm attempting to get a hold of you one last time. I wanted to explain something. . . . Anyway, I just called your home phone and—"

Blythe snatched the portable phone from its charger and quickly pressed the TALK button. "Allie? Hi. . .I was thinking about you this morning."

The pause that followed caused Blythe to grin. "I've been avoiding you," she admitted. "I'm sure you noticed. But I'd like to apologize for my less-than-polite behavior, and. . .and even explain what's happened, if you'll let me."

"Of course I'll 'let you.' And I have some explaining to do myself. I just feel badly that you haven't wanted to talk to me."

"It's not you, personally, Allie. It's that stupid faded photograph you sent. I wasn't ready to deal with the past—or so I thought. But, Allie, a world of good has come out of it."

"That's incredible—and that's sort of why I decided to call, even though I wasn't sure you'd be receptive to it." Allie paused. "Kylie called me late last night and said you'd spent the weekend with her and her grandparents."

"It's true. That in itself is a miracle."

Allie's light laugh resounded from the other end of the line. "Well, just so you know, I was never a blabbermouth. I didn't give Kylie any information, but I didn't lie if she asked me."

"I understand. And that's what Kylie told me, too."

"At my request, Jack found Wendy's address in Wisconsin. I sent the same invitation and photograph to her as I sent to you, only—"

"Only Wendy never got it," Blythe finished for her.

"Right."

"I didn't even know Wendy had died until Kylie showed up here at Precious Things."

"I learned of Wendy's death the week before when Kylie called me with what was supposed to be an RSVP. Unfortunately, the photograph threw her. Wendy led her to believe she'd lived an entirely different existence before getting married."

"I know."

"Well, you could have informed me last November, Blythe. I wouldn't have tried to find Wendy had I known there was a secret to be kept."

Blythe settled back in her desk chair, deciding Allie sounded more hurt than annoyed. "I'm sorry, Allie. Please forgive me. You're right. I could have said something six months ago. But as difficult as it might be to believe this, the mere thought of articulating the truth scared me senseless."

"So you avoided me instead."

"Yes."

"Hmm. . ."

"As I said, I apologize."

"Apology accepted. And I'm sorry, too. I never meant any harm. Quite the opposite. I thought a reunion among old friends would be fun."

Blythe grinned. "Speaking of 'old friends,' what in the world did you do to Jack?"

"What are you talking about? I didn't *do* anything."

"Yeah, sure, the love of a good woman and all that. . ."

Allie laughed again. "Blythe, wait until you hear what God did in Jack's life. It's so amazing that I get the shivers just thinking about it."

"Well, Jack always loved you, Allie."

"I know. . .and I love him with all my heart."

Blythe smiled. "So when's the wedding?"

"This Friday."

"What?" Blythe bolted upright and searched the various neatly stacked papers for the wedding invitation. Hadn't she read the date as being in May? "But this Friday is Good Friday."

"We're aware. . .but Jack and I thought what better day to pledge ourselves to one another than the day in which Christians everywhere pause to remember what Jesus did on the cross for us. It's like Logan said, 'Every day should be Good Friday.' "

"True. . ." Blythe suddenly recalled that Jack's son was a pastor.

"The ceremony is at five o'clock in the evening, and we've invited only family and a few intimate friends."

Blythe found the invitation and relaxed. She was invited to the reception in May and not the ceremony.

"I suppose Kylie told you that she's getting married on Saturday."

"Yes, she did," Allie replied. "I was surprised. Last I heard, she'd broken her engagement. The wedding was off."

"Well, Matt repented and he seems very sincere. I didn't get the impression that he's the philandering type. Anyway, the wedding's back on and now Kylie's giving her loved ones a run for their money." Blythe marveled at her daughter's impulsive nature, although it had been suppressed while Wendy was alive. It was apparent that Kylie was in the throes of *finding herself,* a process that Blythe told her never really ended.

"Kylie said she hopes you'll fly down for the ceremony."

"I want to, but I have to find someone to mind my store, and I need to check airfares. I'm sure prices are outrageous. Everyone goes south the week after Easter."

"That's where Jack and I are headed. South to St. Thomas. I can't wait. I've been freezing to death for nearly half a year."

"Aw, poor California girl." Blythe laughed.

Allie did too. "Hey, can you do lunch today? I'd love to talk some more."

Blythe thought it over; she had no other pressing engagements. "Sure. Can you bring deli sandwiches here to my store? Since I'm a sole proprietress, it's hard for me to get away."

"I understand, and I'd love to. What kind of sandwich do you want?"

Blythe placed an order for chicken salad on a croissant and suggested a favorite delicatessen.

"If you recommend it, Blythe, that's where I'll go. I'm still relearning my way around the Chicago area."

"Okay, see you about one o'clock—and, Allie, I'm really glad you called."

A happy lilt sounded in her voice when she replied. "Me, too."

⊰⊱

Kylie sat at the booth in the new hamburger stand built onto the filling station and stared out the picture window, waiting for Dena to arrive. A glance at her wristwatch told Kylie her friend should have left the bank for lunch by now. . .unless a rush of customers entered. But on a Tuesday morning? It wasn't payday around here, so there shouldn't be lines at the tellers' windows.

At last, Dena's dilapidated white van pulled into the gas station. She parked in one of the spots designated for restaurant patrons, then jumped down from behind the driver's seat and slammed the door shut behind her. Kylie watched with a measure of envy as her longtime friend sauntered to the door in a thigh-high, tight maroon skirt and a revealing white blouse over which she wore a vest that matched the skirt. On Dena, the outfit looked better than its intended polyester bank uniform. But then, with her cute shape and silky blond hair, Kylie figured Dena could wear a burlap sack and still appear fashionable if not downright sexy.

"Hi! Sorry I'm late," Dena said, sliding onto the bright blue seat of the booth. "Thanks for ordering. I'm starved and I have to get back to the bank by one."

"It's 12:20!"

"I know, but my van wouldn't start. Ate up almost half my lunch hour trying to get the blasted thing to turn over. Finally Elmer Jorgensen jump-started the motor for me. But you might have to give me a hand so I can drive back."

"Okay. Matt put jumper cables in the compartment with my spare tire, so I know I have some."

"I own a set, too. Can't leave home without 'em." Dena grinned, her blue eyes twinkling. Then she tore into the paper surrounding her burger.

Kylie folded her hands in her lap, bowed her head, and asked a quick blessing on her food.

"What are you doing?"

"When?" Kylie looked up at Dena.

"Just now."

"Oh. . .I just prayed before I started eating."

"Praying?" Dena took a bite of her burger. "I thought maybe you broke a fingernail or something."

"Nope." Kylie smiled and ripped the wrapper off her cheeseburger.

"So are we friends again?" Dena popped a french fry into her mouth.

"Yeah. We're friends."

"Good."

Kylie bit into her sandwich, chewed, and swallowed. "Thanks for the sweater. It's gorgeous."

"I know. It's totally you. Has Matt seen it on you yet?"

Kylie wagged her head.

"Well, get ready. It's going to be instant turn-on for him."

A sick feeling plumed inside of Kylie. Even in choosing her birthday present, Dena had considered enticing Matt.

She didn't mean it that way, Kylie berated herself. *It's a backhanded compliment, that's all. . . .*

"So you and Matt are back together again, huh?" Dena lifted her cup of cola and sipped the drink through the straw. "You two looked pretty cozy sitting together in church on Sunday morning."

Kylie shook off her unease and nodded. "That's mostly why I asked you to meet me for lunch today. I wanted to be the one to tell you that Matt and I are eloping. . .this weekend. In Sabal Beach."

Dena straightened in the booth's padded seat. "This weekend? As in. . .four days from now?"

"Yep."

"Why the rush?"

"Everybody's asking that." Kylie grinned and lifted her cola, then took a sip.

"Well?"

"Well, I just don't want to wait until September to marry Matt. I know it sounds lame, but—"

"Listen, I wouldn't want to wait to marry him either." Dena winked. "Besides, you two are made for each other. I've said that before."

"I know." Kylie wished she could move beyond the hesitation she felt regarding her friendship with Dena. She wanted to forget what happened between them and go on; however, a check on Kylie's heart still remained.

"I'm disappointed that I don't get to be your maid of honor now."

"Sorry 'bout that." Smiling, Kylie swirled a french fry around in a glob of ketchup.

"What about a reception?"

"Lynellen wants to give us a party when we get back." Kylie didn't add that her future mother-in-law wasn't keen on the eloping idea. Worse, Lynellen disliked the idea of Kylie and Matt moving to South Carolina in the future. She even went so far as to accuse Grandma Kate of influencing Kylie to leave Basil Creek and tearing Matt away from his family's farm.

Fortunately, Kylie had enough sense not to repeat such a fallacy. She figured Lynellen just made a thoughtless remark and would regret it soon enough.

Kylie just hoped Matt wouldn't let his mother's sentiments affect his decision.

"So the two of you will live on the farm after you're married?"

Kylie nodded.

"Yeah, I figured." Dena took a bite of her burger, chewed, and swallowed. "Did you sell your house yet?"

"Not yet, but the Realtor said it shouldn't take long."

"No, I don't suppose it will. What are you asking?"

Kylie told her the amount. "June Littelle came up with the figure. Don't ask me how she did it, though."

"I always liked that house." Dena seemed momentarily pensive. "Well, if it doesn't sell, you can always rent it out."

"I thought about it, but what I really want to do is move to Sabal Beach and live close to my grandparents. They're not getting any younger. I'd like to really get to know them and enjoy their company for as long as I can."

"What does Matt say about that?" Wide-eyed, Dena gulped down several french fries.

Kylie lifted a shoulder. "He's still deciding."

"What if he says he wants to stay here?"

"Then we'll stay here." Kylie prayed that wouldn't happen, but she wasn't so naive to think it wasn't a possibility. She was trying to prepare herself for the worst-case scenario. But what she knew for sure was that she wanted to be Matt's wife as much as she wanted to live in Sabal Beach.

"I'd really miss you if you moved away, Ky."

She smiled out of politeness, wondering if she'd miss Dena. Six weeks ago Kylie would have missed her terribly. Back then, she was so rooted in Basil Creek she would have never dreamed of living elsewhere. Now, however, those proverbial ties that bind were severed, and moving far away and building a brand-new life appealed to Kylie.

Unfortunately, Matt was still bound to his family's farm, and he felt somewhat obligated to look out for his mother. He pointed out that *she* wasn't getting any younger either.

"You're frowning. What's wrong?"

"Nothing. Just have a lot on my mind, that's all."

"Well, you've got no reason to do anything but smile. You're the luckiest person I know." Dena crumpled her trash and set it on the brown plastic tray at the end of the table. "But you've always been lucky. You had terrific parents with money who spoiled you rotten, and now you've got a handsome fiancé who's crazy about you." She shrugged. "I guess some of us have it easy and some of us don't."

"I don't know if I'd call what I'm dealing with 'easy,' " Kylie replied. "You had it rough in your younger years, and I'm having a tough time now."

Dena grimaced. "Sorry. I kind of forgot about your mom and the adoption thing. Yeah, that's got to be a shock."

"It was. . .and is." Kylie forced a tight smile but decided not to elaborate. She couldn't allow herself to get caught up in the past right now. This week she had to focus on her future—beginning with her wedding on Saturday.

CHAPTER FOURTEEN

Here's your change. Thanks for stopping in, and have a great day."

The tall, thin woman with a long face and dark brown hair smiled and made her way out of Precious Things. Blythe watched her go, then saw her uncle enter the store as the woman exited.

"Well, good afternoon, my dear. It's a gorgeous day."

"Yes, it is." She'd taken the garbage out earlier and the April sun on her face felt warm and promising. "I think spring is really here."

"I believe you're right." Garth stepped forward and Blythe noticed that he didn't use his cane today. Obviously, his arthritic hip wasn't bothering him since the weather was so nice.

"How about a glass of iced tea, Uncle Garth?"

"If it's no trouble."

Blythe smiled. "No trouble at all."

She made her way to the back room and into the small kitchen area. Opening the refrigerator, she pulled out the pitcher and poured her uncle a glass of the unsweetened tea she'd prepared around noon. After adding some ice, she headed back into the shop and sent up a prayer that Garth would understand what she had to tell him. She was canceling their plans for Easter Sunday. She knew he'd be disappointed. But after an hour-long conversation with Kylie last night, Blythe decided to attend the wedding this weekend. Kylie assured her that the Chadwyks harbored no resentment toward her, and not wanting to seem insecure or paranoid, Blythe took her daughter's word for it. Next, Lydia agreed to mind the store, albeit grudgingly. She said Blythe was courting disaster, and perhaps that was true. Still, Blythe couldn't seem to help it. She wanted to be a part of Kylie's life no matter what the cost.

Reaching Garth, she handed him the glass of tea.

"I have some bad news." Blythe lowered herself onto a newly reupholstered cane-back settee. "I won't be able to celebrate Easter Sunday with you."

"Oh?" Already Garth wore a disappointed frown.

"Yes. A friend of mine died very suddenly this past January, and her daughter is getting married this weekend. Very spur-of-the-moment, but I was invited. In light of my friend's death, I feel I should go." Blythe stared at the crease in her tan slacks, congratulating herself on conveying at least part of the truth.

"I see. Well, I'll miss you, of course, but you must do what you feel is right."

Blythe lifted her gaze and smiled into her uncle's rheumy blue eyes. "Thanks for understanding."

Garth gave her a slight nod and took a drink of his tea. The ice cubes in his glass clattered after he removed the glass from his lips.

"Lydia said you're welcome to join her for dinner. She's hosting another couple at her apartment. Afterward, she wants to give them a private tour of Precious Things. I told her that would be all right."

"I'll give the offer some thought. Thank you." He grinned. "Now, how's business?"

Blythe smiled. "Business is fine. I sold that Chippendale corner chair." At her uncle's confused expression, she added, "It's the one I found beside the bank's dumpster. The manager threw it away because the seat cover was torn. He said I could have it."

"Hmm. . ." Garth obviously still didn't recall the piece.

"It's the chair that you thought was so odd with its triangular seat."

"Oh, of course. How could I forget it? Did you get a good price?"

"Three hundred dollars."

"Bravo!" Uncle Garth said with a sizable grin. "Blythe, you are a woman after my own heart."

Her smile widened, but inside Blythe prayed her uncle's heart wouldn't change toward her once he discovered the whole truth about her past.

Kylie extracted a cold bottle of cola from the industrial-sized refrigerator. Then, twisting off the cap, she took a long drink before heading outside where she'd left Matt sitting on the front steps of The Light House. The flight had been uneventful this afternoon, and now she and Matt were enjoying the balmy night air—

Until Kylie's thirst got the better of her.

As she entered the dining room, she heard a door slam close somewhere behind her. Curious, she retraced her steps to see who was coming through the back. Moments later, she came face-to-face with Seth Brigham.

Kylie smiled, glad to see her friend again. "Hi, Seth. Hey, your haircut looks nice. But, you're right. It doesn't resemble TJ's bald head at all." She laughed, recalling their phone conversation on her birthday.

But obviously, Seth wasn't amused. He didn't even grin as he wiped the bottoms of his brown leather slip-ons on the rug in the hallway.

"Bad day, Seth?"

"Bad week, I guess."

He stepped into the kitchen and walked around Kylie without saying another word. Pivoting, she watched his retreating form, feeling more than a little confused. He made it as far as the edge of the foyer before turning on his heel and striding toward her again.

"TJ told me to keep my big mouth shut, but you know that's an impossible command for me to keep."

Kylie couldn't help the small grin that tugged at her mouth, except she sensed what was coming.

"I think you're making a big mistake by marrying that guy."

"That guy?" Kylie blinked. "I take it you're referring to Matt."

"Yeah." Seth hiked the strap of his leather computer case higher up onto the shoulder of his white Oxford dress shirt.

"You just got back together and now you're marrying him a week later? What's the hurry?"

"If one more person asks me that question, I'm going to scream."

"If people are asking, maybe it's a sign you'd better think about what you're doing."

"I have thought about it, Seth. I've thought about it and prayed about it a lot."

"Just because you marry him doesn't mean Matt'll be faithful."

"Oh, Matt will be faithful." Kylie arched a brow and stared straight into Seth's brown eyes.

He leaned forward. "How do you know?"

"I just do." Kylie thought about all the recent conversations she'd had with Matt, and she felt convinced he had hurt himself as much as anyone with his thoughtless actions last January. Matt wouldn't be stupid twice.

"I hope for your sake you're sure."

"I'm sure."

"Okay, well. . ." Was it sadness that clouded his dark gaze? "I wish you all the happiness in the world."

Stepping closer, Seth bent and kissed her cheek.

"Hey, what's going on?"

Hearing her fiancé's voice, Kylie felt her face begin to flame with chagrin. Seth had the audacity to look amused. Turning, Kylie peered across the room where Matt stood near the doorway with his hands on his hips and a curious expression on his face.

"Matt, this is my friend, Seth Brigham. Seth. . ." She regarded Matt as he came to stand beside her. "This is my fiancé, Matt Alexander."

"Nice to meet you." Seth's voice sounded flat. Moments later he sauntered out of the kitchen.

Kylie watched him go, feeling bad that she'd hurt him. But she hadn't made him any promises. Seth knew there was a chance she and Matt would get back together.

"He's a *friend*, huh? How come I don't know about that. . . *friend?*"

Kylie peered up at Matt, realizing she had some explaining to do. "Let's go back outside and talk, okay?" She extended her hand and Matt took it. They traipsed through the hallway and the foyer, and then stepped outside, where they sat on the uppermost part of the elegant bowed staircase.

"I met Seth last month when I came here to meet my grandparents."

"Yeah, I figured as much."

"He's staying here at The Light House until he finds an apartment."

"Hmm. . ."

Kylie wondered what to say next. Exactly how much did Matt need to know?

He needs to know everything, her heart seemed to answer.

"Seth and I dated a couple of times, and—"

"You *dated* him?"

Kylie winced at the incredulous tone of Matt's voice.

He leaned into her shoulder in a way that let her know he was angry. "So let me get this straight. While I was waist deep in misery in Basil Creek, you were having the time of your life here in South Carolina, dating. . .*him!*"

"Well, I wouldn't exactly call it 'the time of my life,' but, yeah, I went out with Seth. If you recall, we weren't engaged."

"We were engaged as far as I was concerned!" Matt

straightened, then stood and walked back into the house.

Kylie remained where she was, hoping Matt would give the matter a little thought. Dating Seth paled in comparison to what he did with Dena last January. But Kylie pushed the latter from her thoughts. She'd vowed not to bring up that incident again—and she wouldn't, at least not to Matt.

Sitting there alone, Kylie drank her cola. Again, she felt bad that Seth was hurt. She felt worse that Matt was angry. She drew in a deep breath of the salty sea air. The night was balmy and a thousand stars shone in the black, velvety sky. Down the street, someone had turned up a car stereo, and the *boom-boom-boom* of its bass echoed through the otherwise quiet neighborhood.

Behind her, the door closed and Kylie started. Turning, she saw Matt. He came forward and sat next to her again.

"Okay, so I overreacted. I apologize."

"Apology accepted." Kylie smiled, glad Matt had come to his senses.

"You don't still have feelings for that guy, do you?"

Kylie rolled her eyes. "Do you really think I'd marry you if I had feelings for Seth?" She couldn't help a little laugh.

Then, to her amazement, Matt paused to consider the question. "You know, Ky, I can honestly say without a doubt that you and I wouldn't even be sitting here tonight if you still had special feelings for somebody else. Not after everything we've been through."

"You're right."

He slipped his arm around her and pulled her close to him. "But, um, that's one friendship I'd rather you didn't encourage."

"All right." Kylie felt a little sad over the thought of losing a friend—any friend. But, for Matt, she'd make the sacrifice. He had done the same for her, giving up his drinking buddies.

He kissed her temple. "I love you, Ky."

All seemed right in her world again. "I love you, too."

"TJ!"

Hearing Kathryn hailing him from the upper hallway in the private sector of The Light House, he took the steps two at a time."

"TJ?"

"I'm coming." Rounding the corner, he found Kathryn sitting at her computer at the end of the hall where Lee had constructed a tiny office for her. "You bellowed, madam?" He smirked and gave a little bow.

"Oh, I'm sorry. I sound like a fishmonger, don't I? Well, I'm afraid my tired old bones didn't want to get up and find you."

"Quite all right." TJ grinned. "Now what can I do for you?"

"Oh. . ." Kathryn pointed to the computer. "I got an E-mail from Blythe. She's coming for Kylie's wedding."

"Should we be concerned about that?"

"No. Kylie wants her natural mother in attendance for her wedding and so it shall be."

"Whatever Kylie wants, Kylie gets." TJ couldn't help the quip, although it earned him a look of reproof from Kathryn. "You're spoiling that girl rotten."

"And I'm having the time of my life doing it, too."

"Well, I guess that's all that matters." It sort of bugged him, but TJ didn't exactly feel envious of Kylie. The Chadwyks had "spoiled" him over the years, too.

"Now, about our guest situation, Blythe can room with Kylie and Lynellen. Three's a crowd, I know," Kathryn prattled on, "but it'll be for only one night. On Saturday, after their wedding, Matt and Kylie will spend the night up the street. Martha Owens hasn't rented her cottage out yet, so she offered to let Matt and Kylie use it. They'll return to The Light House for Easter, and then they can stay in the honeymoon suite. But at least the newlyweds will have one evening completely to themselves. Wasn't that kind of Martha?"

"Very." TJ rubbed the back of his neck. The Chadwyks had been home no more than six hours and things seemed out of control. Already, this upcoming wedding had grown from a dozen guests to twenty. Fortunately, most weren't staying here at The Light House.

"Can you pick up Blythe at the airport late Friday afternoon?"

"Don't see why not. I have to drop off Seth at the airport anyhow."

Kathryn smiled. "Thanks for all your help. I honestly don't know what I'd do without you."

He grinned. "It's a two-way street there, Kathryn." Stepping forward, he kissed the top of her head.

After a pleased smile, she went back to her E-mail.

TJ guessed that Kathryn coped with her angst by throwing herself into planning a wedding. Lee, on the other hand, sat downstairs gathering phone numbers. First thing tomorrow morning, he planned to get estimates on how much it would cost to exhume Rob's remains and transport them to South Carolina where his son could have a "decent burial." TJ tried to tell him that Rob wasn't in that "pauper's grave." His spirit was elsewhere. But Lee harbored so many regrets over his parenting that he at least wanted to do right by Rob in this instance, morbid as it seemed.

Both Kathryn's and Lee's emotions were running high. And now that Blythe Severson was slated to arrive in a matter of days, things would get even more intense. TJ grew all the more apprehensive about this coming weekend. When Kylie showed up here six weeks ago, she'd brought happiness to the Chadwyks. Her natural mother, however, had a whole different effect on them.

Forgive me, Lord; I haven't even met her, but I don't like this woman already.

CHAPTER FIFTEEN

On Friday afternoon, Allie stared at her reflection in the bathroom mirror. With her hair rolled up in large hot curlers, she stood inspecting the makeover a friend of Nora's offered to give her. The gal sold a brand of cosmetics, some of which Allie used; however, the Angel Face Cosmetics representative had gone a bit overboard.

"At this rate, Jack won't recognize me when I walk down the aisle."

"Cut it out. You always look glamorous." Nora paused. "It's just. . .*magnified* right now."

Allie's gaze slid to Nora, who stood beside her. They wore identical expressions of certain doubt.

"Better get out the makeup remover."

"Right." Allie opened one of the vanity's drawers and extracted the bottle.

"Give it here," Nora said with outstretched hand. "Allow

me to do the honors since it was my idea to ask Hannah over in the first place."

Allie laughed. "I won't hold it against you. Honest."

Sitting on the side of the bathtub, she allowed Nora to remove the generously applied cosmetics. She thanked God for such a faithful friend.

She and Nora had met last August and became instant confidants. The relationship grew and blossomed, and if Allie ever wanted a sister, it would be Nora Callahan. As it was, they'd be real sisters in a matter of hours. Sisters-in-law. But Allie felt they would be forever friends. They were like-minded committed Christians, although opposites physically. Nora had sandy-brown hair and Allie silvery-blond. Allie's frame was slim, Nora's "pleasingly plump," and Allie towered over Nora by a good four inches. Yet, Allie couldn't say she ever felt such a strong bond with another woman—save, perhaps, Wendy and Blythe years and years ago.

And speaking of Blythe. . .she phoned this morning to say she'd be stopping by. It could be any time now.

As if on cue, Nora's eldest daughter, Veronica, suddenly appeared at the bathroom door. She was a mix of her parents, having Steve's walnut-colored hair and lanky frame and Nora's teal eyes. "Someone's here to see you, Allie."

"Is it Blythe?" she asked with her eyes closed while Nora wiped off the too-bright eye shadow. "I was just thinking about her."

"Yep. That's her."

Allie caught Nora's wrist before she could administer more of the makeup remover. "Would you mind showing her in, Ronnie?" She grinned. "I'll hold court here in the bathroom."

179

Veronica rolled her eyes. "Yes, your highness."

Allie laughed and Nora chuckled.

"That girl is too sassy for her own good."

"You can say that again," Nora replied. "She's blessed with the same sarcastic wit that Jack inherited."

Allie nodded. "So I've noticed."

Moments later, Blythe neared the bathroom doorway. "Allie?"

"In here."

"Oh. . ." She found her way to the master bathroom. "I see I'm interrupting. . . ."

"It's quite all right. Come on in, although I normally don't ask my guests into the bathroom." Allie laughed as she pushed to her feet, then made the introductions.

"I know I look a fright at the moment. Nora is trying to undo what a creative cosmetics rep did to my poor face."

Blythe tipped her head in scrutiny. "It's not so bad, Allie."

She grinned. "You mean there's hope? I feel like a cadaver on the day of her funeral."

Blythe let go a guffaw, then quickly put her hand over her mouth.

With hands on hips, Allie grinned. "Found that amusing, did you?"

"Guess so." Blythe chuckled again.

"I'm glad you stopped by." Allie's gaze did a subtle appraisal of the woman she'd known so well three decades ago. Blythe had turned fifty in a graceful way. From her stylishly cut ebony hair to the fashionable tan slacks and coordinating vested silk blouse she wore, she still had a youthful appearance.

"I wanted to give you something—to wear on your wedding day."

"Listen, I'll leave you two alone for a few minutes," Nora said. She gave both women a parting smile before exiting the bathroom.

Blythe twisted sideways and removed a long white box from her large, brown leather shoulder-strap bag. "Here."

Surprised, Allie stepped forward and accepted the gift. However, she wasn't prepared for the charm and beauty of the sparkling silver bracelet and matching earrings that met her when she lifted the box's lid. "How lovely!"

"I bought it when I lived in Singapore. That bracelet is made with Austrian crystal and the sterling silver beads are from Thailand. The earrings are crystal and silver too."

"Both are exquisite."

"They're yours."

Allie glanced up from the jewelry and searched Blythe's face, unsure of what to make of this unexpected act of generosity.

She smiled. "I'm not superstitious or anything, but tradition mandates that a bride needs something old, something new, something borrowed, and something blue. When you turn the bracelet in a certain way, the light catches so it appears almost blue in color. And it's old—more than a quarter of a century in age. Now, for something new. . ." Blythe fished in her shoulder bag again and pulled out a plastic-wrapped, ivory lace hankie. "I just bought it on my way over here, so it's about as new as you can get, and it might come in handy if you get teary-eyed while saying your vows."

Allie laughed. "I'm sure I'll put it to good use."

"As for borrowed. . ." Blythe extracted another small box from her bag. "This necklace matches the bracelet if you don't look too closely."

Opening the black velvet box, Allie drew in a sharp breath when she saw the delicate silver chain and stunning teardrop diamond pendant.

"It belonged to my aunt, and when she died my uncle gave it to me."

"Oh, Blythe, I'm scared to wear it. What if I lose it?"

"It's insured."

"I know, but—"

"Allie, I've just begun to learn that precious things don't do anyone any good unless they can be used and enjoyed. I want you to borrow the necklace for your wedding day—if you'd like, of course. I noticed your engagement ring is white gold, so I thought the sterling would be something of a match."

"Oh, yes, the jewelry matches perfectly. I'm just a bit overwhelmed by your kindness."

Blythe cast a guilty glance at the tops of her two-inch-heeled ankle boots. When she looked back at Allie, she had tears shining in her dark eyes. "You were once a wonderful friend. I never forgot you, but I did try to run from my past and cover my tracks. I was scared. That's why I never wrote to you in California. I figured you moved away, you were gone, and that was the end of our friendship. What's more, you knew the truth about my past, Rob's death, and Kylie's conception, and I didn't want to face it. Even seeing Jack around Chicago was difficult, and of course, he had his trials."

Allie nodded. Jack's life had certainly been out of control. And, because of his own dire situation, and then losing track of Blythe for a while, Jack had been under the impression that Blythe had spent a year in a sanitarium. They had all laughed together at lunch when she told them such was not the case. She'd lived in Singapore with her aunt and uncle for a few years. It was during that time Blythe became a Christian, and both Allie and Jack had been thrilled to hear the account of her salvation.

Even so, it seemed Blythe's past had kept a strangling grip around her heart.

"Every year when Wendy brought Kylie into the shop," Blythe continued on, "it took me days to recover. But I treasured those scant few minutes when I could get glimpses of my daughter, so I figured the few days of depression that followed were worth it."

Allie's heart twisted with empathy. "Oh, Blythe, I'm sorry things were so tough for you."

"They weren't always. I can recount the endless blessings God has bestowed on me. Besides, things were tough for you too."

"True." Allie couldn't deny it. She'd told Blythe all about her abusive marriage. "But, like yours, my life has been filled with countless blessings. . .like my son, Nicholas, and his wife, Jennifer."

"You'll see them in a couple of weeks, huh?"

Allie nodded. She and Jack had shared their honeymoon plans. First, a trip to St. Thomas, and then a short stay in Long Beach, California, where Allie owned a condo. Decisions had to be made whether to keep the unit or sell it. If she and Jack put the place up for sale, they'd have to pack up all her belongings.

But Allie refused to dwell on all that now. In a few hours, she was getting married!

"I think God, in His infinite mercy and in His perfect timing, is giving us both second chances, Allie—you with Jack and me with Kylie."

"I believe you're right." Allie opened her arms and Blythe stepped into the embrace.

"God be with you, my friend," Blythe whispered in a strangled little voice.

Tears rimmed Allie's eyes now too. "Tell Kylie hello from me when you see her this weekend."

Blythe pulled back and smiled in spite of her misty eyes. "I will."

"And you're planning to come to our reception at the end of May, right?"

"It's marked on my calendar."

"Good." Allie gave Blythe one last hug.

Then, seeing her out, she watched Blythe walk to her van. After a wave of farewell, Allie closed the front door and ambled into the living room, where Nora sat on the floral upholstered couch sipping a cup of hot tea.

"Should we give your face another try?"

"Definitely." Allie laughed. "And we'd better hurry. We've got to be at the church by four o'clock."

"That's almost three hours from now," Veronica said. She sat cross-legged on the floor, flipping through the latest issue of *Today's Christian Woman*. "Please don't tell me it takes you that long to put on your face, Allie."

"Okay, I won't tell you." She winked at Nora, who laughed.

Whirling around on her heel, Allie traipsed down the hallway. As she passed the guest bedroom, she hesitated, unable to keep from thinking about Patrice.

She'd been released from the hospital four days ago, but instead of flying to Oklahoma to live with Kelly, her sister, as was the original plan, Patrice decided to stay in the Chicago area. She liked her job at Parkway Community Church. She said she felt safe there—and loved. And, upon hearing of Patrice's decision, Marilee talked to her former roommates, who agreed to let Patrice move in with them. The apartment was within walking distance of Parkway. But best of all, Patrice would have godly influences in her life during both her working hours and her time-off as the two women she moved in with were Christians and taught at Parkway's academy.

Thank You, Lord, for working out that situation.

Allie's thoughts soon came around to today, Good Friday, a day Christians revered. *Lord, thank You for giving up Your life so that all who believe in You will never perish but have eternal life. How precious a gift, bought with the high price of Your shed blood.*

"Ready, Allie?"

Glancing over her shoulder, she saw Nora coming down the hallway behind her. "I'm ready to finish getting ready," she countered with a laugh.

Reentering the bathroom, Allie forced herself to focus on the task at hand. Nervous excitement fluttered in her abdomen. This was her wedding day! By this evening, Allie would be Mrs. Jack Callahan.

Thank You, Lord, for yet another miracle!

Holding the rim of his favorite tan Stetson, TJ waited by the United Airlines baggage claim, keeping his eyes open for Blythe Severson. Both Kathryn and Kylie had given him specs on the lady, so he figured he'd be able to spot her once she arrived at the luggage carousel. He would be polite, although he wished he could be honest instead. He'd like to tell

Miss Severson that her thirty years of selfishness had shattered an old man's heart. He'd like to inform her that silence had tortured an elderly woman—a mother. But he wouldn't. Unlike Seth, TJ knew how to keep his mouth shut.

TJ thought over that last situation and stifled a groan. Unlike Seth, he knew better than to go around kissing another man's fiancée, too. TJ couldn't believe it when his buddy told him what happened. But at least there hadn't been any fallout. Good thing Matt was a reasonable guy. Even so, it was with a tremendous amount of relief that TJ dropped off his friend ninety minutes ago.

One down, one to go.

Fortunately, TJ didn't have to wait long before he saw a woman who matched Blythe's description. As he made his approach, he decided Blythe was a lot prettier than he imagined. He'd seen the old photograph, the one that touched off Kylie's suspicions about her origins, and he concluded that if Blythe had been lovely in her twenties, she was beautiful thirty years later.

Stepping to her side, TJ inclined his head. " 'Scuse me, ma'am. Are you Blythe?"

She turned and gazed up into his face with shining black eyes. Kylie had those same eyes, and TJ hadn't ever seen anything like them. But Blythe looked startled at the moment, and TJ knew he had that effect on people because of his height and bulky frame. "You're larger than life," Kathryn once told him.

"I didn't mean to sneak up on you," he said, hoping his smile looked as disarming as he intended. Then, in two quick, sweeping glances, he took in Blythe's tan slacks and printed blouse with its coordinating vest. He decided she had that big-city look about her. "I'm TJ McGwyer. I work for the Chadwyks, and they asked that I give you a lift back to The Light House." He stuck out his right hand in greeting.

"Oh, right." She pushed out a hesitant smile. "Yes, I'm Blythe." She slipped her hand into his. It felt cool, small, and fragile, although she had a firm grip. "Blythe Severson."

"A pleasure to meet you," he fibbed out of sheer politeness.

"Likewise."

TJ suddenly recalled what Kathryn had said about Blythe: *a sparrow of a woman.* He wondered at the description. With her ebony hair, worn in a sassy cut, her onyx eyes, and wine-colored lips, Blythe Severson didn't seem "nondescript" to him. He found her quite attractive.

"I hope you had a good flight," he said, trying not to stare.

"I did. Thanks." She turned and eyed the outpouring of baggage before gazing back at TJ. "Less than two hours in the air and not much turbulence."

"Good."

Blythe smiled before inching her way toward the carousel. TJ followed, and when her beige-tone, tapestry-styled bags came around, he plucked them off the conveyor belt. He tried not to laugh when Blythe looked impressed. But her expression made him feel about ten feet tall.

After carrying her luggage to his truck, TJ hoisted each piece into the covered box of his Silverado. Next, he politely assisted Blythe inside by placing his hand beneath her elbow.

"So, how long have you lived in Chicago?" he asked, driving out of the airport's parking lot.

"All my life. I was born and raised there, although I did live in Singapore for a few years."

"No kidding?" A surprised grin tugged at the corner of TJ's mouth. "I was in Singapore once. It was when I was in the Marines. I did a stint in Nam, and my unit was one of the lucky ones that got sent to Singapore for a little R and R."

"What year were you there?" Blythe's voice rang with a note of incredulity.

"Hmm. . .woulda been about '71."

"What a coincidence. I was there from '69 to '72."

"Yeah, that's a coincidence all right." TJ felt himself warming up to this woman in spite of himself.

"I must confess I always felt intimidated, even scared, to pass U.S. soldiers on the street. They'd whistle at me and act like obnoxious males. But, to be fair, I have to say that not all soldiers behaved that way."

TJ grinned. "Yeah, well, I was probably one of those 'obnoxious males' you mentioned."

Braking for a stoplight, he couldn't help a glance at Blythe. He saw her tentative grin before she turned and peered out the window.

The light changed to green and TJ stepped on the accelerator. For some odd reason, he felt like sharing his Christian testimony. Maybe because he didn't want Blythe to assume he was some whacked-out Nam vet, which unfortunately had become a stereotype in this country. But worse, TJ didn't want this woman to think he was still an "obnoxious male."

TJ cleared his throat. "I've changed my life around since those days, although I had to hit rock bottom first. After coming home from the war, I started doing drugs and drinking alcohol, mostly because people made me feel ashamed that I'd gone over to Nam to fight. The draft-dodgers were the heroes in those days. Not us. So I stayed high to forget about the war—and my less-than-ideal upbringing. In a word, I was a mess, a ramblin', gamblin', no-account drifter strung out on drugs. Finally, about ten years ago, I came to the end of the road—and the end of my luck. I wound up on the Chadwyks' doorstep—don't even know how I got there."

He paused, hoping he wasn't boring Blythe or making her uncomfortable.

"Please go on, Mr. McGwyer."

He flicked his gaze in her direction. "Call me TJ. I've really never been much of a 'mister.' "

"I'm partial to first names too. Call me Blythe."

"Will do."

"Now, as you were saying, TJ. . ."

"Right. Well, the Chadwyks took me in, telling me if a man doesn't work, he doesn't eat, so they hired me as their handyman. Over the years, they showed me Christlike love, and in 1992 I believed and became a Christian. Now I manage their bed-and-breakfast. I do everything from bookkeeping to bed making." TJ chuckled. "Correction. I don't do windows."

"A very incredible story. I'm a believer also—happened for me while I was visiting my aunt and uncle in Singapore."

"Well, what do you know? We have our faith in common, too."

TJ glanced her way and saw her smile. He returned the gesture. Then he searched his mind, trying to recall what Kathryn and Kylie had told him about Blythe. Now he wished he had paid closer attention to all their yakking at the lunch table this afternoon.

In any case, TJ felt his earlier dislike for this woman

dissipating like an afternoon rain shower. He wondered if, perhaps, the Chadwyks would soon feel the same way. Forcing himself to relax, he decided this weekend might not be so terrible after all.

C<small>HAPTER</small> S<small>IXTEEN</small>

B lythe slid from the backseat and pulled her purse out of the truck. She closed the door just as Kylie and Matt stepped outside.

"Hey, Matt," TJ bellowed in a voice so deep and resounding it seemed to shake the nearby palmetto trees, "give me a hand, will you?"

Blythe laughed. She had no trouble believing TJ was once a marine.

Matt jogged down the steps to assist TJ, and Blythe's attention was drawn to the stately inn. Built off the ground for obvious reasons like hurricanes and floods, the bed-and-breakfast was erected on what looked like ten-foot stilts. Arched carports had been constructed underneath each side of the home, and a graceful centered staircase wound its way up to the front door. The white spindled rail of the veranda aligned the first floor, while the second story had two large windows on either side and one majestic window in the middle.

Blythe caught sight of Kylie following Matt from the house. When Kylie reached her, she threw her arms around Blythe in a warm embrace. "It's great that you could come!"

"Sure is. Thanks for inviting me." Blythe blinked back sudden tears. She wasn't accustomed to such unexpected affection—especially from the daughter she'd given up at birth.

Kylie pulled back. "I just talked to my friend Marilee. She said Jack and Allie's wedding ceremony was simple but beautiful, and there was a huge surprise. I'll tell you about it later."

"A good surprise, I hope." At Kylie's nod, Blythe grinned. But then she felt a tad confused. "Marilee? Is that Logan's fiancée?"

"Yep."

Blythe nodded. She'd heard all about the Callahan family from Jack and Allie last Monday. Still, it was difficult to keep all the names straight.

"Marilee is so envious that I'm getting married before she is." Kylie's chuckle had a gleeful ring to it. "She said running off and eloping is gaining merit every day. Apparently, her mother is going overboard with all the wedding plans and driving people nuts."

Blythe smiled in reply.

"Well, come on inside. My grandmother will be quite displeased that I've kept you out here in the chilly night air."

"Kylie, it was in the fifties when I left Chicago. This 'chilly night air' is at least twenty degrees warmer."

Kylie leaned closer. "My grandma is a southern belle. Seventy degrees is 'chilly' to her."

"Ah. I see. Well, let's not keep her waiting."

Blythe hooked arms with Kylie and together they walked to the house.

⸺∞⸺

The nose of the plane lifted off the ground and soon the rest of the aircraft roared skyward. Allie clenched her jaw.

"What, are you scared, Miss First-Class World Traveler?"

She lolled her head to the left to find her new husband's teasing grin.

"Now, why would you say such a thing, Jack?"

"Because you've got a death grip on my hand."

Allie loosened her hold and laughed to cover her embarrassment. "Sorry." Then she decided to confess. "I'm not afraid to fly, but I hate takeoffs. Once I'm in the air, I'm fine. I don't even mind landing. But the initial ascent always makes me a little tense."

"Hmm. . ."

"What about you?"

Jack shrugged and straightened in his seat. "Doesn't bother me one way or another. I figure when God says my time on earth is through, it won't matter where I am."

"Well, I agree, and I'm not afraid to die." Allie paused, adding on a facetious note, "I just don't want it to hurt!"

Jack chuckled.

The plane continued its upward glide, and Allie forced herself to relax. She thought back to her wedding, just hours ago. It had been perfect. The ceremony went off with only a slight hitch—and that had been planned by Jack, Logan, and Allie's son, Nicholas.

"I still can't believe Nick and Jennifer showed up!"

Another low rumble of laughter emanated from Jack. "We gotcha."

"Sure did."

Allie still couldn't believe it. Logan was to have presided over the ceremony, but when she arrived at the front of the church, she found her son, Nick, standing there, Bible in hand. Stunned, she had dropped her bouquet. Jack fetched it for her and took her arm so she wouldn't fall over from the shock.

"Hiya, Mom," Nick had said with a wide grin and his blue eyes sparkling with amusement. "Do you really think I'd miss this day?"

At that moment, Allie had wanted to spank him despite the fact Nick was a grown man. For months, she'd begged and pleaded, but Nick said he and Jennifer couldn't rearrange their hectic schedules and they couldn't make the wedding. "We'll have a little something for you here in California," Nick had said, making the whole affair seem trivial.

Allie had started thinking that maybe it was—to Nick. So she didn't push.

But there he stood on the platform, dressed in a dark navy suit and a winning smile. Since Nick, too, was in full-time ministry, Logan had no trouble deferring to him. In fact, the two men performed the ceremony together, and it hadn't been easy for Allie to hold back her tears of joy. She clung to Jack, thinking what a miracle it was that their sons stood side by side officiating the marriage vows. After all the confusion, misunderstandings, heartache, and pain of the past, Allie thought it had been worth every struggle to look at Nick and Logan this afternoon. Both were serving the

Lord, furthering God's kingdom. They had hearts to see lost souls reconciled to the Savior. But had this wedding taken place thirty years ago, as originally planned, neither young man would have been born.

"I'll have you know the big surprise was your son's idea."

Allie smirked. "Oh, sure, blame it on *my* kid. You forget that I know what a prankster Logan is."

"True." Jack laughed. "But this time it really was *your kid* who initiated this evening's practical joke, although I hate to think of what's going to happen when those two guys really put their heads together."

Allie's smile broadened. She was so heartened to learn that already Nick and Logan had become friends.

"What's neat is that Marilee and Jennifer took a liking to each other right away last night."

"I can't believe you kept their arrival a secret from me! I can usually sense when something's up."

"Wasn't difficult, honey. You've been preoccupied for weeks."

"I suppose you're right. I have." Allie expelled a guilt-ridden sigh. "But, Jack, it was worth it. Our wedding was perfect. I'll remember it forever."

"Me too." He brought her fingers to his lips. "And you know what the best part is?"

"What?"

"It was only the beginning."

Blythe's internal alarm clock awoke her at the usual predawn hour. She lingered in bed and prayed, remembering some requests from members at her church. Mrs. Harris and her gallbladder problems. Eileen Sawyer's troubled marriage. Blythe's thoughts soon came around to Uncle Garth, and she prayed that God would give her wisdom as to when and where she should tell him the truth about her past.

Rays of early morning sunshine brightened the windows behind the semi-sheer draperies. They seemed to call to her. Blythe tossed aside her covers and quietly found her blue jeans, a pink T-shirt, and a beige cable-knit pullover sweater. Then, barefooted, she stepped into white canvas slip-ons. She had packed them knowing The Light House was on the beach.

She tiptoed across the floor of the expansive room, which she shared with Lynellen Alexander and Kylie. Lynellen slept in the second double bed, and Kylie snored softly on an inflated air mattress covered with sheets and a comforter. In the bathroom, Blythe washed her face, combed out her short black hair, and brushed her teeth. Next, she silently left the room and made her way downstairs, hoping to find a cup of coffee and watch the rest of the sunrise over the ocean. It had been dusky when she arrived last night, so she hadn't been able to see much of her surroundings.

As she reached the bottom of the stairwell, the rich aromatic smell of brewing java tickled her nostrils. She followed the scent to the kitchen, but as she entered the room and rounded the corner, she slammed into what felt like a brick wall—actually, it slammed into her. Half dazed, Blythe felt herself falling backward when a firm grip on her upper arm halted the process. She looked up into TJ's startling blue eyes, but before she could utter a sound, he covered her mouth with his other large hand.

"Don't scream," he whispered. "We've got a house full of guests."

CHAPTER SEVENTEEN

Even feeling a bit dazed, it really hadn't occurred to Blythe to scream. She didn't find TJ McGwyer to be that frightening of an individual in spite of the fact that his large palm covered half her face.

"I didn't mean to run into you. I hope I didn't hurt you."

Blythe shook her head and he removed his hand.

"I'm awful sorry."

She replied with a soft laugh. "It's quite all right, TJ. I'm fine. Startled, at first, but unharmed."

A look of relief spread across his features.

"I'm an early riser."

"Me, too." He continued to stare at her, and Blythe felt a bit self-conscious. She didn't have a stitch of makeup on. She probably looked a lot better last night beneath the soft glow of the living room lamps. Maybe he didn't recognize her now.

"I was after a cup of coffee." She raked her fingers through her hair, wishing she'd taken more time with her appearance.

"Sure." TJ looked over her shoulder. "It's almost done."

"I thought it would be the perfect start to the day to sip coffee and watch the sun come up."

"I do that nearly every morning, and I know the perfect place. . . . Um, that is if you want company."

"I'd love company."

TJ replied with a pleased smile, then turned on his heel and walked back into the kitchen. Blythe leaned against the doorframe and watched as he pulled down two large and sturdy dark brown disposable cups.

"You married, Blythe?"

She blinked. "What?" She had expected his next question to be whether she liked cream or sugar in her coffee.

"I don't mean to be nosy or anything, it's just that—"

"No, I'm not married." Blythe grinned. TJ McGwyer was about the most adorable lug she'd ever met. "I never married."

"Me neither."

He glanced at the large, industrial-sized coffeemaker, then turned and leaned his backside against the counter. Arms folded across his wide chest, he all but resembled a model for a Mr. Clean commercial except for his green T-shirt. But the whitewashed painter's pants fit the role.

Blythe lowered her gaze and studied the ceramic tiled flooring. She stifled the urge to giggle beneath TJ's scrutiny. *How out of character for me.* Then again, in the past month she'd done a lot of things that were out of the ordinary.

Hearing movement, Blythe looked up to see TJ pouring their coffee.

"Cream and sugar?"

"Yes. A healthy dose of each, please."

Sporting a grin, TJ prepared their morning brew, and Blythe noticed he liked his with just a hint of cream.

Coffee in hand, she followed him outside and down a long ramp leading to the beach. He pointed out the Sabal Beach pier that stretched out into the Atlantic, ending with a two-story gazebo.

"This time of day, the pier is pretty much empty, but around ten it'll be filled with fishermen and tourists."

Reaching the wooden pier, they climbed the steep stairwell, and Blythe felt a bit breathless at its top.

"That's our aerobics for the day." TJ shot her a teasing grin.

They ambled down the wide, planked pier until they came to the gazebo. There they sat at one of the round, built-in wooden tables.

"Would you rather sit upstairs?"

Blythe shook her head. "This is fine."

Actually, the view was magnificent. Gray and magenta were painted across the sky as the sun crept slowly upward.

"Have any hobbies?"

Blythe stared out over the water, hearing the waves lapping against the foundation of the pier while seagulls screeched overhead. "I go junk hunting whenever I find some spare time."

"Junk hunting?"

She nodded. "Rummage and estate sales. Auctions. Curbside trash piles are especially interesting."

"One of those, huh?"

Blythe sipped her coffee, then grinned. "Yeah, one of those."

TJ snorted out a laugh. "Well, I like to chase storms."

Now it was Blythe's turn at surprise. "Chase storms? Like

those crazy people on TV, videotaping tornadoes instead of running for cover?"

"That'd be me."

Blythe thought it over. "In a way, I'm envious." She pondered some more. "I think that for much of the last thirty-one years I've merely existed. Didn't do a lot of living, but I did some. I can count blessing after blessing and friend upon friend. I've taken vacations and had fun. But until recently, there was a dark shadow of sorrow hanging over me, following me wherever I went."

Blythe sipped her coffee, feeling suddenly ridiculous for spouting off such a personal thing. "Forgive me, TJ. That was probably more than you wanted to know."

"Nothing to forgive. It's okay." He looked at her. "So what changed?"

Blythe pursed her lips, wondering how to explain in the briefest of terms. "I made a lot of mistakes in my past that I didn't want to face. But when Kylie walked into my shop that day, asking all sorts of questions, she opened all my festering wounds. It hurt, but I decided not to ignore the pain anymore. With God's help, I chose to deal with it. . .and I am. It's not over yet, either. But I trust the Lord to carry me through."

TJ crossed his legs. "I think that's right where the Chadwyks are. They're wounds have been opened. . .again."

Blythe stared at the top of her coffee cup and said nothing. "I guess I'm to blame for that."

"Oh, I don't know. When they learned they had a granddaughter, they went through a tough time, too. And, if you haven't noticed, the Chadwyks adore Kylie."

"I noticed."

"You, too, huh?"

Blythe nodded. "I have loved Kylie since before she was born."

"So why'd you give her up, if you don't mind my getting personal?"

"No, I don't mind." Without a second thought, she relayed the entire story about how she met Wendy and Rob Chadwyk, fell in love with Rob, and how he was killed.

At the story's end, Blythe felt a bit amazed that she wasn't in tears. Nor was her spirit filled with shame and remorse. Were those signs that after all these years she was finally healing?

"But my uncle doesn't know that Kylie's my natural daughter," she added. "I'm struggling with whether I have to tell him."

Blythe explained that situation, too, after which TJ let out a long, slow whistle.

"I'll keep you in my prayers."

"I would appreciate it."

Blythe finished her coffee, then stood and tossed the cup in a nearby metal garbage can. When she reclaimed her seat next to TJ, she noticed the black, fire-breathing, Oriental dragon on his left bicep.

"Hey, what's this?" Interested, she touched his arm.

TJ glanced down at the tattoo. "I got that in Singapore." He paused. "At least I *think* it was Singapore. I spent a good part of my life drunk or high until Jesus saved me."

Blythe smiled and bent her leg so that her foot rested on the bench. She set her chin on her knee. It seemed she and TJ had a lot in common in the way of blemished pasts and finding Christ.

"You and I have a lot in common."

Blythe laughed. "You just spoke my very thought."

He chuckled. "Guess that proves it."

———— ◦◦◦ ————

"Thanks for bringing me up some breakfast, Grandma Kate. I don't want Matt to see me until the wedding."

"I suspected as much." Kathryn set down a tray filled with eggs, sausage, hash brown potatoes, fruit salad, and baked goodies, a carafe of coffee, two mugs, and a pitcher of orange juice.

"This is enough for ten people!"

Kathryn grinned. "I thought I'd help you eat breakfast."

"That's good. I couldn't do it alone." Kylie eyed the scrumptious-looking fare. "But I'm not really very hungry."

"I can understand. However, we can't have the bride fainting while she recites her vows."

Sitting in one of the two chairs at the small table near the window, Kylie closed her Bible and recalled a friend from college swooning at the altar from stress and nerves on her wedding day. "Guess you're right." She picked off a piece of the blueberry muffin and popped it into her mouth. "Where's Blythe?"

"I'm not sure." Kathryn took a seat in the other wooden chair. "TJ's missing, too." She removed two empty plates that were stacked beneath the one bearing all the food.

Kylie raised a brow, unsure of what her grandmother had just implied. "Maybe he went golfing with Matt and Grandpa Lee."

"Not a chance." Kathryn laughed and the delicate sound filled the room. "TJ hates to golf, remember? Besides, the men are back and having brunch downstairs with Lynellen."

"Hmm. . .well, just because they're both AWOL doesn't mean Blythe and TJ are together." Kylie couldn't picture it. They seemed so opposite. Blythe was sophisticated, well-read, and artsy, while TJ didn't give a wit about fashion and culture. . .although, he was a good photographer when it came to thunderstorms, hurricanes, and lightning.

"I hate to tell you that you're wrong, my dear, but you are. I took my habitual morning walk earlier and spotted TJ and Blythe on the Sabal Beach pier." Kathryn helped herself to some eggs and sausage and then bowed her head for a quick prayer, reminding Kylie she needed to do the same. "Thank You, Lord, for this meal. Bless this food and bless this day, my granddaughter's wedding day. Amen."

"Amen," Kylie repeated. Lifting her head, she looked across the table at her grandmother. "Now back to Blythe and TJ. . ."

"I'm not comfortable with the two of them together. They don't. . .seem right for each other."

"Grandma, they just met. Maybe they're being cordial to one another and simply having a conversation. Big deal."

Kathryn didn't reply but took a bite of her breakfast.

Kylie studied her grandmother's expression. "You don't like Blythe, do you?"

"Now, Kylie, why would you say such a thing? I barely know the woman."

"But you don't like what little you know of her. I can tell, and I think she can, too."

"Nonsense. I am a Christian and I love everyone, just exactly like the Bible tells us." Kathryn set her fork down and jutted out her chin, wearing a look of indignation. "Kylie,

I have gone out of my way to be hospitable to Blythe."

"I didn't mean to offend you. Sorry. My mistake."

Her grandmother resumed eating, but her expression remained closed and unyielding. Kylie didn't ask any more questions. Instead, she gazed out the window and over the sandy beach. It was then she saw Blythe and TJ walking back to The Light House. They appeared to be engaged in a meaningful conversation, judging by the expressions on their faces.

Kylie glanced back at her grandmother and felt a flutter of unease in the pit of her stomach. Prenuptial nerves, perhaps, but Kylie couldn't seem to shake her sudden concern. Had she done the wrong thing by convincing Blythe to attend her wedding here in Sabal Beach?

Blythe and TJ arrived back at The Light House and helped themselves to the breakfast buffet. Blythe hadn't seen anything like the vast selection of foods, ranging from fresh fruit salad to biscuits and gravy, except at upscale resorts. Make that *southern* upscale resorts—and she quickly understood why this particular bed-and-breakfast was a sought-after one-night getaway.

Plate in hand, Blythe followed TJ into the kitchen. The dining room, he explained, was reserved each morning for customers, or "guests," and she, like Matt and Lynellen, was considered family.

Blythe took that as a high compliment, although she got the distinct impression the Chadwyks didn't share TJ's sentiments.

Once in the bright, cheery kitchen, she claimed a chair

beside Lynellen Alexander. After silently asking a blessing on her food, she began to eat.

"How was the golf game?" TJ asked Matt and Lee.

"Just fine." Lee didn't even look up as he replied.

Blythe began to feel uncomfortable. Since arriving last night, she'd sensed a strain between herself and the Chadwyks. For all of Kylie's good intentions, she had it wrong. Blythe could tell that Lee and Kathryn resented her, and they were likely heeding Kylie's wishes because, as TJ said, they "adored" their granddaughter.

"You should have come with us, TJ." Matt grinned across the table at him.

"You couldn't get me on the golf course if you paid me." He devoured an oatmeal-raisin muffin.

"I've tried to convert TJ," Lee explained, "but to no avail."

"That sport isn't more than a glorified game of kick-the-can," TJ said.

Matt's laughter filled the kitchen until Lee hushed him.

"We have guests in the next room. Kathryn will have my head if we scare them off."

Matt lowered his voice. "Sorry 'bout that."

"No harm done."

The cheerful banter was soon replaced by an uncomfortable silence that worked its way around the table. Blythe found she could barely choke down another bite of food. She noticed, however, that TJ had made quick work of eating his breakfast.

TJ glanced at his thick silver wristwatch. "Excuse me, everyone, but this is checkout time." He glanced at Blythe. "If you want to meet me in the foyer in about a half hour, I'll give you a tour of the rest of The Light House."

"I'll do that. Thanks." She welcomed anything that would rescue her from the discomfort here in the kitchen. In the meantime, she picked at the remainder of her breakfast.

Finally, Lynellen stood and began clearing the table. Blythe rose from her chair and began to help. After setting the dishes near the sink, she followed Lynellen out of the kitchen. When they reached the large entryway, Lynellen continued up the stairwell while Blythe walked over to where TJ sat at the French Provincial-styled desk.

"Just two more guests to check out and then we can begin our tour."

"Mind if I nose around down here a bit?" Blythe had only seen the living room last night and then the dining room and kitchen this morning. There were still a few more rooms left to explore.

"Go right ahead."

Smiling, she moseyed into the living room, then the dining room. The guests had cleared out, but hired help were now milling about. In a matter of hours, these two rooms would be transformed into a makeshift chapel and reception area.

Ambling into the enclosed sunporch, Blythe allowed her gaze to wander over the wicker chair and the brightly upholstered sofa and settee. She looked past the room to the sunshine and warm breeze wafting in off the ocean and decided Kylie couldn't have chosen a lovelier day on which to get married.

Retracing her steps, Blythe entered the foyer and noted that TJ was still busy with guests. She headed in the other direction and wandered into what appeared to be a den. A large-screen TV was set inside an encompassing oak entertainment center. Two bold red, navy, and green plaid couches were angled strategically in front of the television set. An area rug partially covered the gleaming parquet flooring. Turning to her left, Blythe noticed an open-ended wooden bookcase that displayed knickknacks and a host of other collectibles, as well as Chadwyk family photographs. . . .

Including what had to be Rob's high school graduation picture.

Filled with a kind of reverence, she lifted the gold-tone frame off the shelf and stared at the picture. Rob, with his kinky brown hair, streaked from the sunshine. He looked just like she remembered him, although in the photo his hair was shorter. Not quite to his shoulders. Blythe remembered giving it a trim. She recalled the feeling of Rob's soft, thick hair as it curled around her fingers. She remembered his kisses and the way his eyes darkened with passion, whether for her or his latest cause. And, in that moment, Blythe didn't think any other man would ever take Rob's place in her heart.

"Okay, are you ready for your tour?"

Blythe jumped at the sound of TJ's booming voice.

"Sorry, I didn't mean to startle you."

In reply, she laughed to cover her embarrassment. Setting the picture back on the shelf, she hoped TJ wouldn't glimpse her sudden misty eyes.

"Well, what do you say? Ready to see the rest of The Light House?"

Blythe shook off the past and faced TJ. She mustered a smile. "Ready."

CHAPTER EIGHTEEN

After her tour, Blythe helped Kylie dress. Lynellen and Kathryn were on hand to assist the bride, too, and Blythe tried to ignore the cold stares Kathryn sent her way. Instead, Blythe focused on Kylie and marveled that she had the privilege of seeing her daughter on her wedding day.

Blythe stepped back and regarded her, arrayed in flounces of pearly lace. "You look sensational!"

Kylie stared at her reflection. "You know, I never did like this dress. Mom picked it out."

"Why, Kylie, it's gorgeous." Lynellen's forehead creased with a surprised frown.

Kathryn agreed. "It's very flattering on you, Kylie."

"I guess I thought so, too. . .when Mom purchased it. But it's. . .well, it looks too childish. It's not me." Kylie turned and peered at Blythe. "I'm a different person now. I've changed."

"Yes, you have." Lynellen gathered Kylie's ebony hair and

began piling it on top of Kylie's head. Then she reached for the bobby pins.

Blythe smiled. "You look anything but childish right now. Which reminds me. I brought you something."

"What is it?"

"Hold still, Kylie." Lynellen clucked her tongue. "You are such a wiggle-worm."

"I can't help it. I'm nervous."

"Don't be, dearheart," Kathryn said. "Everything's going to be perfect. Between Lynellen and me, and with Lee and TJ's help, we'll pull this wedding off yet!"

Blythe noticed her name wasn't mentioned. But, then again, she'd done nothing to help with preparations. Fighting hurt feelings, she rummaged through the zippered pocket of her leather carry-on. Locating the *precious thing*, she pulled it from where she'd tucked it away for safekeeping. Walking back to Kylie, she opened the black velvet box, revealing a string of pearls and a set of matching earrings.

"This jewelry belonged to my grandmother," Blythe explained. "Your great-grandmother. And now I want you to have it."

Kylie sucked in a breath of awe, and Lynellen stepped aside, allowing Blythe to clasp the pearls around her neck. "They're beautiful, Blythe."

"I prayed the necklace would go with your dress, and. . ." She gave the ensemble a speculative glance. "I think it does."

"It'll do." Kathryn gave a curt nod.

"Lovely," Lynellen said, resuming the task of pinning up Kylie's thick hair.

Blythe determined not to let Kathryn Chadwyk get the best of her. "I told Allie that tradition mandates a bride wear something old, something new, something borrowed, and something blue. You've now got the *old*, Kylie."

"The *new* can be your wedding gown," Lynellen suggested.

"Or my shoes," Kylie added.

Kathryn snapped her fingers. "I have a pearl-beaded bracelet you can wear for *something borrowed*."

"And the ribbons in my bouquet are silver and light blue. That's my *something blue*."

"Not that we're superstitious or anything." Lynellen chuckled.

Blythe smiled and even Kathryn grinned.

Kylie still appeared awed as she examined the pearls resting at the base of her throat. "These belonged to my great-grandmother?"

Blythe nodded. "Uh-huh."

"Will you tell me about her sometime?"

"Sure."

Kylie shook her head as if in disbelief. "All of a sudden I've got more family trees than I could ever fit in one album."

"Hold still, young lady," Lynellen warned once more. "You'll have a crooked hairdo if you keep wiggling."

"All right. All right."

With Kylie properly tended to, Blythe showered then slipped into a shimmering burgundy spaghetti-strap dress with matching short-waist jacket. Once her hair was fixed in its stylishly mussed fashion, Blythe applied her cosmetics. After that, she kept Kylie company while Kathryn and Lynellen readied themselves for the wedding.

"I still find it incredible that I'm here for your wedding day. I never dared to dream I'd have this pleasure."

Perched on a high stool, her lacy gown flowing all around

her, Kylie sent Blythe a benevolent grin. "I'm glad you could come, in spite of the short notice."

"I just wish the Chadwyks didn't mind my presence so much."

"Blythe, I don't know what's gotten into them." Kylie's expression was one of sympathy. "I felt so sure they would appreciate meeting you and finally learning the answers to their questions."

She appeared so contrite that Blythe couldn't fault her for daring to hope a friendship would ensue between her grandparents and her natural mother. Although, more and more, Blythe was beginning to understand why Rob and Wendy severed ties with the Chadwyks in the first place.

A teasing gleam suddenly entered Kylie's dark eyes. "So what's this I hear about you and TJ disappearing this morning?"

Blythe laughed to cover her sudden embarrassment. "Oh, we're both early risers, so TJ showed me the Sabal Beach pier."

Kylie arched an inquiring brow.

"There's nothing going on between TJ and me. He's a nice guy. That's it." Standing to her feet, Blythe ambled to the windows and gazed out over the beach. Sunbathers now littered the sandy shoreline. "You've got a gorgeous day for your wedding."

"Sure. Change the subject on me."

Blythe chuckled.

"But you're right. God answered my prayers about the weather. I wanted it warmer here than in Wisconsin, and it is. Grandma Kate said temperatures are expected to be in the eighties today."

Blythe turned away from the windows. "Temps in the eighties would be uncommon for northwestern Wisconsin in April—uncommon for Chicago, too."

"True. And what I'm hoping is that this weekend is like a perfect getaway for Matt and me. I'm also praying that God will work in his heart so Matt will want to move here."

The wind left Blythe's lungs. "You want to relocate to Sabal Beach?" Disappointment shook her to the core. "It's a long way from Chicago." *And your grandparents don't like me!*

"Nothing has been decided yet, but if Matt and I do end up moving here, you and I will stay in touch and we'll visit often. Charleston has a bazillion hotels. You don't have to stay here at The Light House. In fact, if we move, Matt and I will get our own place. I just want to live close to my grand-parents. Not *with* them."

Blythe managed a smile.

"And I can always visit you in Chicago, too."

Sure, Uncle Garth and Lydia would love that, she thought facetiously.

Turning back around, Blythe stared out the window a few moments longer. She forced any remnants of discontent from her soul and, instead, rejoiced that she could take part in this special day.

Then, pivoting, she crossed the room. She looked deep into her daughter's eyes and cupped her face. "Oh, Kylie, I love you so much. I wish you every happiness in the world."

"Thanks." With a smile, Kylie placed her hands over Blythe's and spoke the words Blythe never thought she'd hear from her daughter's lips. "I love you, too."

Four rows of chairs, seated five across, took up much of the living room. Kathryn asked a friend from church to play the piano for Kylie's wedding, and presently the slim brunette warmed up by plunking out an inspiring, contemporary tune that brought a grin to TJ's lips. The flowers were in place, three large vases filled with white roses. One crystal vase sat on the piano and two others had been placed on tables in front of the room where Pastor Ludington would soon perform the marriage ceremony. TJ raised his camera and snapped a couple of shots of the bouquets. As a wedding gift to Kylie and Matt, TJ offered to be their photographer.

Stepping back, TJ realized guests were filing into the makeshift chapel. With everything in order, he decided to see how the groom fared in the den. As he crossed the foyer, he met Blythe, who was on her way to find a place to sit. TJ couldn't help noticing the flattering maroon dress she wore. It matched her berry-colored lips and complemented her dark features.

Blythe gave him a pretty smile as they passed each other, and TJ felt his insides turn to mush.

What in the world is wrong with me?

He gave himself a mental shake as he entered the den. Lee stood chatting with Matt, and TJ snapped a few pictures. Matt didn't seem nervous in the least and, at first, that surprised TJ. But then he imagined himself marrying Blythe, and—

Whoa, I gotta knock this off. I'm thinking like a nutcase! Marriage? I just met her!

"Everything all right, TJ?" Lee gave him a fatherly slap on the back.

"Oh, yeah, everything's fine." *I'm just going crazy,* he added to himself.

And suddenly he felt like a traitor, as though he were giving aid and comfort to the enemy.

Blythe's no enemy. We're all believers. Brothers and sisters in Christ.

Except the Chadwyks' aloofness toward Blythe was as plain to TJ as his bald head.

He sighed, then felt glad for the diversion from his wayward thoughts when Pastor motioned for Matt to take his place. Pastor Ludington had met with the bride and groom twice—once on Thursday and once yesterday afternoon—and, during the sessions, all three became well acquainted if not downright friends. But that didn't surprise TJ. Samuel Ludington was a good-natured family man with a keen sense of humor and a heart for his ministry.

Following Matt into the living room, TJ checked the setup of his video camera, perched on its tripod. Next, he returned to the foyer and snapped several photos of Kylie on her grandfather's arm. He knew Lee's giving away the bride was a task the older man treasured.

TJ smiled at Kylie after taking one more picture. Then, stepping forward, he placed a kiss on her cheek.

"You look like a million bucks."

Her dark eyes glimmered with pleasure at his compliment, and once again TJ saw her resemblance to Blythe. "Thanks. I'm so excited." She bounced up and down on the soles of her white satin slippers. "Is Matt nervous?"

TJ glanced at Lee's intent expression and decided not to tease her. "I think Matt's excitement matches yours."

"Good."

TJ chuckled and gazed at the silver camera in his hand. He patted the pocket of his suit coat, making sure he had more film on hand. "Listen, Matt's a lucky man." He moved forward again, this time lowering his voice in a conspiratorial whisper.

"And if he doesn't take care of you, you let me know."

Kylie giggled at the facetious threat, but it earned TJ a hug.

"You're awesome, Teej."

"Thanks. So are you."

Strains of "The Wedding March" reached their ears.

"I believe that's our cue," Lee said.

"Yep." Kylie gave both men a broad grin.

TJ hustled back into the living room and took his place by the video camera. He began filming the ceremony, capturing Matt's look of wonder when Kylie strolled into the room with Lee. The expression on Matt's face told TJ he truly loved Kylie. A guy couldn't fake something like that.

As the wedding proceeded, Kylie and Matt faced each other and, with her hands in his, they spoke their vows. Lee and Kathryn stood in as witnesses.

The "I do's" were said, and shortly thereafter the ceremony came to an end. Kylie and Matt sealed their promise "to have and to hold" with a kiss. Everyone applauded. TJ stopped the film in the video camera and proceeded to move his equipment into the dining room where the bride and groom would greet their guests and soon slice their wedding cake.

"How much would you charge me for a copy of that video?"

TJ glanced up and saw Blythe standing before him. He grinned. "I wouldn't charge you a cent. I'll make you a copy for free."

"Well. . .thank you." She gave him a smile.

He smiled back, then watched her enter the dining room with the other guests. Returning to his task, TJ caught sight of Kathryn several feet away. A flick of her disapproving glance said she'd seen the exchange between him and Blythe. Once more TJ felt troubled.

Things shouldn't be like this, he thought. Next, he wondered what it would take to set matters straight.

⸘⸘⸘

Clinging to her new husband, Kylie felt as though she were moving in slow motion through a delicious dream. People surrounded them with congratulatory hugs and handshakes while TJ's camera flashed, securing each precious memory so Kylie could relive this day over and over again.

At last the small throng of guests, many of whom Kylie hadn't met before today, dispersed. People began helping themselves to the finger sandwiches and other hors d'oeuvres that were spread out on the white lace-covered table. Then the cake and punch were served, and Kylie laughed, anticipating that Matt would shove a piece of it in her face—as was the tradition at some weddings. But he surprised her and fed it to her in a slow and easy way that made her blush.

TJ snapped a picture, then gave them both an exasperated shake of his bald head. Next, he crossed the room. "Listen, feel free to sneak out of here any time now. Temperature is pushing eighty and I'm getting warm in this suit."

"I hear ya." Matt tugged at the stiff collar of his shirt.

"Oh, and before I forget. . ." He pulled a blue plastic key ring from his trouser pocket and handed it to Matt. "Here's the key to my truck. You and Kylie are welcome to use it tomorrow morning if you want to attend the Easter service. I'll be driving folks over to Seaside Baptist in the van the Chadwyks rented, but Lee insisted on staying behind to check out guests, so he'll be here if you need anything."

"Thanks." Matt smiled and closed his fist around the key ring.

"In fact, use my truck if you decide you want to go out for dinner tonight."

"Maybe we will, although we've been told that the place we're staying tonight has a stocked kitchen. Might be fun to make Kylie cook for me on our wedding night."

She gave him a playful sock in the arm and TJ chuckled.

"Scoot, you two. Beat it. Vamoose. You know where the cottage is. About half a mile up the road."

Matt winked at Kylie.

"The honeymoon suite will be waiting for you when you get back tomorrow."

Given the green light, Matt grabbed Kylie's hand, pulling her toward the room's archway.

"Have fun."

Turning, Kylie blew a sisterly kiss to him then followed Matt out of the room.

CHAPTER

NINETEEN

Evening settled around Blythe as she stared out over the Atlantic. She watched the whitecaps crash into the shore and realized how amazing this body of water truly was. It sustained life and brought about death. It captured imaginations and struck terror into hearts and minds. For Blythe, the magnificent ocean inspired her to be brave even though Kylie, who'd served as a sort of buffer between herself and the Chadwyks, had left for her wedding night. Kylie's absence caused Blythe to feel somewhat vulnerable, although TJ was around. She felt like she had a friend in him.

The patio door slid open, and Blythe turned to see Lynellen Alexander step out onto the deck. She had changed her clothes and now wore white cotton slacks and a multicolored striped top.

"In spite of all the rush, the wedding was lovely."

"I agree." Blythe grinned as Lynellen came to stand beside

her. She decided she had a friend in Lynellen, too.

"What a view!" the redhead exclaimed. "How can anyone doubt there's a God when they look at the ocean?"

"Good question."

Lynellen clucked her tongue. "And to think 'Mother Nature' gets all the credit. Ha!"

Blythe chuckled. "I share your sentiments."

A few moments of amiable silence went by before Lynellen turned toward Blythe. "With Matt and Kylie married now, I guess that makes us mothers-in-law."

Blythe shook her head. "No, I don't deserve that title. I'm happy to be just another friend."

"I don't think Kylie wants it that way."

Blythe raised her shoulders in a quick up-and-down motion.

"I've gotten to know all my kids' in-laws. We're friends. I like to think of us as a blended family. They've come to the farm at Christmastime and we've had such fun. I want you to consider yourself part of our family, too."

"Thank you." Blythe felt so touched that tears filled her eyes. "There's just one problem."

"What's that?"

Blythe whispered her next reply. "The Chadwyks don't like me."

Lynellen leaned forward. "That's *their* problem."

Blythe grinned in spite of herself.

"Kylie wants you to be a part of her life. She was very close to Wendy. Their lives were intertwined. They did everything together. Like best friends. But since Wendy died, and now that Kylie and Dena had a falling out, Kylie seems to be searching for a new *best friend.*"

"That honor is Matt's, not mine."

"True. And I don't mean to imply that he won't take that place in Kylie's heart. I believe he will. But there's room there for you, too." Lynellen grinned. "That's my point."

"Thanks. I feel very blessed that Kylie wants to get to know me." *But how do I keep her a secret from Uncle Garth? Oh, Lord, do I really have to tell him?*

The patio door slid open again and TJ appeared. He, too, had changed clothes and now wore faded jeans and a navy blue T-shirt. "If you ladies are interested, I'll show you some of my storm-chasing videos just as soon as I get back from returning the folding chairs that we borrowed from church."

"Storm chasing?" Lynellen shook her head. "No thank you. I've experienced enough floods and tornadoes in Wisconsin to last a lifetime."

"Well, in that case, I'm sure the Chadwyks will be happy to coerce you into a card game once their guests are settled for the night."

"Now that's more my speed." Lynellen chuckled.

TJ grinned. "Blythe? What about you?"

"Um. . ." She regarded him and thought TJ seemed as eager as a boy. Suddenly she didn't have the heart to turn down his offer. True, she would have much rather dined in Charleston and attended an art show or the theatre afterwards. Then again, she'd never met a "storm chaser," much less watched his adventures on video. Could be interesting. Besides, she wasn't about to spend the evening with the Chadwyks. "Sure. I'll watch your adventures."

He sent her a winning smile. "Great. I'll be back in a half hour or so."

"I'll be here."

TJ reentered the house and Blythe had to chuckle at his exuberance.

"Storm chasing?" Lynellen shook her head and a frown creased her russet eyebrows. "What kind of man does something like that for kicks?"

Blythe pursed her lips in thought. "Good question." She laughed. "When I figure it out, I'll let you know."

Some time later, Blythe sat back, folding her legs beneath her, and continued to watch the video of TJ's storm chasing. The recording took her to Kansas and Oklahoma where TJ and three of his buddies followed some of the most wicked weather Blythe had ever seen—even on TV. TJ played commentator and described the action as it occurred on film. He even reminisced a bit and talked about how he and his friends camped in a "pop-top" trailer and what they did to occupy themselves between storms.

"We played poker—but not *real* poker," he quickly amended. "The stakes in our games weren't very high. Usually the loser had to buy supper."

Blythe smiled and realized she had learned a lot about this man in a relatively short time. What's more, she found TJ's transparency refreshing.

"You sick of watching this?" he asked after a good part of an hour lapsed. "I can throw in a movie or we can watch something on one of the cable networks. In fact, we don't have to watch anything at all. We can go sit in the sunroom or out on the deck."

"I'm fine. I enjoy watching your storm-chasing adventures.

I like hearing about them just as much as seeing them."

"Really?" TJ arched a brow, looking doubtful. "Don't lie just to be polite now, Blythe."

She lifted her chin and assumed a regal stance. "I will admit to occasionally fibbing in order not to hurt a person's feelings, but this is not one of those times."

"Okay, then. . ." TJ grinned. "Once I get started it's hard to shut me up."

"I'll consider myself fairly warned."

Looking pleased, TJ resumed his annotations. One particular segment wasn't about bad weather at all, but TJ on vacation. The tape showed him parasailing in Mackinaw City, Michigan. The next set of film was TJ hang gliding, and when Blythe saw him take a running jump off the cliff her heart did a plunge of its own. Of course, TJ hang glided off into the sunset.

"You are a daredevil!" Blythe declared.

He wore a look of chagrin when he replied. "Yeah, maybe just a tad. So, tell me about the most exciting thing you ever did."

Blythe mulled it over for a few long moments. "One year I traveled to France with my mother and the two of us spent a day touring the Louvre Museum. It's magnificent!"

"Mmm. . .I feel a yawn coming on."

Blythe laughed before giving TJ a playful swat on his shoulder. In many ways, he reminded her of her beloved friend Twila. "Do you really think touring museums is boring?"

"Haven't done a whole lot of it, to be perfectly honest. But I s'pose it'd all depend on who's on the tour with me."

The reply sounded a bit suggestive, and Blythe rather thought she'd enjoy viewing paintings and sculptures with

TJ. He would certainly put an unusual spin on things.

"Like I said this morning, I haven't done a lot of living. Real living. I believe meeting Kylie, coupled with your influence, has made me see that I need to incorporate a bit of excitement and daring into my own life. I have a friend in Houston who's been telling me something similar, it's just that I've been too afraid to. . .to step out."

TJ pursed his lips and squinted in thought. "Maybe you just need someone who's willing to step out with you."

"Or push me off the cliff," Blythe added, thinking of TJ's hang gliding episode.

"Or out of the airplane." Remote control in hand, he fast-forwarded the tape. "I'll have to show you the video of me skydiving. A friend chickened out, so I had him film me from the airplane."

Her jaw dropped along with her stomach. Skydiving was definitely not her thing. "You know what, TJ? Maybe I'll stick to art museums."

He laughed and the sound seemed to ping-pong off all four walls.

"I'm glad to see you two are enjoying yourselves." Lee Chadwyk's deep voice resounded from the den's doorway.

Blythe felt a sudden nervous swell rise up inside her. Was it just her imagination, or did Lee's tone have a disapproving ring to it?

In either case, TJ seemed to care less. "Come and join us, Lee—although you've seen these videos before."

"Numerous times over."

Blythe turned to look at Lee as he replied when, from the corner of her eye, she glimpsed the image of Rob's face smiling from inside its gold-tone frame. She found herself wishing for a copy of the photograph, especially since she'd given Rob's things to his parents.

Lee followed her gaze, then rubbed his hand over his chest. "Rob's senior class picture. It seems like only last week when that photo was taken."

"You feeling okay, Lee?" TJ asked.

"Fine, except for a bit of indigestion."

"Would you like me to fetch some antacids?"

"Just on my way to do that very thi—"

Lee suddenly gasped and staggered against the doorframe. Blythe pushed to her feet and ran forward, grasping Lee's arm, steadying him. With wide eyes, she watched him grow deathly pale.

TJ was beside him in the next instant. He helped Lee to a chair. "Get Kathryn. Tell her to call the paramedics."

Blythe nodded, then raced through the house. She found Kathryn and Lynellen on the enclosed sunporch. "It's Lee," she managed on a breathless note. "Something's wrong. TJ said to call for an ambulance."

Kathryn flew into action. Blythe and Lynellen made their way to the edge of the foyer, both wanting to be of some assistance but feeling helpless. Lee was conscious and chiding TJ for making such a fuss over him. Blythe thought that was a positive sign.

The emergency medical personnel seemed to take a lifetime in coming. Finally they arrived, but the sirens and flashing red lights drew guests from their upstairs rooms and neighbors from their homes. After examining Lee, hooking him up to a monitor, and giving him medicine intravenously, the medics gurneyed him out to the awaiting ambulance. Kathryn decided to follow in the car.

"I'll drive you," TJ announced. "You've had a shock."

She didn't reply but stood in the foyer, tight-lipped and hugging herself. But in the next moment, her hazel eyes found Blythe.

"If he dies," she snapped, her gaze darkening, "I'm holding you personally responsible! You've brought us nothing but stress and strain, and now Lee could die!"

"Enough, Kathryn!" TJ quickly stepped between her and Blythe. Placing an arm around the older woman's shoulders, he spoke to her in a low voice that only she could hear.

Meanwhile, Blythe's mind whirred at the implication. Almost as bad was the fact there were still neighbors and guests milling around. They had likely overheard Kathryn's unwarranted edict.

Lynellen stepped to her side. "Come on, Blythe, let's go upstairs."

With Lynellen's arm hooked around hers, Blythe ascended the steps. Then the two made their way down the hallway and into the room they shared.

"It's been a long day. We should probably turn in for the night."

Blythe plopped down on one of the double beds as Lynellen headed for the other. She felt so numbed by Kathryn Chadwyk's angry words that she was barely aware of the time that passed while Lynellen showered and prepared for bed.

At last, she sat next to Blythe. "Whatever is wrong with Lee is not your fault."

"I know, but it still hurts." She turned to look directly at Lynellen. "What did I ever do to deserve the Chadwyks' hatred? I gave them the information they had been seeking. I've tried to meet them halfway."

Lynellen nodded. "I think this is a classic case of shooting the messenger. Lee and Kathryn are probably wounded and angry over the fact their kids wrote them off like a bad debt. Since Wendy and her brother aren't around anymore, you're getting the brunt of it."

"Just what I *didn't* want to happen!" A tear leaked from the corner of Blythe's eye and made its way down her cheek. She swatted it away. "I had such high hopes of things turning out differently."

"They still might."

Blythe shook her head. "No, I'm emotionally unable to endure any more. This has been just as hard on me as it has been on the Chadwyks."

"I'm sure it has, but. . ." Lynellen put a sisterly arm around Blythe. "Try to imagine how they feel—not that they're right by any stretch of the imagination—but, think of being a parent and how total rejection from your kids would feel." She shook her auburn head. "I can't begin to fathom the sorrow I'd live with if one of my adult children decided he or she never wanted to see me again. I'd be devastated."

"Well, in Rob and Wendy's defense, there is a flip side. It's likely the Chadwyks' behavior drove their children away. Lee and Kathryn have no one to blame but themselves."

"That may be true, but don't let bitterness eat away at you, Blythe—not like it's eating at them. As for what happened downstairs, Kathryn owes you an apology, that's for sure. And, believe me, I'll see that you get one."

Blythe waved off the promise. "An apology won't do anything. The damage is done."

"Perhaps, but God can fix it." Smiling, Lynellen gave her a little hug, then rose and padded across the spacious bedroom where she crawled into the second double bed. "If you feel like talking, I'm happy to listen."

"Thanks. I'll be fine."

The knot in Blythe's stomach belied her remark, but she didn't want to discuss the matter further. All she knew was that as much as she loved Kylie and was glad to attend her wedding, she had made a terrible mistake in coming here.

Now she couldn't wait to get away.

CHAPTER TWENTY

TJ and Kathryn sat on hard plastic chairs in the stuffy exam room while the EKG monitor bleeped with every beat of Lee's heart. The ER doctor said it appeared Lee had suffered a mild heart attack. Now he would have to stay overnight for observation. If tests went well tomorrow, he could go home as soon as Monday.

"What a lousy way to celebrate Easter Sunday," Lee groused from where he lay in bed. "I've barely been sick a day in my life! I don't want to stay in the hospital. I can recover at home."

"You'll do whatever the doctors say," Kathryn argued.

TJ said nothing but continued to flip through the outdated fishing magazine in his lap. His felt bad for Blythe and he couldn't get the image of her horrified expression out of his head. There was little doubt in his mind that Kathryn's words had maimed her.

"What's wrong with you, TJ?" Lee wanted to know. "You've hardly spoken a word in the last two hours."

"TJ is upset with me."

Hearing her remark, he glanced at Kathryn.

"I gave Blythe a piece of my mind and TJ didn't like it."

"That wasn't 'a piece of your mind,' Kathryn. What you said was plain ol' meanness."

She lifted her chin and clucked her tongue.

"And pride goes before a fall," he said, leaning closer to her.

Neither of the Chadwyks spoke, and TJ felt his blood pressure rising. He hated the very idea of Lee being pleased with Kathryn's behavior.

He stood. "You know I've never said anything like this before, but I'll say it now. I'm real disappointed in the two of you."

Lee drew his white bushy brows together. "Why's that?"

"Because you're both wonderful, caring, Christian people, but you haven't shown that side of yourselves to Blythe. She's not to blame for any of the hurt you're feeling. Rob and Wendy are responsible."

"TJ, I think—"

"Hush, Kathryn. Hear me out."

Two pink spots appeared on her cheeks, but she pressed her lips together.

"Let's assume Rob and Wendy told Blythe the very worst about you. Let's say they told her you're the most hard-hearted folks in all the world. Blythe was their friend, not yours. She had no obligation to contact you. That wasn't her responsibility. And yet you're acting like it was. Furthermore, she's a very sensitive woman, and she risked a lot by agreeing to meet you and tell you everything you wanted to know.

Now she's probably regretting it. Worse, she's probably thinking that Rob and Wendy had good reason to cut their ties with you. By being standoffish and distant—and by blaming her, Kathryn, for Lee's heart attack—you both have proved Rob and Wendy right."

TJ knew his words met their mark when tears formed in Kathryn's hazel eyes.

"You blamed her, Kathryn?" Lee's voice was soft.

"Well, not exactly—"

"She blamed her, all right." TJ turned to Lee. "Kathryn promised to hold Blythe personally responsible if you died. I know Blythe is devastated."

"Oh, you can't possibly know how she's feeling at the moment. I was upset. I said something I shouldn't have. If she's any sort of decent person, she'll understand." Kathryn stood and faced him. "And after all we've done for you, TJ, I should think you of all people would be compassionate. Look what Lee and I are going through emotionally."

TJ wasn't swayed a bit. "After all you've done for me, Kathryn, I feel I owe it to you to point out the truth. You both are acting like spoiled children, and I'm ashamed and disappointed. What's more, Kylie will hear about this. Lynellen overheard everything tonight, and if Blythe doesn't tell Kylie, her mother-in-law will. I've lived long enough to know how women talk. Are you going to make Kylie choose between her natural mother and her grandparents, Kathryn? What if Kylie starts thinking maybe Wendy had good reason to separate from you after all?"

Kathryn blanched.

"You'd better shape up, Mama Chadwyk," TJ said, using one of his pet names for her. "There's a lot at stake here, and it goes beyond your pride and indignation." He turned to Lee. "And I'd wager it's your bitterness that caused your heart attack. Blythe didn't have anything to do with it."

TJ gave them each a stern look before exiting the exam room. He headed for the lobby and the vending machines, thinking a cup of coffee might be in order. He wished he could talk to Blythe. He'd like a chance at encouraging her. Deep down, the Chadwyks were wonderful people, and maybe if Blythe would give them another chance she'd see their virtues for herself.

Glancing at his watch, TJ saw it was nearing midnight. Blythe was likely sleeping. He sighed. Any conversation would have to wait until breakfast.

The next morning, Blythe took her time showering and dressing. She didn't want to face Kathryn Chadwyk, although it seemed inevitable. She couldn't leave without saying a perfunctory farewell. She wouldn't be rude. What's more, she wanted to tell TJ good-bye.

Lord, help me with this situation. I didn't do anything wrong—except come here on a lark without even praying about it first. Now I've got to ask You to bless my mess!

Squaring her shoulders, Blythe packed her suitcase and carry-on. With the task completed, she called a cab from her cell phone. Her plane wasn't scheduled to leave until tonight; however, Blythe was determined to get on an earlier flight or wait it out in the airport. The latter seemed ever so much more appealing than spending the next eight hours at The Light House.

After placing the call, Blythe sat on the edge of the bed and took several minutes to regroup. She knew she was going to have to give *some* explanation to *someone* before taking her leave. She only prayed she wouldn't fall apart in the process.

At last, she made her way downstairs. Several guests were checking out with TJ's assistance, so Blythe parked her luggage off to the side and went to find Lynellen. She discovered her and Kathryn sitting on the sunporch, sipping their morning coffee.

"Church is at ten thirty," Lynellen said with a smile. "So you've got plenty of time for breakfast."

"Thanks, but I have to catch a plane." Blythe glanced at Kathryn. She dared not ask about Lee, fearing the worst of reactions. "Thanks for everything."

"I thought you didn't leave until this evening." Kathryn's reddish-brown brows knitted together in a frown.

"Change of plans."

"Oh, but I don't think we can get you to the airport—"

"I've called a cab."

Kathryn slowly rose from the armchair. "Kylie will be disappointed if you're not here for Easter dinner. I've got a ham in the oven."

"I apologize for any inconvenience, but I need to go."

Blythe forced a grin, then plucked her wallet from her purse. She realized her only regret about leaving in such haste was not seeing Kylie again.

She looked back at Kathryn. "Do I owe you anything for the two nights' stay?"

Surprise and possibly insult spread across the older woman's face. "No, of course not. You were our guest."

"Well, thank you very much. You have a lovely place."

"Glad you enjoyed your visit." A note of uncertainty rang in the older woman's voice.

Blythe ignored it and moved on to Lynellen. "Good to see you again."

"Likewise. We'll be in touch."

Blythe bobbed out a reply. She then clasped Lynellen's outstretched hand in farewell before wheeling around and heading out of the room.

When she arrived back in the foyer, it was empty. Blythe quelled her disappointment. She had hoped to say good-bye to TJ, but the cab would be here any minute. Connecting her suitcases so that the smaller of the two rode piggyback, she pulled them along toward the front entrance.

"Whoa! Lemme help you!" TJ's deep ex-marine voice shot through the foyer.

Smiling, she turned around and watched as he stopped dead in his tracks.

"Blythe?"

"Morning, TJ."

"I didn't realize it was you, lugging those bags toward the door. Where are you going?"

"I have a plane to catch."

Wearing a frown, TJ moved forward. "I thought you were leaving tonight."

"I changed my plans."

A knowing look lit his blue eyes. "How are you planning to get to the airport?"

"Cab."

"That's going to cost you a fortune."

"I don't care."

TJ extracted the suitcase handle from Blythe's grip. "Why don't you let me drive you? Later. I'll take Kathryn and Lynellen to church first and then I'll—"

"No." Blythe shook her head. "I've made up my mind. I'm leaving. Now."

"Because of what Kathryn said last night?"

Blythe shrugged and zeroed in on the shiny brass handle gracing the front door.

"Listen, I had a talk with her and Lee, and I think you should know that—"

"How's he doing, by the way?"

"Lee?" TJ's sudden grin dispelled his glum expression. "He had a mild heart attack, but the prognosis looks great. He'll be back on the golf course in no time."

"Good." Blythe meant it from the bottom of her heart, too. "Will you carry out my luggage now?"

"Yes, but I'm not happy about it. I don't want you to leave. It's Easter."

"I know, but I'm going to be stubborn about this one, TJ."

"That's what I thought." Lifting her bags, he headed out the door and Blythe followed him down the bowed staircase. At the bottom, he set the suitcases on the sidewalk.

"Blythe, I wish you'd reconsider. Give Kathryn another chance. Lee, too, although he probably won't come home until tomorrow."

She shook her head. "My mind's made up."

"All right." He puffed out his broad chest before expelling a long breath. "I can't exactly force you to stay. I just hope this wasn't a wasted trip for you."

The remorse in his voice touched Blythe's heart. "I was able to attend Kylie's wedding. That was worth the trip right there."

TJ sent her an ambiguous nod as he gazed out over the palmetto-lined street.

"And I had the opportunity to meet you and make a new friend. That was a bonus."

Her remark brought a grin to his face. His gaze met hers. "I enjoyed meeting you, too, Blythe."

She smiled and then the taxi turned the corner and pulled alongside the curb. Blythe felt almost disappointed.

Almost.

The driver climbed out and sauntered around the vehicle. He collected Blythe's luggage and jammed it into the trunk.

She turned to TJ. "If you're ever in Chicago, look me up."

"Will do."

Blythe stepped closer, intending to give TJ a parting hug; however, a chaste embrace somehow became a kiss that lasted a moment or two longer than mere friendship allowed.

"Do you have E-mail?" TJ wanted to know when Blythe lowered herself off her tiptoes.

She nodded, still feeling dumbfounded by what had just transpired.

"Well, what is it? Do you have a business card on you?"

The smirk on TJ's face caused Blythe to snap out of her girlish daze. Laughing at herself, she unzipped the side of her carry-on and fished out a card. Then she handed it to TJ.

"Have a safe trip," he said as the driver opened the door to the backseat.

"Thanks."

Throwing her carry-on and purse into the taxi, Blythe crawled inside. She sent TJ a parting wave when, at last, the vehicle pulled away from the curb.

But for some crazy, mixed-up reason, the only thing she could think about on the way to the airport was TJ's kiss.

CHAPTER TWENTY-ONE

Kylie stood in front of the large bathroom mirror and took the curling iron to her hair. Out of the corner of her eye, she watched Matt draw the electric shaver across his cheek and over his chin. Standing just two feet away, bare-chested with only his black trousers on, he made an attractive sight—and Kylie couldn't seem to get her fill.

Matt glanced at her through the mirror, then did a double-take. "What are you staring at?"

"You." She laughed to cover her sudden embarrassment.

Matt looked a bit self-conscious but grinned and continued gliding the razor up and down his jaw. At last, he shut off the buzzing device and placed it in its charging unit. He tickled Kylie in the ribs before making his way to the door. "You're not running late, are you?"

"Nope. I'll be ready on time," Kylie promised. "I'm almost done."

"Me, too."

Kylie got a whiff of Matt's tangy cologne as he passed by. Then her gaze followed him into the next room where he pulled a white undershirt over his head before donning a pale purple cotton dress shirt.

His gaze met hers while his fingers worked the buttons. "The way you're scrutinizing my every move, you're going to give me a complex."

"I can't help it. I'm just totally in love with you." Kylie's heart filled with the sentiment even as she spoke.

He smiled. "I'm totally in love with you, too."

Closing the distance between them, Matt kissed her before returning to the bedroom and continuing to dress. Kylie found herself wishing they hadn't decided to attend church this morning. She'd much rather stay here and "scrutinize" her new husband some more. But on the other hand, she felt glad that Matt and Sam Ludington got along so well. Maybe if Matt were impressed by Pastor's sermon this morning, he'd want to move to Sabal Beach.

"So what do you think of this place so far?"

"So far? It's okay."

"Just okay?"

Matt sent her a sheepish grin. "Yeah, just okay. Everything in the cottage smells kind of musty, you know?"

Kylie rolled her eyes. "I didn't mean *this place* as in *this cottage*. I meant Sabal Beach. Do you like it here?"

Matt's grin became a smirk. "Yeah, it's okay."

Kylie smiled but let the subject drop along with this silly game of cat and mouse.

She finished her hair and unplugged the curling iron. Then, after applying her lipstick, she reentered the bedroom and helped Matt pack up their things. This afternoon they'd move back into The Light House for the remainder of their honeymoon.

"So, what if I don't want to live here in Sabal Beach, or anywhere in South Carolina for that matter?" Outside the cabin, Matt deposited their luggage by TJ's truck. "You going to divorce me?"

"How can you even tease me like that?" Kylie felt more than a tad insulted. By now, he should know how much she loved him.

She glanced down at their things, feeling more hurt now than anything else.

"Hey, I was just kidding around." Matt cupped her chin and forced her gaze to meet his. Then he pressed a kiss on her lips. "I just want you to be happy, whether we live here or Basil Creek."

Kylie nodded out a reply but couldn't imagine ever feeling content in Basil Creek again.

"Are you ready to go?"

Again, she nodded.

The drive to Seaside Baptist Church didn't take long, and Kylie was quick to point out the scenery that she found so inspiring.

"Sabal Beach might have the ocean in its back yard, but we've got the mighty Mississippi in ours."

Kylie flicked her gaze upward. "It's not the same. I assure you."

Matt didn't reply, and in that moment something strange and undefined seemed to work its way between them. However, before Kylie had a chance to explore the matter, Matt turned into the church's parking lot. He parked and they climbed out of TJ's pickup. After collecting their Bibles, they made their way inside the redbrick building and into the sanctuary. Kylie spotted her grandmother and Lynellen at once. Slipping her hand into Matt's, she walked up the aisle beside him to the polished wooden pew in which the two ladies sat.

"Well, if it isn't the newlyweds!" Lynellen smiled up at them, and she and Kathryn scooted over to make some room. "We weren't sure if you'd show up this morning."

"It's Easter Sunday," Matt said. "It just didn't seem right if we skipped church."

Kylie moved into the pew and sat next to her grandmother. Matt slipped in, occupying the space on her left.

"Where's everybody else?"

"Well, let's see. . . . TJ is checking out the last of our guests and"—Kathryn set her hand on top of Kylie's—"your grandfather is just fine, but he had a mild heart attack last night. He's in the hospital."

"What?" Apprehension engulfed her. "Why didn't someone call me?"

Lynellen sat forward, looking around Kathryn. "Because it was your wedding night and Lee is going to be okay. We would have contacted you if he'd been critical."

Matt slipped his arm around her shoulders and Kylie felt herself relax. "Is he coming home today?"

"No. But maybe tomorrow."

Kylie settled into Matt's embrace, deciding things didn't seem as terrible as she'd first feared.

But then she realized one other person was unaccounted for.

"Where's Blythe?" Kylie couldn't contain a smirk, thinking about how Blythe and TJ were "AWOL" yesterday morning.

Had she stayed behind at The Light House to keep him company?

"Blythe decided to leave this morning," Kathryn said.

A deep sense of regret permeated Kylie's being. "Why did she do that? I thought she wasn't returning to Chicago until tonight."

"She didn't give me any explanation." Kathryn held her gaze straight ahead. "Blythe just announced she was leaving and thanked me for the hospitality."

Something didn't sound right. Sitting forward, Kylie glanced at Lynellen, who'd begun leafing through the delicate pages of her Bible. Kylie turned to Matt, and he produced one of his wide-eyed expressions that said her instincts were correct. There had been trouble last night.

Blythe purchased a book and a bag of pretzels, wishing she could have gotten onto that last flight out. Now, she would have to wait until four o'clock when the next one took off. But she'd been aware of the circumstances and the odds against switching flights when she made her choice to leave The Light House, and she wasn't sorry about her decision. She only hoped that Kylie would understand.

Heading for her gate, she realized attending service and spending the remainder of Easter Sunday with her uncle would have been more enjoyable than sitting in the airport all afternoon. As much as she wanted to start living, like she mentioned to TJ, she saw how unwise it had been to act on impulse. Blythe wouldn't do it again. She'd be more careful in the future, praying over each situation and thinking each one through. Kylie's impetuousness had rubbed off on her—and the same thing had happened thirty-plus years ago. Rob had been a tremendous influence on her.

Shaking off the melancholy that suddenly threatened, Blythe tried to focus on the positive side of life. She felt blessed to have seen Kylie's wedding. Kylie looked so happy, so in love. As for today, Blythe was relieved that Garth had accepted Lydia's invitation to come over for dinner. They still planned to tour Precious Things this afternoon, and Garth would be in his glory, showing off various treasures to Lydia's friends. As the silent partner, he took pride in the shop's success.

Reaching the appropriate gate, Blythe found an empty chair and sat down. Opening her book and her pretzels, she decided to make the best of the hours that loomed ahead of her.

∞∞∞

Kylie glanced around the dining room table at TJ, Lynellen, her grandmother, then Matt. She thought it was sad that Grandpa Lee's place was vacant, but they planned to visit him in the hospital once supper was over. At the moment, however, no one was saying much of anything, and Kylie presumed it stemmed from her probing to discover what happened last night with Blythe.

"So no one is going to tell me, huh?"

"You are one persistent young woman." With a huff, Grandma Kate set down her fork. "All right. I'll come clean. It's my fault. I said something to Blythe I shouldn't have. I was worried about Lee and I lashed out at her. I was wrong."

"What did you say?"

"I would prefer not to repeat it. It's bad enough that

I have to admit to such a thing."

Kylie glanced across the table and saw Lynellen's pinched expression. It troubled Kylie that Blythe's feelings got hurt.

She looked back at her grandmother. "Did you apologize?"

"I never got the chance, dearheart."

That bothered Kylie all the more. But something else began nibbling at her peace of mind.

"I hope Blythe doesn't decide I'm more trouble than I'm worth."

"Oh, I'm sure that's the furthest thing from her mind," Lynellen said.

However, Kylie wasn't so sure.

As the afternoon progressed, Kylie felt all the more perturbed. Even visiting her grandfather and hearing that he'd passed his stress test didn't rid her thoughts of Blythe.

Finally, that evening, Kylie decided to give her a call. Sitting on the deck outside the honeymoon suite, while her husband of twenty-four hours lounged in the Jacuzzi, she punched in Blythe's number using her cell phone. No answer at her home. She dialed Blythe's mobile phone but only reached a recording.

"Hey, Ky, get your suit on and come join me. Man, does it feel great in here." Matt leaned his head back. "I think this is a little taste of heaven on earth."

She smiled and decided sitting in a hot tub with Matt was an offer she couldn't—and wouldn't—refuse. "Okay, I'll be right back."

Giving up on contacting Blythe for the moment, Kylie went inside and changed. Heading out again, she paused when she glimpsed her cell phone on the table beside her purse. On a lark, she decided to try Blythe at her shop. Maybe she stopped there on her way home from the airport. She did seem like something of a workaholic.

But much to Kylie's disappointment, an answering machine picked up. This time, however, Kylie left a message. She figured if nothing else, Blythe would hear the message tomorrow morning.

"Hi, Blythe, it's Kylie. Listen, I don't know exactly what my grandmother said, but I'm so sorry your feelings got hurt. I don't blame you for being angry, and I probably would have left early, too, if it were me." She paused to collect her thoughts. "But I hope you haven't decided we can't be friends. Getting to know my biological mother is one of the foremost desires on my heart. You're such a sweet, sensitive person and I love you already. Will you call me on my cell when you get this message? You've got my phone number. Bye for now."

Smiling, she pressed the END button on her phone, set it down, then made her way outside to the deck.

CHAPTER TWENTY-TWO

After a delayed flight, Blythe landed at O'Hare International around nine o'clock that night. She phoned Lydia first thing, just as they'd planned, and Blythe couldn't wait to get home and take a hot bath and crawl into bed. It had been an emotionally trying weekend, and Blythe was exhausted.

"I'm on my way," her mother said. "But, I should warn you. I've got very bad news."

"What is it?"

"I'll tell you on the way home—and, hopefully, we'll have a home in the future."

Standing on the escalator as she made her way to the baggage claim area, Blythe felt a heavy frown crease her forehead. "What are you talking about?"

"You'll find out soon enough."

With that, Lydia disconnected.

Finding the appropriate carousel, Blythe waited for her bags and tried to imagine what was eating her mother. Had there been a fire? A flood? Some other natural disaster? Collecting her luggage, Blythe headed to the designated meeting place. As she awaited Lydia's arrival, Blythe tried not to fret.

At last, her mother pulled up to the curb, and Blythe wheeled her luggage to the car. Lydia got out and helped load Blythe's belongings into the trunk.

"So what's the crisis?" Blythe couldn't help but ask as Lydia drove out of the busy airport.

"It's Garth. He knows about Kylie."

"What?" Blythe felt her heart plunge into the pit of her stomach.

"We were at the shop very late this afternoon, having a perfectly lovely time, sipping champagne and discussing artwork. Then the phone rang. Of course, none of us answered it. Precious Things was closed. But Garth had seated himself in your office because he was disgusted that my friends and I were drinking an alcoholic beverage in his presence. Suddenly I heard talking so I went into the back to check on him, and would you believe Kylie had the nerve to leave a personal message on your business answering machine? Garth heard every word." Lydia hit the steering wheel with both palms of her hands and cursed. "I knew that girl was going to ruin our lives!"

Blythe felt stunned. "Wh–what did she say?"

"Oh, nothing much." Sarcasm dripped from Lydia's voice. "Just that she wanted to get to know you, her biological mother—she used those exact words, too."

Blythe closed her eyes. She felt sick. "And Garth's reaction?"

"He asked who Kylie was and I said he needed to get the details from you. He wanted to know if you were, indeed, her 'biological mother,' and I told him I wasn't at liberty to discuss such matters. My response angered Garth, who was already in a snit, and he threw everything off your desk, your files, coffee cup, pictures, phone, and answering machine— all of it. I've never seen him so mad."

Blythe covered her face with her hands, appalled by the scenario. She'd never seen Garth lose his patience. Never!

"I told Garth I didn't think he was behaving very Christian-like."

"Oh, no!"

"Blythe, you know how champagne makes me mouthy." Her mother sniffed with an air of indignation. "Well, in the end, Garth stormed out of the shop, and I haven't seen or heard from him since."

"I hope he's all right."

"You hope *he's* all right! Ha! You should be worried about *us!*"

Blythe didn't reply, but she was worried. Very worried.

An hour later, Blythe found herself at home in her apartment. She was unpacking when the phone rang. One check of the Caller ID told her Garth was at the other end of the line. She momentarily debated whether to answer the call, but then decided it was foolish to put off the inevitable.

"Well, I'm glad you arrived home safe and sound."

Blythe didn't think her uncle sounded upset. "I haven't been home for very long."

"Did Lydia tell you what occurred this afternoon at Precious Things?"

"Yes." Blythe held her breath.

"Your mother's friends are foul-mouthed and ignorant. I regretted spending my Easter Sunday with them."

"I'm sorry it turned out badly for you."

"As you must know, the day ended even worse."

Blythe wasn't sure of what to say.

"Tell me about this woman named Kylie. Who is she?"

Blythe wet her lips and paced the living room. She searched for the perfect words, but finding none, she blurted out the truth. "Kylie is the daughter I gave birth to thirty-one years ago and then gave up for adoption."

"Who's the father?"

"Rob Chadwyk. He's the one who was killed in the riot back in '68."

"Ah, yes. I remember." A moment of silence passed. "So you gave birth to a child, and all these years, you hid the truth from me. You deceived me."

"Not intentionally. . .at least not at first. I thought you knew about Kylie. You knew about my emotional breakdown. Rob's death and giving away my baby were the reasons for it, also the reasons why Pete and Lydia urged me to visit you and Sabina in Singapore."

"Your boyfriend's death I knew about. But I had no idea you'd given birth out of wedlock."

Shame and humiliation pervaded Blythe's being. "It happened before I became a Christian."

"You still should have said something. Why didn't you?"

Blythe ceased her pacing and lowered herself into a nearby armchair. She let out a deep sigh. "I was afraid."

"Of what?"

"Losing everything I'd worked so hard to achieve. You see, it wasn't until years later that Lydia learned of the terms in my contract with you, and that's when I discovered you didn't know the truth about my past."

"It was at that point you should have told me."

"You're right, and I wanted to, but Lydia begged me to keep the secret. She'd invested in Precious Things and didn't want to lose her money."

"And how would she lose her money, Blythe?"

By his tone, she could tell he was goading her. "You know very well how she could lose everything. I stand to lose even more."

"Hmm. . ."

Blythe wondered if her uncle enjoyed the feeling of such power. He held the future of two women in the palm of his hand.

"We'll discuss this matter further tomorrow. I'm sure you're just as exhausted as I am. Let's get together for dinner at that family restaurant I like so much."

Blythe knew the one but dreaded the meeting. Even so, she agreed to it.

Wishing her uncle a good night, she hung up the phone. However, she knew tonight would be a sleepless one.

The following day, Kylie sat between her dozing husband and her mother-in-law on the flight back to Wisconsin. She wished the honeymoon would have lasted forever. Realistically, she would have preferred a few more days. But they'd already been gone since last Wednesday, and Matt needed to get back to the farm. Kylie was just glad she'd been able to say good-bye to Grandpa Lee before they left. He came home from the hospital and assured her they'd return to Basil Creek soon. After all, his car was still parked in Kylie's driveway.

"Lynellen, don't you ever wish you lived somewhere else besides Basil Creek?"

"No, I'm happy. But I understand from Matt that you're not. He told me last week that you wanted to move closer to your grandparents."

"They're not getting any younger, Lynellen. They haven't ever been a part of my life, and I'd like them to be a part of it now."

"Are you sure? In all honesty, honey, I think it's disgraceful how they treated Blythe."

"I agree, but in all fairness, my grandparents have been under a lot of stress."

"I'm sure they have. So have you. But would you tell someone that you'd hold them 'personally responsible' if your husband died?"

Shocked, Kylie turned to Lynellen. "Who said that?"

"Kathryn. When Lee had his heart attack, she told those very words to Blythe. The poor woman was mortified."

Kylie felt numbed at the news. "My grandmother said that?"

The exclamation roused Matt. He peered at Kylie through sleepy blue eyes. "What's wrong?"

"Nothing, sweetie," she whispered. "Your mom and I are just talking."

Matt sniffed, rubbed his nose, then repositioned himself so his head rested on Kylie's shoulder.

"So glad I make a good pillow."

"Mm-hmm, you do."

At Matt's remark, Kylie grinned at Lynellen. But all the while, she was still digesting her grandmother's awful remark. What's more, Kylie hadn't heard from Blythe and hoped that didn't mean the worst. Of course, Mondays could be busy days for her. Maybe Blythe hadn't found time to call. Or maybe she called after Kylie turned off her cell phone in preparation for the flight home.

"Kylie, your mom was my best friend. We talked about a lot of things. Before this last weekend, I figured that Wendy had harbored bitterness against her folks and that's why she never contacted them and made amends. But then after seeing how the Chadwyks treated Blythe, I started to wonder. . . ."

"But Grandma Kate said they weren't Christians when Rob and Mom ran away from home. That's one of her deepest regrets."

"That may be. But Christians are just as prone to holding grudges as unbelievers."

Thinking it over, Kylie began to see a pattern emerging. Her mother had resented her parents and blamed them for Rob's death. Her grandparents resented Blythe and blamed her for their decades-old hurt and sorrow. It made no sense to Kylie. As far as she was concerned, if she could forgive Matt and Dena, then everyone else had a cakewalk!

Now if only she could help her loved ones see that for themselves.

"Wow, sounds like it was quite a weekend."

Walking to his truck after fetching Seth at the airport, TJ could only nod. He was pleased that the timing worked out so he could drop off the Alexanders and then pick up Seth in one trip.

"I'm glad Lee's okay."

"Me, too. He's home from the hospital, but he has to see the cardiologist again tomorrow."

They reached TJ's Silverado and climbed in. TJ started the engine and pulled out of the parking structure.

"So when are the Chadwyks returning to Wisconsin?" Seth wanted to know.

"Probably as soon as Lee gets the go-ahead from his doctor. I'm guessing in a week or so."

"Hmm. . ."

"But I need to warn you. . . . I'm sort of in the doghouse right now. Both Lee and Kathryn are miffed at me for spouting off to them. In a way I feel disloyal." TJ's gut twisted into a painful knot. He loved the Chadwyks and would do anything for them. "Except, I can't help but think how Lee and Kathryn did Blythe wrong and she went back to Chicago a wounded sparrow."

"A. . .*what?*"

"Oh, nothin'. I was making reference to something Kathryn once said. Never mind." TJ shot a look at his buddy. "But I will say this. I've never seen the Chadwyks act so brusque to one of their houseguests."

"Me neither."

"They must be hurting something terrible."

"That'd be my guess." Seth cleared his throat. "Kinda like me all last week."

"Yeah, you were hard to live with."

Seth chuckled. "Well, don't worry. I've gotten over it."

"That's good, because Kylie's a married woman now."

"For better or for worse."

TJ smirked. "Doesn't sound like you're over anything."

"Nah, I'm just kidding."

TJ braked for a stoplight and an idea hit. "Hey, why don't you ask Lissa out?"

"Lissa?" Seth frowned. "Lissa Elliot? The blond who works part-time at The Light House?"

"The very one. She's hardworking, pretty, a widow, and she's got a good head on her shoulders—for the most part, anyhow."

"Then why don't *you* ask her out?"

"She's too young for me." The light switched to green, and TJ pressed on the accelerator. "Lissa was in diapers when I was in Nam. That's what I call *too young*."

Blythe's face suddenly filled TJ's memory. She'd recently turned fifty. TJ was fifty-two. She'd never married, just like him. Maybe he'd send her an E-mail tonight. . .

"Yeah, well, I'll think about it."

"Think about what?"

"Dating Lissa."

"Oh. Right. You do that."

TJ shook himself, deciding he had best stop thinking about women and concentrate on his driving—and on how he could set things right with the Chadwyks once he got back to The Light House.

CHAPTER TWENTY-THREE

M onday proved a long day for Blythe. It began with straightening the back office where Uncle Garth had strewn her papers and other items all over the floor. The answering machine was broken, so she placed an order for another one, and things just spiraled downhill from there. It was Murphy's Law revisited: "If anything can go wrong, it will." Of course, it didn't help matters that Blythe was sleep-deprived and tense, anticipating the meeting with her uncle.

But, finally, the time came to lock up Precious Things. Blythe climbed into her Montana and drove to the restaurant. As she pulled into its parking lot, she noticed it wasn't quite dark outside yet, but that time between twilight and nightfall. Killing the engine, she cupped the top of steering wheel then rested her forehead on the backs of her hands.

That's right where I am, Lord. I'm in a twilight place in my life. I'm scared, Lord, and I need Your help. Please go with me into this meeting with Garth. Go with him also, Lord Jesus. In Your precious name, I ask these things. . . . Amen.

Taking a deep breath, Blythe did her best to cast her cares on God as she climbed from her minivan. When she entered the restaurant, she spotted her uncle immediately and began walking toward him. But then she realized he sat with another man, and a moment later she recognized him as Archibald Baylar, Uncle Garth's attorney.

Blythe's step faltered. Her stomach knotted and her throat went dry.

"Trust in the Lord with all your heart, and lean not on your own understanding. . . ."

Those revered words from Proverbs managed to overcome the fear in Blythe's heart.

"He shall give His angels charge over you, to keep you in all your ways. In their hands they shall bear you up, lest you dash your foot against a stone."

The passage from Psalm 91 calmed the last of Blythe's jangled nerves. Ironically, she had her uncle to thank for prodding her to memorize Scripture after she became a Christian.

She had her uncle to thank for so much. . . .

Having collected her wits, she approached the table with a smile. The men stood, and Blythe kissed her uncle's cheek. Then she gave Archie a smile and politely took his hand in a formal greeting. Garth pulled out a chair for her, and she sat down.

"You're looking well, Blythe."

"Thanks, Archie." She gave the slender man with the long face another smile. In a way, he reminded Blythe of Stan Laurel during the Laurel and Hardy heyday.

The waitress showed up and handed Blythe a menu.

"Did you want something to drink?" Garth asked. "Archie and I are drinking decaf."

She glanced at the waitress. "Ice water with a slice of lemon will be fine. Thanks."

The woman scurried away with her request.

Blythe sent her uncle an expectant look. "Perhaps we should get down to business."

"Let's pray first."

All three bowed their heads, and Garth said a simple but sincere-sounding prayer, ending it with, "And may all we do here tonight glorify You. In Jesus' name. . ."

Blythe lifted her head, glancing at both men while trying to quell a new onset of anxiety. She knew it wasn't happenstance that Garth's lawyer was present at this meeting.

"I filled in Archie on the situation just as you relayed it to me last night." Garth raised his cup and sipped his coffee without a sound. "I see no reason to beat a dead horse, unless you have something to add, Blythe."

"No. . ."

Archie pulled up his briefcase from where it sat beside his chair. He placed it in the vacant setting at the table for four. "Your uncle asked me to read the contract you signed almost twenty-seven years ago. I brought a copy with me tonight." He opened the attaché case. "Your uncle feels that you violated the moral turpitude clause, and you're aware of his reaction, correct?"

Blythe narrowed her gaze at Garth. "Am I aware? I don't recall you telling me about your. . .reaction."

"I feel you deceived me over the years, and I'm a man of principle. My belief is that for every decision we make in life, there are consequences. You, Blythe, chose to keep silent about something I feel I should have known about. You should have told me. Instead, I had to find out by accidentally overhearing a recorded message. Therefore, I'm declaring our contract null and void. Precious Things is now mine."

Blythe felt the blood drain from her face. Everything she feared was becoming reality.

"Your, um, uncle asked me to present a couple of options to you," Archie said, although he sounded hesitant.

Blythe didn't reply. She couldn't. Her world had just come crashing down around her feet.

∞

Kylie woke up in Matt's bedroom the next morning. It felt rather strange to be lying in his bed. It felt almost *wrong*. But, of course, it wasn't, and Lynellen, bless her heart, had practically stripped the room bare last week and scrubbed it from ceiling to floorboard. She even insisted Matt sleep on the sofa one night when she didn't get the cleaning all done. Still, the deep blue paint on the walls was too dark for Kylie's taste. The quilt and bedspread were Lynellen's handiwork and veritable treasures, but they didn't match the curtains quite right.

All in due time, Kylie told herself. She was the one who pushed up the wedding and now she'd have to live with the décor in what could someday be her home.

Oh, God, please don't let that happen! Farm life doesn't bother me, I just want out of Basil Creek.

Now, if only Matt would decide he wanted the same thing.

Heavy footfalls on the bare wooden steps caused Kylie to hold her breath. They seemed to shake the whole house. She wasn't accustomed to the sound, and it frightened her for a few seconds until she realized Matt was on his way up. And if it wasn't Matt, she'd better figure out where the shotgun was kept!

Moments later, Matt burst into the room. "Hey, Lazybones, time to get your carcass outta bed." He sat on the edge of the bed and gave Kylie a playful shake. "What, do you think you're still on your honeymoon or something?"

"Yes, but obviously you plan to dispel that myth."

"You got it, babe."

She laughed and stared up into his unshaven face, noticing his windblown hair. Next, she noticed his appalling attire. He must have grabbed whatever clothes were handy and dressed in the dark because he wore a purple T-shirt under a battered mint-green and orange striped shirt.

"I think the fashion police have a warrant out for your arrest." Kylie tugged on the front of his shirt.

"Who cares? I don't have to be fashionable while I'm doing chores."

"You always looked good when I saw you."

Matt smirked. "I always tried to clean up and change before you came over."

"Oh. . ." She thought it over and somehow felt kind of melancholy at the prospect of her new husband not caring what he looked like around her anymore. "I guess the honeymoon really is over."

Matt's blue eyes widened. "Don't look so glum, Ky. You make me feel bad."

"Sorry." She stared up at him as he leaned over her, and she fell in love with Matt all over again. "You're the best-looking slob I ever laid eyes on."

"Slob? Oh, yeah?"

The way Matt's gaze darkened told Kylie she was about to get tickled until she couldn't breathe. But instead, he helped her into a sitting position. After she straightened her nightgown, one of several her grandmother bought her as a wedding gift, Kylie pushed her hair out of her face.

"I would love nothing better than to horse around with you, but I've got a billion things to do, and Jim Kruger is on his way over with some stuff I ordered. But the most important thing I need to tell you is the Realtor called and said she's got an offer on your house. It's a good one, too, Ky. I think you should take it."

"She sold the house?"

"Well, honey, you have the final say."

"I know, but. . ." Kylie was still trying to grasp his meaning. "But, basically, the house is sold?"

"Uh-huh, supposing the new owner has his or her ducks in a row."

"That's good news."

Matt lowered his chin, giving her an intent look. "You're sure you want to sell, Ky? I mean, you grew up in that house. We could just rent it out."

She shook her head. That house only brought her sadness now. It reminded her of everything lost and nothing gained. She realized she felt the opposite of Blythe, who surrounded herself with "precious things." Kylie wanted no reminders of the past—including the house. "I want to get rid of it."

Matt took her hand and studied her fingers. "Mom asked me to tell you to reconsider."

"Why?"

"Because she thinks you're acting out of emotion and not

common sense. She said that house is where you learned to take your first steps, had your birthday parties. . ."

"She's right. But, Matt, my whole life"—Kylie widened her gaze for emphasis—"was all a lie."

His expression fell and compassion pooled in his eyes. He gathered Kylie in his arms, and she clung to him, knowing every time she drove past her childhood home she'd cry, whether she sold it or not.

It was just one more reason she wanted to move away from Basil Creek. It seemed her entire future, including her happiness with Matt, depended on it.

⁂

Somewhat dazed and feeling depressed, Blythe put another stack of magazines and miscellaneous files into the cardboard box on her desk. She never thought she'd be packing her office in preparation for leaving her shop behind. She had no idea of Garth's plans for the place, although it'd be sheer folly for him to run it himself. Blythe figured he'd probably sell it. In the meantime, he was calling in his loan. After thinking over the options presented to her at last night's dinner meeting, Blythe chose to pay him back ten cents on the dollar. Since a bank loan was out of the question, as Garth acquired the shop, she'd have to exhaust her retirement fund and savings. But worse, she was now forced to sell the two-flat she owned with her mother, and Lydia was furious about it, to say the least.

I've lost everything, she thought, lifting the box and carrying it out the back door and to her minivan. When she returned to the shop, her phone was ringing. Blythe almost decided against answering the call, since the shop was closed to the public. But at the last minute, she picked it up anyway.

"Blythe? It's Kylie."

In spite of the woe in her world, Blythe smiled. "How's the new bride? Back from your honeymoon already?"

"Yes. We got back late last night." Kylie paused. "I've been waiting for you to return my call. I left a message Sunday night."

The message. Blythe lowered herself into the desk chair. "I'm sorry, Kylie, my answering machine broke, and I'm sort of having a—a crisis."

"Is it because of what my grandmother said to you? I'm really sorry that happened."

Blythe had to laugh. She hadn't given Kathryn Chadwyk a single thought. "No. It has nothing to do with your grandmother. I'm. . .I'm closing my shop." Sudden tears clouded her vision.

"You're closing? Why?"

"Remember the vow I mentioned?"

"Yes." There was a hesitancy in Kylie's voice.

"Well, I broke it. The end result is losing my shop."

There was a long pause before Kylie spoke again. When she did, it was a whispered reply. "It's my fault!"

"No, Kylie, it's not. It's not your fault at all. Get that notion out of your head. It's mine. I wasn't honest. I withheld information from my financier. He found out and he's taking action against me."

"What was the vow? Can you tell me?"

Blythe drew in a steadying breath and then relayed the whole story, beginning with how she'd signed her uncle's contract with its hazy moral turpitude clause that spanned past, present, and future transgressions.

"That doesn't seem very fair." Kylie's voice rang with indignation. "Can't you get a lawyer or something?"

"I suppose I could, if I thought I was justified in what I did. But that's not the case. I was wrong."

Kylie ignored the explanation. "Blythe, don't you dare give up your shop without a fight. You have to do something."

She grinned, thinking Kylie inherited her father's tenacity.

"Promise me you'll get some legal counsel. If you really don't have a case, fine. Drop it. But maybe you do. It can't hurt to at least find out."

"All right. I'll check into it." Blythe had her doubts it would do any good, but Kylie had a point—some legal advice couldn't hurt either.

Sitting forward, Blythe opened a desk drawer and began emptying it. "Let's change the subject. How's married life?"

CHAPTER TWENTY-FOUR

"We have to help Blythe!"

Matt looked up from the engine he was working on and wiped the perspiration from his brow with the back of his dirty hand. It was hot and stuffy in the corner of the barn where Matt worked. His blue jeans were soiled and his sleeveless, white, ribbed undershirt was stained with sweat. "What's going on with Blythe?"

"She's losing her shop." Kylie leaned against the piece of machinery that Matt was tinkering with. "She said it's not my fault, but I feel like it is. I mean, I barged into her life, asking all sorts of questions, and now her uncle, the guy who's part owner of Precious Things, is calling Blythe on the carpet for violating the moral turpitude clause in their contract. But, see, she really didn't violate anything. I was born years before she ever signed the agreement."

Matt frowned. "Sounds complicated."

"I told Blythe to get a lawyer."

"Probably a good idea." Matt stood, tossed the wrench on the ground, and then stretched. "Looks like Bruce is going to have to come back out here and fix this stupid thing." His gaze met Kylie's.

She smiled.

He grinned.

Then he stepped toward her. She took in his sweaty, greasy appearance and held out a hand as if to forestall him.

"Oh, no! You're gross. Stay away."

His grin broadened and he lunged at her. Kylie shrieked and ran from the barn, sprinting across the yard with Matt right on her heels. Before he could catch her, however, Kylie ducked under the rows of clean laundry hanging out to dry. Lynellen stood at the far end of the clothesline, pinning up the last of it.

Kylie grinned triumphantly. She knew Matt was no fool.

Lynellen's gaze passed between them and she chuckled. "Kylie, are you still planning to go over to your house after supper and pack?"

"Yep." She sobered but kept a wary eye on Matt. Finally, he gave up and sauntered into the house.

"Did Matt tell you what I suggested—that you rethink selling the place? You grew up there."

"I know, and I gave it some more thought." Kylie tipped her head. "Do you want to move into the house, Lynellen?"

"No way. I'm fond of the place and always admired how your mom kept it neat and decorated, but I have my heart set on having a little mobile home on the other side of the orchard."

Kylie nodded. She knew that already. Lynellen had been

talking about her "mobile home" ever since Matt proposed last Christmas. "Say, how 'bout a mobile home on a beach?"

Arching an auburn brow, Lynellen shook her head. "Kylie, I swear, you have a one-track mind." Bending, she scooped up the large wicker laundry basket from off the springtime brown grass.

"We could all move to Sabal Beach and live happily ever after."

"Honey, if we all moved to Sabal Beach, life would be one big soap opera."

In spite of herself, and her quest to leave this sleepy Wisconsin town, Kylie had to laugh. Then she traipsed into the house behind Lynellen.

During their early supper, which Lynellen served every night at five without fail, Kylie mentioned her desire to help Blythe again. She explained the circumstances to Lynellen before looking at Matt. "Maybe I should tell her she can rent my house."

"Do you think someone who's lived in Chicago all her life is going to want to move to the country?"

"My mom did—of course, that's not what she told me." Kylie tamped down the hurt brought on by the realization that she'd been raised believing a string of lies.

"And what if we end up selling the farm?" Matt sliced off a piece of his baked chicken. "Is Blythe going to follow us wherever we go?"

"Matt! You're not really thinking of selling, are you?"

Kylie noted that her mother-in-law wore that familiar pinched look, the one that said she disapproved.

"This farm has been in the Alexander family for two generations. Your grandfather built it. In fact, the original part of this house came in pieces on a flatbed railroad car in 1910."

"Mom, I'm just exploring options, that's all. Nothing's been decided."

Kylie glanced from Matt to Lynellen then back at Matt. He had showered and changed into a navy polo shirt and a clean pair of jeans. He looked just as handsome now as he did this past weekend. However, Kylie realized her husband was in a rather prickly position. The decision to stay would appease his mother, but the one to move would please his wife. While Kylie sympathized, she hoped Matt would opt to sell the farm. He'd earned a degree in business. He'd never planned to be a farmer until after Rochelle and Jason died. His childhood home had been a place of refuge after life delivered Matt a terrible blow.

But that was all over now. He had a brand-new life and opportunities looming before him.

Kylie only hoped and prayed that Matt saw their future the same way she did!

<hr>

"Twila, I just don't know what to do," Blythe lamented. She leaned against the glass counter, peering into the Japanese porcelain tea set encased below. "Lydia is barely speaking to me, and my uncle expects me to hand over the keys to Precious Things tomorrow morning."

"You know what? I say tell your uncle and mother 'adios,' and move down here. You can work for me. Do you know how much fun we'd have?"

Blythe grinned. They'd have a ball.

"Maybe losing your shop is a blessing. You have been tied

to that place for half your life. Isn't it time to start really living?"

Her friend's words echoed through Blythe's being. Hadn't she decided to start living again?

"Blythe, I vote you take charge of your life and move to Houston. What do you have to lose?"

"My relationship with my daughter, for one thing. Now that she's found me, and I finally have a place in her life, I want to be close to her."

"Remind me. . .where does she live again?"

"Wisconsin."

"Cheese and Green Bay Packers."

"That's it, except Kylie has high hopes of talking her new husband into moving to South Carolina so she can be near her grandparents. The only problem is, they're not too fond of me."

"Who cares? South Carolina has plenty of hotels."

A little smile tugged at Blythe's mouth. Kylie had said much the same thing on Saturday.

"So you travel from Chicago or from Houston. What's the difference? Besides, thanks to the Internet and telephones, the world's a lot smaller place these days."

"True." Blythe thought it over. "Just curious, Twila, how far is South Carolina from Texas?"

"I dunno. Look at one of those map places on the Internet."

Blythe was already halfway to her office. Everything was packed except the computer. Since it was the property of Precious Things, Blythe couldn't take it with her.

Sitting down at the desk, she typed each city into the computer while Twila tried to beguile her with a position at her art gallery.

"Hey, we'll shop at Old Town Spring once a week or until you're tired of it."

"I can't imagine tiring of that quaint little place."

"Well, after a while the mall looks pretty good, especially when it's 110 degrees outside."

Blythe grimaced. "I don't think I could stand 110."

"Nobody can. That's why there's central air-conditioning."

She laughed and the numbers came up on her computer. "Hey, according to this, Houston is 225 miles farther away from Sabal Beach than Chicago."

"Hey, who's counting? You wouldn't want to drive all that way anyhow. Blythe, if you work for me, I'll pay you enough so you can fly."

"Keep talking, Twila. Tell me some more." Somehow, the idea of starting over fresh in a new city suddenly appealed to Blythe.

"Okay, here's my idea. For quite some time, I've been toying with the idea of expanding my gallery into Galveston. . . ."

After supper, Kylie, Matt, and Lynellen drove over to the two-story wood-framed house that Kylie had called home for thirty-one years. The Realtor said she'd be bringing by the prospective buyer who had already toured the place. Kylie had ditched her idea to rent the home to Blythe, even on a temporary basis, although she still longed to help her natural mother in some way.

"Matt, you start on the garage. Kylie and I will tackle the closets. Closets are a good place to begin." Lynellen strode through the dining room and living room then paused near the front door. She slid open the door to the entryway closet. "Goodness! I forgot what a pack rat Wendy was!"

Kylie nodded and grinned at Matt. "Wait 'til you see the garage."

He groaned.

The hum and rattle of a vehicle in need of repair reached Kylie's ears and summoned her to the windows. "It's Dena and the kids—and the Realtor will be here any second." She took a step back. "I'll get rid of them."

She turned and glimpsed Matt's wide-eyed stare.

"Politely," she amended. "I'll *politely* get rid of them, especially since Dena has the kids with her."

Matt chuckled and Lynellen clucked her tongue while Kylie jogged to the back door. By the time she reached the driveway, the Realtor had pulled in and parked.

Dena and her two children, who weren't so little anymore, stood near the dilapidated white van.

"Hey, guys, I'm expecting a prospective buyer for my house." Kylie knew Dena could take a hint. "See, here's the Realtor." She smiled. "Hi, June."

Attired in a printed dress and navy blue blazer, the older woman waved as she pulled an attaché case from her trunk.

"Ky, I'm the prospective buyer."

Halting in mid-stride, Kylie stared at Dena. "You?"

Dena nodded.

Amber, her twelve-year-old daughter, sauntered up to Kylie and put an arm around her shoulders. "Are you surprised, Aunt Kylie?"

Kylie regarded the preteen, thinking it didn't seem that long ago when she and Ryan were both in diapers. But now Amber stood eye-to-eye with her.

Kylie feigned an indignant look. "When did you get so tall?"

Amber laughed and gave her brother a taunting smirk. "I'm taller than Ryan."

"You are not!" Blond with hazel eyes, Ryan favored his mother right down to his slight build—although, at fourteen, he still had a lot of growing left to do.

"So how's the kitten you got for your birthday?"

Ryan smiled at Kylie's inquiry. "Good. I named him Slugger."

She grinned. Ever since Ryan was a toddler he loved animals, and for years he'd been talking about becoming a veterinarian when he grew up.

Won't be long. He'll be a freshman next year. This place is a lot closer to the high school. . . .

Kylie brought her gaze back to Dena. "You really want to buy my house?"

She nodded. "But I'm hoping you'll knock a few bucks off the price for me."

"Please, Aunt Kylie," Amber pleaded, tightening her hold. A curly, auburn tendril flopped down onto her forehead. "This house will be perfect for us. The one we've got now is cramped for space."

Kylie knew that was true. Dena and her kids lived in a trailer park on the edge of town. Their mobile home wasn't even a double-wide, like the models Lynellen had been considering, and as Ryan and Amber got older, Dena's house seemed to get smaller. What's more, it had no basement or laundry room. Dena washed clothes at the Laundromat.

"Mom's been telling us all the cool things she remembers about this place," Ryan said with a nod toward the Cape Cod structure.

"Yeah, like happiness."

Kylie peered into Amber's freckled face.

"Mom said this house was always filled with happiness and that's what we want for us." Amber looked at her mother. "Right?"

"Right." Dena's eyes suddenly looked misty.

"And me and Amber remember coming here all the time when we were small," Ryan added. "It's been like our second home, so we might as well buy it."

Kylie felt so flabbergasted, she didn't know what to say.

June Littel, the Realtor, cleared her throat. "Shall we go inside and discuss this matter further?"

Kylie led the small entourage in through the back door.

"The dining room is a good place to sit and discuss business," June suggested.

Dena shooed the kids into the den to watch TV. "You don't mind, do you, Ky?"

"Not at all."

Matt entered the room and Kylie watched Dena's expression. But nothing out of the ordinary wafted across her face.

"Hey, Matt."

"Dena." He inclined his head. "What's going on?"

"She's our prospective buyer." Kylie pulled out a chair and sat down. The Realtor had opened her briefcase and was unpacking forms, pens, and a calculator.

"No kidding?" Matt's surprise matched Kylie's.

Lynellen overheard and stood in the entryway that joined the dining room and living room. "What a perfect arrangement!"

"Well, it's not a done deal yet." Dena looked at Kylie. "Since I work at the bank, I get some perks. But, like I said, I'm hoping you'll come down on the price."

"I've informed Ms. Hubbard that the price is already

quite low," June said. "We set it that way so the house would sell. I don't recommend coming down any further, Kylie."

She glanced at June, then Matt. He sat across the table from her, and the expression in his blue eyes said he wasn't sure she should come down any lower either.

Slowly, Kylie slid her gaze to Dena, who was seated opposite the Realtor.

"I want the house, even if you don't lower the price."

Kylie wondered what she should do. A month ago she would have charged Dena double just to spite her. Now, Kylie wanted her to have the house—for the kids' sakes, if nothing else. What's more, she knew Dena was a single mother. She worked full-time, and Todd, her ex-husband, wasn't always on time with his alimony checks.

She once was my very best friend, next to my mother. . . .

"I remember when your mom wallpapered the kitchen with the brown and orange geometric paper. Remember that stuff?"

Kylie smiled. "How could I forget? There are still rolls of it out in the garage."

"No way!"

"Yeah way, Matt." Kylie glanced at her husband. "And, just to give you an idea of what you're in for, the crib I slept in is stored in the rafters. It's probably so warped it's unusable. I don't know why Mom didn't get rid of it."

Matt collapsed onto the table and Kylie laughed at his antics.

June cleared her throat to get everyone's attention. "So the price stays as is?"

"I'll come down ten thousand dollars," Kylie blurted. She turned to Dena. "Do you want the appliances, too? Stove and refrigerator are about seven years old, but the washer and dryer downstairs are practically new."

"Um. . .yeah. I'd love 'em! Oh, Kylie, thank you!"

"Sure." She looked at Matt, suspecting he might send her back a disapproving frown. But instead, he winked.

Dena stood and hovered over Kylie before wrapping her in a grateful embrace. Within seconds, Kylie felt choked with unshed emotion. Her eyes filled. She didn't even know where the tears had come from.

"Kylie, you've always been my best friend in the whole world," Dena began, "and I remember the love I felt in your home. I wished I was your sister and lived with you."

Memories of special times with her mom and dad scampered through Kylie's mind. She missed her parents so badly her heart crimped, but the pain wasn't as terrible as even a week ago.

I'm healing. At the same time, she sensed her relationship with Dena was on the mend. Gone were those intense feelings of animosity. In their place was a calm and peace.

Standing, Kylie hugged Dena back. Soon they were both in tears. For Kylie, the release felt therapeutic.

And suddenly this house didn't seem so glum and sorrowful. Like her, it appeared to have a bright and shining future.

CHAPTER TWENTY-FIVE

B lythe managed to get an appointment with an attorney the following day. A friend who owned the clothing store around the corner from Precious Things had recommended the lawyer, so Blythe gave her a call. She'd convinced herself it wouldn't hurt. Besides, she promised Kylie. . . .

"I'm wondering if there's a loophole somewhere," Blythe said, after explaining the situation.

The impeccably dressed woman read the contract and then peered at Blythe from over her violet-framed bifocals. "It appears your uncle dotted every *i* and crossed each *t*. But that doesn't mean you can't take him to court and pursue the matter. You were young and naïve when you signed this document. The judge may rule in your favor. Then, again, he might not."

It was a gamble. Blythe decided she might as well roll the dice. The verdict could swing either way, and if she lost, she would have to pay out legal fees on top of what she owed her uncle. And, yet, her shop defined who she was as a person; Precious Things had become her very existence. How could she lock its doors and hand Garth the key at the end of the month as he'd mandated at their dinner meeting?

But as she drove home that evening, Blythe prayed about it and felt no peace about taking Garth to court. She remembered then that God's Word discouraged such things. Christians were to work out their disputes in love and among themselves. Blythe realized that, before throwing herself on the mercy of the court, she needed to ask for Garth's mercy.

"What did the lawyer say?" Lydia wanted to know. Dressed in a fawn-colored suede outfit, she had a commanding presence for one so petite.

Blythe stepped into the two-flat they owned. "I can't file a lawsuit against Garth."

"She said that? Why can't you?"

"No, the attorney didn't tell me that. . . ." Blythe weighed her reply. Finally, she decided on the truth in spite of the fact her mother wasn't a Christian and wouldn't respect her views. "I've changed my mind. It wouldn't be pleasing to God if I took Garth to court."

Lydia cursed, making Blythe wince as she took the steps leading up to her apartment.

"I want to see how this God of yours is going to get us out of our present predicament."

Yeah, me, too. Blythe unlocked her door and walked inside.

TJ worked on a broken patio door upstairs for most of the morning. When he came down for some lunch, he passed the den and paused for just a moment, seeing Lee and Kathryn.

They stopped talking.

Immediately, TJ felt the friction that had lingered between them for almost a full week now.

Saying nothing, he continued on to the kitchen.

"TJ, please come back here."

At Kathryn's beckon, TJ whirled around and retraced his steps.

"We'd like to speak with you for a moment."

"Sure, Kathryn, what's up?"

"Last night we heard from Kylie," Lee began. He was seated in one of the wing chairs. "She gave us the proverbial good news and bad news."

"We'll give you the good news first." Kathryn mustered a smile that didn't quite brighten her hazel eyes. "Kylie sold her house."

TJ grinned. "That is good news."

"A friend bought it." Lee cleared his throat and sat up a little straighter in his chair. "Same friend who cheated on her months ago, but Kylie told us she's having victory in the forgiveness area."

"Well, she didn't actually say 'victory,' " Kathryn amended, "but it's apparent she's winning that battle against bitterness and resentment."

"Unlike Wendy—and many others who never resolve their differences."

Kathryn and Lee regarded each other then looked at TJ.

"And we might as well point the finger at ourselves, too." Upon the admission, Kathryn turned misty. "I never understood how some people can call themselves Christians and hide such evil in their souls. It must eat them alive."

"Or give them heart attacks."

TJ smirked.

Kathryn continued on. "I've held a grudge against Blythe practically since I've known of her. I realized it began that day I didn't find her in her store when Lee and I walked in. I wanted answers, and I was miffed when I didn't get my way. I never once considered Blythe's feelings or what she might be going through."

"I'm guilty as well."

TJ leaned against the doorframe and fought against shouting *Hallelujah!* "At least you've both realized your mistake before it's too late to do something about it."

"Well, it is too late for some things. And that's the bad news we have to tell you." Kathryn strode to one of the end tables and plucked a Kleenex. She dabbed her eyes. "Kylie said Blythe lost her shop. She'd signed something years ago and made a vow. That's why she didn't want anything to do with Kylie at first. But then she changed her mind, and her 'financier,' as Kylie termed it, found out. Now he's closing Precious Things down and wants his investment paid back."

"The amount is staggering," Lee said.

TJ winced. "Yeah, Blythe mentioned some of this to me last week, although I didn't know the outcome. She hasn't returned my E-mails." He didn't add that he'd been feeling rather bummed out about the latter. But now he understood why she might be too preoccupied for idle chitchat via the Internet.

"Kylie said Blythe sacrificed everything in order to have a relationship with her, and here Lee and I were feeling smug and justified in our contempt of that poor woman." Kathryn shook her head and swatted an errant tear. "I feel horrible."

"I have her E-mail address if you want to write an apology."

Kathryn lifted her chin. "I'll have you know, TJ, that I had Blythe's E-mail address long before you did."

He grinned. Things were starting to sound like normal. Kathryn's feigned regal air proved it.

"Actually, TJ, we'd like to do more than just apologize," Lee said. "But we're not sure that a monetary gift is the answer. We couldn't give her very much. The amount would be like spit on a bonfire."

"Aw, you both know what to do. Pray. God'll give you the answer. I'll pray, too." TJ pushed away from the doorway. "Might be that just offering Blythe your love and support will be all she wants and needs—and that won't cost you a cent."

The Chadwyks both bobbed out contrite-looking replies. TJ smiled and headed for the kitchen again. While he felt glad and even relieved over Lee and Kathryn's change of heart, he was sorry for Blythe's loss.

Lord, You raised Lazarus from the dead, healed the sick, and went to the cross to save mankind. Blythe's situation pales in comparison, but You care about even the littlest things in our lives. Will you show her that? Work a miracle, Lord, 'cause it sounds like Blythe could sure use one about now.

───◦◦◦───

On the first day of May, in accordance with their latest agreement, Blythe turned in the key to Precious Things. Archie Baylar, Garth's attorney, wanted her to stick around until her uncle arrived. Garth had requested a meeting. However, Blythe wasn't up to seeing him just yet. What would she say to the man who had ripped her livelihood out from under her?

Driving back to her apartment, she thought of the inventory left in her shop. Per their contract, Garth acquired all of it, leaving Blythe to feel like a mother who had lost all her children. She had taken special care of the items in her store. Many of them she personally and lovingly refurbished.

"I told you this would happen," Lydia said, following Blythe up the stairs to her apartment. The climb left the older woman breathless, but not deterred. "You vowed this wouldn't happen, Blythe. You promised me."

"I promised I wouldn't tell Uncle Garth and I didn't." Weary, Blythe unlocked the upper doorway and entered the apartment with her mother right behind her. "*That* was my biggest mistake. I should have been honest with him the moment I learned he didn't know about Kylie."

"Big deal. You would have lost your shop eighteen years ago instead of today."

Blythe set her purse down and shrugged out of her suede jacket.

"What's going to happen to us now? We'll have to sell the house, of course, and any profit will go to Garth—but then what? Where are we going to live?"

Setting her hands on her hips, Blythe studied the tops of her leather shoes. "I–I don't know."

"Well, you'd better think of something." Lydia shook her head. "Maybe God will send you a check for a quarter of a million dollars." She laughed and it rang with bitterness. "You have a better chance of winning the lottery."

"Lydia. . ." Blythe couldn't keep the exasperation out of her tone. "I doubt God will send me a check, but He could. He's able to do anything—He's *God*. What's more, my situation, as dire as it seems right now, hasn't shaken heaven in the least."

"Humph!" Lydia raised a defiant chin. "Well, if your God behaves like Garth, who needs Him?"

Blythe's heart twisted in grief to think this situation might have blackened her Savior's name in Lydia's mind. "I guess this is really all my fault. The very fact that I was afraid to tell Garth the truth proves my lack of trust in the Lord."

"Self-pity won't solve this problem."

The reply stung. "I wasn't attempting to feel sorry for myself. I was just being honest."

"Yes, well, look how far your honesty has gotten you now."

Blythe threw her hands in the air. "Lydia, what was I supposed to do? Uncle Garth heard Kylie's message. He heard her say I was her biological mother."

"Like I said, look where your honesty has gotten you."

Blythe raised her brows. "Do you think I should have concocted some sort of outlandish story in an effort to conceal the truth?"

Lydia gave her a pointed look. "Successful businessmen and women can't afford to operate on honesty. They do what they have to do—as long as it's not illegal."

Blythe bit back a reply, deciding it would do no good to argue the point. But she understood from what Lydia said that, in her mother's eyes, she was a failure.

For the next few days, as Blythe considered her future, a dark depression threatened to consume her. The feeling was frightening because she'd gotten swallowed up in that desolate abyss once before. But she kept reminding herself that the difference between then and now was Jesus Christ in her life. He was her hope, even when things appeared hopeless. Despite all the wrongs in her past, Blythe reminded herself that Christ cared about her future, and her faith was affirmed as she read through Lamentations in her Bible. *Through the Lord's mercies we are not consumed, because His compassions fail not. They are new every morning; great is Your faithfulness. . . .*

Then Kylie phoned and Blythe's spirit rose all the more.

"If you're not running Precious Things, what are you doing?"

"I'm praying about whether to accept a friend's job offer while Lydia and I get the two-flat ready to put on the market."

"Oh, Blythe, I'm so sorry you have to sell your house. I feel responsible."

"Nonsense."

"But—"

"Kylie, stop right there." Blythe loaded the last of her dishes into the dishwasher, added soap, then turned on the machine. "I made my choices, knowing the consequences. If anyone is to blame, it's me."

"What about your uncle?"

Blythe walked to the living room and dropped into one of the overstuffed armchairs. "He's been calling me and one afternoon he stopped by. But I haven't answered his calls and I didn't answer the door." A sigh escaped her. "I feel so many things when it comes to Uncle Garth, but I'm not sure what to label those feelings. As soon as I figure them all out I'll be able to speak to him without dissolving into tears or spouting off in anger."

"Understandable. Well," Kylie hedged, "I guess I was hoping you had nothing to do."

"Oh?" Blythe grinned in spite of herself. "Why's that?"

"I had this fleeting notion that maybe you'd come and help me pack."

"Hmm. . ." Blythe thought about it.

"I could really use your help. There's so much stuff that I'm not sure of what to keep, what to sell, and what to throw away. But you'd know."

She needs me. . . . "I guess I could come for a few days."

"How 'bout a week?"

Blythe laughed. "Let's play it by ear, okay? But I'd love to spend some time with you."

"I'd love to spend time with you, too. We'll gab while we empty the attic."

Blythe chuckled again and decided that, perhaps, a trip to Wisconsin was just what she needed.

———

"What are you up to?"

"Huh?" Kylie whirled around and looked at Matt. He sat at the kitchen table, sipping a cup of coffee while she washed the lunch dishes. "How do you know I'm 'up' to something?"

He grinned. "I've known you practically all your life, that's how I can tell."

"Well, you're right. *This time.*"

Matt chuckled. "Okay, lemme guess. . .you bought a house in Sabal Beach."

"No, but how about we make that a reality?"

Matt rolled his eyes.

Kylie laughed but chose not to park on that subject. She didn't want to push Matt too hard, fearing he'd decide against moving just to get her off his back.

"Blythe is coming to help me pack. She'll be here Friday."

After a gulp of coffee, Matt raised one blond brow. "Think that's a good idea with your grandparents in town?"

"Blythe can stay here at the farm with us, and my grandparents are at my house—make that *Dena's house.*"

"Kylie—"

"Matt, they have to talk to each other sometime, and my grandparents are eager to apologize." Kylie tossed the dishtowel over her shoulder. "You heard my grandmother last night."

"Yeah, that's true, but—"

"And TJ's coming this weekend."

"So?"

"So! TJ and Blythe *like* each other."

Matt smirked. "You little matchmaker."

With a smile of her own, Kylie turned back to the sink full of suds and finished a load before setting the frying pan into the water to soak. "I don't know how your mom has survived all these years without a dishwasher."

"I never heard her complain about it."

Kylie wiped her hands and took a seat next to Matt. "You probably weren't listening."

He sat back in his chair. "Honey, I'll buy you a dishwasher. Just say the word."

"Dishwasher."

"You got it." Matt sent her a charming grin. "See how easy that was?"

Kylie gave him a smile. She'd said "Sabal Beach" plenty of times, but Matt hadn't given into that request.

Yet.

He finished his coffee and stood. "I suppose we should go back over to the house and help your grandparents."

"Yeah, guess you're right." A cloud of gloom suddenly seemed to loom overhead.

Matt kissed the top of her head. "Thanks for coming

home to make me lunch. That was sweet."

While glad for the compliment, Kylie's heart sank hearing the word "home." This farm didn't feel like her home—and neither did the place she and her grandparents and Lynellen were packing up and cleaning out. She stared at the crooked picture on the wall and suddenly felt lost and very alone.

"Hey, c'mon." Matt held out his hand.

Kylie swiveled and gazed up at him. At last, she set her palm into his calloused one. Helping her out of the chair, he took one look at her misty-eyed expression and pulled her into a snug embrace. He held her so tightly she almost couldn't breathe.

"I kinda figured that's why you came home at noon. It's all getting to you over there, isn't it?"

Kylie nodded, her nose in the shoulder of his battered blue and white Milwaukee Brewers T-shirt. But in spite of those feelings of forsakenness, she had to admit she felt right at home in Matt's arms.

CHAPTER TWENTY-SIX

As Blythe sped down the highway, she sang along with an ancient James Taylor cassette that she'd found in a desk drawer when she cleaned out her office. "Fire and Rain." "You Can Close Your Eyes." "Rockabye Sweet Baby James." She wished she knew Scripture as well as these old songs! They whisked her back to a tumultuous time in her life, and at first, she'd been terrified to insert the tape, afraid the recorded words and music would resurrect the past in a way in which she wouldn't be able to cope. But then she thought about TJ and his hang gliding and skydiving and the next thing she knew, James Taylor's voice was crooning through her stereo speakers. What's more, singing harmony with the tape felt somewhat cathartic.

My past is no longer a frightening, dark shadow. The realization made Blythe feel remarkably free.

Now if only she could decide on her future.

Lord, won't You write an answer in the heavens for me to see?

Go to Texas. Stay in Chicago.

Blythe mulled over her options. She knew of dozens of art galleries in the Chicago area. With her contacts, she ought to be able to land a position at one of them.

But is that what You want, Lord, or should I accept Twila's offer?

Above her, the azure sky was devoid of even a single cloud. No answer written there.

Driving on, Blythe shifted her thinking and noted the changes in the scenery since the last time she'd driven this route. The treetops were now shrouded with tiny green buds, the dormant brown grass was coming back to life, and every so often clusters of brightly colored tulips graced the side of a farmhouse.

At last, she arrived in Basil Creek, and minutes later, she pulled up the gravel driveway leading to Kylie's house—rather, her former house. Climbing from behind the wheel of her minivan, Blythe stretched. She noticed the garage door was open and various items, including a few bikes, a tractor-mower, and other lawn equipment, occupied the car space. A large, formidable, blue Dumpster lurked nearby, and Blythe immediately wondered what sorts of items Kylie had thrown away. She decided she'd peer inside the thing later.

Proceeding to the house, Blythe's step faltered as the back door swung open. Then she came to an abrupt halt as Kathryn Chadwyk stepped onto the narrow walkway.

"Good afternoon, Blythe, and welcome." Kathryn smiled, but Blythe found it difficult to return the gesture. "You're just in time to join us for a late lunch."

"No, thank you." Blythe had to fight the urge to get back in her van and leave. Only one person kept her in place. "Is Kylie here?"

"Yes, but I persuaded her to let me have a few words with you before we go inside." Kathryn inched forward. "Blythe, I want to apologize for the rude way in which I've behaved." She wagged her chestnut-brown head, wearing a look of shame. "I'm truly sorry. Ever since Kylie appeared in our lives, Lee and I have struggled with our children's rejection, Wendy's especially. We took it out on you—rather, I did. Lee tends to suffer in silence, as it were. And what I said to you the night of his heart attack was inexcusable. Yet, I stand here asking for your forgiveness."

"Let's just forget it, okay?" Blythe waved off the act of contrition, wondering if Kylie put her grandmother up to it. *And that little stinker didn't say a word about Kathryn's being here.*

The back door opened again, and this time Lee emerged from the house. Blythe wanted to groan. Instead, she pushed out a polite grin.

"I'm glad you arrived safely, Blythe."

"Thank you. I trust you're feeling better."

"Oh, much better. I'm as good as new." His mouth curved upward and his features brightened. Blythe glimpsed the resemblance Rob had to his father. Odd, but she hadn't seen it until just now when he smiled. "I hope there are no hard feelings between us, Blythe. I'm sorry for offending you."

"No worries," she fibbed, but all the while, she couldn't shake her unease. Did these folks have some ulterior motive for apologizing? Maybe they wanted more information.

"Well, let's all go inside, shall we?" Kathryn's hazel eyes brightened with the suggestion. "Kylie will be wondering what's keeping us."

They walked into the house, through the back hall, and into the kitchen. A plate of bagels sat in the middle of the table, and four varieties of cream cheese in Styrofoam cups surrounded it.

"Hi, Blythe!" Kylie popped out of her chair and skirted around Lynellen. After a hug, she offered Blythe some lunch.

"No, thanks. I'm not hungry."

Matt smiled and waved a greeting, and Blythe smiled back.

"Good to see you again, Blythe."

She smiled at Lynellen. "Nice to see you, too."

"Well, I'm finished eating," Lynellen said to all around the table, "so I'll show Blythe what we've accomplished in the last couple of weeks." With a wide-eyed look, she added, "And everything we have left to do. Wendy was quite the saver."

Blythe managed a grin.

"I never even knew that about my own daughter." Kathryn lowered herself onto a chair next to Matt.

"People change." Lee glanced at his wife and smiled. "We only had Wendy around for seventeen years. She was forty-nine when she. . .died."

Looking glum, Kathryn nodded. Blythe felt a sudden stab of pity for the lady.

"After more than thirty years, one would think Wendy would have wanted to contact us and make amends. She was a Christian."

Kylie attested to that fact with several bobs of her head.

"Even if she didn't want a relationship with us—"

"Let it go, Kathryn," Lynellen said. "You're going to make yourself crazy. The answers to your questions died with Wendy, so there's no use in asking them over and over."

"She's right, dear." Lee reached over and covered her hand with his.

Kathryn sadly lowered her gaze.

Blythe shifted her stance and looked from the Chadwyks to Lynellen. She felt out of place here. Had it been a mistake to come? Unlike her trip to South Carolina, Blythe had prayed about this one. She hadn't felt that God said "no."

Lynellen touched her forearm and inclined her head. Blythe followed the woman into the dining room. The table-top was cluttered with glassware and dishes. Blythe paused and turned over a plate and read the company signature on the back.

"These are worth quite a lot of money."

Lynellen drew closer. "I thought maybe they were, and I managed to convince Kylie to keep them for when company comes. She'll have a houseful on the holidays. Take this November, for example. Every one of Matt's siblings had planned to come to Basil Creek for a wedding in the fall. Since that's already done, they've all decided to come for Thanksgiving. Kylie's going to need all those place settings." Lynellen smirked. "I'll be in my new mobile home by then, enjoying peace and quiet."

Blythe smiled. "So she and Matt plan to stay in Wisconsin?"

"No. Nothing's been decided yet."

Blythe pivoted at the sound of Kylie's voice behind her.

"Matt's still thinking about it."

Lynellen turned and walked into the living room without another word.

"Obviously, my mother-in-law doesn't want us to leave."

"Kylie, I think selling the farm is a big mistake," Lynellen declared from the adjacent room. "The place is rich with our family's history."

"Maybe one of your other kids'll buy it. Why does it have to be Matt who's stuck there forever?"

Lynellen's face contorted with a mixture of shock and indignation. Then she walked into the hallway and out of sight.

Blythe's sympathies went with her.

She turned to Kylie. "Heritage isn't something you want to throw away, Kylie. It's hard to reclaim. Don't you want that farm for your children?"

Kylie hung her head back. "I just want to get out of Basil Creek."

"Why?"

"Because I hate it here."

"Why?"

At the challenge, Kylie brought her dark gaze back to Blythe. "The memories hurt me. Everywhere I go in this town, I remember Mom and the things we liked to do together. Then I remember that she lied to me my entire life. My *heritage* has been nothing but a sham."

"No, it hasn't. Wendy lied to you about *her* past—and mine. But she loved you more than anything, and neither of us ever meant to wound you." Blythe slipped an arm around her shoulders. "I'm so sorry."

Kylie hugged her back. "I know."

"And just for the record," Blythe said in a whisper as she leaned nearer to Kylie, "memories have a way of following you wherever you go. You can't run from them. I've learned that much in the past two months."

"So you don't think Matt and I should move." Kylie looked suddenly forlorn.

"I don't know what you should do. I wouldn't be so presumptuous to try and tell you your business, either. All I'm saying is that there are some precious things you ought not to turn your back on." Blythe glanced around the room. "I have a feeling this whole house is full of them." Looking back at Kylie, she frowned. "Oh, by the way, just what is in that Dumpster outside?"

TJ exited the aircraft, anticipating that Matt Alexander would meet him at the baggage claim. But, instead, it was Blythe who had come to drive him to Basil Creek from the Madison, Wisconsin, airport. TJ had to admit to feeling both surprised and somewhat thrilled at seeing her again.

"Wasn't expecting to find you here." He grinned then gave her a friendly hug. He thought she looked stylish if not downright trendy in her black skirt, beige sleeveless shirt, and ebony sweater that was slung around her slender shoulders.

"I've been banished from the house-packing. They've had it with me already, and I only arrived yesterday."

"Oh?" TJ's smile widened, seeing the spark of amusement in Blythe's dark eyes. "What happened?"

"Well, I just can't stand to watch perfectly good and useful items get thrown away. For instance, we found an adorable wooden washstand in the attic. It's a little warped from years of summer heat, and I'll be the first to admit it could use a new coat of paint. A more ambitious person might strip, stain, and varnish it." Blythe stopped, hearing TJ chuckle. "Oh, fine. Laugh. But now you know why I was. . .*banished*. I imagine while I'm gone today Matt will fill up the Dumpster and haul it away before I can rescue anything else."

"Rescue, huh?" TJ chuckled again.

Blythe sent him a withering look but then smiled to let him know she was kidding.

"Seriously, it's nice to see you again, Blythe." TJ moved toward the carousel and watched for his luggage before adding, "Even though you didn't answer my E-mails."

Blythe followed him, a little frown creasing her brows. "What E-mails?"

"The ones I sent you, of course."

An expression of chagrin shadowed her features. "Um. . . I . . .well, I haven't been online for weeks."

"Good, then I won't take it personally."

"No, please don't." A slow smile spread across her face. "But since we've got an hour-and-a-half drive to Basil Creek, you can feel free to talk my ear off."

"Yeah, okay, I just might do that." TJ winked before lifting his bags off the conveyor belt.

Together they walked to Blythe's van. After setting TJ's luggage in the back, they climbed in and buckled their seatbelts.

"So have you and the Chadwyks been getting along all right?"

"They apologized to me."

TJ settled against the seat and watched Blythe as she paid the parking attendant. A moment later, she drove out of the structure. "That wasn't an answer to my question."

"I know, but it's the best I can give you right now, TJ." She flicked her gaze at him. "I've always been a very forgiving person, but for some odd reason I'm really struggling with the concept now. I know God commands us to forgive, just as we have been forgiven. I've accepted Lee and Kathryn's apology, and yet I don't feel like true forgiveness has really taken place in my heart."

"I think I know what you mean. I went through something

similar with my folks. I grew up in a hick town in Tennessee. My daddy died in his sin, I've got a brother in jail, and my mother's a drunk—always has been as far as I can remember. Her liver's shot. It's amazing she's still alive at all—at least, I *think* she's still alive." TJ paused, marveling that the situation still stung. "I haven't talked to her or any other family members in a very long time."

"Why not?"

"Well, my mother and the rest of my family saw how Jesus changed my whole life, and it made them resent me. I used to send money back home, but I stopped years ago. The Chadwyks helped me see that I was actually harming my kin by giving them money to buy the very thing destroying their lives. Booze. Except the consequence for cutting them off was their complete rejection. Now my own mother won't even speak to me."

"I'm so sorry, TJ."

"I am, too. That is, I wish things were different." He turned and regarded Blythe. "But reality is what it is. I can't change anybody else. So, once I accepted that fact, I had to forgive my family. Wasn't easy, but now I'm committed to praying for them on a regular basis."

Blythe sent him a tremulous little smile. "You've given me a lot to think about."

He snickered. "Well, you did give me permission to talk your ear off."

"Yes, I guess that's true." Blythe laughed. "So, how's the weather in South Carolina?"

TJ noted the abrupt subject change. He supposed he hit a nerve. "It's a lot warmer there than here."

"Forecasts call for temperatures near eighty and humidity

the next two days. You'll feel right at home." She smiled. "And, you're in for a real treat. Meteorologists are predicting thunderstorms for tomorrow and Monday."

"You know, I almost didn't bring my cameras. But at the last minute, I stuffed them into my carry-on. Just in case."

Again, Blythe smiled. "Once the storms have past, or perhaps before they blow in, Matt said he'll take you and Lee fishing in the Mississippi."

"What kind of fish are worth catching in that river?"

"Don't ask me. I'm from Chicago." She laughed once more. "We've got Lake Michigan, but I'm no fisherman—make that fisher*woman*."

"Politically correct, are you?"

"Of course."

TJ sported another grin. He rather enjoyed the bantering.

Suddenly he felt glad he made the trip. Not only could he drive the Chadwyks back home and not worry about Lee behind the wheel all that distance, what with his recent health issues, but TJ could spend some time with Blythe and get to know her better. In truth, she had consumed his thoughts more times than he cared to count. Maybe God would use him to be a blessing to Blythe in the forgiveness area she admitted struggling with.

TJ had to grin. Top all that off with a good thunderstorm, and life couldn't get any more perfect.

───※───

With dinner in the oven, Blythe and TJ on their way from the airport, Matt and Grandpa Lee on the golf course, and Lynellen and Grandma Kate chatting in the living room,

Kylie found a few minutes to log on to the computer and check her E-mail. Scanning her in-box, she found a post from Marilee Domotor and quickly opened it to read what her dear friend had to say.

Hiya, Kylie,

I can't believe my wedding is just a couple of weeks away. I'm so excited. I'll finally be Mrs. Logan Callahan! Write back and let me know how married life is going for you.

Did I tell you Patrice lost her baby? It was all so sad. Patrice was more disappointed than either Logan or I, and, of course, our first and foremost concern was for Patrice's health. But she's feeling better now. She's still working at church and really likes it. I'm grateful God has allowed her to stay in a Christian setting.

As for children, Logan and I are focusing on the youth group, and we're planning several community outreaches. God has also been working in my heart about foster care. So many kids in the Chicago area need stable environments in which to live, and while Logan and I wouldn't push our faith on anyone, we could show these children Christlike love. Even though I can't have babies of my own, I sense that God is going to fill my world with many, many children.

Kylie sat back and smiled. Had it really only been two months since she and Marilee took their trip to South Carolina? They'd laughed most of the way there. And though they hadn't known one another before their little escapade, Kylie and Marilee had bonded in a way that seemed to seal their friendship forever. Even now, Kylie laughed to herself when she thought of how everyone said she and Marilee were crazy to take off on that trip. However, only the Lord knew that it was journey of healing—for both of them.

Oh, God, that's what my grandparents need. And Blythe, too. They need to heal from all their hurts. I have no idea what that's going to entail. Kylie grinned. *But You do!*

CHAPTER TWENTY-SEVEN

W ait!"
Kylie pivoted on the sidewalk and frowned. "Blythe,
you are not going to stop me from throwing this box of stuff
in the Dumpster."

"I'm afraid I am." Blythe gave her a pleading look. She'd
fairly chased Kylie from the second floor. "The contents of
that box came from Wendy's closet. Let me just look through
it before you toss it, okay? I'd hate for you to lose something
valuable."

"Not a chance, and I already rummaged through it. All
that's in this box is crumpled up notebook paper and outdated magazines."

"Why would Wendy hang onto those items if they
weren't important?"

"Good question." Kylie arched a dark brow. "It's one that
Matt, Lynellen, and I have been asking for weeks."

Blythe smiled. "Please, Kylie, let me look."

"Oh, fine." With a roll of her eyes, she deposited the box into Blythe's arms and headed for the house.

The items, however, proved heavier than Blythe realized, and she dropped the cardboard container on the gravel driveway.

"Oh, I'm sorry." Kylie rushed back to help her.

"This weighs a ton. How did you manage to carry it?"

"I'm just strong, I guess." Kylie sent her an impish grin. "How 'bout I carry it to the picnic table for you?"

Before Blythe could answer, TJ emerged from the garage. "You ladies need some help?"

"Well, I don't, but Blythe does." Kylie elbowed her and smirked.

Blythe sent her a quelling look. She could tell her lovely daughter had matchmaking on her mind; however, Blythe didn't feel sure she was interested. She liked TJ very much, but her future seemed so uncertain. A romance was the last thing she needed to contend with.

TJ was suddenly standing beside her. "What can I assist you with?"

"Um. . .this box. Would you carry it to the picnic table for me?"

"Sure thing."

He lifted it off the ground and Blythe smiled to herself. TJ might have replied, *Your wish is my command.* He sort of resembled one of those fabled genies who appeared from out of a magic lamp. Then again, Blythe had never known genies to wear dark blue jeans and a light blue polo shirt.

"I'll leave you to your picking," Kylie quipped, making her way into the house.

She disappeared through the back door and Blythe hovered over the box, lifting out exactly what had been described to her as "crumpled notebook paper and outdated magazines." She lifted the glossy publications out and noticed the dates on each one. 1992.

Blythe pointed it out to TJ. "If I'm not mistaken, that's the year Josh died."

"Hmm. . .maybe saving those magazines was Wendy's way of remembering what was happening in the world at that time."

"Could be."

"Say, would you like a cup of coffee?"

"No thanks." Blythe shook her head in a simultaneous reply. She tried not to indulge in anything containing caffeine after dinner. Now, seeing that it was nearly 7:15, she knew if she drank coffee she'd never sleep tonight. "But if you're going into the kitchen, I'll take a glass of ice water."

"You got it."

"Thanks, TJ."

Smiling at his retreating form, Blythe had to admit he was a kindhearted guy and the likes of him weren't easily found in this day and age. Even so, she felt hesitant about pursuing anything more than a friendship.

Back to the task at hand, Blythe pulled out the crumpled spiral notebook. It appeared to have been haphazardly tossed into the box. Flipping through the pages, she noticed some penciled writing. It had faded with the years and was nearly impossible to read.

Dear Mom,

Blythe made out those two words easily enough. She wondered if Kylie had written them.

But then she discerned the bulleted points and the chicken scratch beneath them. Her heart skipped a beat.

- *Rob died 8/28/68*
  (Relay details.)
  I don't blame you and Dad anymore. Rob and I made decisions independent of anything you said or did. My only true regret was that Rob died never knowing Christ.
- *My conversion*
  I'm a Christian. Happened December of '68. My friend Jack Callahan showed me from the Bible how to be "saved." Being saved is more than just the religion I grew up with; it's all about knowing Jesus Christ like I know my best friend. (Elaborate.)
- *Josh*
  I married a wonderful man. Josh is a Christian and a medical doctor. He's the center of my life, along with our daughter.
- *Kylie*
  She's 23 and almost finished with college. She's smart, but sometimes, like today, she reminds me of you, Mom. Other times, I see glimpses of Rob.

Blythe blinked back the tears gathering in her eyes. She carefully tore the pages out of the notebook and tried to smooth away their wrinkles. She guessed this was a rough draft of a letter Wendy had once intended to send Kathryn.

"Kathryn." Blythe spoke the name out loud, realizing this letter would soothe the older woman's broken heart. Blythe felt oddly privileged to be the one to have discovered it. She hugged the pages to her chest just as TJ stepped outside. She gave him a smile. "I'll be right back."

"You okay?"

She nodded as she passed him.

Traipsing through the house, Blythe ran up the steps and then dodged plastic garbage bags lining the hallway.

"Kathryn?"

"In here."

Entering what was once Wendy's bedroom, Blythe paused, seeing Kathryn's expectant look.

"What is it, Blythe?"

"I, um, found something you need to see." She held out the creased notebook paper.

"What did you find?" Kylie asked, coming behind Blythe.

"It's a letter. From Wendy. . .to you, Kathryn."

"What?" The older woman dropped the dust rag she'd been holding and crossed the room. She took the proffered pages, and a tentative frown creased her brow. "Dare I read this missive?" Her mournful gaze searched Blythe's face.

"Actually, no. On second thought, you shouldn't read it. The print is much too light. You'll never make it out or you'll strain your eyes trying." Blythe grinned, unable to squelch the excitement that plumed inside of her. "I'll read it aloud so you both can hear."

She reclaimed the papers and, after a smile at Kylie, proceeded. When she finished, tears streamed down Kathryn's age-lined cheeks.

"Let me see." Kylie took the notebook paper and inspected each sheet. "Yep. This is Mom's handwriting."

Blythe smiled at Kathryn. "You see? Wendy didn't hate you. She attempted to write to you. This is all deductive reasoning, of course, but my thinking is Josh got sick, then died, and Wendy forgot all about this draft. From the looks of it, the magazines were tossed in the box on top of the notebook." Blythe watched Kylie give the letter back to her grandmother. "The magazines were dated the year Josh died."

"Really?" At Blythe's nod, a rueful shadow crept over Kylie's face. "My dad went so fast that Mom and I were in shock for months afterwards."

"I know the feeling." Blythe put an arm around Kylie's shoulders. "But when Josh died, I was in New York at an art show. I sent Wendy my condolences, knowing even if I were home it wouldn't have been appropriate for me to attend Josh's funeral."

"Understandable, given the situation."

The two exchanged sad smiles before looking at Kathryn. Despite her heartrending expression, the older woman's hazel eyes shone with something akin to happiness.

"This is answered prayer," Kathryn announced. "It's what has kept me here, in Wendy's house, among all her things." She held up the notebook pages, crimped with time. "These. I asked God to let me find *something*, something that would put peace in my soul. This—this letter, even though it's unfinished and unsigned—it means the world to me. It's now my most prized possession."

Kathryn glanced at the letter again, then headed for the bedroom door. "I must show Lee. . . ."

Seconds of silence ticked by as Blythe and Kylie regarded each other.

"And to think I almost threw out that box."

Blythe laughed, feeling glad she'd made a nuisance of herself over the tossing away of such. . .*precious things*.

"Guess I'd better be more careful." Kylie became momentarily pensive. "What might seem like trash on the outside can turn out to be something valuable on the inside."

"That's right." Blythe smiled. "I've made my living on that very premise."

Kylie smacked her palm against her forehead. "Yeah, duh!"

They both laughed.

———◦◦◦———

The next morning, the delectable smell of coffee and fresh-baked cinnamon rolls awoke Blythe. Throwing off the bedcovers, she padded to the door and peeked into the hallway. Seeing it was empty, as was the bathroom at the far end, she decided to shower and dress before making her way downstairs. When at last she did reach the kitchen, some forty-five minutes later, Blythe met Lynellen, Kylie, and Matt, all sitting around the table.

"I guess I'm the last one up, huh?"

"We're all early risers, Blythe." Matt grinned. "Milking's already done by this time every day."

"Yep, and when Matt gets up, everybody gets up." Kylie leaned over and touched his arm. "Right, honey?"

He replied with an annoyed look and Kylie laughed.

"Blythe, sit down," Lynellen urged. "I'll get you some coffee. Help yourself to a frosted cinnamon roll."

"Mmm, my mouth has been watering for the last hour."

Smiling, Lynellen strode from the room, and Matt sat forward.

"I thought we'd attend church in La Crosse this morning. I already phoned the Rollinses' place and told the Chadwyks and TJ. They should be here any minute."

"Sounds fine."

"The Rollinses' place. . ." Kylie shook her head. "You're going to have to quit calling it that. The Rollinses don't exist anymore."

"Sure they do." Blythe licked off icing stuck to her lower lip. "They exist through you and all of us who loved them."

"Yeah, Ky." Matt tossed a challenging glance in his wife's direction. "And just for the record, Blythe, I don't insist Kylie get up with me at the crack of dawn. She's a light sleeper."

"Matt!" Kylie frowned, looking insulted.

He shrugged. "I just wanted to explain."

Blythe waved off the remark, not wanting to offend either one or land in the middle of a spat.

In the next moments that passed, she took in the décor of the dining room. She'd been admiring the old farmhouse for the last forty-eight hours.

Lynellen entered the room.

"You'll have to give me the lowdown on this place," Blythe said. "I'm enthralled by it."

"I'd be happy to." Lynellen set the steaming cup of coffee in front of Blythe, then seated herself next to Kylie. "I'm proud of this house. Parts of it are ninety years old, and I'm sure you're able to tell by the way the floorboards creak."

Kylie nodded and Matt sent her a hooded glance. In reply, she sent him a sassy grin.

Blythe couldn't suppress a wide smile. She'd noticed on several occasions how Kylie and Matt teased each other. But Blythe had witnessed the more serious moments between them, too. It was apparent that Matt was good for Kylie and vice versa—just as Wendy had said. What's more, it did

Blythe's heart good to see two people so in love.

Just then, voices filled the kitchen, and TJ's thunderous laughter made its way into the dining room.

"Well, it sounds like everyone's here now," Lynellen said as she pushed back her chair and stood. "As soon as TJ and the Chadwyks have some breakfast, we'll be good to go."

She sauntered off toward the kitchen, and Kylie and Matt got up to make room for the entering guests. Blythe scooted her chair over to the right to aid their efforts.

"Good morning, everyone!" Lee was the first to enter the dining room. He looked quite dapper in his dark, charcoal-colored suit with French-blue shirt and coordinating tie.

Blythe smiled a greeting and sipped her coffee.

TJ entered next, wearing black trousers, a graphite-colored suit coat, and a burgundy band-collared shirt. His blue-eyed gaze roamed the room and settled on Blythe.

She grinned at him.

"Man, you guys are dressed to the nines." Matt let out a long, slow whistle for emphasis. "Guess I'd better change clothes."

"Yeah, me, too."

Kylie followed Matt out. Both still had on blue jeans and T-shirts.

Wonder if she's had any luck convincing Matt to move to South Carolina. Blythe sipped her coffee as she pondered the question.

"You seem miles away," TJ remarked, sitting down next to her.

Blythe laughed, embarrassed that he noticed. "Oh, it's Kylie and Matt. They amuse me."

TJ grinned.

"Ah, yes, young love," Lee said, sitting down across the

way. "It's enjoyable to watch it bloom and grow."

Blythe wondered how the Chadwyks would feel if Matt decided to stay in Wisconsin. On a number of occasions, Blythe had overheard Kathryn encouraging Kylie to move by listing Charleston and Sabal Beach's many attributes. Blythe was determined to stay out of it; she had her own selfish reasons for hoping Kylie stayed on this farm—although, if Blythe took Twila's offer and relocated to Houston. . .

"Blythe! I just heard about Wendy's letter!" Lynellen strolled into the dining room with Kathryn at her side. "Good thing you didn't let Kylie pitch that box of stuff."

Blythe smiled.

"A godsend to be sure," Kathryn added. "Although, I have been wondering why Wendy never got around to actually writing the final version and mailing it." That strained, fretful look had reentered her hazel eyes.

Blythe's heart went out to the lady.

"Maybe Wendy *thought* she sent it," Lynellen replied. "Maybe in all the hustle and bustle, she had a memory lapse. I mean, I can vouch for the fact Wendy got a little spacey after Josh passed away. Call it shock, part of the mourning process—label it whatever you want. I got that way, too, after my husband died."

Blythe lowered her gaze and stared into her coffee. She'd lost at least the three months following Rob's death, probably more. What a blessing that Wendy had taken it upon herself to look after her—and unborn Kylie.

"Oh, my soul! Is it worse to think Wendy believed we never replied to her letter?"

"Kathryn, stop torturing yourself." Lee stood and pulled

out a chair for his wife. "Sit down and eat something. Have a cup of coffee."

Kathryn did as he bid her.

Meanwhile, a sinking feeling settled over Blythe. Was it going to be her fault that she found Wendy's unfinished letter? Another thing against her in the Chadwyks' eyes, not that Blythe really cared what the older couple thought of her. But it would be nice if they could get along, seeing they each desired a relationship with Kylie.

Blythe moved her chair back, picked up her dishes, and left the room. Setting her plate by the sink, she took her coffee and wandered outside. The air was thick, laden with humidity, and the raw, defining smell of cows, mud, and fertilizer converged on her senses. Deciding it wasn't unpleasant, just very natural for the country, Blythe made her way across the yard. She paused to admire the pastoral scenery before her, a gently rolling hill, a cluster of blossoming apple trees below it, just a glimpse of the gray ribbon of highway behind the orchard. Little wonder that Lynellen had chosen that location for her mobile home.

"Blythe!"

Hearing TJ's deep, resounding voice, she turned and watched as he strode toward her.

Reaching her, he set his hands on his hips, breathed deeply, and gazed out over the yard. "Mmm, love that smell of cow pies."

The sarcastic quip made Blythe laugh.

TJ shook his smooth, bald head. "I don't know how Matt does it. I'm not much of an animal lover myself, and I'm partial to seafood over beef, cheese, and milk."

"Some men are made to farm and some aren't."

"Amen to that."

Again, Blythe chuckled. TJ was another person who amused her.

His blue eyes suddenly regarded her with an intense light. All humor vanished. "I sense you got offended by something that just happened in there," he said, inclining his head toward the house. "Kathryn was ecstatic over that letter last night. This morning she's singing the blues again. But I'm thinking it's just her way of dealing with all the pain she's carried around for thirty-plus years."

"I'm sure you're right."

Blythe shifted her gaze to the apple orchard and took a sip of her now-lukewarm coffee. She felt weary of extending leniencies to everyone else when she herself hadn't been afforded a single one! Garth had dealt with her with an iron fist. Blythe was still reeling from the blow.

Molten-hot tears burned in the backs of her eyes, but she blinked them away. Maybe instead of attending church this morning, she should drive back to Chicago and start figuring out what to do with the rest of her life.

Suddenly she felt TJ's hand on her shoulder. "Thanks for allowing God to use you, Blythe. You've blessed the Chadwyks in a lot of ways, giving them Rob's things, finding that letter Wendy started to write. Lee and I were discussing it last night after you returned here to the farm, and we both agreed you didn't have to do any of the things you've done. But I know the Chadwyks are grateful. I am, too, because I care so much for Lee and Kathryn."

"Not a problem," Blythe replied out of a sense of propriety. But obviously, TJ wasn't a mind reader.

"Now what can we do for you?"

"What?" She glanced his way, wearing a confused frown.

"You, know, with the situation involving your uncle—what can we do to help you?"

She shook her head. "Nothing. There's nothing anyone can do, but thanks for the offer."

Blythe dumped the remainder of her coffee onto the lawn and stepped out from under TJ's touch. She felt like dissolving into tears. Perhaps it was a good thing profound acts of kindness didn't come her way too often. She'd be a blithering idiot.

Without another word, she strode back to the house.

CHAPTER TWENTY-EIGHT

TJ sat in church, not paying as much attention as he should while the good pastor expounded on a passage in the book of Isaiah. But his thoughts were in a jumble over Blythe. TJ sensed she'd erected an emotional fortress around herself and he felt bad about it. The Chadwyks had hurt her and her uncle had decimated her. Shoot, given the circumstances, who wouldn't struggle with forgiveness? He thought of their ride home from the airport and decided it was to her credit that she could even admit it. However, she was about to flee this morning. TJ was just glad Kylie managed to talk her into staying and attending church with them. It seemed Kylie was the one person who still had access to Blythe's heart, and TJ rather wished he shared the privilege.

He gave himself a mental shake. How odd for him to feel that way. There was good reason he was fifty-two years old and still a bachelor. No woman had captured his interest long enough for him to think about a serious relationship. Then Blythe came along, a little sparrow of a woman with shining dark eyes and a gentle disposition, and suddenly TJ found himself smitten—and he hadn't even wanted to like her in the first place.

Ah, the ironies of life. . .

"Even to your old age I am He, and even to gray hairs will I carry you."

TJ glanced at his Bible, hearing the reading from the Scriptures. He smiled. Those were some powerful promises. He stole a glance down the pew at Blythe. Maybe they'd touch her heart the way they touched his.

Walking out of the Sunday morning worship service, Blythe felt like sobbing, and not because she still felt sorry for herself, but because God was so loving and merciful. If Blythe longed for grace, she'd received it fourfold. The Lord was able to provide and protect. Blythe was reminded her future was safe in His hands.

Blythe slipped in behind the wheel of her minivan. Since she possessed the largest vehicle, Kylie requested that Blythe drive so they could all ride to church together—that was after she convinced Blythe not to leave this morning. Buckling her seat belt, Blythe decided Matt was in big trouble. How could he deny his bride a single thing?

Blythe started the engine as TJ climbed into the passenger seat. The Chadwyks sat in the middle bench seat, while Kylie, Matt, and Lynellen filed into the farthest backseat.

Once everyone was settled, Blythe pulled out of the church's parking lot.

Lynellen called directions to Blythe, who drove to the restaurant. Eating out after church, Lynellen explained, was an Alexander tradition.

They supped at a quaint local eatery, and afterward Blythe took everyone back to the farm. The rest of the day's plans called for a change of clothes. Then she and the Alexanders would head over to Kylie's former home where they'd meet TJ and the Chadwyks. There, they would all finish packing and setting up for the giant estate sale scheduled to run for a week, beginning next Saturday. Blythe decided to go along with the setup. She could return to Chicago tomorrow. It wasn't as if she had a job she needed to get back to— or a shop to run.

Forgive me, Father, for sinking into self-pity again.

By the time they arrived at the home in which Kylie had been raised, the sky had turned a dismal gray. The weather didn't appear threatening, although it did look like rain.

"I'm all about a good thunderstorm," TJ said, rubbing his palms together in anticipation.

"Tell you what," Lee offered, "I'll go into the den and flip on the TV so we can check out the latest forecast."

As the older man sauntered out of the kitchen, TJ winked at Blythe. "It's really time for his catnap. He has no intention of watching the weather."

"I heard that!"

Blythe smiled at TJ's chagrined expression.

"You know," Kathryn said with a remarkable look on her face, "for a man his age, Lee's hearing is really quite good."

Everyone laughed, and so went the beginnings of the

afternoon. Blythe busied herself with helping Kylie in the upstairs bedrooms. Kathryn sorted items in the adjacent attic space. However, within the hour it had grown eerily dark outside.

Kylie peered out the window. "I think we're in for a doozy."

Kathryn stepped out of the attic area. "We're going to get some rain, huh?"

As the words left her lips, TJ appeared at the doorway of the master bedroom. His handheld video camera was strapped to his palm. "Who wants to come watch the storm brew? The National Weather Service has issued a tornado watch and everything!"

"No, thank you." Kathryn shook her head.

"I'm not interested, either. Blythe, you go."

She sent Kylie a knowing glance. *The matchmaker strikes again*. Turning to TJ, she, too, refused the offer. "And if this watch becomes a warning, I'll be the first one in the basement."

"Ah, c'mon, you chicken." TJ crossed the distance between them and tugged on the belt loop of Blythe's jeans.

She sent him an annoyed look.

His blue eyes twinkled. "I recall a certain discussion we had about a month ago—something about having a *pushy* friend. You remember?"

Blythe felt her cheeks warm with embarrassment. She remembered, all right, although she didn't feel like relaying their private conversation to Kylie and her grandmother, who both now regarded her with curious stares. And Blythe had a feeling her sweet daughter would get it out of her, too.

"Yeah, well, um. . ."

A faint rumble of thunder sounded from not too far off.

"C'mon, we're gonna miss the show!"

TJ grabbed Blythe's hand and pulled her into the hallway. As they descended the steps, she heard Kylie's laughter.

"TJ, I'm really not a storm-chasing person."

"Maybe I'll convert you."

She rolled her eyes, but then gave in. TJ was about as insistent as Kylie.

"Now, listen, if there's a tornado, I want you to get a picture of me with the twister in the background."

"Are you crazy?" Blythe jogged alongside him as they headed for the road. "If there's a tornado, I will be running for the basement—or the nearest ditch."

"Ah, Blythe, be a good sport. I have a friend in Oklahoma who runs a storm-chasing business. He and I are always trying to one-up each other and he just sent me the coolest photo—"

"Where are we going?"

They had crossed the highway and were presently descending a short embankment. A wooded area lay ahead of them.

"Matt said there's an open field on the other side of this woods. . .said it'd be a good place to see the storm come in."

"Yay."

TJ laughed at her sarcasm. "Now, Blythe," he chided her in fun, "I'm the friend who's gonna push you off that proverbial cliff and help you do some real living. Remember? That's what you said you wanted."

"I know, but I'd like to eat my words right about now."

He chuckled again as they tromped through the brush. Then they reached the edge of the trees and skirted several boulders. They traipsed over fieldstones. TJ took Blythe's hand and helped her up a rocky incline before they finally arrived in the grassy pasture.

About half a mile later, he stopped and pointed off to the

right, where giant black clouds roiled towards them. TJ filmed the sight for a few minutes and Blythe was mesmerized. Part of her felt frightened, tempted to run, and yet she felt rooted by the magnificence and power she saw in the sky.

"Listen."

Blythe strained to hear. Nothing. All was still. "God's creatures have more sense than we do, TJ."

He just laughed.

Blythe, on the other hand, didn't think it was funny. She glanced off to her left and determined that it was ten minutes back to the house. This was a very stupid endeavor.

Suddenly a bolt of lightning ripped through the heavens.

"Oh, that's awesome!"

"TJ, that was right over our heads!"

Thunder crashed and shook the very ground on which they stood. Another fork of lightning lit the sky.

"That's it. Too close for comfort." TJ shut off his camera. "We're outta here."

Blythe turned around to go back the way they'd come, but TJ caught her wrist.

"This way."

"What?"

The wind picked up and whipped around them. A painful blend of raindrops and hail began to fall.

"We'll take shelter in that barn over there."

"What barn?"

Blythe didn't recall seeing any such thing, although she didn't protest as TJ led her down a grassy slope.

At the bottom, she saw it. Not a barn, but the ruins of a barn.

She halted, tugging at his hold on her hand. "I'm not

going in there." Icy droplets pelted her face and shoulders, causing her to grimace. "It's not safe!"

"It's not safe out here, either. The way I figure, this barn already fell down, and since it butts up against a hill. . ."

Blythe couldn't make out the rest of his sentence as he pulled her through an opening in the stone foundation. Soon they found a place where the structure's wooden floor had caved in, forming a triangular shelter. However, it was standing room only in a space that was never intended for one human being, let alone two.

Meanwhile, the rain fell in torrents, and the hail bounced off the rotten wood above them, sounding like a shower of Ping-Pong balls. The temperature had turned from balmy to chilly in a single gust. Wearing only a short-sleeved shirt over her jeans, Blythe wished she would have thought to grab a sweatshirt. She shivered from both the cold and dampness and from the fear that the remainder of the barn would crash down on their heads.

Lord, if You let us live, I promise I'll never complain again!

She almost laughed at the childish prayer, but it was all she could think of at the moment.

TJ wrapped his large arms around her. The camera he held in one hand rested on his opposite forearm.

At the physical contact, Blythe tensed. She wasn't accustomed to such closeness. She didn't like it.

Why? She was fond of TJ. He was just being kind.

As if to prove it, he asked, "Are you all right, Blythe?"

"Yes." It was a fib. Her insides were anything but "all right." She wanted out of TJ's embrace and this dilapidated barn.

She wanted out of this situation!

Oh, God. . .

For whatever odd reason, every date she had in the last twenty years flashed before her eyes. None had ever resulted in more than polite good-night kisses. When the relationship heated up to a point that warranted commitments, Blythe's blood ran cold and she broke things off.

Out of fear.

But fear of what? Happiness?

Blythe had never considered the root of the matter until now. In the past, she cited the weaknesses or character flaws of the male pursuants as the reasons for the breakups. But had it been her fear of loving someone, then losing him, like she'd lost Rob, that kept her from giving her heart to another man?

Now, as she contemplated the issue, she wondered what would happen if she allowed herself to enjoy this moment in TJ's arms.

Maybe the barn really would fall in on them.

And then she realized it: She feared God's wrath the same way she had feared her uncle's all these years. Her parents', too. Lydia's. But it wasn't a healthy sort of fear, born out of respect. It was a fear that God, like all other authoritative figures in her life, would punish and reject her the minute she displeased Him.

No, Lord, I know that's pretzel logic. Twisted thinking. You're the One who said, "I have loved you with an everlasting love. . . ."

Her spirit warred against demonic lies. Closing her eyes, Blythe recalled a New Testament passage that stated, "Perfect love casts out fear."

Another loud clap of thunder resounded. It seemed to shake Blythe to her core. She winced and TJ's arms tightened around her. When the last of the ancient barn didn't collapse, she forced herself to relax.

"It's getting lighter. Won't be long and the storm'll be over."

He was right. Daylight had returned; however, the rain still poured down.

"I can now relate to the disciples when they became afraid in the boat during a storm on the sea."

"And what was Jesus doing the whole while?"

Blythe grinned. "Sleeping."

"When the disciples woke Him up, He calmed the wind and the waves and said—"

" 'Oh, you of little faith.' "

"Yep. Nothing like a good storm to strengthen a person's trust in the very God who created it."

"Thanks for the illustration."

Smiling, Blythe managed to turn around and face TJ. Immediately, she realized her mistake in doing so. He was close. So close. . .

His blue eyes searched her face for an instant. Then he bent his head until his lips touched hers. Delightful tingles shimmied down her spine. But suddenly, a thunderous crack shattered the moment.

Blythe jumped back. Wide-eyed, heart pounding, she stared up at TJ.

He grinned. "That was some kiss!"

She blinked, confused.

He explained. "There are those folks who hear birds singing or bells ringing. We hear thunderclaps." His gaze darkened, and he whispered, "Guess it's meant to be."

Before Blythe's brain could even form a reply, he kissed her once more. She lost herself in the heady sensation and decided at this rate, it could rain for hours. But all too soon, they heard the drone of a vehicle's engine, and then Matt's pickup came into view. He'd driven into the field from the opposite direction.

Releasing Blythe, TJ handed her his camera before stepping out into the rain. Putting two fingers in his mouth, he produced an ear-splitting whistle that stopped the truck. Matt spotted them and backed up.

TJ opened the passenger-side door and motioned to Blythe. She shielded the camera under her shirt. Then, with a strange mix of relief and regret, she dashed from out of the decrepit, falling-down barn.

<hr />

Kylie lay in bed with her brain going a mile a minute. She thought of TJ and Blythe. They liked each other a lot. She grinned and thought of her grandparents. Things seemed to be better between them and Blythe.

Stretched out on her right side, Kylie yawned. Her back was to Matt, but she could tell he wasn't sleeping either. He'd be snoring otherwise. But now the darkened room seemed all too quiet as their thoughts kept them awake.

At last, Kylie's curiosity got the better of her. She rolled onto her back.

"What are thinking about, Matt?"

"How do you know I'm thinking?"

"Why do you always answer my question with another question?" The habit really irritated her. Kylie rolled onto her side again.

"I don't *always* do that."

Kylie mouthed the word *whatever* in a silent reply.

The minutes ticked by and she tried in vain to sleep.

"Hey, Ky?"

"What?"

"You sorry we got married?"

"No!" She frowned and flopped onto her back once more. She lolled her head in Matt's direction. "Why are you asking me that?"

"Because every night you sleep with your back to me."

"I do?"

"Yep."

Kylie thought it over. "I don't mean anything by it. I guess I just prefer sleeping that way. Should we switch sides of the bed? Then I'd sleep facing you."

"Yeah, maybe."

A tide of compassion rose up in Kylie and she snuggled against Matt. "I love you. Don't ever think I don't."

He kissed the top of her head. "I love you, too. And I want you to be happy. But every time you make a wisecrack about the farm or this house, it's like a knife in my gut. I'm supposed to be the provider, and I haven't provided what you want."

"Matt, that's not true. We just got married. We're figuring things out as we go. And. . .I'm happy." Kylie hated the tentative note she heard in her own voice when she spoke those last two words. She cleared her throat and tried again. "I'm happy being married to you."

"But you're not happy *here,* are you?"

"Well. . ." She searched her heart. "I'm not as unhappy as I was a month ago."

"Guess that's something."

With her head on his shoulder, her arm draped across his midsection, Kylie heard Matt's deep, resigning sigh.

"You know, I love you more than anything, Ky. More than this farm. More than Basil Creek. If you really aren't happy here, and you truly want to move, then we will."

"Really?" Kylie smiled and raised herself up on her elbow. "Really, Matt?"

"Yep. If you're not happy, I'm not happy. I've known that for some time—since the day I fell in love with you, actually. But I realized it again just now."

"Oh, thank you!"

She peppered his face with kisses until he laughed. Then she nestled beside him. In a matter of minutes, she felt drowsy, and Kylie was certain she'd fall asleep with a smile on her face before long.

CHAPTER TWENTY-NINE

Monday morning dawned with blue skies and sunshine. Yesterday's thunderstorm was but a mere memory—and a fond one at that. Blythe didn't think she'd ever forget it.

In the kitchen of the farmhouse, she helped Lynellen prepare breakfast. They ate together and shared sections of the daily newspaper. After their meal, Blythe offered to wash dishes. It took a bit of cajoling, but Lynellen finally accepted. Once the task was completed, Blythe ambled outside and pulled her cell phone from her van. Turning on the device, she listened to the recorded voice messages.

Three of them were from Garth. The latest came in this morning.

"I really must speak with you, my dear. Every day the shop is closed costs me money. I've set up a meeting at Archie's office for two o'clock this afternoon. I trust you'll be there."

Blythe glanced at her wristwatch, noting it was after nine. She'd never make it to Chicago by two, and she didn't quite understand why Garth hadn't opened Precious Things—unless he had no one to run the place. If that was the case, Blythe decided it wasn't her problem. However, out of courtesy, she phoned Archie's office.

"No, we can't postpone the meeting," the attorney said, once she got him on the line. "I'm in court the rest of the week."

"Archie, you don't understand. I'm visiting friends in Northwestern Wisconsin. I can't get to Chicago by two o'clock this afternoon."

"Can you make it by five? How 'bout six? I'm working late tonight anyway. If Garth agrees—"

"All right. Six it is. And my uncle has no choice but to agree, unless he can meet me somewhere other than your office and without you in attendance."

"No, that won't work. There are legalities involved."

"What sort of legalities?" Blythe couldn't stem her curiosity.

But Archie dodged the question, shrewd lawyer that he was. "We'll discuss them this evening. See you later."

With that, he disconnected.

Blythe ended the call on her mobile phone. Somewhat agitated, she reentered the house and climbed the stairs. In the bedroom she'd been occupying, she packed her things. Funny how twenty-four hours made a world of difference. Yesterday she'd wanted to leave, but today the thought of returning to Chicago saddened her.

Carrying her suitcase downstairs, she happened upon Lynellen, who was getting ready to drive over to see if Kylie and Kathryn needed help. She wore a melancholy expression, and after Blythe explained her situation and her need to return home, Lynellen appeared downright miserable.

"It's been nice having you here."

Blythe smiled. "I've enjoyed my stay."

"I don't know if you heard, but Matt decided to sell the farm," Lynellen said as she and Blythe walked from the house to the driveway where their vehicles were parked. "He's in the barn and told me the news just now."

At once, Blythe understood the reason behind Lynellen's remorse. She didn't know what to say, so she hugged the woman, hoping the embrace would make up for her loss of words.

"Keep in touch, okay?"

"I will."

"Are you following me over to the other place?"

Blythe nodded. She had more good-byes to say.

Lynellen slid behind the wheel of her Buick. Likewise, Blythe climbed into her minivan and started the engine. She recalled what Twila said about the world being a smaller place, what with the aid of cell phones and the Internet. Blythe supposed that's how she and Kylie would have to stay in contact after she and Matt relocated to South Carolina.

And what about me, Lord? Where will I spend the rest of my life?

Minutes later, Blythe pulled in the drive of the two-story house and parked behind Lynellen. TJ stepped out of the garage, tossed a box into the Dumpster, then gave Blythe a sheepish grin.

"Don't worry. It wasn't anything valuable. It was a hedge-trimming unit that didn't work. I tried to get it running, but—"

"Save your breath." Smiling, she held out her hand, halting

further explanation. "That's more than I want to know."

The glib reply made Lynellen smile. She turned and blew a kiss in Blythe's direction. "Drop me an E-mail once in a while."

"Will do."

She watched as Lynellen strode to the house just as TJ stepped forward.

"Going somewhere?"

"Actually, yes. I came over to say good-bye."

TJ moved in closer, then leaned against the open door of her minivan. "Hope it wasn't anything I said—or did."

"No." Blythe grinned. "It was actually something my uncle said. He wants to meet with me at his attorney's office this evening. I don't know what's up, but I guess I'll find out this evening."

TJ stared across the yard and pursed his lips for a long moment. "Well, I hope all goes well."

"Me, too."

He looked back at her and Blythe saw the questions in his blue eyes. She tore her gaze from his. She didn't have any answers.

"I'll be in Chicago with the Chadwyks at the end of the month for a wedding. We're driving back to Sabal Beach from there. Can I call you?"

"Sure. I'd like that." She smiled and glanced at him.

"Well, now, wait a sec. Maybe I can do better than that."

Blythe chuckled. She could practically see the gears turning inside his shiny, bald head.

"Will you attend the wedding with me. . .come as my date?"

"Whose wedding?"

"Marilee Domotor's. She's a friend of Kylie's. The two of

them stayed at The Light House this past March, so that's how the Chadwyks and I got invited."

"Hmm, well, I don't personally know Marilee or her fiancé, Logan Callahan, but I know Logan's father, Jack. Both Jack and his wife, Allie, were once close friends of mine. Allie and I graduated from high school together."

TJ grinned. "Small world. So will you come?"

"I'd be honored, although I do have one small favor to ask in return." Blythe's mental gears were turning equally as fast as his. "Jack and Allie just got married, and I've been invited to their reception. It's on the twenty-seventh—the Saturday before Marilee's wedding. Will you escort me?"

TJ scratched his jaw and folded his arms across the front of his red T-shirt. "Hmm. . .I don't know, Blythe. You're asking kind of a lot. I mean, if I escorted you to that reception, I'd probably have to hang around Chicago for an entire week until the Chadwyks drove down that following Friday."

Blythe smiled at his teasing. "I'm sure I can think of ways to keep you entertained. There's Navy Pier, the Museum of Science and Industry. . . But don't worry, I won't drag you through any art galleries."

"Whew!" Despite his sigh of relief, there was acquiescence in his smile—and maybe something else.

"Okay, you're on, Blythe. I'll be your date on the twenty-seventh and you'll be my date on June third. . .and maybe we'll be each other's dates a few times in between there, too."

Blythe felt a blush warm her face. "All right. Deal."

"Should we shake on it?" TJ held out his right hand and Blythe grasped it.

Then he leaned towards her and kissed her cheek in gentlemanly fashion.

"Blythe, are you really leaving?" Kylie's voice echoed across the yard. "Lynellen just told me."

TJ dropped her hand. "I'll talk to you later, Blythe." He headed for the garage, then turned around and pointed at her. "And don't forget to check your E-mail."

"Yes, sir." She saluted.

By then Kylie had reached her. Blythe explained the situation, just as she'd told it to TJ.

"But I'll see you soon—at Marilee's wedding." Blythe smiled. "I'm going as TJ's *date.*"

Kylie beamed.

"We're just friends."

"Whatever you say, Blythe."

They hugged, and Blythe felt so privileged to hold her daughter in her arms. It was more than her fondest dream come true. It was an answer to an unspoken prayer from the depths of her heart for the last thirty-one years.

"I love you, Kylie," she said before placing a kiss on her cheek.

"I love you, too, Blythe. I mean it. And I'm so glad we got to spend the weekend together." Her ebony eyes shone with sincerity. "Thanks for all your help."

"My pleasure. Tell your grandparents good-bye for me, all right?"

A moment's hesitation, but at last she nodded.

Another quick embrace, and then Blythe was on her way.

⊲∘∘∘⊳

Kylie picked at her supper while Grandma Kate chatted amicably with Lynellen. Matt had told his mother of his decision to move to Sabal Beach, and so far, she'd taken the news without incident. But Kylie hadn't yet informed her grandparents and TJ, even though she knew they'd be ecstatic. She couldn't tell them. Suddenly leaving this little nothing town on the Mississippi just didn't seem right.

"Ky, want some dessert?" Matt stood and picked up his empty dinner plate.

She shook her head and handed him her all but untouched meal. "I'm not hungry."

After a quizzical look, he walked into the kitchen. A moment later, she excused herself and followed him.

"You okay?" Matt began making a pot of coffee.

"Yeah, I'm fine. . .physically. I'm just having reservations about moving to Sabal Beach. Isn't that weird? I got what I wanted, but now I'm not sure it's really what I want."

Matt gave her a patient grin. "Well, we don't have to move immediately. I mean, I do have to sell this place. That could take awhile."

Kylie mulled it over and backed up to the sink, leaning against it. "This afternoon I started thinking about Ryan and Amber and how they're going to spend the rest of their growing up years in the house I grew up in. It's neat. . . . I mean, I helped raise those kids. Amber is going to have my old bedroom. But if we move, I'll never get to see Ryan's eighth-grade graduation. I'll never see either of them graduate from high school or get married or have kids. . . ."

Matt laughed. "Ky, that is so far out in the future. How do you know we won't have moved back to Basil Creek in that time? Besides. . ." He chuckled again. "There's this invention called an airplane. It takes people long distances in short periods of time. You can fly in and visit Dena any time you want to. . .maybe. . .if I let you."

"Very funny." Kylie noticed her husband certainly seemed to think so. He laughed again and she rolled her eyes.

"Ky, nothing has to be written in stone, okay? If you're unsure, we'll just keep thinking about it. In fact, we probably should be praying about it together." A sheepish look shadowed his features. "But, listen, you've been through a lot, so let's just take things slow."

He kissed her then gave her a playful shove so she'd move out of his way and he could get to the faucet. Once he filled the coffeemaker with water, he flicked the switch and turned to Kylie again.

"I just want you to be happy."

Cupping her face, he gave her another kiss, and it occurred to her that happiness wasn't a place. It was a state of mind.

"You know what, Matt?"

"Hmm?" He smiled into her eyes.

"I think I'll be happy anywhere—as long as I'm with you."

The trip back to Chicago seemed to take hours longer than the drive to Basil Creek. After getting stuck in rush-hour traffic, Blythe didn't even get a chance to stop at home but went directly to Archie's downtown office. At least, in the time she'd spent on the road, she'd come up with a plan, a roadmap for her future. It was one she believed God sanctioned, and one even Lydia would approve as well.

But first things first. Blythe realized she owed her uncle an apology.

Garth stood as she entered the dimly lit boardroom with

its mahogany table surrounded by ten sturdy, matching chairs.

"I'm glad to see you arrived safely," he said.

"Me, too. Traffic was terrible for a Monday." Noticing that her uncle's attorney was temporarily preoccupied in the hallway, Blythe took the time to address the personal matter on her heart. "Uncle Garth, before we get started, I want to say that I'm truly sorry I deceived you. And I did. It's true. I might have had my reasons, but I realize now even they were skewed. Worse, I wasn't trusting the Lord, and I've disappointed you. Will you forgive me?"

"Of course. I forgave you almost immediately. I consider you my very own daughter." One of Garth's dusty gray brows dipped in a frown. "But that doesn't eradicate the consequences."

"I know. I know." Blythe sat and then held out her hand. "I don't need a reprimand."

Before Garth could reply, Archie entered the boardroom. He handed Garth a small stack of papers, then seated himself at the head of the table.

"I'm just here to answer any legal questions," he said. "So, Garth, go ahead and begin whenever you'd like."

"Very well." Garth cleared his throat. "Blythe, as you know, I declared our contract null and void for reasons previously discussed."

She bobbed out a weary reply.

"But had you returned my phone calls, you would have discovered long before today that I never intended to close the shop permanently or let you succumb to poverty as Lydia accused me of this past weekend." Garth gave an indignant sniff. "However, I did what I had to do. It was a matter of principle. That done, I asked Archie to create a new contract for us. The old one is useless, given what occurred; however, this new one will put us both back in business. . .together."

With a satisfied grin, Garth slid the copies of the contract across the table to Blythe, who could only gape at her uncle.

"You did. . .*what?*"

"Which part didn't you hear, my dear?"

"Actually, I heard every word." Blythe shook her head, trying to clear it. "Uncle Garth, I—this is unbelievable."

"No need to thank me; just sign the contract. We'll celebrate by going to Stefani's for dinner. I've already made reservations."

Thank him? She wanted to strangle him! She'd nearly had another nervous breakdown, but he had his principle!

However, her reasoning slowly returned and Blythe admitted that everything she'd endured had been for her own good. God had showed her many things over the last few weeks. He might have allowed her to walk through the fire, but He had walked beside her.

Lifting the contract, she skimmed it. It certainly did seem to her that her troubles would end as soon as she signed, but she couldn't help wondering what her uncle would say if he discovered she'd been holed up inside a ramshackle barn where she kissed TJ with pure abandon. Would he deem that morally wrong? Would he find her a disgrace and declare this new agreement "null and void"? There were many aspects to morality, and Garth tended towards fanaticism. Where did he draw the boundaries? Blythe knew where she drew hers. But she didn't think she wanted her life to be an open book that her uncle had the right to scrutinize.

She pushed the contract and its copies back across the

table. "I can't. . .I won't sign this."

"What?" He sat forward, arms on the table. Then he shook his head. "You don't understand, my dear. Once you sign, you no longer have to pay me back. You won't have to sell the two-flat."

Blythe still refused, although her practical side called her a fool.

"Why won't you sign, Blythe?" Archie drummed his fingers on the polished tabletop. His expression spoke of his impatience.

After a glance at the wiry attorney, she looked back at her uncle. "Uncle Garth, it's very simple. I don't want anyone owning my conscience. Business agreements are one thing, but stipulations and conditions that pervade the soul are another."

"I see. And may I assume you're referring to the moral turpitude clause in this contract?" At Blythe's nod, he said, "I put the condition in all my business treaties. I want to know the people I'm dealing with are on the up-and-up. I have to be a good steward of my funds. I can't invest in dishonest louts who delve into corruption."

"I understand. I really do. I wouldn't dare to tell you to change the way you conduct business. You're very successful. I just know that for me, Jesus Christ has to be Lord of my life and I need to answer to Him—and only Him."

Blythe stood.

Garth stood as well. "But if you don't sign this contract, what will you do?"

"I have a plan. Twila has offered me a position in Houston. I'm going to accept it. Then I'll see my banker and ask for a line of credit. Twila will give me a reference. I'll use that money to get Lydia settled in a new apartment and pay for my moving expenses. Meanwhile, with the sale of the house and after I cash in some mutual funds, I can repay you the sum we agreed on."

"But that's so unnecessary." Her uncle smirked. "Unless you're planning to live a racy lifestyle like your mother and her friends."

Blythe's jaw slackened. "I can't believe you just said that. Well, more's the reason we shouldn't be in business together. If you don't know my heart by now, you never will."

"I'm sorry, Blythe." Garth appeared genuinely contrite. "My last remark was uncalled for."

Her ire up, she strode to the door. Placing her hand on the knob, it suddenly occurred to her that she had expected him to forgive her when she entered this room minutes ago. Now the tables were turned.

She wheeled around to face him. "Apology accepted."

"Good. Now, what about the shop?"

"It's yours. Do whatever you want."

"No, it's yours. It's *you*."

"Not anymore," she replied with a vehement shake of her head. "Maybe once. But, you see, I have a beautiful daughter." She took a step toward him. "I've loved her from the moment I discovered that I carried her in my womb. Developing a relationship with her is priceless to me. If it costs me my shop, my home, my savings, so be it. I'll still be a wealthy woman."

"Funny, that's how I feel about you, Blythe. Our relationship is. . .priceless."

Her uncle's words met their mark and all the fight went out of her. Nevertheless, the sentiment left a bittersweet taste in her mouth.

Archie came up behind her and reached around to open the door. "I'll leave you two to discuss the rest of this matter in private. I'll be in my office down the hall if you need me."

Once he'd gone, Blythe watched her uncle slowly sink back into his chair. She realized they'd never exchanged endearments. She had spent three years with him and Aunt Sabina in Singapore but never fully shared her heart with either of them. After returning to the States, their correspondence largely consisted of letters, phone calls, and then, eventually, E-mails. Most often, they discussed business and rarely personal matters.

"I'm an old man, and Houston is far away."

Blythe felt a stab of guilt, knowing she and Lydia were all the family he had left—and Garth wasn't particularly fond of Lydia. "You're welcome to visit me. You've met Twila. You said you liked her."

Judging by his expression, Garth wasn't appeased. "I've left everything I own to you, Blythe. Archie has my will right here in this office."

"Why are you telling me that? I don't love you for your money, although I have greatly benefited from your generosity. I'm grateful, but—"

"I love you, too, Blythe."

She blinked. She hadn't even realized she'd told her uncle she loved him. The words had just tumbled from her lips.

He loves me, too. . .

"Now then, about the shop. . ."

Blythe drew in a deep breath.

"If you're adamant about a sole proprietorship, how about if you buy Precious Things from me? I can't imagine what I'm going to do with an antique shop, and I abhor the thought of selling it to someone else."

Blythe smiled, feeling suddenly unfettered. She closed her eyes. *Thank You, Lord.* Then she gazed back at Garth. "Name your price."

He rattled off a figure.

Blythe laughed. Her shop was worth three times as much. What's more, the amount was well within her means, although it would take a little bit of doing. But Precious Things was a solid business, and she was well established in the community.

Her confidence grew. "What about the building?"

"You can rent from me." He quoted an amount. "Is that too steep?"

"N—no. I think I can manage it." Again, Blythe wanted to hoot. It was about a quarter of the price of rents near Michigan Avenue. "You've got a deal, Mr. Severson."

"Ah, good. And would you like to borrow off your inheritance?"

"Nope." Blythe lifted her chin. "I'll see my banker in the morning."

Wearing a smirk, her uncle shuffled to his feet. "You're a woman after my own heart, Blythe. I'm proud of you."

She smiled and her spirit soared. Garth's praise was definitely better than his disapproval. "Thank you."

"Would you like to have dinner with me?"

"I'd be happy to." She laughed and hooked her arm through his. "I'll even let you buy."

CHAPTER THIRTY

"Good afternoon, Precious Things."

"Blythe?"

Hearing her daughter's voice, she smiled. It had been several days since they last spoke and almost two weeks since they last saw each other. "Yep, it's me. Hi, Kylie."

"Guess what?"

"What?"

"I closed on my house today, and the estate sale is going great! Dena can't wait until it's over so she can move in."

"Really? Congratulations. We both have cause to celebrate. This morning Garth and I signed the contract that *my* lawyer drafted. Precious Things is really mine!"

"Hooray! That is so cool."

"Oh, Kylie, it's more than cool. It's a veritable miracle. Lydia is still in shock, but I told her God would come through for me. . .for us. He did. What's more, my uncle's testimony has been restored in her eyes. I think Lydia is beginning to wonder if there might be something to Christianity after all."

"I'm smiling so hard right now, my face hurts."

Blythe laughed. "Garth wants to meet you."

"He does? Awesome. I want to meet him, too. My great-uncle."

"Uh-huh. And eventually I think Lydia will come around."

"I'm ready to meet her whenever she's ready to meet me. Now let me tell you some more good news on my end."

"Fire away." Portable phone in hand, Blythe seated herself near the display case she'd recently purchased from a local store soon to be remodeled. "What's up?"

"Matt and I are staying in Basil Creek. On the farm. We're not moving."

A slow smile spread across Blythe's face. She was thrilled to hear it. All along, she'd hated the thought of Kylie moving so far away from her. "But I know you wanted to live in South Carolina. What made you change your mind?"

"You and Matt."

Blythe frowned, feeling confused, and Kylie went on to explain.

"You're two people who really love me. You've made mistakes, but you've also sacrificed for me. You were willing to give up your shop, lose it if it came to that, and Matt was willing to give up the farm—all for me. So when it came down to choices, I picked Basil Creek because I know it's where Matt feels most at home. He wants our kids to grow up on this farm and play in the same yard that he and his siblings romped around. Basil Creek is also closer to Chicago and to. . .*you*."

Joy filled Blythe's heart. "Kylie, I. . .I don't know what to say other than I'm deeply touched. And happy. Really happy." She blinked back sudden tears but then thought of the Chadwyks. "I imagine your grandparents are disappointed."

"Yeah, but they're handling it. They're going to visit us every summer, and Matt and I have promised to visit them twice a year. In January and in fall because TJ said hurricane season is the best time in Sabal Beach."

Blythe hung her head back and laughed. "Oh, and speaking of TJ. . .I'd better scoot. I'm closing the shop right on time so I can meet him for dinner. I have to stop home and change first."

"Getting all dolled up, eh?"

"Well, I want to look my best."

"Just friends, huh?"

Blythe smirked at the teasing; however, she loved every second of it. "Kylie, you're more precious to me than any *thing* I own."

"Ditto. Hey, tell Allie and Jack hello from me when you see them tomorrow night."

"Will do. Good-bye for now." Smiling, Blythe disconnected the call. She didn't think she could ever feel any happier than she did at this precise moment.

<hr />

One week later, the *ting, ting, ting* of glassware rang throughout the magnificent banquet hall. Logan Callahan grinned before gathering his bride in his arms and placing a kiss on her lips. He took his sweet time about it, too, while guests cheered him on.

"Isn't Marilee beautiful?"

Blythe looked to her right at Kylie, then back at the now-blushing bride. "Yes, she is. Marilee and Logan are a stunning couple." Blythe smiled. "Logan looks just like his dad when Jack was that age." She shook her head. "Unbelievable."

"This room is unbelievable," TJ muttered from where he sat at the table to Blythe's left. He looked up. "Get a load of that mammoth crystal chandelier."

Blythe lifted her gaze. "Yes, I was admiring it when we first arrived."

"Marilee's mother wanted the finest wedding for her daughter," Kylie informed them, "bar none."

"I'd say she outdid herself." TJ shook his head. "She even hired a string quartet."

"Those four guys are from Logan's church. Isn't that cool?" Kylie grinned. "As a wedding gift, they offered to play tonight."

"Pretty nice." TJ took a sip of his Diet Coke. "The only musician I know is this guy in Charleston who plays the harmonica."

"Don't even go there," Blythe said with a grin. After spending much of the week with TJ, she could tell when one of his sappy jokes was coming on. Two nights ago, he'd had her laughing so hard at the restaurant she almost choked on her deep-dish pizza. In the course of the last seven days, he even managed to charm Lydia and impress Garth.

Just then, Allie approached their table. Since marrying Jack, she looked so contented. Her sapphire eyes, the same color as her two-piece outfit, shone with a special light. "TJ, would you mind doing me a favor and taking a couple of snapshots?"

"It'd be my pleasure."

Blythe hurled a glance upward. "Allie, you and your pictures."

"She's a troublemaker, all right." Jack stepped up from behind his wife and slipped his arm around Allie's waist. "But I hate to think what my life would be like had she not returned to Oakland Park."

A swell of gratitude filled Blythe's being, and she fixed her gaze on Allie. "You've impacted my life for the better, too."

"Thanks, but all the glory goes to God. I obeyed Him. That's it. And even when I doubted Him with regards to coming back to Chicago, the Lord gave me a consulting job here at a time when I happened to need the work. So thank Him, not me."

"I do thank Him, Allie, but He used you."

She smiled. "Just goes to show you, God really does use broken things. That'd be me."

"Me, too," Kylie admitted. She glanced at Blythe and TJ as Matt put his arm around her shoulders and pulled her close. "All of us."

Next to Blythe, TJ nodded.

Allie smiled. "Now about that picture. . . Don't distract me. Blythe and Jack. . ." She looked at him.

"I know. I've got a job to do. It's as good as done."

He kissed her cheek then took off. TJ stood and lifted his large black leather camera case while Allie pointed to a less-populated corner of the room.

"Okay, pictures. I want one of Blythe, Kylie, Jack, and me, and then a group shot."

Kylie looked puzzled. "Me? Why do you want me in your first picture?"

Allie sent her a wry grin. "Well, you were in the first one, you know?"

Blythe felt her face flush, but she winked at Kylie.

Allie turned back to TJ. "In the second photo I'd like all of us—you, Blythe, Kylie, Matt, Mr. and Mrs. Chadwyk, Logan, Marilee, Patrice, Jack, and me."

"Fine, Allie. I have a timer on my camera, but you'll have to round up everyone."

"Remember that 'job' I sent Jack on?" She smiled. "He's rounding up the troops as we speak."

"All right then."

Blythe pushed her chair and stood. Then, she and TJ walked over to the designated area of the banquet hall. The Chadwyks had been visiting with another older couple, but at Jack's bidding, they strode to the far end of the room. For the first shot, Jack and Allie stood to Blythe's left and Kylie on her other side while TJ set up his tripod and positioned his camera.

"Remember how I told you Matt and I decided to stay in Basil Creek?" Kylie's voice was but a whisper into Blythe's ear.

"Yes."

"Well, it's also going to be awesome that you're within driving distance, because you'll want to visit often once the baby comes."

Blythe wasn't sure she'd heard correctly. "Baby?"

With a smile splitting her lovely, round face, Kylie nodded. "Matt and I are pregnant. We just found out." Her dark eyes clouded with emotion. "Oh, Blythe, it's such a blessing. After Matt and his first wife tried for years and spent thousands of dollars to have a baby, we got pregnant in our first month of marriage." She smiled in spite of her misty eyes.

"Matt is totally excited. I am, too. We've only told a few people for now, but I had to let you know because. . .you're going to be a *grandma!*"

Blythe's heart skipped a beat. "A grandma? But. . ." She paused, thinking she'd given up her rights to motherhood and yet her daughter now offered her a chance to be a grandmother. Tears filled Blythe's eyes, and she wrapped Kylie in an embrace. "Will you really let me be a grandma?" she whispered.

"Of course!" Kylie pulled back. "I'm expecting you to be a grandma."

"Who's expecting?" Allie asked, leaning into Blythe.

"Not me," Blythe teased. "That was in the *last* photograph you took of us together."

Jack overheard and chuckled. "Blythe, I never realized you had such a good sense of humor."

"Oh, I guess certain people just bring it out in me." She looked at TJ and grinned.

He caught her gaze and winked. "All right, people, get ready." His deep voice boomed over the din of the banquet hall. "Jack, keep those ladies from chattering so they hold still."

"Yeah, right. Want me to lasso the moon while I'm at it?"

Everyone laughed and TJ snapped the picture. Next, he took a couple of shots with Allie's camera and simultaneously continued the sarcastic banter with Jack. The two men had hit it off almost immediately at last week's reception, and now with the quips zinging back and forth, smiles grew wider. Blythe was hard-pressed to keep from wiggling as she giggled, and beside her, Allie was having the same problem.

At long last, they were ready for the group snapshot. They huddled together for the pose. TJ stood behind Blythe and put his large hands on her shoulders. Matt took his place next to Kylie. The Chadwyks stood next to him. Logan, Marilee, and Patrice sat in chairs and formed a front row.

"It'll be fun to see where we all are in another thirty years," Allie said.

"Well, let's not wait that long to see each again."

"For sure." Allie smiled. "Want to do lunch next week?"

"Love to."

Allie slipped an arm around Blythe's waist, and Blythe wrapped her arm around Allie's.

"We're sisters in Christ."

"Sisters, indeed." Blythe smiled and the camera flashed.

"Don't move," TJ ordered. "There's another one coming."

The directive left Blythe's ear buzzing; however, she honestly believed she was falling for the adorable galoot. Perhaps she'd already fallen. Time would tell. Meanwhile, she and TJ had committed to a long-distance romance, complete with letters, E-mails, phone calls, and intermittent visits.

And in that very moment, as she stood encircled by loved ones, Blythe was amazed, yet again, at God's handiwork in her life. The good Lord had plucked her from a frightened existence, surrounded by things no more precious in His sight than wood, hay, and stubble. God caused her to realize precious people and her relationships with them were what mattered most in this life. Inanimate objects couldn't follow her into eternity, but people would. With that truth finally rooted in her soul, God set Blythe's feet on the path to becoming the woman He wanted her to be.

Blythe's heart was now filled with unspeakable joy.

And to think it all started with a faded photograph. . . .

ABOUT THE AUTHOR

ANDREA BOESHAAR has been married for twenty-six years. She and her husband, Daniel, have three adult sons. Andrea attended college first at the University of Wisconsin–Milwaukee, where she majored in English, and then at Alverno College, where she majored in Professional Communications and Business Management.

Andrea has been writing stories and poems since she was a little girl; however, it wasn't until 1984 that she started submitting her work for publication. In 1991 she became a Christian and realized her calling to write exclusively for the Christian market. Since then Andrea has written articles, devotionals, and over a dozen novels for **Heartsong Presents,** as well as numerous novellas for Barbour Publishing. In addition to her own writing, she works as an agent for Hartline Literary Agency.

When she's not at the computer, Andrea enjoys being active in her local church and taking long walks with Daniel and their "baby"—a golden Labrador-Retriever mix named Kasey.

What readers are saying about *Broken Things*...

Broken Things. . .is what Christian fiction should be.

C.R.

I happened to pick up a copy of your book *Broken Things*. . .and passed it on to a friend. It has ministered to her in ways I never thought possible. Thanks for sharing your wonderful gift of writing with us—I cannot wait to read *Hidden Things*.

S.K.

Outstanding! *Broken Things* is a wonderful story of how God uses people and situations from our past and present lives to bring us back to Him and to restore in His time and his way those tattered and torn relationships.

S.M.

What a fantastic read! I enjoyed it from front to back.

J.M.

Broken Things is an inspiration! I have endured many rough spots in life and have to admit that reading this [book] put it all in perspective for me.

D.F.

It was good to read about broken hearts and relationships being mended. I'll be looking for the next book.

V.C.

This is a wonderful story, and so masterfully written. You had a perfect blend of everything—great story and story elements.

Y.L.

Andrea Boeshaar has outdone herself with her first women's fiction novel. Through the weaving of a wonderful story, Andrea brings out the message of God's unconditional love and willingness to forgive.

P.M.

Very interesting story and very well written. The faded photograph theme is a great way to tie a series together. I will look forward to reading the next one.

C.T.

What readers are saying about *Hidden Things*...

I just finished *Hidden Things* and didn't want it to end. I am eagerly waiting for *Precious Things*.

P.S.

Kylie won my heart with her life struggles and the search for herself, love, and the true meaning of Christ's love.

D.L.B.

I loved *(Hidden Things)*. Compelling. It just sucked me in and dragged me along.

M.C.

I just finished *Hidden Things*. I've been praying and crying since. I've been struggling with hearing from God and trying to find my "place" in my own life—trying to figure out who I am. Reading the characters' struggles helped me with my own.

C.C.

I just started reading *Hidden Things* yesterday while waiting for my son at the orthodontist's. I am almost done with it, and I'm thinking, "How in the world did I miss this author and the first book?" Good grief, I love this book!

C.M.

BROKEN THINGS

Favorite **Heartsong Presents**
author Andrea Boeshaar
takes us into the world of a
woman who courageously
faces the failures of her
past when she finds a
faded photograph of the
Chicago cop she once
loved. . .but left. When
Allie Littenberg returns
to make amends for
broken relationships
of more than twenty
years earlier, she finds she is
not the only person who has changed. Instead
of the tender beau she'd left, Jack Callahan has turned
into a bitter man, angry at a God who failed him. Can
God use Allie to minister healing in Jack's shattered
life and broken family?

ISBN 1-58660-756-1

Available wherever books are sold.

Hidden Things

Kylie had her life all planned out—with marriage to Matthew and a "happily-ever-after" in their sleepy Wisconsin hometown. But when she opens a wedding invitation and a decades-old faded photograph falls out, she uncovers a side of her mother Kylie never suspected. As she digs into the past, Kylie uncovers a whole world of hidden surprises—including

grandparents she never knew existed. Suddenly, Kylie faces a choice between two worlds. . .and doesn't feel she fits into either. As the past changes, so does her whole foundation of security. Will Kylie learn who she really is and where she fits into God's plan?

ISBN 1-58660-970-X

Available wherever books are sold.